NEW BEGINNINGS

In the treatment room, I scrutinized my face under the fluorescent light. What hidden facets would Signor Eduardo bring out in the glamorous new me? Passion? Suppressed desire? Cool competence?

I didn't really care, so long as my face wasn't a signboard for the real truth: Middle-aged. Separated. Abandoned. Scared.

No wonder I needed a makeover.

My mother-in-law had bought me the session about a year before the separation three months earlier, and she asked about it every time I saw her, managing to make me feel guilty.

The unspoken rebuke was that if I had acted more quickly, my perilous grip on a shaky marriage might never have faltered, and her son might not be spending his weekends squiring flight attendants around the breakwater on the firm's yacht, leaving his children to run wild in the streets of La Jolla.

Catherine Todd

Making Waves

AVON BOOKS  NEW YORK

This is a work of fiction. Names, characters, places, and incidents either are the product of the author's imagination or are used fictitiously. Any resemblance to actual events, locales, organizations, or persons, living or dead, is entirely coincidental and beyond the intent of either the author or the publisher.

AVON BOOKS
A division of
The Hearst Corporation
1350 Avenue of the Americas
New York, New York 10019

Copyright © 1997 by Catherine Todd
Published by arrangement with the author
Visit our website at http://AvonBooks.com
Library of Congress Catalog Card Number: 96-97082
ISBN: 0-380-78773-3

First Avon Books Printing: April 1997

AVON TRADEMARK REG. U.S. PAT. OFF. AND IN OTHER COUNTRIES, MARCA REGISTRADA, HECHO EN U.S.A.

Printed in the U.S.A.

RA   10   9   8   7   6   5   4   3   2   1

For A. E. L. M.

ACKNOWLEDGMENTS

For several of the ideas and images appearing in Chapter 1, I am indebted to a HERS column in *The New York Times Magazine* entitled "Face to Face with the New Me" by Dava Sobel, April 16, 1989, page 26.

I would like to thank my agent, Denise Marcil, for her editorial help in preparing the manuscript and for all her efforts on behalf of the book. I would also like to thank my editor at Avon Books, Ellen Edwards, for her first-rate editorial advice and encouragement.

Sean Hutchins very kindly gave me background and advice on the retailing business, and Bruce Campbell of Radio Shack consulted on recording devices. Any errors or adaptation of the facts are entirely my own.

A book is very much a collaborative effort, and I would like to express my appreciation to everyone involved in the publication of *Making Waves*.

1

I WAS A blank slate. My name tag, which had "Caroline" printed over a background of muted peach and salmon, had no other information, certainly not my history or my taste in books (Jane Austen and Barbara Kingsolver) or whether I had always dreamed of being a blonde (I hadn't). The receptionist, her voice carefully neutral, balanced a minuscule pot reverently on her outstretched palm and offered it to me with perfect pink nails. "This is our own specially formulated cleanser," she breathed, in a tone suitable to one offering frankincense at the Virgin Birth. "If you would like to step into the Treatment Room and remove all your makeup, Signor"—she gave it the Italian pronunciation—"Eduardo will be with you in just a few minutes. His other appointment has not arrived yet."

With two slim fingers, she lifted a plastic package from a bowl on her desk. "This is a bandage to pull your hair back from your face." She shook her own glossy, perfectly cut hair—into which no gray would make insidious advances for at least a decade and a half—and smiled sympathetically. "It is

1

not flattering, but Signor Eduardo wants to study your bone structure. Step this way, please."

Inside the Treatment Room, I scrutinized my face under the fluorescent light. What would this person whom I was trusting to unearth the new me find there? Despite years of scarcely disinterested inspection, I hadn't a clue.

Well, that's not quite true. There were hints enough—the little runways of gray at each temple, the blotch of brown pigment on my forehead, the lipstick oozing into the tiny crevices the years had formed around my lips. Still, I didn't really know what I looked like. Pictures usually startled me. My nose was bigger and my hair shorter than I remembered, though the general effect was not displeasing. But whether or not Signor Eduardo could find any characteristics on my face that I had failed to observe on my own, I couldn't say. What hidden facets would he bring out in the glamorous new me? Passion? Suppressed desire? Cool competence?

I didn't really care so long as my face wasn't a signboard for the real truth: Middle-aged. Separated. Abandoned. Scared.

You might think "sex-starved" or some other cliché for the newly partnerless would not be inapt, but the fact is that ever since my marriage had succumbed to domestic attrition or whatever it was, the south end of my body had pretty well closed up shop. Fear and humiliation were scarcely the most potent aphrodisiacs, despite the unsuitable opportunities that almost immediately presented themselves, just the way all the books said they would. The prospect of a quickie with the mailman was scarcely the appropriate tonic to my battered pride. No wonder I needed a makeover.

Still, I was more than a little embarrassed to be

handing over the task of renovation to an image consultant. I had always distrusted interior decorators, despite the hulking black leather couch that took up too much space in my family room and other mistakes that, presumably, expert advice would have saved me from. Look at all those pictures in *Architectural Digest*; not a single perfect room ever contains more than three books or a few discreetly arranged magazines, even if the owner is Susan Sontag. Besides, decorators always want to put sago palms or pampas grass or some such thing in the living room, and I am really bad with plants. So how could I trust a total stranger—albeit a highly paid and, as I was shortly to discover, extremely confident one—to turn me into something I liked better than what I was?

Because I was desperate.

Not only that, but my mother-in-law had bought me the session about a year before our separation three months before, and ever since then she had not failed to ask me about it every time I saw her. The message was scarcely subtle, and she had gotten a deal on the makeover because the cosmetic company that employs the image consultants is one of the law firm's biggest clients, but nevertheless she managed to make me feel guilty. The unspoken rebuke was that if I had acted more quickly, my perilous grip on a shaky marriage might never have faltered, and her son might not be spending his weekends squiring flight attendants round the breakwater on the firm's yacht, leaving his children to run wild in the streets of La Jolla.

She might even have been right. So add "guilty" to middle-aged, desperate, etc, etc.

Signor Eduardo's origins were probably a lot closer to Guadalajara than Fiesole, but his mauve silk shirt and slim-cut Italian pants exuded an enviable air of fashionable certainty. His hair was pulled back in a ponytail. He raised one slender wrist and frowned at his watch in disbelief. "My clients are never late. Never!" His accent, like his style, hovered somewhere between two continents. He was a half hour late himself.

I smiled apologetically, although it was not my fault.

He did not appear to be mollified. "We must begin," he announced, with the air of a symphony conductor raising his baton. My renovation could not wait a moment longer, apparently. "Clarice," he said, reopening the door of what I had come to think of as the Examining Room, "when Signora Hampton arrives, if she arrives, please show her into Giorgio's room. She must begin with him."

I started. "Signora—Mrs. Hampton? Is that Eleanor Hampton?"

He consulted a typed card surreptitiously. "Signora Eleanor Hampton, sí. She is a friend, perhaps? If so, I may make an exception and allow her to come into my session late. I have found that my ladies are more confident in the company of friends."

I shook my head, more to clear it than in denial. I was trying to find a way to explain Eleanor Hampton. "Her ex-husband and my . . . husband are partners in Eastman, Bartels, and Steed."

He looked politely blank.

"It's a law firm," I told him. "They do the legal work for this company."

His nostrils quivered a little, as if I had presented him with a piece of moldy cheese. "I do not concern myself with such things," he said with finality. "I live only for beauty and loveliness. I find beauty in every woman," he added firmly, though I was not inclined to dispute it. I did wonder, though, what he would find in Eleanor Hampton.

Eleanor Hampton was the divorced woman's Dorian Gray. The portrait, not the character. Every wounded feeling, every urge to hurl the *spaghetti al vongole* in the bastard's face, every outraged rebellion against being quietly replaced with some pliant bimbette, was magnified and given (ample) flesh in Eleanor Hampton. Ever since Barclay had left her for his legal assistant, she had made Medea look like Anne of Green Gables. Her obsession with her ex-husband, his new wife, and the life they had stolen from her was her only topic of conversation, and the lengths to which she would go to harass and pursue them (sample: She had hired herself out as an assistant to the florist who furnished her husband's wedding, and then she sneaked ragweed into the bridal bouquet.) made her a social pariah. I don't suppose too many people sat down to dinner with the Furies, either. Still, she served as a kind of a safety valve for the rest of us. She did what we could only imagine doing, and her excess reassured us that no matter how neurotic we felt, we still had not "gone too far," like Eleanor.

Like me, Eleanor lived in a Mediterranean-style villa in La Jolla, except that hers was on the view side of her street, which added a generous collection of zeroes to its value, and the part of the Mediterranean it emulated was Cap d'Antibes. The walls were thick with bougainvillea—the salmon-colored type, not ordinary Barbara Karst—but the garden was so meticulous that not a single messy blossom ever found its way into the pool. In palmier days the Hamptons had done quite a bit of entertaining, mostly outdoor affairs with lots of margaritas and ceviche and quesadillas with papayas and Anaheim chiles. Once they had a woman in a brightly embroidered blouse who patted out fresh tortillas and cooked them on a *comal* in front of the guests. Those were law firm events. The charities probably got California champagne and lobster quenelles, but I never went to any of those. Still, they were good parties.

"You have good bones," said my mentor, apparently studying the arrangement of these objects with some care, "but your hair is too short. You must grow it out, but while you are waiting we will give you a cut with more style. And it should be red."

There was a limit to my complicity in this process. I gasped.

Signor Eduardo frowned. "I do not say some vulgar red which screams 'Here I am,' or even the flaming color of Tiziano." He carried this off as if Titian had been his next door neighbor in Old Trastavere. "That would not be you. But we will add highlights—yes?—the color of rubies or fine wine."

Or rust.

He studied my expression in the mirror with disapproval. "Your hair is pretty and very thick. But dark brown—and a little gray, yes?—is too dull for you. Your eyes—so beautiful, so intelligent—deserve more."

He was expecting a response, but I couldn't answer him. I was too overwhelmed at the thought of becoming a redhead to succumb to flattery.

His tone became more distant and almost parental. "If you are happy with the way you look, why are you here?" he asked reprovingly, clucking his tongue. "We will discuss your clothing later—"

My heart sank to the tops of my Neiman Marcus

pumps. I had worn something very expensive and, I thought, very tasteful.

"It is very tasteful, very expensive, yes? But it does not *speak*. The real you does not come through. It is very safe to dress so, but it is not *chic*. To be chic you must be uniquely yourself, no one else. Trust me, and I will make you a very striking woman."

I thought some of Signor Eduardo's pep talk would not have been inappropriate at a motivational conference for car salesmen or, at the very least, between the covers of the latest self-help manual, but I fell for it anyway, for a number of the aforementioned reasons. Besides that, my closet was full of an embarrassing array of expensive mistakes, so how could I resist someone who promised to endow me with that most mystical of European qualities, chic? So what if his version was a south-of-the-border hybrid? It was closer than I was likely to get on my own. And anyway, hair dye would always grow out, wouldn't it?

"All right," I agreed, hoping I did not sound cowed.

"Mrs. Hampton is here," announced Clarice brightly from the doorway.

Signor Eduardo was not so involved with beauty and loveliness that he had lost all his business sense. He looked up. "Excellent! Have her begin with Giorgio and I will look in while Signora James is having her shampoo."

Clarice remained where she was, her smile—all gloss and lip pencil—frozen on her face. Even I could see that she was tense.

Signor Eduardo raised one delicate eyebrow. "Is there a problem?"

"Mrs. Hampton insists that her appointment is

with you." She hesitated. "I told her you had already begun with another client and she . . ."

"Yes, *cara*?"

"She said she would not mind sharing you with Mrs. James."

I laughed.

Signor Eduardo looked flustered. "You do not mind, Caroline?"

I considered telling him the truth, that I did in fact very much mind spending the rest of the day in Eleanor's exhausting company, but it would only have put him in a difficult position, as he was unlikely in any case to emerge from this skirmish victorious. I sighed. "No. Of course not."

He exhaled. "*Va bene.* Clarice, please tell Salvador that Signora James is ready for her shampoo." He flashed me a smile in which I caught a glint of gold. "For you, I think, we will use the Blanc de Noir. All of our shampoos are made from the finest champagne. You will see how it adds body and shine to your hair without drying it out. Step this way, please."

I did, just as the door opened on Eleanor Hampton. She was wearing a beautiful pink suit, but a size sixteen in Chanel is still a size sixteen. One of the things she had done since Barclay left her was eat. I certainly didn't blame her for that, but one of her weapons against him was to reproach him with the past of her own body and her now-burgeoning hips and thighs. She liked to say that she would still be a size six if Tricia Lindera Hampton had never come on the scene, although I had known her for several years before that event and she was more like an eight or a ten. Still, since Steve had moved out, I had more than once been tempted by the prospect of an orgy of Häagen-Dazs Belgian Chocolate Chocolate, but the thought of Eleanor Hampton had kept my spoon firmly anchored on the table. It was bad enough to have incipient varicose veins like little raisins, without giving them thighs like rice pudding to float around in.

"Hello, Eleanor," I said, extending my hand.

She took it and looked at me oddly, I thought. "Caroline?"

I'd forgotten that I was makeup-less and had my hair skinned back from my head. I nodded. "This is the 'before' look."

"You are the chrysalis—yes?—before the butterfly emerges," offered Signor Eduardo.

I was disappointed that he would say something so trite, but then I decided it was undoubtedly the sort of thing they taught you in image consultant school.

"Good God," said Eleanor. "I haven't seen you since your son-of-a-bitch of a husband moved out. Are you all right?"

"Of course," I told her.

"Caroline," said Signor Eduardo rather hurriedly, "Salvador is waiting for you at the hair station. Step this way, please."

From underneath the delirious froth of bubbles created by the Champagne of Shampoos, I could hear snatches of Eleanor's consultation. I had to hand it to Signor Eduardo; his enthusiasm for his Galateas appeared to be boundless and not at all tarnished by what must appear to less loving eyes as a challenge. We might both have been in hot demand as *Vogue* models instead of fortyish matrons with too much avoirdupois around the hips.

"You have such lovely proportions," I heard him

tell Eleanor, who was at least thirty pounds overweight. "You must not wear pink."

"Why not?" asked Eleanor, the defensive note in her voice not entirely unwarranted, since she was, I knew, the possessor of a number of very expensive pink outfits in addition to the Chanel.

"It is a lovely color—yes?—and the suit is bee-utiful," he said soothingly. "But it is what everyone expects with your pale blond coloring, so there is no mystery. Besides, Eleanor, pink is the color of ingenues, and you are a woman of experience and sophistication, is it not so?"

"Not black," said Eleanor suspiciously. "I hate black."

"Did I say you must wear black?" he asked huffily. "You must wear rich shades—plum, burgundy—which reflect your confidence, your desirability . . ."

I didn't want to hear any more. I didn't want to know if Signor Eduardo researched his clients or just made educated guesses about their psychological vulnerability. Most of all, I didn't want to discover the Wizard pulling levers behind the curtain.

The Champagne of Shampoos, according to my husband, Steve, who had not worked on Naturcare's incorporation himself but had "heard all the stories," was inspired by one of Diana Vreeland's famous "Why don't you's" in *Vogue* magazine in the 1930s: "Why don't you rinse your child's hair in 'dead' champagne as they do in France to keep it gold?" It was the first of a line of all-natural products (although it might be stretching it a bit to call champagne a natural product) touted as environmentally sound and sensuously indulgent. Naturcare was politically correct even before that term was invented. The salespeople had fundraisers for Save the Rainforests and "volunteered" their time planting trees in parks and protesting the massacre of dolphins. The product line was quite expensive— a one-ounce jar of sea urchin cream for dry skin (extracted, perhaps, under duress but never requiring the "ultimate sacrifice"—besides, had anyone ever seen a dry sea urchin?) cost about sixty-five dollars—and phenomenally successful.

In the several years since the company's incorporation, the founders—Cindi Meadows, a onetime animal trainer at Sea World, and her husband, Michael, a financial planner—had made their fortune many times over, so that they were constantly talking about moving the business to Utah or Nevada or some such place where personal income taxes were negligible or nonexistent. The only thing was, most of the products were made or processed just over the border in Mexico, where the wages were even lower than they were in Utah, and Michael believed in hands-on management. Besides, Cindi told me once, when their success was still new enough for them to invite their lawyers to their parties, "In Utah everybody's Mormon, and in Nevada they're all pale from spending so much time in casinos. And anyway, I'd, like, miss the ocean."

Their prosperity hadn't done the law firm any harm, either. Michael Meadows had been a minor client and sometime tennis partner of Barclay Hampton, and when he had asked Eastman, Bartels, and Steed to incorporate his wife's "little business," it was more in the nature of requesting a favor. "Just have a paralegal do it," he'd said. "That way we can keep the costs down." There was no reason to expect that Cindi's business would be anything but an indulgence and a flop; after all, he had mar-

ried her more for her perfect California look and the
way she graced a wet suit in the Petting Pool than
for her education, which was minimal, or her intelligence, which was not much better. But her idea
came along at the right time, and Michael's financial
acumen, once his attention had finally been caught,
turned it into something big.

The stock had just gone public, and the product
line was about to go into department stores, so the
lawyers at Eastman, etc., were salivating over the
prospect of a second Mercedes in the garage or a
little Aspen condo that didn't have to be time-
shared. When we were still talking to each other,
Steve had told me that Henry Eastman, the firm's
senior partner, was worried about so many legal
eggs being put into one basket, but in the "Nasty
Nineties," a huge, ongoing, and successful client
was like the proverbial 600-pound gorilla. (Question: What does a 600-pound gorilla do on his birth-
day? Answer: Anything he wants.)

Barclay Hampton's elevation to firm superstar by
virtue of his connection to Naturcare had been the
beginning of the end of his marriage to Eleanor. He
bought the aforementioned stunning home, complete with its own tennis court, in the best area of
La Jolla, where he spent so many hours practicing
for his games with Michael Meadows that he accidentally lost fifteen pounds, got fit, and acquired a
not-unattractive little crinkle around his eyes from
too much looking into the sun. He bought a new
wardrobe to go with his new body. He acquired a
Jaguar to go with the wardrobe. He was so
swamped with work that he insisted on hiring his
own personal legal assistant, selecting—instead of
one of the decorous and professional paralegals already employed by the firm—the unfortunately

decorative Tricia Lindera, the receptionist. Their working rapport soon necessitated a number of after-hours conferences and, increasingly, private celebrations. It was your basic wife's nightmare, however scathingly *Ms.* might disapprove. Barclay was a bit too well-bred to fondle her ass during depositions, but let's just say that no one was surprised when the Hamptons split up about eight months after Tricia's "promotion."

The awful thing was, as much as you would have liked to hate Tricia, she really wasn't such a bad person. Somewhat dim at times, and a little bit too breathlessly pleased at finding herself the second Mrs. Hampton, but it didn't take too long in Eleanor's company before you could sort of see Barclay's point. If I had to be trapped in a makeover for hours with one or the other, for example, I would have picked Tricia, hands down, even though her Italian bombshell body and her fifteen-year advantage would have made her a hard act to compete with. I bet Signor Eduardo would have liked to play Pygmalion with her, and he wouldn't have had to strain to come up with compliments about her sophistication and symmetry, either. All in all, though, her lack of conversation might have been restful, compared to Eleanor.

Now that I was separated from Steve, I had apparently crossed over into Eleanor's territory. "How are you?" she asked with a new and terrible intimacy, as our facial pores steamed beneath hot towels.

Without waiting for my muffled reply, she said, "I know how you feel. Men are such shits. Ten to one he's sticking it to some twat with an IQ smaller than her bust size and talking about 'finding himself.'"

"I don't think—" I began.

"That's what Barclay did," she said, as the "facial technician" removed the cloths and began the light tapping motion of her fingers on the skin that is supposed to stimulate the circulation. "He took off with his new car and his new suits and his new wife, and he hopes it will make him a new man. He said I was carrying around too much baggage, too much of our past, and that it was holding him back. Well, Tricia could carry around her past in a bottle cap, and now she's living my life! She has my husband, she goes to all the parties I used to go to, and he takes her to all the same restaurants. She even reads the same books I do!"

"How do you know that?" I asked her, curious. My voice vibrated a little because of the massage.

"I saw them on her bedside table."

"Oh." I decided I didn't really want to pursue that further, so I succumbed to the ministrations of the attendant, who was rubbing attar of jasmine or some such thing into the hollows around my eyes. It smelled delicious, and if the circular motion could not ultimately subdue the "laugh lines," at least it was cool and incredibly soothing.

"Have you seen a lawyer yet?" she asked sharply.

"Ummm," I offered noncommittally. I hadn't, and it was going to cost me a fortune by the time I finally got the divorce, but the way the legal profession screws women was one of Eleanor's hobbyhorses. She had a point, but if you got her started you could wind up hearing the entire history of *Hampton v. Hampton*, and there were still six hours or so left in the day.

"You need someone savvy and tough as nails," she continued, undeterred. "Whatever you do, don't let some jerk-ass at the firm handle it for you.

I'll bet you anything Steve will suggest it because it would 'save you both so much money.' Don't fall for it. It's just another way of staying in control, and you'll end up getting screwed even worse than you will anyway."

As a matter of fact, Steve *had* made that suggestion, and I'd told him I'd get back to him about it. It seemed to make sense: a nice, amicable divorce, with as few fights as possible over division of the spoils. But my income-producing capacity was currently pretty low, and then Steve started making noises about selling our house and moving me and the kids into a condo in Mira Mesa or someplace—in La Jolla parlance—"east of 5," the magical barrier of freeway that bifurcates the upscale coastal communities from the unhip and more middle-class areas of inland San Diego. I actually liked the interior, with its warmer weather and easier accessibility (La Jolla is purposely constructed so that there is only one main two-lane access road, and getting in and out of the place at commuting hours or in the midst of weekend beach traffic can be bloody Hell), but moving would have meant disrupting the kids' school lives, and besides, the house was my security against the future.

"When Barclay and I got married, I quit teaching as soon as he finished law school so we could start a family," Eleanor continued. "That was just what you did. I stood by him through every single bad thing that ever happened to him, I took care of his house and his children, and look what I get. I thought I had a lifetime of safety, and instead I have to depend on whatever pittance he and the rest of the asshole lawyers decided I deserve for eighteen years of marriage. He's stolen my whole life, and I'm supposed to think it's fair!"

"Please, Mrs. Hampton," the technician murmured, "you are removing the cucumber moisturizing cream."

"I'm not going to let him get away with it," she insisted.

Right. Barclay Hampton stories now circulated at the country club, at legal functions, even at the schools the Hampton children had attended. Like some Joanie Appleseed, Eleanor sowed them everywhere. Barclay gave himself such a bad rash with Retin-A that he had to tell everyone he was going to a conference in Washington while the dermatologist cleared it up. Barclay insisted that his undershorts had to be ironed. Barclay dyed his chest hair, but it turned out to be a bad match to the rest of his body.

It wasn't the stuff of *The Count of Monte Cristo*, but as revenge went, it wasn't all that unsatisfying. The trouble was, it didn't put money in the bank. And money, after all, is the bottom line. Money, or the ability to get more of it, is what gives you the capacity to walk away from your problems, the way Barclay and Steve did. When you don't have money, that is the problem. Eleanor had a lot more money than, say, your average grocery clerk, and in the grand scheme of things it was hard to feel sorry for her, but it is humiliating to be dependent on someone who resents every dollar he is forced to give you and persists in regarding you as a Youthful Mistake. Not only that, it is hard to have a lot of money one day and not much the next. Stockbrokers have jumped out of windows for less.

"I told Barclay he had better come up with more per month, and you know what he told me?" she said, committed inevitably to telling her story to the end, though I'd heard most of it already.

"No, what?"

"He said he was thinking about leaving the firm and becoming a judge. He said if he did, he'd only make eighty thousand a year, so I'd better get used to living on less, not more. He said there'd be less for the kids, too. Can you believe the nerve of that asshole? I don't for a minute believe he'll do it, because he just loves being Mr. Hotshot-corporate-lawyer-who-brought-in-Naturcare, but if he even thinks about it as a way to get me, I'm going straight to Henry Eastman."

"What could he do about it?"

She gave me a look that, despite the cucumber cream around her eyes, made me feel extremely stupid and naive. She sighed, her bosom heaving under the smock. "Caroline, you had better wake up and smell the coffee before it's too late. Don't you realize they're all in this together? Don't you think Henry had to approve it when Barclay moved all his partnership income into a bonus that wouldn't be paid till after our financial settlement? They're out to screw every one of us! They rewrite the divorce laws of the state of California to suit themselves, and they help each other do it through the biggest old-boy network you can imagine."

"Would it help to get a woman lawyer?" I asked her. As obsessed as she was with the topic, I was still afraid she might be right. As Henry Kissinger is said to have remarked (or paraphrased), even paranoids can have real enemies.

"Some," she conceded. "But the real problem is that Steve or Barclay can use all kinds of legal tactics you never heard of just to harass you, and you have to keep paying *your* lawyer, whoever he or she is, to fight them. Finally it just gets too expensive to go on, so you have to give in. Do you know what I owed my lawyer by the time my divorce was final?"

"I'm sure it was a lot."

"Over one hundred thousand dollars."

Oh. Behind me, the technician dropped one of her very expensive tiny gold pots of crushed abalone shell foundation, smearing it all over the floor.

Well, but. The Hampton divorce might have been the messiest in La Jolla history, so it wouldn't be so shocking if it were one of the most expensive as well. Still . . .

"When I got on to what Barclay was doing with that tramp," she continued as we walked to the station where Signor Eduardo's makeup expert would exercise the full extent of his artistry on our naked faces, "I made copies of his keys to the firm and went over there at night to go through his files. I went through everything at home, too. I had *piles* of paper, but my lawyer wouldn't look at any of it. He said it was privileged information and that I shouldn't have taken it. He said it wasn't in my best interests to do anything to hurt the firm, because how could Barclay pay me what I was asking if I did anything to jeopardize his income? So I went along with him, and the prick screwed me anyway. And what did I find out a week after our settlement? That my lawyer and Barclay had become racquetball partners!"

"Really? Before or after your divorce?"

"What difference does it make? If my lawyer had made Barclay squirm and own up to his obligations as a husband and father, do you think they would have felt chummy enough to be out on the court together?" The look in her eye would have made Savonarola quail. Her breath was coming fast, as if she were hyperventilating.

"It took me ages," she said, gulping air, "to go through all the material. I don't care what happens to the goddamn firm. I wouldn't care if they all ended up bankrupt and in disgrace. I don't give a flying fuck what happens to Barclay and that hot little number he dumped me for. To tell you the truth, I don't much care what happens to me. But goddamn it, I just don't want to get screwed anymore!"

"Oh, Eleanor." Full of real sympathy, I reached out and touched her arm. She looked so weary and depressed.

"Ladies, please," interjected Signor Eduardo, who had come to check on how our transformation was progressing, "you must be positive. You must smile. You must let your inner beauty come through. Ernesto, I think Signora Hampton needs a warmer tone of blush. Eleanor, we must soften your look a bit. Ah, Jimmy, that is the perfect eye shadow for Signora James." He beamed approvingly. "It brings out the copper highlights of your hair. It is a whole new look. I know you will be pleased."

I had not seen a mirror since the Treatment Room and I had forgotten I was now, apparently, a redhead. "Eleanor," I asked, when Luigi or Jimmy or whoever the latest magician was had removed the lip pencil from the contour of my lower lip and had gone in search of the perfect gloss and I could speak again, "how does my hair look?"

She pursed her lips, considering. "Your inner beauty is coming through."

"Shit."

"Actually, you look terrific."

As a matter of fact, when the unveiling finally came, I found the look unsettling. The sum total of hair-care products and makeup expended on my new look was $427, if I cared to duplicate it myself, at a today-only discount. What I would get for that was, if not quite a stranger, someone who looked unfamiliarly cool and sophisticated with a stylish haircut (something like a very mature Demi Moore), high cheekbones (how had they done *that*?), and aggressively bronzed lids and lips. They had refurbished me in I. M. Pei when I am fairly certain I had walked in in John Nash. Well, as Signor Eduardo had said, what had I come for if I didn't want to change?

He, at least, was full of enthusiasm. "How do you like your hair?" he asked, his head tilted to catch all the angles of, apparently, the exciting new me.

"Well, I—"

"Did I not tell you that the red highlights would make you look more vibrant, more exciting? It has taken years from your age."

Next they would be asking me for my ID in bars. Not that I ever went to bars. Still, I couldn't help falling for it just a little, and I peered at my reflection with more tolerance.

My mentor was full of suggestions. "Now you must stop dressing so traditionally, Caroline. Wear brighter colors, bolder clothes. Your clothes look as if you hide in them. You do not need to throw everything out, but you must combine your outfits with more flair and daring. Use the sketches and the samples I gave you." He flashed his golden smile again. "Be brave, *cara*. Live it up a little."

By contrast, I really thought Eleanor looked great. He had loosened her hair style into soft curls around her face and warmed up her ash blond color to something like honey. She looked far more approachable and yet, as Signor Eduardo had promised, worldly as well.

"Eleanor, you look fantastic," I told her admiringly, as we met at the counter to pick up our purchases. Not $427 worth, naturally—I couldn't have spent that even if I had emerged as a dead ringer for Demi Moore—but the minimum required to keep the makeover pump primed.

"Do I?" she asked, frowning a little. "I think I look bizarre."

"No, seriously. You look great. Really."

"Thank you." She laid a hand on my arm. "I've been thinking—"

"Yes?"

"You should write it up."

"What? This?" I swept my hand around the soft-hued room, with its thick carpeting and gleaming counters running the entire length of both walls.

She shook her head impatiently. "No. About *them*. Lawyers. How they use their influence with the system to fuck their families. I've thought about doing it—God knows somebody has to—but I'm not a writer. *You* are."

"Oh, no. I mean, I'm not that kind of writer. I've only done a few articles and some historical novels and"—blush—"some Regencies. . . ."

"What difference does *that* make? I have piles of material. I'll send you copies. You just won't believe the stuff they've pulled. Besides," she said, sizing up my discomfort rather shrewdly, "some of it may help you when your turn comes. And I promise you, it will come."

Once I read an article by one of the hostages in Lebanon who described his first meeting, after long isolation, with another hostage. Instead of the expected joy at finding himself with, at last, a longed-for companion, he was surprised to discover that he felt wary and reticent. He thought he was too vulnerable, with too many exposed nerves, to open up to somebody else.

Or maybe he just didn't like the looks of the guy and thought he would tell endless stories about all the other men his wife would be seeing, or his son's problems with coke. If you tell too much, too often, you lose your friends. You wear them out. If they weren't your friends to begin with, watch out.

"Well, thanks," I said.

"You'll do it, then?" she persisted.

"I'll be happy to look at anything you send me, Eleanor. But frankly, I'm not sure I'm the person . . ." I trailed off meekly. My mother, who had raised me to be polite to everyone no matter what, would have been so proud. I couldn't just tell Eleanor that I was afraid of catching her obsession with getting screwed, like some dreadful contagious disease. Mental herpes, that was it.

"If enough of us speak out, maybe we can stop them. There are lots of us, believe me. I'll call you soon."

"Great," I agreed. Anyway, I was too tired to do anything else. The process of transforming me from worm to butterfly (or maybe just an exalted moth) had taken about six and a half hours, and I was too exhausted to take my new face and hair any place but home to bed. Luckily the kids were with Steve's parents that weekend, so I wouldn't have to face their exacting scrutiny. I was stricken by the thought of washing off two hundred and fifty dollars' worth of makeup before anyone other than Eleanor could see it, but I didn't think that stopping off at the deli to pick up a dinner salad exactly qualified as a grand unveiling.

Eleanor was fishing in her purse for the keys to

her Land Cruiser. She looked up. "Maybe we could have lunch some time."

"Sure," I said, trying not to sound too encouraging. A moment later, a wave of guilt swept over me. She must be very lonely. I didn't have to ask myself how I knew that.

We stepped out into the street. It was a typical La Jolla summer night, which meant that the fog was already coming in. I smiled. "That would be nice," I said more heartily. I touched her arm. "Eleanor?"

"Yes?"

"You really do look fantastic."

"Thanks." She gave me a tiny wave and opened the car door. I shivered a little in the damp air. "I'll be in touch," she said.

I never saw her again.

2

ONE OF THE things I was going to have to figure out was how to transform myself into a career woman at the age of forty. It was true enough, as Eleanor had said, that I was a writer, but I was hardly one of the approximately eleven people nationwide who make a real living that way. I was a few steps beyond all those guests at cocktail parties who, José Cuervo Gold in hand and gazing mistily out over the Pacific, would tell you that they were thinking of writing a book, if only they could find the time. Actually, most people in La Jolla, if they weren't living off their trust funds, were probably connected to real estate in some fashion or other, but they all seemed to fantasize about being writers. Now that the boom had gone bust in California, their dreams of retiring to the garret with the PC would apparently have to be deferred.

My own modest output consisted of some travel articles, a novel about Henry VIII, a sequel on Elizabeth I, and a couple of Regency romances. These last, written under a pseudonym, fell into the category of guilty pleasures. All that passion suppressed and restrained under a cloak of propriety and elevated language is an acquired taste. You either get off on sentences like "Time had done more to expand her waistline than her horizons" or you don't. I had always thought Elizabeth Bennet and Mr. Darcy generated a lot of wattage beneath all those elegant manners, but perfectly intelligent people have found *Pride and Prejudice* dull because nothing happens in it.

The trouble is, even if you concede the pleasure of that kind of writing, there isn't any money in it. And it's not like you're really writing literary masterpieces that everyone will still be reading in fifty years, either. On the other hand, you can't quietly chuckle and say you've "sold out" for commercial reasons, since a less commercial sort of genre doesn't exist. Mostly you just don't say anything.

All this was all right, or even better than all right, when we were living on Steve's income. My schedule was "flexible," I was home a lot with Jason and Megan, and I was available at a moment's notice for whipping up a dinner party or spending a weekend in the Napa Valley. Besides, the historical novels got good reviews—though no one read those, either—and people in the firm dutifully went down to Windsor's bookstore during the books' (more or less) three-week shelf life and purchased a copy. Steve even found it rather charming, though not, of course, significant. His income paid for the trips that made the research and the travel articles possible, and whatever I earned from my writing. I could keep for myself.

With a divorce in the offing, however, the charm had worn thin. Well, marriage keeps changing, too: One morning you wake up next to your husband and listen to his gentle snoring, and you think,

"How precious!"; another time you can barely refrain from smothering him with the pillow. The problem with divorce is, it takes all the worst moments and carves them in stone. Nowadays, every conversation I had with my husband was about how I was going to make some "real" money to support myself and the kids. I would have an as-yet-unspecified settlement and a closet full of a wardrobe for occasions I no longer attended (clothes which, I now knew, were inappropriate anyway). What I didn't have was a career.

Even so, I wasn't about to make one out of taking on the legal establishment à la Eleanor Hampton. The box she had UPSed me waited like a coiled rattler next to my desk. It was brown and square, like an ordinary box, but I could almost feel the venom oozing from it. So far I lacked the courage either to open it or just throw it away.

"Oh, Missy James, what about that box?" Maria, the maid, asked me when it had lain bristling and defiant in its spot for two weeks. Dust refused to settle on it, but it offended Maria's sense of order. I hadn't yet had the courage to tell her that soon I would no longer be able to afford domestic help, but she had been so fierce in her attacks on the house's apparent squalor that she must have figured it out.

She had been coming once a week since the children were little, and she supported a mother and two sisters in a village near Oaxaca. Her husband had disappeared into *el Norte* some years before she crossed the border to join him. As far as I know, she had never found him, and she didn't like to talk about it. Steve and I had hoped that Jason and Megan would learn Spanish from her, and they did—until the day they figured out, despite our best egalitarian efforts, that Spanish was "Maria talk" and not the language of power and affluence. Mexico was only twenty minutes away, and the furthest they ever got was *hamburguesa, por favor*. Now I was going to be putting her family in jeopardy. Clearly I would have to find her another job, and soon.

"Just leave it," I said, sighing. "Mrs. Hampton sent it over, and I haven't had the chance to look at it yet."

She rolled her eyes and shrugged. I knew what that meant. Maria's cousin worked for Eleanor as a gardener, and the Hamptons did not enjoy their professional approval. Eleanor was messy. Eleanor yelled at the help. Eleanor swam in her pool in the nude and did not care if Manuel could see. Fortunately, Manuel was precluded from having to hear the story of the Hampton divorce by the fact that he couldn't speak English. Whether or not he could really appreciate the extent of this extraordinary good fortune, I didn't know.

The box was still unopened a few days later when my neighbor, Rob Holland, knocked at the door. My son, Jason, 16, had just prepared a postprandial snack of gargantuan proportions and taken it up to his room to eat while he finished *Catcher in the Rye*. It was one of the few books he had really enjoyed reading at school, especially because he had heard from last year's juniors that the word "fuck" appeared at least six times. Now he was apparently busy making sure he didn't miss a single occurrence. One day he would probably be able to turn it into a master's thesis.

Megan, 14, and the real student of the two, was at a soccer game. Typical La Jolla school night.

Rob was not exactly grinning, but he wore an enigmatic smile. "Have you heard the news?"

"Apparently not," I said, opening the door wider so he could come in. Rob was discreetly gay, very smart, and an inveterate gossip. His lover was a younger stepbrother acquired when his mother married for the third time. Rob had made a minor pile in real estate and was a shade unscrupulous, but he was very amusing.

"Guess who turned up dead this afternoon?" he asked cheerfully, settling himself on my living room couch.

Melmoth, the cat, eyed his Dockers and the silk couch with equal longing, assessing the risk, and finally compromised on a safer position at Rob's feet.

"Jesse Helms," I ventured.

He snickered. "No such luck. Try a little closer to home. Eleanor Hampton."

I set down the coffee cup I had been holding with a clatter. "What?"

"The very same. The Lilith of La Jolla popped a few too many pills with a bottle of Bâtard-Montrachet '85 and drowned in her hot tub. Kenny"—Rob's lover and a San Diego policeman— "said Barclay's housekeeper was bringing their boys back to Eleanor's this afternoon and found the body then."

"How—how terrible," I managed to croak, trying to take it all in.

"Yes, I gather it wasn't a very pretty sight. She'd been in there the whole night, apparently. All that boiled and mottled flesh, and not a stitch on to cover it. Why Eleanor of all people should have felt it appropriate to disport in the nude, I can't imagine. It shows the most dreadful lack of foresight."

"Kenny seems to have been remarkably forthcoming about the details," I remarked.

He grinned. "It made a *big* impression," he said. "And anyway, I have my ways of making him talk. Strictly speaking, he wasn't supposed to divulge the particulars, like what kind of wine she was drinking or that she had left a pair of those hideous hairy pink bedroom slippers right by the edge of the tub, so don't spread it around." He bent down and ran his hand along Melmoth's chin, which vibrated with delight. "It's funny," he said meditatively, ruffling the cat's fur. "I always pictured a really dramatic and bizarre ending for Eleanor. Like getting dorked by an amorous dolphin and drowning in the cetacean petting pool at Waikoloa. Or getting poisoned when she barbecued hot dogs on an oleander branch by mistake. . . ."

"Rob!" I protested, a little shocked by his callousness.

"What?" He looked at me expectantly, sighed, and folded his arms. "Oh, you're not going to turn hypocritical on me, are you? You know you disliked her as much as I did. The woman put me through the torments of Hell when she and Barclay were trying to sell their house."

"You mean when Barclay was trying to sell it out from under her," I reminded him. One of the things that most enraged Eleanor was Barclay's attempt to get a "four-hour notice," which, with court permission but against her will, would have forced her to accept a pending offer on the house. He'd failed, but Eleanor had never forgiven him for it and had withdrawn the house from the market altogether.

"Oh, come *on*, Caroline. I spent weeks, and I mean weeks, trying to find her a buyer at her price. I warned her she was asking too much, but you couldn't tell her anything. When I finally found someone who came in just five thousand dollars below her asking price, she refused to even consider it. *Five thousand dollars!* That's nothing! It was perfectly obvious that she did it just to annoy Barclay, and I don't blame him a bit for trying to force the issue. That house was much too big for her, and it's costing him a fortune in upkeep."

"You sound like Steve," I told him.

He made a face. "Don't get paranoid. But don't expect me to shed any tears over Eleanor Hampton, either. I would rather have had my nipple pierced with a safety pin—a *rusty* safety pin—than do any more deals with her. Maybe she was pathetic, but she was a vindictive harpy, and I'm not sorry she's gone. And you didn't like her, either, so don't give me any lectures."

I had to smile. "I won't. But you're not exactly unbiased. Real estate agents always say their clients are unreasonable if they won't cut a deal. And anyway, I saw Eleanor lately, and I did feel sorry for her, in spite of everything. She seemed lonely."

"So are vampires. Probably for the same reason." He stood up, causing Mammoth to glance at him reproachfully. "I have to go. I just wanted to be the bearer of good tidings. It will probably be all over the papers tomorrow anyway: 'La Jolla *Bain-Marie* Steams Socialite.' "

I bit my lip. "You're awful," I told him.

He put his arm around me. "I know," he said sympathetically. "That reminds me. Let me at least partially redeem myself in your hypercritical eyes by making a suggestion."

"I'm all attention," I told him.

"You remember I told you about that investment course I'm taking at UCSD?" he asked.

"Not the one where they talk about being 'wealth impaired' and everybody sits around complaining about how hard it is to have all that money?"

He laughed. "Not that one, no. That was my mother. Anyway, that was a seminar, not a course. And believe it or not, there *are* some problems with having lots of money. You just don't get any sympathy for them."

"Apparently not," I murmured. Rob's mother was seriously impaired with old money. Her search for sympathy had so far necessitated the acquisition of four husbands, and number four was reputedly on shaky ground. Rob's father, husband number one, was the CEO of an oil company, and he lived like a pasha courtesy of his shareholders. But living on somebody else's money was not the same as having heaps of your own.

"Anyway, this is really a good course. We have a different speaker every week."

"Rob—" I was about to tell him that Steve handled all our investments when I caught myself up short. I would have my own stocks and investments now, and I didn't have a clue what to do with them. I didn't much care for the idea of letting Steve continue to manage my money for me, but I wasn't very comfortable with my own judgment either. I sighed.

"I want you to come with me next week. You don't have to commit yourself or anything like that," Rob said with amused understanding, "but if you're interested, you could sign up for it next semester. Besides, the guy who's speaking next week is a friend of my brother's."

"Kenny?" I asked incredulously.

"Certainly not," he said with a smile. "My real brother—Ben—went to business school with this guy. His name's David something or other, and he's a short. You know what that means, don't you?"

I nodded. "Sort of. They make money betting on the stock prices to go down, right? But Steve always said that was risky," I added apologetically.

"It is risky. Everything's risky nowadays. But Ben says this guy's fund made money all through ninety-one, when all the other shorts took it on the chin. Anyway, there's a lot more to it than that. Why don't you just come and hear him talk? It won't cost you anything, and you really ought to know more about this stuff. Besides, he's supposed to be quite a hunk."

I winced. "I hate that term. And I thought you were supposed to be happily monogamous."

"That, my dear, is an oxymoron. Anyway, I don't believe he's of my persuasion. I was thinking of you."

"Rob," I said, horrified, "you're not trying to fix me up?"

"Take it easy. Do I look like somebody's maiden aunt? If I want to fix people up, I'll get a turban and diamond earrings and advertise 'Discreet Introductions' in the *In Print Light*."

"They wouldn't take your ad," I told him.

"The *Union-Tribune*, then. Whatever. There's no point in going to all that trouble unless you're going to make money at it. Look, I know the financial world isn't your strong point, and I thought that if the guy looked good it might make the subject matter more attractive."

"Stimulate the brain through the hormones, is that it?"

"It's one of the proven tenets of learning theory," he said smoothly. "And don't look at me as if I've insinuated that you were some air-head cheerleader. If you don't want me to introduce you to attractive, eligible men, I won't. It's your funeral. Speaking of which, I'll be your date for Eleanor's, if you don't go with Steve." I must have looked dubious, because he added, "I promise to wear deepest mourning and make only appropriately reverent remarks."

"It isn't that. I was thinking that under the circumstances, if I were the family I'd want a very private service."

He wrinkled his nose. "Want to bet? Well, time will tell. You'll probably hear before I do, so keep me informed. I don't expect anyone will think to call me, so I'm relying on you."

When he had gone, I stood for a moment studying my empty coffee cup for inspiration. Then I went into the kitchen and accelerated as I headed toward the phone, which was, wonder of wonders, apparently unoccupied. As I reached for it, I almost collided with Megan, who was coming in the back door clutching a bundle of her soccer clothes. It was a warm night, and her hair was spiky and damp with sweat. "Good practice?" I asked her, simultaneously leaning out the door to wave a greeting at Janine Carson, whose Ford Explorer was backing out of our driveway. The soccer moms' carpool required an organizational structure NASA might have envied, and it was utterly reliable. The full-page schedule was posted on the bulletin board by the phone.

She shrugged. "Yeah, but we had to wait to use the field, so it took twice as long as it should have."

Megan's coach was a fanatic who kept the kids for hours after school, despite a number of parental protests. Only her genuine horror of my interference, and her promise that sports would not interfere with her schoolwork, kept me from pulling her off the team, but I was still appalled. "I'm beat," she said wearily. "I think I'll take a shower and go to bed."

"Homework?" I queried, as gently as I could.

She gave me a long-suffering look of resignation. "I finished it before I left. I told you."

"Just checking," I said lightly. "Sleep well."

"Susan," I said when she had picked up the phone after a dozen rings, "when's the funeral?"

Susan Goldman was my best friend, a transplanted New Yorker who managed Eastman, Bartels, and Steed's paralegals and clerical staff. She regarded California and Californians with a New Yorker's jaundiced eye, but she had moved here after a broken engagement and was determined to be a good sport. My separation from Steve occasionally put a strain on our relationship, but I still managed to talk to her at least once a week.

"I see you've heard the news," she said, with just a trace of the outer boroughs remaining in her speech. She thought she sounded like a native California, an accent she described as "newscaster nasal." She didn't.

"Look," she said, "I'm sort of tied up right now. Could you call me tomorrow at work?"

"Sure," I said, my heart sinking. "Or you could call me."

"Right. Talk to you tomorrow then, okay?"

Why did I hate calling the law firm so much? The only thing worse was going there, and nothing short of divine intervention could get me to do that. I hated the curiosity I imagined I heard in the receptionist's voice—or worse, the pity. If Steve's secretary said he wasn't there, I imagined him standing behind her, gesturing that he was tied up, out, unavailable. I started wondering all sorts of things. In short, I was paranoid, and I felt well on my way to becoming like Eleanor Hampton. The only way I could cope with it was to avoid it altogether, and usually I did just that.

I didn't exactly want to admit any of this to Susan. How could you tell someone who was eminently practical and apparently fearless that you were nervous about calling your husband's office? Susan was fairly reserved on the subject of her past, but one story I had learned was that by the time her fiancé, a doctor in Connecticut, had decided to call off the wedding, the invitations had been sent and the arrangements for an elegant reception at his country club had already been made. The caterer refused to return even a portion of their payment, so Susan chartered a bus, rounded up sixty homeless people on the streets of Manhattan, and ferried them all up to Connecticut for the sit-down dinner. You really had to admire somebody who would do that.

I stood there, lost in contemplation of this elegant revenge, holding the phone in my hand. I turned around to find Megan watching me. Her hair was wrapped in a towel. "I thought you went to bed," I told her.

She shrugged. I expected her to push past me on her way to the peanut butter and jelly or the stash of Fig Newtons that usually fueled her study sessions, but she stood her ground. She looked slightly worried.

"What?" I asked her.

She looked away. "Nothing."

Uh-oh. "Is there something bothering you?" I waited. If you aren't careful with teenagers, you can crush the life right out of the conversation before you even know what the conversation is about. I tried again. "Is there something you want to talk to me about?"

She shifted her feet and then finally met my eyes. "Have you talked to Dad lately?" she asked me.

It was my turn to squirm. "A few days ago," I said. "Why?"

"Did he say anything about Jason and me?" she asked in a tentative voice. Her careful demeanor, in combination with the topic, was beginning to make me uneasy.

"Like what?"

"Like about us spending more time with him," she said, looking away.

My heart started pounding in my chest. "He didn't mention it, no," I said, as calmly as I could.

"Oh."

"What did he say to you?" I inquired.

Her eyes flicked back and forth. "Not much. He said he just wondered how we would feel about spending more time with him. He wasn't very specific."

"How much more time?" I tried to keep the incipient panic out of my voice. I had just assumed, and Steve had never contradicted the assumption, that the children would continue to live with me on a full-time basis. My husband's long hours and newly liberated lifestyle seemed to make any other arrangement unthinkable.

"I don't know, Mom. Maybe you should talk to Dad about it."

"Well, he hasn't seen that much of the two of you lately," I told her. "He's been so busy at the firm. They worked day and night taking Naturcare public." I could hear myself babbling, but I couldn't stop. "He probably just wants to make it up to you. It wouldn't hurt to spend more time with him. He probably gets lonely, too. I'm sure that's all he meant."

"I guess you're right." She gave me a dubious smile. "So we won't be moving soon, or anything like that?"

It was all I could do not to clutch my heart and fall stricken to the floor. "Of course not," I said as firmly as I could.

"Relax, Mom. Don't get paranoid." She rubbed her hair with her towel and yawned. "Good night, then," she said cheerfully and left me alone in the kitchen.

Don't get paranoid. How could I help it? I had so much to lose. My age, my lack of earning power, and most of all my children made me exceptionally vulnerable. I wondered, as I stood in my kitchen trying to second-guess the husband who had become a stranger to me, if this was how Eleanor Hampton had felt, if this was how she had begun to believe the entire world conspired against her. Even Medea had had to start somewhere. *I am not Eleanor,* I told myself. It made me feel a little better.

"Susan Goldman's office," intoned her assistant with chilly dignity, the next morning.

"Jonathan?"

"Jonathan is on a break," said the voice patiently. "This is Richard. How may I help you?"

"I'd like to speak to Ms. Goldman, please. Caroline James calling."

He sniffed. "One moment, please. I'll see if she's in." He managed to make it sound like a major favor.

"Jesus," I said when she had picked up the line, "who was that, the butler?"

She laughed. "The Xerox operator. He fills in when Jonathan's out. He has aspirations."

I didn't doubt it. Everybody at Eastman, Bartels wanted to be something else. The go-fers wanted to be secretaries. The secretaries wanted to be paralegals. The paralegals wanted to be lawyers. The lawyers wanted out.

"Look," she said, "I'm sorry about last night, but I had company."

"I hope it was amusing," I told her. Susan had a tastefully varied social life. When I was married, we never talked much about it, but now I had an unbecoming lust for details. If I were ever going to go in for Middle-Age Dating, I wanted to scout the territory first.

A whole lot has been written on this topic, so I don't really need to go into it here. If you're old enough to remember that the last time you were going out with someone men were still supposed to open the doors for women (though not all of them did, even then), you'll understand what I mean when I say that fear of dating has probably kept a lot of terminal marriages on the life support system.

Everybody has horror stories. My personal favorite happened to a friend of mine in New York. (Susan and I had a running debate on the virtues of New York versus California, but even she would admit that this could never have happened in La Jolla.) My friend was invited to a Halloween party given by her date's family, and when he picked her up, he thoughtfully provided her with a fireman's outfit to wear as a costume. He was wearing one, too. When they got to the party, it wasn't a costume party at all, and there were the two of them, arrayed as firemen, amid a large group of disapproving and more conventionally clad aunts and uncles. Her date told her he had just wanted to see if he could get her to wear what he had brought. And this was a thirty-eight-year-old woman! It was definitely the sort of story to put minor marital annoyances in perspective.

The thing I really wanted to know about middle-age dating was what to do about sex. The pseudo-fireman was clearly out of the running, but what about everybody else? It was all so much more complicated than it used to be. Even if you took away the Saturday-night roulette and the blood tests and the etiquette of condoms, it was still a minefield of potential embarrassment and mistakes. How were you supposed to go from years of suppressing the desire to sleep with strangers to falling into the sack with the first thing in a suit that invited you for a *chile relleno* and a margarita?

And then there was the body problem. I mean, long gone was the day when everything was fixable, when you could get your flat stomach or thin thighs back just by skipping dessert for the next few days. I had to admit that Signor Eduardo had done a lot for my exterior, but under the paint job, the model was no longer deluxe. Maybe I would have to go into training, like an athlete. The thought of investing the necessary hours in the gym was depressing, and the only sport I liked—or was any good at—was swimming. To tell the truth, an excessive interest in fitness had always seemed a trifle unimaginative.

Freud said (or might have said) that there are no innocent questions, and Susan was certainly no dummy. "You mean, 'did I sleep with him?' " She laughed softly. "Don't worry, Caroline, we were very careful."

"Great," I said, as embarrassed as if I'd been caught snooping in her drawers. "Sorry if I sounded nosy."

"No, just like my mother."

Susan's mother was a petite but overbearing widow who lived in Florida and called at least once a week to express her displeasure with her errant daughter's rootless lifestyle. She was about as subtle as a freight train. "Susan, your mother *is* nosy," I told her.

"True," she admitted, "but at least you're not so disapproving."

"No, I'm envious," I confessed. "But look, I did have a serious reason for calling. I want to know what you know about Eleanor Hampton."

"It's certainly topic A around here. The police called the firm almost as soon as they hoisted the body out of the water."

"It's so humiliating. I mean, how would you like to be exposed like that to a bunch of strangers?"

"Not much," she said, not sounding particularly bothered. "Now you know why our mothers always warned us to wear clean slips in case we got into an accident. At least she might have put on a bikini, if she could have found one she could get into. Anyway, I really don't know much about it. Apparently she was on some kind of sedative—Valium or Librium or Xanax or something like that—and she combined it with too much wine. They found the pills and the wine bottle right by the hot tub. She must have passed out and then slipped down into the water."

"Is there going to be a service?"

"Oh, yes." She sounded surprised I would ask.

"This Saturday." She paused. "I'm sure Steve will call you. Everyone at the firm will be going. Barclay is taking care of everything."

"I'm sure he's disfigured with grief," I said.

"He seems to be genuinely upset, Caroline," she said calmly. "In my position, I hardly like to inquire beyond that. Why does this bother you so much, anyway?"

"I don't know. Maybe because she thought he took everything away from her, and now he's taken over her death."

"I see what you mean, but there really isn't anyone else. Her parents live in Maine, her brother's in the Midwest, and the children are too young to plan anything." She paused tactfully. "I don't think she's very close to anyone in her family."

"That doesn't surprise me," I admitted.

"No. Well. Tricia's staying in the background, naturally, but Barclay will host a reception afterward for the mourners. They've suggested contributions to the La Jolla Alliance against Substance Abuse in lieu of flowers, but of course the firm will send both."

"Hmmm," I said, noncommittally.

"It'll be fine," Susan said reassuringly. "You'll see."

I thanked her and hung up, and I was standing in the kitchen rolling out the crust for a quiche Lorraine (I know, I know. It's out of style and definitely bad for you, but I like it anyway.) when it hit me. Barclay was getting in one last dig at Eleanor with his suggested contributions to the La Jolla Alliance, et al. It was as good as proclaiming that she was a pill junkie. Well, maybe she was, though I never saw evidence of any addiction other than the desire for revenge on her ex-husband. I stood there pulling pie crust off the cool marble and pictured Tricia Lindera Hampton stepping into her walk-in closet on the morning of the funeral and pulling out the perfect Second-Wife dress: something sympathetic but not hypocritical. Dove gray, not black. And Barclay, greeting the guests with a firm handshake and eyes ever-so-slightly moist.

And I just knew Eleanor would have hated it. *Hated* it.

I decided the time had come to have a look at the contents of that box.

3

READING THE CONTENTS of Eleanor's box was like perusing the diary of a distraught and somewhat neurotic adolescent. Jason would have called her a "real dork." If you ever kept a diary as a teenager, you'll know exactly what I mean.

When I was fifteen, I asked a boy from another school to go to our spring formal. These days, girls call Jason with daunting regularity, determination crackling in their voices like static on the line, but back then it required courage to brave his mother's courteous but slightly disapproving tone when she summoned him to the receiver (how well I understand that, now that I am the one fielding the calls!), and to brazen out the automatic presumption of forwardness that always attended any act where the girl made the first move. I found myself apologetic and hideously embarrassed. The phone was slick in my hand. My face was hot, and my voice was breathy and nervous.

How do I remember all this? Because any time I want to, I can relive every painful moment of that call by rereading my diary. I don't want to very often, but sometimes I do, so that I can remind myself how turbulent and dreadful (and bittersweet) adolescence can be. It's a useful reminder with two teenagers in the house.

The point is, I didn't leave anything out. It is all there: he said, I said (that was before the "he goes, I go" era, thank God), how many rings it took before the phone was picked up, what I was wearing as I sat on my bed, pushing my damp finger into the rotary, et cetera. I had had a monumental crush on this person for at least a year, and love, apparently, finds no detail too insignificant for scrutiny.

Neither, it would seem, does hatred, which just goes to show that all those psychologists and philosophers who go on about how closely related those two emotions are, are probably right. Certainly the scorching passion that animated Eleanor's collection of every piece of Barclay Hampton/Eastman, Bartels trivia she could lay her hands on had its roots in some kind of obsession, which might even, under the right circumstances, be called "love."

I would not have wanted to be the object of it.

In addition to collecting every document of relevance to her divorce and Barclay's remarriage, and a thick file of Eastman, Bartels client papers—which, I assume, had pertinence to Barclay's compensation and to her own rightful share of his earnings—she had edited some of the letters and documents with marginalia written in bold print with a scarlet pencil.

Dear Mrs. Hampton, began one letter, an apparent attempt by Barclay's attorney to stop her from spreading stories about her erstwhile husband all over La Jolla, *We have been notified by the manager of the La Jolla Sport and Water Club that on Saturday, May*

16 of last year, you became very irate when Mr. Hampton appeared at the club's swimming pool with his wife, whom you were overheard to call a "two-bit bimbo." Witnesses have attested that you then screamed that my client, Mr. Hampton, was a "thief and a liar" who "would not have a single client left if the truth were known about him." After this, the club manager asserts that you threw an ashtray at my client, which, while failing to strike Mr. Hampton, only narrowly missed making contact with Mrs. Hampton's head.

The letter went on to point out the inadvisability of such statements and behavior, and to threaten legal action if Eleanor did not desist. Someone, presumably Eleanor, had scrawled "*I* am Mrs. Hampton" and "she *is* a two-bit bimbo" in the margin, and "Too bad" under "narrowly missed." "Thief" and "Liar" were underscored so hard there was a hole in the paper.

I wondered fleetingly where Eleanor had found an ashtray at the Sport and Water Club, since hardly anyone smoked these days, but otherwise I felt a little chilled. It was worse than reading someone's diary; it was almost like living out another person's bad dream. Like my old adolescent self, Eleanor seemed to have no consciousness of how she came across. Even she, for all her anger, must have shied away from the obsessed, vindictive persona who emerged from the pages, had she had the objectivity to perceive it.

Dear Eleanor, began another letter, dated only a month before she died, *I know your first reaction to this letter will be a violent one, but I hope you will calm down before you take any actions which might embarrass yourself or our children any further. Your threats, which are based on a matter you have misunderstood entirely, are nothing short of blackmail, and I intend to treat them as the workings of a sick mind. If you do not desist in this harassment and persecution of myself and my wife, I will be forced to secure a restraining order against you.*

I hated that shabby-genteel "myself." But there was more. *Not only that,* he wrote, *but you will never get a red cent out of me without a court order. If you stand in my way, I have a number of means of cutting your income. You had better think twice before you follow through on your threats.*

I could see that lawyerly Barclay had given way to Barclay the irate and irritated. I wondered what threats Eleanor had made against him, since he appeared to be holding all the cards.

I felt like a voyeur, or like a guest at one of those dinner parties everyone seems to have endured at least once where the host and hostess engage in a verbal sparring match for the apparent entertainment of themselves and their audience. I thought of all the fights I had had with Steve before he had left the house, even in the years when our marriage still had vitality, and I knew how much I would hate it if any of it had been in writing for someone else to see. I wondered why Eleanor had wanted me to look through the box. I wouldn't have wanted my vulnerability so exposed—my privacy shredded and my emotional needs subjected to scrutiny.

I thought about stopping right then, but it was like stumbling on someone having sex in public— embarrassing and inappropriate, but you couldn't help looking. I decided to put aside the personal letters for the time being in favor of a sheaf of more official-looking papers fastened together with an incongruous hot-pink plastic clip. I didn't recognize the name on the letterhead, but the text was decipherable, so I knew they couldn't be legal documents. *Dear Mrs. Hampton,* read the letter at the top of the stack, *Our records indicate that the balance of your account, $2,500, is more than six weeks overdue. We have received your written request for further investigation into the matters we discussed, but, as I outlined for you at the time of your initial consultation, we will be unable to proceed until the balance is paid in full. Without further documentation, the information we provided may not stand up in court, and with this in mind we feel sure that you will want to follow through with our services. . . .*

Intrigued, I flipped through the rest of the pile. There were two more bills. Beneath them was a written report of Barclay's financial activities around the time he had separated from Eleanor. These were heavily edited by Eleanor's red pencil. *July 26* ("Six days before he left me!" Eleanor had written next to the date), *Mr. Hampton wired $300,000 to his brother, Mr. Thomas Hampton. June 5, Mr. Hampton withdrew $170,000 from a business account. August 10, Mr. Hampton made an unsecured loan of $500,000 to his brother, Mr. Thomas Hampton. Mr. Thomas Hampton is believed to have deposited these sums in an account in the Cayman Islands, where access to further information is currently impossible.* Eleanor had scrawled across the page in very large, angry red letters, "None of this money—*my money, too*—was mentioned in the financial statement he submitted to the court!"

No wonder Eleanor was monumentally pissed off. I remembered her saying, "I just don't want to get screwed anymore." I remembered my condescending reaction and how I'd both pitied and been revolted by her paranoia.

There was one more letter under the clip.

Dear Mrs. Hampton, it read, *The material you sent from Eastman, Bartels, and Steed was most helpful, but*

I am afraid that at this time we are unable to support the conclusion that Mr. Hampton's bonus was more than the $4,500 he indicates. The law firm is a partnership of professional corporations, and it is very easy for any one partner to hide his assets. Your lawyer can obtain a court order to copy the firm's documents, but by that time, frankly, it is likely that such an action would be useless. A careful and confidential examination of all your husband's financial records and transactions may provide what you desire, but before we proceed with such an investigation we would need to have an additional payment from you of . . .

The year in which Barclay Hampton had claimed that his bonus was $4,500, I knew that my husband Steve's bonus had been over $50,000. Given that Barclay was already moving up to firm superstar status by that time, the discrepancy seemed unlikely. I saw what Eleanor had been trying to explain at the makeover: Barclay had manipulated his finances to avoid giving her her rightful share. If she could prove that he had done it, it seemed very likely that he was guilty of willful fraud. I was outraged on her behalf, and the fact that she was dead did nothing to assuage my anger. She had overreacted, certainly, and the venomous, aggressive pose she adopted had scared off anyone who might have sympathized or helped her. But damn it, she had had a case.

The phone rang.

"Susan said you wanted to talk to me," my husband said in the succinct tone he used for most of our conversations these days. It found the golden mean between chilly and cordial.

Still lost in my contemplation of Barclay's perfidy, I forced myself to concentrate. "I wondered if you were going to Eleanor Hampton's funeral," I asked him.

"Of course I'm going. The whole firm is going." He sounded annoyed.

"I'm going," I told him.

"Ah. Well, I can't take you, Caroline, because I have to work tomorrow. As it is, I'll probably be late."

"That's okay. I'll go with Susan." Rob had developed a real estate commitment and canceled our "date." Some brewery barons from St. Louis were shopping for a summer place in the Muirlands, and if he didn't take them immediately he was afraid they'd go to Rancho Santa Fe instead.

"I could meet you there," he said grudgingly.

"All right."

"You sound angry," he added.

"Not at you."

"Then what, for God's sake?" He sounded exasperated.

"It's just . . . Eleanor," I said slowly. "I saw her a few weeks ago, and she sent me some papers to look at. I was just going through them. I think Barclay—"

"Listen, Caroline, I'd love to hear about, it but I have to go now. We'll talk tomorrow. There are some things I'd like to discuss with you anyway. And please, don't waste a lot of sympathy on Eleanor. We need to put on a decent show of mourning tomorrow for Barclay and the children's sake, but believe me, the world is a happier place without her."

"But—"

"Gotta go. Bye."

Eleanor's words sounded in my head like some persistent and unwelcome ghost. *Wake up and smell the coffee before it's too late. Don't you realize they're all in this together? They're out to screw every one of us!* I shook my head to clear it. Steve wouldn't do that, I told myself. Not Steve . . .

The Hamptons' church owed much more to New England than San Diego, favoring deep wood paneling and the most tasteful and restrained of crosses instead of Latin excess. There was no planted courtyard to hint at an embarrassing fertility, no gaudy messiness of votive candles. An affluent lobster fisherman would have felt quite at home. Well, make that a very affluent lobster fisherman.

The minister had a full head of white hair, like a television preacher, but he seemed a lot more sincere. His voice was plummy, with just a hint of a British accent—a West Coast Alistair Cooke. "Eleanor Mary," he said, gesturing toward the coffin that was sleek, dark, and costly, like his robe, "has found peace at last, the eternal peace and rest of our Lord Jesus Christ." He cleared his throat, which the perfect acoustics of the sanctuary carried all the way to the back pews, where I was sitting. "In her final months, he said, almost apologetically, "some of us who knew her could see that she was troubled and unhappy."

To put it mildly. The minister looked pained, and I had visions of Eleanor filling his ears for all that time with the Sins of Barclay. I tried to catch a glimpse of how Barclay was taking this, but he was up front, in a sea of suits.

It was just as well. After my immersion in his letters to Eleanor and my discovery of the way he had cheated her, I doubted if I could have witnessed any ostentatious outpouring of grief with equanimity or self-control.

The minister shook his head sadly. "Perhaps we could have done more to help her in her time of need. Sometimes we are so busy, so committed to our own schedules, that we do not have time for another person's pain. Perhaps, if we had been more attentive, this tragic loss—to her family, to her friends, to her community—might have been prevented."

My attention, which had wandered off to inspect the Victorian-style stained glass representation of, if I am not mistaken, the miracle of the loaves and fishes, suddenly jerked back to my pew. I tapped Susan on the arm.

She leaned over inquiringly.

"They're making it sound like a suicide," I hissed, sotto voce.

She shrugged slightly, looked into my face, and put an admonitory finger to her lips. Arguing with the minister was not the most tactful of funereal demeanors.

"But Eleanor would not want us to dwell on the things in her life that made her unhappy," he intoned. "She was a loving mother who wanted the best for her children. Randy, Barry, Jennifer, above all she would not want to cause you any grief."

There was a short, stifled sob from the front row. "That will be Jennifer," the woman in front of me proclaimed knowledgeably to her companion.

Jennifer was a sophomore at UCSD. She was blond and pale, with a perpetually exhausted expression. Perhaps her parents' fighting had wrung all the spirit out of her. Next to her, her brothers, twins, appeared to be pummeling each other, although in fairness I couldn't really see them all that well. Randy and Barry, were, I regret to say, monumentally unlikable children. Every time I ever saw them, mostly at firm functions, they were executing some sly prank (like putting butter on the chairs) designed to get some other luckless child into trouble. They were younger than Megan, a fact for which she and I were both profoundly grateful, as by no stretch of the imagination could they be deemed suitable playmates. I thought that now they would be living with Barclay, and I wondered how Tricia would like having her stepsons in the house.

"And Barclay," the minister intoned, in a sort of cheery, Norman Vincent Peale–ish manner, "what would Eleanor say to you, if she were here with us today?" He paused dramatically.

I smiled, imagining what Eleanor really would say.

"That she wants him to come home?" whispered Susan.

I shook my head. "Only if he arrived in a hearse."

We looked at each other and laughed. "Right," Susan said.

"And dripped embalming fluid on the carpets."

From behind me, I could feel Steve glaring at my back. You develop a sixth sense about those things when you have been married for a long time. At first it is charming: You can always find each other in department-store crowds, and you can read the other person's mood just by a glimpse of his body. Now I felt his disapproval, and it made me uncomfortable. I fought the urge to turn around and look at him, which I knew he was willing me to do.

I got so wrapped up in contemplating marital ESP that I forgot to listen to what Eleanor would be saying to Barclay, if she were here.

". . . forgiveness," the minister was saying. "That despite your new family and responsibilities,"—I could imagine Barclay giving Tricia's hand a proprietary squeeze—"she was aware of your concern for her well-being, even of your abiding love for her as the mother of your children and someone who had traveled with you along life's road."

Right.

He spread his hands in a benevolent gesture that encompassed the entire congregation. " 'Man that is born of a woman hath but a short time to live, and is full of misery. He cometh forth like a flower and is cut down.' " He paused. "Now Eleanor's worldly journey has ended. Let us remember her with love and gladness. Let us be happy that she has laid down her burden and left behind her pain. Let us take away with us today a renewed determination to attend to the ties that bind us together, to take time to show that we care. If we can do that, then Eleanor's death will not be in vain. And I think she would have liked that very much."

Suicide, definitely.

I wondered why, when I had first heard the news, I had not considered it. I lit on the image of Eleanor washing down pill after pill with sips of 100-plus-dollars-a-bottle wine and, literally, going gentle into that good night. A second later I knew why it seemed wrong, why Dylan Thomas had popped into my head. It was the rage; that was it. Depression might lead you to end it all, but rage, the kind Eleanor had seemed to harbor, led you into action. Eleanor had wanted revenge, not peace.

Besides, parading in the nude, uncaring, before the domestics was one thing, but knowing that your friends and half the fire department would get an eyeful of your sandbag ass and cottage cheese (large curd, definitely) thighs was something else. If I were going to off myself, I'd do it in my best Noel Coward–style lounging outfit and wear my most expen-

sive and tasteful underwear to boot. It's definitely
your last chance to make a good impression, and
why go out like a slob?

On the other hand, there was that Bâtard-
Montrachet. I had been to a few dinner parties
where the hosts offered, or the guests brought, wine
that expensive, but when they did, it was always
served with the requisite amount of cork sniffing
and swirling around the glass and slurping noises
that are supposed to signify urbane enjoyment and
appreciation. I didn't know anyone who sipped it
for routine hot-tub refreshment. So maybe it was the
Last Tipple, Eleanor's farewell gift to her palate, after all.

"Caroline."

I turned to find not Steve but Henry Eastman, of
Eastman, Bartels, and Steed, who had possessed
himself of my elbow with as much reverence as if
it were a holy relic. I smiled. Henry's manners were
courtly, and he had the charm of an old-world gentleman. "Hello, Henry."

"You look wonderful, Caroline. Beautiful, in
fact," he said in his soft Southern voice. He had not
seen me since Alyson Wallandi had wrought his
magic on my person. "You've done something to
your hair, haven't you?"

I could have gratified him by giving all the credit
to Naturcare, but I didn't feel like it, even though I
was genuinely fond of him. He was one of "them,"
and I was an outsider now. Besides, he spoke to me
with that false heartiness with which people address the newly diagnosed. Henry did not feel comfortable with marital rifts. He had been married to
the same woman, a slender socialite blonde, for
thirty-five apparently blissful years.

"Thank you, Henry. I'm a redhead now," I informed him, in case he couldn't put his finger on it. "Pamela couldn't make it today?"

He shook his head sadly. "She's on the committee for the Onyx Ball, and she just couldn't miss the meeting this afternoon." The Onyx Ball was the county bar association's annual formal. I realized with surprise that this would be the first year in ten that I wouldn't be attending.

"Pamela's the chairperson," Susan supplied helpfully.

Henry shrugged modestly, as if not quite able to believe his good fortune in being allied to a woman of such accomplishment. I began to see why Susan was so good at her job. I glanced at her; she looked amused.

"Of course," I mumbled. "She must be very busy."

"Caroline," breathed Steve solicitously in my other ear, "I'm so sorry we couldn't sit together. Hello, Henry. Susan." He reached for my hand, and Henry obligingly relinquished my elbow.

I couldn't decide whether to be diverted or annoyed by this unexpected display of spousal attention, clearly designed to show the senior partner that all the appropriate husbandly attributes were still intact, notwithstanding a mere inconvenience like our separation. "Hello, darling," I said cheerfully.

I had my reward. He had to struggle to keep from wincing and ruining the whole effect. "You look great," I added with what I hoped sounded like a note of adoration.

As a matter of fact, he did. Steve reminded me of the title character of *Richard Cory*: "clean shaven, and imperially slim." His blond hair had just the right amount of gray for distinction, with a kind of controlled dishevelment that made him look younger than his age, which was forty-two. His eyes were hazel and intelligent, and their expression used to be warm. Now it was coolly assessing. "Thank you," he said, but his eyes flashed me a warning.

"I haven't spoken to Barclay yet," said Susan equably. "Shall I see you later?"

"I'll take you home, Caroline," Steve interjected. Henry smiled.

"I'll call you tonight," I told Susan, giving in.

"Poor Eleanor," said Henry, when Susan had gone to join the mourners surrounding the grieving ex-husband and his new wife. "It isn't nice to say so, but it will be so peaceful now that she is gone. I must confess I won't miss her little visits to the office."

"Did she come to the office?" I asked him, surprised.

"Jesus, Caroline, she was there two or three times a week," Steve told me. "The crazy bitch was always on about something."

I ignored him and looked inquiringly at Henry.

"Oh, yes," he said, nodding gently. "I'm afraid that in Eleanor's mind her personal problems and our legal affairs were one and the same. She was rather, ah, insistent that we become involved in certain matters that were much better resolved between herself and Barclay." I remembered that Eleanor had alleged that he must have colluded in Barclay's hiding his bonus, if, as seemed likely, he had hidden it. Henry, however, seemed genuinely sorrowful. Besides, he was one of the most honorable people I had ever met, and it was much more likely that Barclay had engineered his financial arrangements on his own.

"Insistent!" said Steve, the edge of his mouth twisting up in disdain. "She had full-fledged tantrums. She was sure we were all out to screw her personally, and she wanted everyone between here and Palm Beach to know about it."

"Still," said Henry sadly, "I regret the pills. I can't help feeling a little bit responsible."

"Don't be silly, Henry," said Steve adamantly. "What could you have done to stop her? Besides, the real truth is that she did us all a favor."

"The children," murmured Henry.

"Well, we all know what kind of a mother she was."

Did we? I wondered. "Why is everyone assuming it wasn't an accident?" I asked aloud.

The two of them looked at me as if a potted plant had spoken. "What do you mean?" Steve asked with a frown.

"I mean, why would she want to kill herself?"

"Isn't it obvious?"

"Apparently not to me."

Henry did not like the way the conversation was going. "My dear, you know she was very unhappy," he said in a soft voice. "Maybe she just didn't like her life very much anymore."

"Wasn't that what she was trying to do at your office? Change her life?" I asked him. "Why would she want to give up now?"

Henry gave a small shrug, and my husband glared at me. "She was crazy, I told you," Steve said. "Caroline, we should go say something to Barclay before we leave. I have to go back to the office this afternoon."

Whether that was true or merely meant to impress Henry, who was the head of the compensation committee, I couldn't tell. In any case, it reminded me of all those weekends—years and years of them—that Steve had spent at the office while the children and I entertained ourselves at home. Weekdays were even worse, because there isn't a significant law firm in the country that shuts down before six, and most of the partners and associates stay long after that, acolytes in the religion of Billable Hours. When Steve did get home, he washed down dinner with half of an expensive bottle of wine, retired to his study to read the paper or prepare for the next day's exertions, and then fell exhausted into bed. Lawyers don't sleep well, either. There is always something that can go wrong, some lurking variable that tugs hard enough at the subconscious to trouble it into wakefulness. Once a problem gets its hook into you at three A.M., you can kiss the rest of the night good-bye.

"Are you crazy?" Steve hissed at me as we made our way across the floor to where Barclay stood, a half-drunk cup of coffee in hand, the center of a solicitous crowd. "Why couldn't you leave well enough alone? You could see that Henry already feels guilty enough as it is."

"Really?" I hissed back. "He sounded more relieved than anything else. It seems to me that people are overly pleased to give Eleanor her celestial discharge and forget about her. She may have been a pain in the ass, but she did have a point." He glared at me, which was usually the prologue to an epic of snide remarks, but he couldn't find anything to say that would not make him—us—members of that ill-bred company of persons who quarreled in public.

"Besides," I added for good measure, knowing I had a captive audience for a moment more, "if Henry feels so guilty about it, he should be pleased to think that not everyone assumes that she committed suicide. And if she did do it, Barclay's the one who should be feeling bad."

Barclay, as a matter of fact, looked as if he were afflicted with a stupendous hangover: watery eyes, green-tinged skin, and a squint indicating that the light might be too much for him. Still, since he had had his conversion on the road to Del Mar or wherever and become the husband of Tricia, he was notoriously abstemious, so maybe it was only the flu. I knew most of the people around him, but the man he was talking to—a fleshy, ineffectual towhead with pale, sad eyes—I didn't recognize.

"Of course it doesn't matter that we divorced," Barclay was saying earnestly. "I've told you, the firm will take care of everything. Henry Eastman is sending someone to go through all the papers tomorrow."

The flaccid man murmured something I didn't catch, and Barclay gave a reassuring little laugh. "You know Eleanor was always disorganized, and God only knows where she put the stock certificates and important papers. She didn't even make a will, for Christ's sake, after we got the divorce. Naturally I won't have anything to do with handling her affairs. The firm is doing it all on behalf of the children."

His listener nodded morosely. "I don't see any harm in that." The voice was flat. Midwestern.

"Barclay, I'm so sorry," said Steve, extending his hand to offer the sincere handshake that passes for condolences among men. Their eyes locked, and Steve patted Barclay on the arm with his other hand.

"Thanks, Steve." He noticed me. "Caroline, how nice of you to come. Tricia's with the children.

They're taking it very hard, naturally."

I leaned forward to give him a formal kiss on the cheek. I had considered what I was going to say. "This must be very hard for all of you."

I thought I sounded wonderfully sympathetic, but Steve gave the inside of my arm a little pinch.

"Well, yes, it is," Barclay said, his eyes turning a little glassy and his lips whitening. "I'm sure you can appreciate that, in spite of everything, I still had feelings for her." He looked as if he might want to throw up or faint.

"Would you like to sit down?" I asked him. *Lying hypocrite*, I thought.

He straightened. "No, I'm all right. Excuse me. Where are my manners? I'd like you to meet Eleanor's brother, George Johnson. Caroline and Steven James."

George extended a predictably clammy hand and regarded us dolefully. Susan had hinted that Eleanor was not on very good terms with her own family. I began to see why. I guessed that Eleanor had bullied poor George as a child. She had probably choked him when she was forced to baby-sit, and left him brain-damaged or just permanently sullen. He was no doubt overjoyed that she was gone but had some dim notion that he should struggle not to show it. Well, in that, he wasn't too far different from anyone else in the room. "I'm happy to meet you," I told him.

"Likewise."

We took our leave just as one of the secretaries in the firm teetered up in a too-tight purple acetate dress and four-inch heels. "What can I say, Mr. Hampton?" she said, dabbing her mascara delicately with a tissue. "It's so sad about your wife."

Barclay looked embarrassed. "You mean my ex-wife. But thank you."

"Oooh, sorry. But I just want to say—"

We left them to it, stopping only to greet Tricia, who clearly had her hands full with her new charges. She looked harassed, though quite lovely, in a navy blue suit. Her lustrous black hair and warm brown eyes would have complemented a grocery sack, and a recycled one at that. In spite of myself, I felt sorry for her. There is no easy way to be the new wife at the old wife's funeral, and Tricia was a bit short on imagination. She looked puzzled and kept casting stricken glances at Barclay, who seemed not to notice.

"This is awful," she said, disarmingly.

"Yes," I agreed.

4

"DID YOU HAVE lunch?" I asked Steve when he slid behind the wheel of the Porsche. The car was used, so the leather on the seats was supple and broken in. He bought it the week he moved out of our house. I would have liked to ask him if he didn't regret doing something quite so trite, but civility was too precious a commodity to be squandered on a sports car. I didn't even want to begin to guess what it cost for a tune-up.

"I didn't have time," he said shortly, fitting the key into the ignition, which was cocooned in a minor forest's worth of expensive wood. The engine turned over and promptly died. "Shit."

"Would you like to get something? We could talk."

He glanced at me sidelong, apparently dismissing the possibility that I was about to throw myself weeping upon his shoulder and beg for his return. The car turned over once more, caught, and came to life. "Have you found a job yet?" he asked.

I crossed my legs, no mean feat in that front seat, and looked out the window. "No."

"Oh. The kids all right?"

"Yes. They miss you."

"Jesus, Caroline, I see them every other weekend."

"Yes, if you don't cancel."

He sighed with exasperation. "That was only once."

"Three times in as many months."

"Are you counting?"

"Jason does."

"Jason also wants a car and an expensive college education, courtesy of his father. Sometimes I just have to work; you know that."

"I know."

There was a silence, thick as the carpeting beneath my feet. Steve maneuvered the car down Prospect, dodging the crowds of shoppers and bon vivants out for a day on the town. An occasional diver, encumbered with gear, moved ponderously down the hill toward the cove. The gulls and pelicans swooped overhead, coming to rest on their favorite rock, an expensive piece of real estate fronting the ocean, from which emanated nonetheless the acrid and unmistakable odor of gull guano. It was one of the few messy spots in La Jolla, and no one had figured out a way to bring the birds up to code.

Steve cleared his throat. "Since when did you get to be such a buddy of Eleanor Hampton's?" he asked, swerving to avoid a minivan with New Jersey plates that had backed out of a parking place directly into our path. His tone of voice told me that he had been going to say something else. I felt a prickle of uneasiness along my neck.

"What do you mean?" I asked him, temporizing.

"Jesus, Caroline, I thought you couldn't stand her," he said, giving me a sidelong glance. "I mean, it's one thing to be a little charitable at her funeral, but the way you were defending her to Henry just now sounded like you were long-lost sorority sisters or something."

"I wasn't in a sorority," I reminded him. Stanford didn't have them when I went there. I knew what he was worried about, though. He was wondering if I had caught Eleanor's virus, if he would have to start posting a security guard outside his office at Eastman, Bartels, and Steed.

He watched me in tight-lipped exasperation, an old trick. I could never outlast him, no matter how determined I was. I gave in now.

"I didn't really like her," I conceded with a sigh. "But you didn't have to be her soul mate to feel sorry for her. And I'm sorry, but I don't think Barclay is as guiltless as everyone at the firm would like to pretend. He took her whole life away from her, and then he expected her to thank him for every support check he sent."

"Well, why the hell shouldn't she thank him?" Steve sputtered. "It's not as if she did a goddamn thing in her life to earn it. Just look at her—she got at least thirty pounds beyond pleasingly plump, and, let's face it, the children are a disaster. What kind of life is that to come home to? And then she never even tried to get a job, to make something of herself after she and Barclay split up. She's damned lucky she died before he could petition the court to reduce her support payments and really give her something to be pissed off about."

"Was he going to do that?" I asked, shocked.

He shifted his gaze quickly back to the windy road and muttered something unintelligible, so I knew that he had instantly repented this revelation. It was probably part of the firm strategy Eleanor had mentioned, and I wondered how much else of what I had discounted as exaggeration might really be true. Right then I decided I wasn't going to say anything definitive to Steve about Eleanor's box until I figured out what to do with the information.

"I heard he might be quitting the practice to become a judge," I said, testing the waters.

Steve downshifted, throwing the car into too low a gear for the rpm. The grinding was deafening. "Christ," he said. "Where did you hear that?"

"I saw Eleanor a few weeks ago. We were talking about . . . the firm. She mentioned it then."

"What did she say?" he asked sharply. "Is that what you started to tell me about last night? Something about some materials she sent you?"

"It was nothing much," I told him. "She was thinking about writing a book and wanted me to look at the first chapter." I shrugged. "You can imagine what it's like. I haven't had the heart to read beyond the first page."

I knew I had hit on the perfect way to trivialize Eleanor's information. His voice softened. "I don't know about the judgeship thing. Barclay wants to spend more time with Tricia, maybe start a new family. It's been mentioned, that's all." He reached over and put his hand on my arm. "Look, Caroline, I'm not Barclay, and you certainly aren't Eleanor. I know you're worried about the future, but you can trust me. I won't do anything to harm you or the children. I hope you believe that."

I wanted to believe him. I had wanted so many things from him. Wanted him to ask me out, wanted him to want to marry me, and later, wanted him not to be angry or bored. I hadn't wanted him to leave, either. Now it had come down to just wanting to believe that he didn't want to screw me. "Thank you," I said.

"You'll be happy with the settlement, I promise you," he told me. "There is one thing, though."

Marital ESP worked both ways. My sensors went on instant alert. I waited.

"Maxine thinks she has someone who might be interested in the house," he said casually. Too casually.

I longed to scream "*What?*" and scratch his face with my fingernails, but after a lifetime with Steve I had learned that he thrived on confrontation and was rarely bested in it. Maxine was the real estate agent who had sold us our house. I forced myself to stay calm. "Our house?" I inquired, as if the notion were preposterous.

He had enough shame left to look away. "She thinks she can get a very good price for it," he said. "The way the market is now, it might not be a good idea to wait to sell."

I twisted my wedding ring around on my finger and clenched my fist, so that the diamonds bit into my palm. "I didn't know," I told him in a measured tone, "that it was necessary to sell it at all."

"Come on, Caroline. The house is worth a lot of bucks. If we do get a divorce, how do you think you can pay me for my half of its value if we don't sell?"

"Am I going to?" I asked him, appalled. Still, I noticed that he'd said "*if* we get a divorce." Talk about clutching at straws.

He shrugged. "The courts usually see that as fair."

"Even though you have all the earning capacity, and I haven't a prayer of being able to afford another house in this school district on my half?"

"No one's stopping you from getting a job, Caroline."

"And no one's going to give me one that pays enough to buy a house in La Jolla, either. What about Jason and Megan? They're upset enough about the separation without being uprooted from their school and their normal routines."

"I've been thinking about that," he said.

Now we're getting to it, I thought. But I didn't say anything.

"I thought maybe the kids could live with me while you . . . relocate."

He coughed. "Temporarily, of course."

This time I did scream *"What?"* It had the usual effect.

"There is no need to get angry," he said, the voice of reason. "It was merely a suggestion. I thought it might *help* you."

"You thought it might help me to give up the kids, sell the house, and move somewhere else?"

"You're purposely misunderstanding me, Caroline." He sighed. "You are going to have to face this sooner or later, you know. I'm just trying to work it out the best way for all concerned. The courts have frequently agreed that the children can benefit from living with their father. It isn't so automatic anymore."

"The children stay with me, Steve," I said through a haze of panic. "Don't even think about suing for custody."

He must have picked up on my mother-bear ferocity. He backed off. "Did I say anything about suing for custody? You're being ridiculous."

"Am I?" I demanded. "Didn't you say something to Megan about spending more time with you?"

"Certainly I did," he said in a superior tone. "I

miss her. Of course I'd like to spend more time with her. And Jason, too."

"Then I suggest you start keeping your scheduled visitation times," I told him. It was dangerous, though, to try to get the last word.

"It is clear that you are in no mood to be rational on the subject," he said loftily. "All I ask is that you at least consider what I've said. We have a number of issues that we have to work out, and it won't make it easier if you go flying off the handle all the time."

I looked out the window, counting to ten and plotting my response. I had it. "That reminds me," I told him, watching the bases of the palm trees flash by. "Rob wants me to go to his investment class to hear some guy talk about selling short."

I heard a strangled sound from the driver's side. I turned to face him; he was pale as yogurt. "You can't be serious," he gasped.

"It's just a class."

"But short selling is *risky*. You don't know anything about it. You would be just throwing our money away."

"Steve, you're always telling me I should find out more about these things. I'm not going to start commodity trading or investing in Bolivian gold mines. Rob thought it might be interesting for me to learn more about managing my own money."

"Rob!" my husband said with contempt—and more than a whiff of homophobia. "Besides, I thought you'd want me to continue managing it for you."

"I don't know what I want," I said truthfully. "It's just a class," I repeated.

"Do what you want," he said, pulling up in front

of the house and turning off the motor. "Just don't expect me to bail you out."

"I won't," I told him, fumbling with what appeared to be a highly intricate door handle.

He leaned across me to open it and hesitated. "Oh. Did you offer to fix me some lunch? I'm running a little late, and I don't have time to grab something."

"I haven't got anything in the refrigerator," I told him and pushed open the door.

I raced up the stairs to Jason's bedroom, possessed of an irrational desire to make sure he was still there. He was sitting on the bed listening to music that spilled out of the headphones in an appalling screech. His eyes were shut in bliss. I patted his knee.

He opened his eyes and smiled. "Hi." I had to will myself not to throw my arms around him, sobbing. "How was the funeral?" he asked.

"Sad," I said truthfully. "Listen, would you like to go to a movie later? You can pick."

He opened his eyes wide. "Anything?"

"Well, no," I said, recovering momentarily. "Anything appropriate." I had to laugh at his expression. "I'll be tolerant, I promise."

"Is Megan coming?" he asked suspiciously.

I shook my head. "She's spending the night with Marcie. It'll just be the two of us."

He considered. "Okay, I guess."

"Great. I'll catch you later."

My domestic tranquillity temporarily secured, I raced downstairs again in search of outside reinforcements.

"Gene," I breathed into the phone, trying not to reveal that I was trembling on the brink of a full-blown anxiety attack, "can you possibly do me a favor and come over for a few minutes?"

I heard static and the honking of horns. He was talking from his car phone. "Gee, Caroline, I was on my way to the office."

Gene Stewart was one of our oldest friends together. He had gone to law school with Steve and, like my husband, had joined a corporate firm in San Diego. Unlike Eastman, Bartels, and Steed, Gene's firm had not made it into the big leagues, but he was reasonably content and comfortable. We had had an easy friendship with him and his wife, Mary Ann, until she went away to med school and never came back. Gene didn't seem very worried about it and courted an amiable string of casual girlfriends. He made sympathetic noises when Steve moved out on me, but he hadn't exactly said, "Call me if you need anything." I'm not even sure if he'd implied it. Still, I thought I could trust him, and I needed advice.

I looked at my watch. It was five o'clock on a Saturday afternoon. "It's important," I told him. "It won't take very long, I promise. I could meet you somewhere, if that would save time."

His tone changed. "Is everything all right, Caroline? I mean, is everybody okay?"

"Nobody's sick or anything like that," I told him. "But I really don't want to go into it on the phone."

"There's a coffee shop across the street from the firm," he said. "I'm almost there now." He gave me the address.

"Thanks. Oh, and Gene . . ."

"Yes?"

"If you should happen to run into Steve, don't mention that I called."

I could almost hear him swallow at the other end

of the line. He said something I didn't catch and then there was a crackle, and the connection was severed.

I took the bulk of Eleanor's papers and put them into Steve's second-best attaché case (he took the best one with him when he moved out). I looked at myself in the mirror: I was still in my funeral garb; with the case in hand I looked deceptively professional. Would it be enough to persuade a judge that I wasn't dangerously hysterical or hopelessly irresponsible, or would he see that Steve had much more to offer Jason and Megan than a premenopausal mop-squeezer with an attitude?

Gene was sitting at a booth in the coffee shop, gazing reflectively into his water glass. I slid in across from him. He looked at me with speculation—tinged, I thought, with alarm. "You didn't have to dress up," he said politely.

"I went to Eleanor Hampton's funeral today," I told him.

"Oh, right." Silence. We couldn't seem to get beyond a certain unease. What was wrong? I had known this man for years, and while we hadn't exactly engaged in a lot of soul-baring bull sessions, at least we had never been uncomfortable. The waitress approached. "Would you like anything?" he asked, gesturing at the oversized laminated menu.

I was far too nervous to eat. "Just water," I said. In California, you always have to ask. The waitress gave me a disgusted look. "And some tea, please," I amended hastily.

"Coffee, black," Gene said shortly. "Now," he said when she had gone, "what is all this about, Caroline?" He sounded just like a lawyer, with an acre of desk between us instead of two feet of Formica table. It occurred to me that maybe he had adopted a distant tone in order to set me straight just in case I was coming on to him, but I dismissed the idea as preposterous. And anyway, I didn't care. I *was* desperate, but not for male companionship. At least not at the moment.

I took a deep breath. "I think Steve might try to take Jason and Megan away from me."

He shrank back in horror. "I'm not a family law attorney," he said.

"I know that. But you're a friend."

He seemed less certain of that than I was. "Caroline, I *really* don't want to get involved in your breakup with Steve."

I clutched at his sleeve. He looked as if he'd have liked to jerk his arm away, if only good manners didn't forbid it. "I don't want you to get involved," I assured him. "I really don't." Although I wouldn't have minded if he'd insisted. "Please, Gene. I need someone to talk to."

"Okay," he agreed reluctantly. He glanced around furtively, as if Steve might come popping out of the men's room at any second, accusing him of treachery.

I was beginning to get the picture, but I told him about the house, and Steve's comment about Megan and Jason moving in with him, and just about everything else that had happened since Steve moved out, except for my discoveries about Eleanor and Barclay. I was saving that for the coup de grâce.

"You're paranoid," he said with a smile, when he had heard me out.

"That's it? That's the verdict?" I asked him disbelievingly. "I'm paranoid?"

His smile broadened. "Well, you *asked* me for my opinion, didn't you?"

"Yes, but—"

He put his hand over mine, the first really friendly gesture he had made so far. "Okay, then. Steve hasn't engaged a lawyer, has he?"

"Not that I know of," I admitted.

"Then he's probably hoping you might still work things out."

I shook my head. "If that were true, why would he want to sell the house?"

He shrugged. "At least you shouldn't dismiss the possibility."

"Is it true that I'd have to buy him out if I wanted to keep it?"

"Not necessarily. But you'd probably have to trade his half for other assets, and then you might not be able to afford the house anyway. I'm not an expert in these things, but that's usually the way it seems to go. If the house is community property, half of it is definitely Steve's."

"Did Mary Ann buy *you* out?"

He nodded. "Eventually."

"Oh." I paused. "What I can't understand is why Steve would even consider having custody of the children in the first place. Even joint custody seems like too much for him."

He frowned. "Don't you think he loves his children? Couldn't he just want to spend more time with them?"

"Sure, he loves them. I'm not saying he doesn't. But he works all the time." I sighed. "Well, in fairness, he worked all the time before he left me, too. But he schedules days or weekends to see them, and then he doesn't show up. I think he might have this idea that because they are teenagers they don't need any real attention, but it's not true."

Gene pulled at his earlobe and looked unhappy

again. "Caroline, I feel incredibly disloyal to Steve in saying this, and in fact this entire conversation makes me extremely uncomfortable, but you have to realize that it's a *huge* financial advantage to be the custodial parent. I'm not saying that's what Steve's motivation is. I'm sure it couldn't be. But many men think their child support payments are outrageous, and they feel a lot less resentful if they have custody. In a lot of ways, it's profitable for the wife, too, because otherwise fathers can lose touch with their children."

"Profitable?" I sputtered.

He shrugged. "Beneficial, then. Advantageous. Get a grip, Caroline. Steve is an honorable man. He makes a good living. He can afford to pay a decent settlement, and I'm sure he'll do right by you."

I studied my empty teacup. "Maybe you're right," I told him, "but the problem is, I don't know how to protect myself if you're wrong."

He shook his head. "You aren't going to need that kind of protection. What do you think he's going to do? Kidnap the children from their beds? Turn you out into the street? What?"

"Maybe not those things," I admitted. "But . . ." I took a breath. "What if he moves our assets around so I don't know how much he has? What if he lies about his bonus? What if he makes phony loans to his relatives?"

He made a dismissive gesture. "Ridiculous."

"It's not ridiculous. That's what Barclay Hampton did to Eleanor."

He uttered a very refined version of a snort. "I've played tennis with Barclay. He's a nice guy. He wouldn't do that sort of thing."

"Well, he did."

"Who told you that? Eleanor?" He seemed almost

amused. "It was Eleanor, wasn't it? Good God, Caroline, everyone in town knows she's nutty as a fruitcake. You shouldn't take her word about anything."

"Was."

"What?"

"*Was* nutty as a fruitcake. They buried her today, remember?"

"Oh. Right."

"And anyway, she had proof." I patted the attaché case meaningfully. "Some legal documents she took from the firm, and an investigator's report. As a matter of fact, I—"

Gene was no dummy. He knew what was coming next, and he welcomed it with all the enthusiasm he might have shown a black widow spider in the woodpile. He looked away. "Don't ask me, Caroline."

"Why not?" I asked, sounding like a child.

"Lots of reasons. Because ten to one Eleanor took those documents illegally. Because in any case, even if it's true, it has nothing to do with you. Because I said I didn't want to get involved in your problems with Steve, and I meant it."

"Then you won't help me?"

"I'll help you, but I will not look at those documents." I started to protest, and he gave my hand another avuncular pat. Then he tore a page out of the front of his pocket diary—lawyers always carry pocket diaries, even on weekends—and wrote a name on it. He handed it to me.

"What's this?"

He smiled. "The name of the lawyer who handled my divorce from Mary Ann. When you do need to see someone—or if you do, I should say—this guy is very conciliatory. You may not think so, but that's important. He won't go charging in aggressively, doing things like getting a court order to copy law firm documents or emptying out the bank accounts. That would just put Steve's back up, and it's the kind of thing that starts divorce wars and lets them escalate out of control. Don't you think it's better for everyone concerned if you and Steve stay friends?"

I had to admit that it would be.

He looked at his watch and stood. He put a five-dollar bill on the table. He gave me a perfunctory hug. "Have some faith in your husband, Caroline. No matter what happens, I'm sure there will always be a part of him that still loves you." I said nothing and he gave me a searching look. "Besides, you wouldn't want to end up like Eleanor Hampton. . . ."

I didn't want to think about what he meant by that.

5

I HADN'T MADE love with Steve in almost a year. The only vaguely male attention my bodily parts had received in all that time was when Melmoth drooled on my thighs while kneading my lap into a suitable resting place.

You could hardly count that.

I had known there was something wrong for months. You can't lie next to someone night after night feeling his body go rigid with anger, his mind somewhere remote and bent on escape, without knowing. I would listen to him breathing—in, out, in, out—and try to analyze it, telling myself it was just a mood, a midlife crisis, like something out of a book that could be categorized, resolved, and worked through. I wouldn't turn over or touch the blankets for fear of irritating him further. *It's a phase*, I told myself, feeling the sheets cold and stiff between us. We'll get through it.

On the last night we made love, we were lying naked beneath the comforter like two parked cars. I reached over tentatively and ran my hand along the warm skin of his side. When he did not cringe or turn over, I stretched out alongside him, pulling close. If he had let me, I would have melted into him, swamping our little boat in a rush of desperate, restless love.

But Steve was not interested in a tsunami of passion. His hands slid over my breasts with all the fervor of an internist conducting his yearly exam, looking for lumps. He brushed my nipples impersonally with his thumb. I put my hands to his face, searching for his mouth in the dark.

His lips were warm on mine but not comforting. Once, when we had loved each other unconditionally, a kiss could be so much more—teasing, gentle, suffocating, combustible—but now it was just mouth on mouth. He pushed my hand down his stomach, kept flat and firm by hours of lunchtime workouts. I closed my hand around him, and he muttered softly. I stroked. He placed a finger in me experimentally and sighed. "Relax," he told me.

I had wanted this so much, but I couldn't. I felt rejection in every line of his body, even as he lowered himself (with difficulty) into me and began to thrust. He made no sound, moving mutely to his own rhythm, going away from me. I clung to his back in misery, my eyes wet.

He finished silently, in a spurt of hot fluid. I held my breath. He shrank away and went into the bathroom, returning with a wad of tissue, which he handed me.

"Steve," I began.

"Good night," he said neutrally, but with finality.

When we were still friends, Steve once told me that I invested every act with too much significance. Since I wasn't even a psych major in college and had never been to a therapist in my life (Susan thought I should, after Steve moved out, but then, she's from New York, and people in New York see a therapist for their hangnails), I was sure he was exaggerating, but it's only fair to warn you that the tendency may exist. Still, I don't think it's an accident that that was the last time we had sex. What I realized was that we had stopped making love a long time before. When I remembered how it used to be between us—the hours of sex, the little jokes and nicknames, the tenderness, the playfulness and joy—I felt so sad I could hardly breathe.

You might say love is deliberate, an outgrowth of the intellect as much as the body. You could think that it's some irresistible biological tide sweeping you off your feet despite yourself. Or you might just believe that the real thing is reserved for God and Mother Teresa, while everything else is either habit or fodder for trashy novels. One day you might believe one thing, the next day another.

Either way, it didn't matter. It finally struck me that, body or mind, Steve didn't love me anymore. It didn't matter what I did, whether or not I still loved him. It didn't even matter whether he felt guilty. He had stopped, and I hadn't. There was nothing in the world I could do about it. And it was very unlikely that he was ever coming back.

"Jesus," Rob said when I answered the door. "You look like you're dressed for a blind date with Claus von Bulow."

I was wearing a black sweater and slacks and a leather jacket. "I like black," I said defensively.

"I thought the Matamoros Magician or whoever he was told you to loosen up and wear more colors."

"He did. I have. But tonight this is me."

"You mean this is you feeling sorry for yourself," he suggested.

"If you choose to ignore the fact that I look sleek and sophisticated, that's up to you," I told him. "Susan says women in New York wear black all the time."

"Yes, because they're all in mourning for someone they lost to a mugger," he retorted. "I've heard it's the same in Sicilian villages."

I laughed. "Well anyway, what difference does it make? Who goes to financial planning lectures looking flamboyant?"

"Someone who wants to meet a man," he offered.

"You're not still going on about that, are you? I've told you, I don't think I could cope with dating right now. Besides, I'm thinking of joining the National Chastity Association. I'm already a de facto honorary member."

"How perfectly lovely for you. Do they have a group for the nouveau dull, too?"

"This is the nineties, Rob. You're morally deficient if you don't work out six times a week. Cheesecake is out and yogurt is in. Nobody's having fun anymore. I'm just keeping up with the trend. Besides, isn't it better than constantly wondering if last Saturday night is going to kill you?"

"You're behind the times, as usual. And anyway, it's just a lecture, Caroline, not some garish infidelity."

"Right," I told him. "So let's get going."

"The bad thing," the speaker was saying, as we slipped into the back of the room, "is not that the eighties are gone." He paused. "The bad thing is that the thirties are back."

The auditorium was full of eager young men and women on the make, leaning forward in their seats to catch any passing financial windfall. Their enthusiasm bordered on the excessive, like the opera fans at the Met who rushed out at intermission to critique the latest soprano's performance from the phones on each level. (The San Diego Opera played in a theater where there weren't many phones, and the only place people rushed out to at intermission was the restrooms. My Met stories come from Susan, and from a few weeks Steve and I spent in New York and New England one wonderful fall.)

"Still, most of the people who went short in 1991 were devastated," continued the speaker. "We watched the stocks go from overvalued to wildly overvalued to something that could only be called absurd." He paused for effect. "And then they doubled."

The man speaking was slender, dark-haired, and Continental-looking, like a Spaniard or an Italian. Mild nearsightedness made it hard to discern more than that; mild vanity made me refuse to take out my glasses so I could bring him into perfect focus.

He cleared his throat. "A lot of us—the shorts, that is—were lucky if we could only measure our losses in the single digits. People who correctly bet on companies that went bankrupt, like Continental Airlines,"—50 glossy heads bent over their attaché cases, and pens scribbled furiously—"continued to hold their positions instead of paying tax on their gain. But speculation in distressed securities unexpectedly drove up the prices, and Continental, for example, went from one dollar to five dollars a share. A lot of us got beat up on that."

I remembered how Steve had blanched when I told him I was going to an investment lecture on short selling. That reaction alone made my presence worth it, but it was obvious that the kind of speculation where even the so-called experts got badly burned was not for me. Still, I sat there with my pen poised over my notebook, just for fellowship's sake.

The woman next to me daintily licked the tip of her pen, sighed, and recrossed her slim legs beneath her pencil-thin skirt. I wondered what she would do with all the money she would make from her investments. I wondered how she managed to look so elegant and intelligent at the same time. I wondered if she had small children at home who left shit stains on the couch. I wondered if she had multiple orgasms. I wondered if she was a lawyer.

"With the market the way it is now, we have to be a lot more careful than we were in the eighties," the speaker was saying. I looked down at the program to see what his name was. Sanchez. David Sanchez. Well, not Italian, then.

"Still, I think it is safe to say that the sorts of things we have always shorted—the companies that have overhyped or misrepresented their prospects or their true earnings—will continue to be with us in the nineties. We will be watching the stocks that are ripe for a corrective decline in price. And we will make money."

I was sure that, all around me, well-manicured hands were underlining "Make Money" in their notebooks. I wished I didn't find the subject so formidable and alienating. It was inconvenient, to say the least. Now I knew how all those people who had trouble distinguishing the parts of speech or basic linguistic patterns—abilities at which I had displayed an undeniable but quite useless proficiency—had felt. Steve had always said that a large component of business success was luck, however much the firm's corporate clients wanted to believe otherwise, but I couldn't help thinking there was some basic instinct to it as well, a kind of careless confidence that attracts money to it and makes it stick, like flypaper.

After the lecture, Rob said, "Let's go up to the front." He was already moving away from me, down the aisle of closing Tumis and Atlases and newly capped pens.

David Sanchez was leaning comfortably against the lectern, apparently debating the decline of the Fesbach brothers with a knowledgeable but unpleasantly avid short zealot who was particularly interested in the role of Scientology in the brothers' rise and fall. As I knew next to nothing about any aspect of the subject, my eyes began to glaze over while I stood beside Rob, who was waiting for a polite moment to intrude. I lifted my eyebrows meaningfully at him, but he wouldn't budge.

At length Mr. Sanchez disengaged himself from his dialogue and turned inquiringly in our direction.

Up close, he exhibited none of the air you expect to find in tax attorneys and accountants—that of a child who lines up every pencil in the box by color before he puts them away. There were no visible signs of anal retentiveness. Nor did he look like a pressure cooker–loving, swashbuckling pirate of the financial seas.

His eyes were warm and brown and a little tired. His black hair was streaked with gray, and he looked about forty-five. If he had been a Regency hero, I would have described him as "tolerably handsome," although if I had done so in a book I would have been compelled to go on to describe how the hero's powerful thighs stretched out his tight-fitting stockinet pantaloons. I hadn't a clue as to whether David Sanchez's thighs were powerful or not; beneath his suit pants, they looked approximately normal.

Rob seized his moment. "I just wanted to touch base with you, tell you how much I enjoyed your lecture," he said. "I'm Ben Holland's brother."

The zealot drifted away. David Sanchez extended his hand. "Of course. Ben mentioned you. Rob, isn't it? I'm David."

Rob shook his hand and turned to me. "This is Caroline James."

David's handshake was firm and warm, neither timid nor bone-crushingly hearty.

"Caroline is my friend and neighbor," explained Rob. "She's looking for ways to expand her investment portfolio."

"Are you trying to diversify your holdings, Ms. James?"

"Caroline. I'm getting a divorce." It was out of my mouth before I realized I had finally said it out loud to somebody. I wondered, observing the remark dispassionately, what had moved me to utter it just then. It was true that I had a secret agenda— I'd been sizing up David Sanchez as a potential reader of Eleanor Hampton documents, despite the discouragement I had received from Gene—but this, to use a riding expression, was cramming the fences. It was far too soon to bring it up, and I bet it sounded pretty odd as a conversation opener.

David Sanchez's experience must have encompassed a wide variety of unusual confessions, because he handled this, too, with aplomb. "In that case, you might want to be very careful about getting into short selling, even into a fairly cautious managed fund like ours." He managed to sound reasonably uncondescending, if a bit too practiced. "We generally prefer that our clients have a continuing high income stream, or enough assets so that putting a considerable amount at risk will not cause an immediate hardship."

I saw that he had sized *me* up, correctly, as a woman whose husband was the one who made all the money. Well, it was true, but it still rankled.

"Can I buy you a drink or a cup of coffee?" Rob asked him.

David consulted his watch, which I was glad to see was not a Rolex. "I have to be getting back soon," he said. "But some coffee would be nice."

The coffeehouse was self-consciously arty, with rotating B-plus paintings on the wall and a clientele that dressed in a combination of underworld trendy and California exuberant. The tiny tables all had black vases containing a single flower that looked forlorn and desiccated amid so much opulent color. The coffee came in tall slender cups and was very expensive.

Rob and I crowded together on one side of the table across from David Sanchez. Beside so many mummers, he looked like a person of substance and solidity, upright among the slumped. In addition, he was probably the only man in the room wearing navy blue socks.

"I've been thinking," Rob was saying between sips of his mocha caffè latte, "that being a short seller is almost a metaphor for the nineties."

"How's that?" David asked politely, as if he had never heard of the concept.

"Cleaning up the excesses of the eighties," Rob said succinctly.

"Ah," said David.

"I'm not sure I get it," I confessed. It bothered me. I was usually good at metaphors.

They both turned toward me politely.

"The big gains in the eighties were fueled by leveraged buyouts or junk bond speculation or a lot of things that didn't have a lot to do with real increases in productivity or assets," Rob told me. He looked at David, who nodded encouragingly. "In the end, it was all a hollow shell. The future got downsized. Shorting relies on the same principle— selling at what you think is an inflated price and waiting some period for the price to sink before you buy back."

I looked at David, who was surreptitiously rubbing his eyes with the back of his hand and looking at his watch at the same time. He caught me looking and smiled. "Essentially, you're a pessimist, then," I said to him.

His smile broadened. "I prefer to think of myself as a realist." He shifted in his seat. "There's more to it than just sitting around waiting for things to go bad. About a third of our firm's employees are in research."

He said the magic word: "research." I didn't even wait for him to finish. "Do you ever take on work that isn't just related to a company's value in the marketplace? Research for private clients?" It had occurred to me that he would be the perfect person to review any prospective financial settlement, once he had seen, via a peek at Eleanor's documents, what could be done through creative accounting. He had the intelligence, the background, and the objectivity. Best of all, he didn't seem to be a lawyer. Besides, I really wanted someone else to confirm that Barclay was the rotten pond scum I thought he was.

"Like what?" he inquired politely.

"Private financial documents, such as personal loan transactions or . . ."

This time his smile had just a touch of condescension. "Documents relating to a divorce settlement, for example?"

I was annoyed at being so transparent. I looked at my napkin and nodded.

"We don't do *that* kind of research, Ms. James . . . Caroline. What we do is a little broader. We pore over a company's financial documents; we call their competitors, suppliers, and customers. We look for weaknesses or outright lying. Sometimes we hire private investigators."

I considered this and decided to pay him back a little for making me feel like a fool for asking. "But if word leaks out that you're investigating a company, couldn't that turn your negative opinion into a self-fulfilling prophesy? I mean, rumors could start, and then investors would lose confidence, and—"

"I know what you mean," he said in a decidedly chillier tone of voice. "But, in our opinion, investors are far more likely to get hurt by companies that hype their projections or tout favorable developments and then fail to live up to them. Besides, if we smell something fishy, we tip off the regulators, and then they investigate."

Which doesn't help the stock price either, I thought.

"It was a short who uncovered the fraud at ZZZ Best," said Rob eagerly. I could tell Rob was disappointed in me, and I was sorry, because he had gone to considerable trouble on my behalf. "You remember ZZZ Best, don't you?"

I didn't, as a matter of fact, though by now I know quite a bit about it. ZZZ Best was a carpet-cleaning company in the L.A. area that faked a pile of contracts and essentially made money in a gigantic pyramid scheme. The whiz-kid founder, who was Wall Street's darling before the truth was uncovered, went to jail. Before I could open my mouth to reply, David said, "This has been nice, but I have an early day tomorrow."

"Looking for bad guys?" I asked him.

"Jesus, Caroline," Rob muttered under his breath.

David stood and raised a graceful black eyebrow in inquiry. "Are you by any chance a Republican, Ms. James?"

It was the first personal question he had asked me all evening, but since he had spent most of it implicitly blaming the party of Lincoln for the financial mess that was currently making his fortune, I was scarcely flattered. He was stereotyping me again, this time inaccurately.

"As a matter of fact, I'm not."

"I'm sure La Jolla is a hotbed of Democratic activism," he assured me.

Well, he had me there. I don't suppose there were more than a few dozen residents who hadn't voted for the GOP at least since the days of Eisenhower, and some of those were probably live-in domestic help. Still, you couldn't really tell for sure. Bumper stickers, like FOR SALE signs, were too vulgar for display within the town limits.

"So nice to have met you," I told him with what I hoped was unruffled savoir faire. His confident manner and superior assumptions (however accurate) had gotten under my skin, but not so much that I wanted to seem like a shrew. Why is it that when men are well-disposed toward you, they argue for the sake of argument and the men all accept that, but if a woman disagrees with a man, she's a bitch?

Mr. Sanchez had the air of one politely but firmly extricating himself from a situation that was an obligation rather than a pleasure, like a family reunion or a PTA meeting. "Thank you for the coffee," he told Rob. He shook both our hands formally.

"Christ," said Rob, when he had gone. "No wonder you want to join Undersexed Anonymous or whatever it was."

I let that one pass.

"I mean, you practically went for his balls. Did you mean to accuse him of planting misinformation so that the stock price collapses?"

"Of course not. I didn't say that."

"You didn't say it, but you implied it. All the short sellers are sensitive about that kind of thing."

"Well, his sensitivity may have been dealt a mortal blow by my failure to admire his life's work, but I somehow doubt it. Besides, what's the big deal? All I did was ask him a question. The SEC must have at least prepared him for that."

He gazed meditatively into his empty coffee cup and then looked up at me. "What's really bothering you?"

"Nothing."

"Was it what you asked him about looking at private financial documents?"

"No, not really." Pause. "I told you I wasn't ready."

"You didn't have to go down on the guy. All you had to do was sound reasonably interested. Your social skills haven't atrophied that much."

"Well, he was too sure of himself. It got irritating."

I didn't have to see his expression to know how that sounded.

"Admit you were snide," he commanded.

"I was snide," I conceded. "But he deserved it."

"Caroline, he was perfectly decent. He didn't brag about his millions. He didn't blow cigar smoke in your face or make sexist remarks. I could have gone for him myself, and I'm far from desperate."

"And I am?"

"Of course you are. This evening just proves it. Listen, short sellers aren't shrinking-violet types, but you're carrying on as if he were Attila the Hun, trampling your virginity underfoot with his terrible swift sword or some such thing."

"That's a mixed metaphor."

"You're taking refuge in nonessentials," he accused.

"Why does everything have to be about sex?" I asked him.

He slipped a twenty-dollar bill under the vase with the check. "Because everything *is* about sex," he replied.

6

THE PORCH LIGHT was on. Melmoth strode purposefully out from under the azalea bush, stalking miniature wildebeests. He swatted futilely at an ichneumon fly and rounded the corner of the house. That was as much of a greeting as anyone ever got from him while he was patrolling his perimeters, unless it was one of his frequent mealtimes.

Jason was sitting in the living room, his feet slung over the arm of the chair. A magazine was open in his lap, but I could see that he had not been reading, that something was troubling him. I felt a pang for that moment, not far away, when I would no longer be able to read his expressions and his body language, when I would see only what he chose to let me see. Already he and Megan kept so much secret. This was the moment at which every mother wanted to shout, "I bathed you! I changed your diapers!" and snatch her offspring back into childhood.

"Hi, Jas," I said.

Unaware of his transparency, he attempted nonchalance. "Hi, Mom." He sat up and yawned. "What time is it?"

The antique wall clock was not five feet from his head. "Almost ten thirty," I told him.

His eyes widened and shifted and then came back to my face. "Dad's here," he said with a little shrug.

The apprehension in his look pierced my heart. No matter how many times you vow not to involve the children in your marital struggles, no matter how many divorce workshops you go to where the speakers tell you all about creative parenting and enhanced self-esteem, you know. It hurts them. You throw a great big wrecking ball into their lives and then you ask them to pretend they believe in this comfortable fiction you weave in which Daddy loves you and Mommy loves you and nothing fundamental is going to change in the family structure except that Mommy and Daddy won't live in the same house anymore. We'll all be so much happier now that there's no more fighting.

Right.

I had never anticipated putting the children I loved through the domestic version of Bosnia and Herzegovina, but here I was, causing my son to look at me anxiously and wonder how I would react to his father's presence in the house.

"Great," I said with determined cheerfulness. "I didn't see the car."

He watched me carefully, testing the weather. "It's in back. He couldn't get in the garage."

I smiled through clenched teeth. I thought: What the fuck is Steve doing here at ten thirty at night, and who the hell does he think he is, trying to open up the garage without asking me first? What I said was, "Is he with Megan?"

Jason shook his head. I saw that part of his problem was that whatever the purpose of Steve's visit, it had nothing to do with his children.

"He's in his—the—your office," he said finally. I had converted the guest room where Steve had retired—occasionally at first, and then, toward the end, on a nightly basis—to finish the day's legal work, read his photography magazines, and work out on his exercycle, into my office and library. I had to resist the impulse to run down the hall and yank open the door.

"How long has Dad been here?" I asked him.

He shrugged again. "About an hour, I guess."

"Maybe I'll see if he wants anything to eat," I offered casually. "Would you like anything?"

"No, Mom," he said sadly. "You go ahead."

When the office had been Steve's, I had never entered it without knocking, not so much because he demanded it but as a talisman, a gesture that I could hold up against his growing need for solitude and privacy. Invariably he would look up from his work, his magazine, his book, etc., etc., with an expression of controlled annoyance. It wasn't that he snarled "What do you want?" at me or anything like that. He was always very courteous. Still, he made me feel as if I were bringing him a drawing from my coloring book, something he could promise to put on the refrigerator door before going back to his grown-up work.

Old habits die hard. My hand was poised in its little fist to knock, ready to set the routine in motion again. I caught myself just in time and jerked on the doorknob instead.

The assertive woman comes into her own.

There were papers everywhere—on the floor, on the desk, spilling out of the filing cabinet like survivors of a shipwreck. Steve whirled at the sound of my entrance, and a manila folder slipped from his fingers. He did not look annoyed, he looked flustered.

I was too much taken aback to do more than mouth "What are you doing?" in a squeaky voice.

"I—I lost a file I needed at work. I thought it might be here." He averted his eyes. Was he actually embarrassed? I decided to stick to the moral high ground.

"If you had let me know, I would have looked for you and saved you all of . . . this." I looked meaningfully at the mess on the ground. "I thought you cleaned out all your files when you moved out. I haven't seen anything of yours for months."

"I know," he said, recovering a bit. "I'm sorry, but it was really urgent, and you were out."

"You called first?"

"Yes, Caroline, I called. What is this, an investigation? I've said I'm sorry about the mess, and I'll clean it up before I leave, so let's just leave it at that, okay?"

"Not okay. Those are my papers you're going through."

He folded his arms. "You have secrets now? For Christ's sake."

I made a conscious effort not to look away. "I expect you to respect my privacy. Why don't you tell me what it is you're looking for, so if I come across it I can let you know."

"Some documents for Naturcare." He waved a hand dismissively. "But don't bother; I've already looked through everything here."

"I moved some things out to the garage," I suggested.

"Maybe I'll look there before I go," he said distractedly, as I hoped he would.

I shook my head. "Not tonight. It's late, and the kids and I need to get to bed. And next time, ask me before you start going through my office."

He glared at me with disgust, having fallen into the trap. I savored my mean little victory on the postmarital playing field, but it gave me small satisfaction. I felt diminished, and I relented a little. "Would you like some coffee while you clean this stuff up? It would only take a minute."

He gave me the cold look that only someone with light-colored eyes can properly effect. He had often told me the best negotiating position for a lawyer is to be sitting on his opponent's chest. When had he become so unyielding, so hard? Toward the end of our marriage, he laid out his clothes every night—his suit first, then his shirt and tie, his socks and underwear on top. Did it comfort him to have this tangible reminder of his "real" identity so close? Did it smooth his entry into the world of important issues and big-time compensation? Did it speed his exit in the morning?

He hadn't always been that fastidious. His dorm room at Stanford, where he was a senior and I a sophomore when we met, was predictably chaotic. It was stacked with books, of course, and papers and all the normal detritus of a liberal arts education, but there were athletic trophies, too, and cast-off clothes piled beneath the Miró print on the wall. Not just a bookstore poster like the rest of us had, but an honest-to-God signed and numbered lithograph. I took it as a signpost of "true culture," like Steve's ability to discuss Camus in well-accented French (though he was only taking the twentieth century French lit class to fill a language requirement for his Poli Sci major) or to introduce Kierkegaard into a conversation without sounding pompous. He was a Renaissance man, well-rounded and proficient, and law school would be the key to unlocking opportunities for exercising the broad scope of his talents. He scorned corporate law and making money; he would be a great jurist like Felix Frankfurter or a politician like Earl Warren, but either way, the only place to be was the Supreme Court.

I liked it that he didn't feel he had to pick up the room for me (though his roommate, a meticulous transfer student from Princeton, moved into an available single about four weeks into the term). We had to shift *Principles of American Government* and *Roosevelt: The Lion and the Fox* and *The Great Depression* off the bed and onto the floor, so we could progress from protracted mouth exploration to more serious anatomical discoveries. Swooning back against the dusty pillowcase, nearly beside myself with excitement, I moaned when his fingers made electric arcs beneath my shirt. In no time at all, his hands were sliding down inside my jeans with what seemed like amazing expertise.

"Take them off," he whispered.

I could scarcely catch my breath to answer him. Still, common sense had not entirely deserted me. "Do you have anything?" I asked him. I was not on the pill, and my education was costing my parents so much a year that I was not about to take foolish chances.

He looked up from what he was doing and frowned a little. "No. Don't you?"

I shook my head.

Even then, Steve was not easily defeated. "It doesn't matter," he said and tugged at my jeans.

"Steve—"

"Trust me."

Volumes can be written about women who have fallen for that line, but I was not yet old enough for a disinterested assessment. I slipped out of my jeans, which suddenly seemed unnecessarily burdensome and restrictive, and when his fingers gently eased off my underpants as well, I made no protest.

I was not so yielding, however, when he knelt on the rug beside the bed and pushed my legs apart. "Don't, Steve," I said, clamping them together again so that the sponginess of my inner thighs would not show.

"Are you sure?"

This was a difficult one to answer. While I was thinking about it, Steve took the initiative. In a short time, I stopped thinking altogether.

"Jesus," I gasped.

"Did you like it?" Steve asked a while later, while I applied a wad of tissue to strategic areas. The rough dorm blanket chafed my bare backside, and the sheets were all the way down to the foot of the bed.

"Jesus," I said again.

"Jesus, Caroline," my husband said coldly, interrupting my reverie. His fingers curled around the edge of the desk. "You really are manipulative, you know?"

"*I'm* manipulative?"

"What would you call it? And while we're on the subject of manipulation, I don't appreciate your going behind my back and complaining about me to one of my oldest friends. I wasn't going to say anything, but when you act like this—" He broke off in apparent exasperation over my perfidious behavior.

You rat, Gene, I thought. Still, I remembered his

idea about not throwing gasoline on the fire with aggressive tactics and tried for moderation. "I didn't know who else to talk to," I told him candidly. "After our last conversation about . . . about the house, and about Jason and Megan, I was a little upset. I needed to talk to someone who cares about both of us and get his opinion."

"From what I hear, you were throwing around accusations about Barclay Hampton as well." His mouth was tight and ungenerous.

I shrugged. "I just said that it looks like Eleanor was right: Some men do take advantage of their wives."

"You got all this from the book Eleanor was writing?"

I squirmed. "More or less."

"And you believe it?"

Yes. "I don't know," I told him.

"Caroline, I am seriously worried about you. This obsession you have with Eleanor Hampton is unhealthy, to say the least. I can't believe you would drag one of our closest friends into our personal affairs on the basis of the rantings of that lunatic woman. You're imagining this whole thing!"

"Did I imagine that you want to sell the house and take custody of Jason and Megan?"

"Look, I know I rushed you on that. It's too soon; I see that now. Christ, we don't even have a legal separation yet. I know you need some time to think things through. But face it, Caroline, you've got to get on with your life. Look forward. You might enjoy the challenge of living somewhere new, starting a new career without anyone to worry about except yourself."

"You *bastard*."

He sighed. "Have it your way, Caroline. But one

way or the other, things will move forward. It would be better for everyone if they proceed harmoniously, but it's really all up to you. If you want to fight me on every issue, you'll have to pay a lawyer a lot of money to do it in court, and that will put a big drain on your resources. Think about it."

I was so frightened and angry I couldn't get my breath to answer him. I stood leaning against the doorsill, arms folded, unwilling to give him the victory of leaving him alone in the office.

When he had put all my papers and books and things away (not back, because that would imply that he put them where he had found them, and of course he didn't), he pushed past me in the doorway. He stopped in the hall and looked at me. "One more thing, Caroline. Leave this thing with Barclay and Eleanor alone. Forget about it, and get on with something else."

I drew in a breath to tell him he made it sound like a threat, but he put out a hand to silence me. He always had to have the last world. "Don't make a big thing out of it," he said with a sigh. "I'm just telling you for your own good."

I resisted the urge to chase him down the hall hurling epithets and presently was rewarded by hearing him converse with Jason for a minute or two in well-modulated tones. Then I heard the car start up, and he was gone.

I was about to shut off the light in the office and go to bed when I paused, my attention caught. There was something different about the room, something more than just the reordering Steve had done in the aftermath of his search. As a matter of fact, there was something missing.

I looked around dully for a few moments. I was very tired, and unless you have a photographic memory, trying to identify the missing piece of the puzzle is like trying to reconstruct a map of the United States totally out of your head. Try it. I shifted things around mentally a bit and then I had it: I couldn't locate Eleanor Hampton's box.

I had stubbed my toe on it every day for a week, and then, gradually, it had become part of the office furniture. When I thought about it, I couldn't really remember the last time I had seen the box. It might have been gone two hours or two days. I had transferred most of the contents to the attaché case I had taken to coffee with Gene, and as far as I knew, that was still upstairs in my closet, where I had left it. All that was left in the box were a few of the most vitriolic letters, the ones I had already gone through carefully and decided should never see the light of day.

Still, it bothered me that the box was missing. It occurred to me that if Steve had stumbled across it, he might have destroyed it in a fit of pique. I briefly considered calling him to ask whether he had done anything with it, but I did not particularly want to remind him of its existence, and it seemed likely, given his loathing for anything having to do with Eleanor Hampton, that he would have given it a wide berth.

Then a more sinister thought occurred to me: What if he was *looking* for something that had been in the box? I had told him it was just Eleanor's fictional ramblings, but Barclay might have known that Eleanor had documents that would show he had tried to defraud her. What if Steve had mentioned that she gave me some materials, and Barclay had asked him to find out what I had? I wondered how damaging the documents would be if they got out.

You're paranoid, Gene had told me. Like Eleanor.
Maybe I was seeing the bogeyman in the closet, but
first thing in the morning I was going to find a copy
machine and file a second set of the documents in
a safe place. It couldn't hurt, even if I was wrong.
The whole thing seemed like a bad spy novel, and
I couldn't really believe the scenario I had created,
but there was no doubt that, in addition to behaving
belligerently and making some pretty nasty implied
threats, Steve had acted rather strangely.

That reminded me of something else I wanted to
check. "Jason," I called out when I heard him going
up the stairs to his room, "what time did Dad call
to tell you he was coming over tonight?"

The heavy tread stopped. "I didn't talk to him,
Mom. He just came. He said he had to look for
something important. I thought it would be all
right. I mean . . ."

"It's fine," I said in a reassuring tone. "It doesn't
matter."

"Did he find what he was looking for?" he asked
anxiously.

"I don't think so."

I followed him up the stairs and down the hall.
The light was showing under Megan's door. I
opened it gently. Her bedtime was usually about
9:30, but she often fell asleep before that beneath a
pile of books or, occasionally, Melmoth.

Her hair was spread out on the pillow, and her
eyes were tightly closed. She looked absurdly
young and vulnerable, and there was none of the
budding confidence she exhibited while awake. Her
fingers still marked her place in her geography
book, tracing the tributaries of the Mississippi. I
raised her hand, heavy with sleep, and removed the

book. She turned on her side and opened her eyes a little.

"Hi, Mom. What time is it?"

I told her.

She stirred. "Sorry. I fell asleep. Was Dad here, or did I dream it? I thought I heard his voice downstairs."

"Yes, he was here."

She sighed. "Why didn't he come up, then? I would have liked to see him."

I smiled and pulled the covers up around her chin, as if she were four instead of fourteen. "He wanted to. I told him you were sleeping."

"Oh. Okay. Good night."

"Good night."

They were so natural, these lies. I'd scarcely noticed when I'd begun to cover for Steve's lapses with Jason and Megan, to reinterpret, excuse, fabricate. I had been doing it for a long time before he moved out. Occasionally, in a mood of extreme truthfulness or a bout of self-criticism, depending on your interpretation, I had to wonder whether part of me did not relish the fact that Steve was not as good a parent as I was. Having to cover for him was proof of that, wasn't it? Mostly, however, it just made me angry. How could a man who couldn't even take the time to come upstairs to see his daughter have the gall to suggest that he take custody, just because the arrangement would benefit him financially? *No way, Steve.*

So much anger, so little time. No wonder the kids looked apprehensive every time the subject of their father came up, despite my best efforts at insouciant cheer.

I had one other inquiry to pursue before I rested from my labors for the night.

I went down the hall to our—my—bedroom and closed the door. I loved this room. An interior decorator friend had hand-painted a Mexican motif along the base and top of the walls, and I had added south-of-the-border touches in the throw pillows and terra cotta pots of dracaena and sansevieria. Wide casement windows opened onto a tiled balcony. It was spacious and light, and in summer and early fall, night-blooming jasmine perfumed the air.

I walked to the bedside and pressed the message button on the answering machine.

Beep.

"We'd like to interest you in our Med-Alert system, which ties into your phone line and enables you to signal for help if you fall down and can't get up—"

Beep.

"This is Doctor Kronberg's office calling to remind you that your last dental checkup was more than six months ago. I'll call again to schedule an appointment—"

Beep.

"Caroline, this is Susan. I just called to find out if you still want to go to the Old Globe Theater next week. The firm is picking up the tickets but . . ."

Beep.

Once, in a frenzy of English-major-style speculation (and doubtless under the influence of one too many margaritas), I came up with the theory that the answering machine is the perfect metaphor for the deconstructionist's view of reality: i.e., that reality is incomplete if viewed from any one point of view, and incoherent if viewed from all points of view at once. Still, the sum of my messages gave me a pretty coherent, if scarcely upbeat, view of my new life overall, like those experts who are supposed to be able to reconstruct your entire personal universe by sorting through your trash.

I pressed the message button again, just in case.

Nothing.

Steve hadn't called first.

Another lie.

7

◡◡ DEAR ELEANOR, READ one of the letters I took out of the case to copy, *As I tried to explain to you last week, you are liable for one half of the losses on our investments out of your settlement figure. The debt accrued until the day of the divorce and will be approximately $700,000. The value of our community property was frozen at the date of our separation, so it is not reasonable for you to keep insisting on a larger portion of my interest in the law practice just because it has recently increased in value. You are still left with a sum that should be more than enough to support you and the children in comfort.*

This letter is also your official notice that your personal coverage under my medical plan is canceled as of today's date, and from today forward you are responsible for paying the premiums on the children's coverage as well, as per our settlement agreement. To help you in this, I have outlined the amounts and expiration dates of the premiums as follows . . .

Eleanor,

I write to inform you that in view of your refusal to stop slandering myself and my wife through de-

liberate and malicious lies about our personal lives, I will in future reduce your support by $500 for every instance that is reported to me.

Yours sincerely, etc.

Dear Mrs. Hampton,

Thank you for your inquiry into the possibility of our representing you in connection with your divorce proceedings. I regret that I am considering leaving the practice of law to become a judge, and while a final decision has not yet been made, I do not feel that it would be fair to represent you under the circumstances. Nevertheless, I wish you all the best.

Very truly yours,
Jay Thompson, Esq.

Dear Mrs. Hampton,

We have received your request for postponement of payment of country club membership dues for the coming year. We are sorry to inform you that your husband, Mr. Barclay Hampton, sold your membership in October. Divorce is always a sad and complicated matter, and we regret the necessity of informing you in this fashion. Should you wish to purchase a membership in your own name, please contact our membership secretary at . . .

Dear Mrs. Hampton,

As a follow-up to our conversation of last Tuesday, I would like to reiterate the point I made to you at

that time. Although I understand the source of
your rage at Mr. Hampton, your anger must be
diverted through more legitimate channels. The
slanderous attacks against Mr. Hampton, Miss
Lindera, and Eastman, Bartels, and Steed must
stop. If you cannot live within the guidelines I have
set down, I will cease to represent you. I cannot
spend my time and talents attempting to justify
your unjustifiable behavior to the courts. Moreover,
I feel that it is my duty to suggest that psychiatric
counseling might be of great potential benefit at
this stressful time.

Wishing you all the best, yours sincerely, etc.,
etc.

Dear Eleanor,

Believe me when I tell you how truly sorry I am
about the way things have worked out between you
and Barclay. We at the firm are all fond of you and
hope you will stay in touch, particularly if we can
be of any service to you or the children. At the
present time, however, I'm afraid I cannot be of any
further assistance with regard to Barclay's bonus.
That is a confidential firm matter arrived at between the partner himself and the compensation
committee, but of course it is also a matter of record
with the IRS. If you really feel it necessary to do
so—and I cannot believe, dear Eleanor, that it will
be—you could have your attorney subpoena the tax
records. At all events, the matter is out of my
hands. We at Eastman, Bartels, and Steed are sincere in wishing you all the best.

Sincerely,
Henry J. Eastman, Managing Partner

Boy, was I getting depressed reading all this stuff. It didn't seem criminal, just terribly sad, and scarcely reassuring to someone about to enter the "Valley of the Shadow" herself. Even Henry's compassionate note had been, in the end, a refusal to help. No wonder Eleanor had been goaded into the kind of obsession I had witnessed during our makeover. It made me feel so bad I seriously wondered whether it would be healthy to go on reading any more. It also awakened me to the dangers of excess, even in the face of justifiable anger. In any case, before I could dive in again, the phone rang.

"You didn't call me back," said Susan.

"Sorry. There's been a lot going on," I told her.

"You sound annoyed."

I caught myself up. I had been annoyed, a little, but not at her. You could hardly immerse yourself in an afternoon of Eleanoriana without some of it rubbing off. "Sorry," I said again. "Just preoccupied."

"With what?" she asked kindly.

I told her about the investment class, Steve's visit, and Eleanor's files.

"My, you have been busy," she breathed into the receiver. "Ummm . . ."

She had not been my friend for years for nothing. "What?" I asked her.

"I know you have this fascination with Eleanor Hampton," she began.

"I don't," I protested, bristling a little. "I didn't *ask* her to send me all this stuff."

"Whatever you say, Caroline. Relax."

"I am relaxed. What's the 'but'?"

"What?"

"I heard a 'but' in your voice."

She sighed. "Okay. I just wanted to say that this

might not be a very good time to bring up Eleanor Hampton and all her problems, particularly with the firm."

I waited. She didn't go on. "Talk to me, Susan," I prompted her, after a minute.

"I shouldn't be telling you this. I would lose my job."

At least she didn't say, "Promise you won't tell anyone." We knew each other too well for that. I held my breath.

"Steve's contacted Jay Thompson," she said at last.

"Who's that?" I asked her. I had heard the name recently, but I couldn't quite place it.

Susan's tone was neutral. "He's a big-time divorce attorney."

I had it. "Oh, that's right. Eleanor asked him to represent her. Didn't he become a judge?"

"No, Caroline. He represented Barclay."

I finally understood what she was saying. "Oh." It was all I could think of to say. I had known this moment would come, of course, but until it had, I hadn't realized how weak my defenses were. It was like the difference between a rehearsal and a play, between imagining someone's death and actually feeling the loss. It took my breath away.

"Caroline?"

"He's found someone." My mouth was so dry I could scarcely frame the words. After all our recent conversations, I realized that Steve probably had finances on his mind more than flings, but it was the first thing that popped into my head anyway.

I had read an article by a woman who said that whenever she was really angry with her husband, she pictured meeting him with his new wife and baby. She would run into him in some public place—a park or a museum—and she would be un-made-up, carelessly dressed, vulnerable. The new wife would have slim hips and tight jeans, in spite of the baby who bestrode the world like a colossus from a carrier on the husband's back. The husband and new wife would be polite in their inquiries after her well-being, but their intimacy, their little gestures and looks, were like physical blows. She would excuse herself quickly and run off, while they looked after her with pitying glances.

It never failed to make her want to keep him, she said. She swallowed her anger before her scenario became reality, before she pushed him into the seas where all those potential second wives were trolling, their high, firm breasts and tight buns like bait upon the hook. No matter if the fish had prior, inconvenient attachments.

"We don't know that," Susan insisted. "I haven't seen him with anyone or heard anything to suggest he's seeing anybody seriously. And you know how the office talks."

"Would you really tell me if you knew? Well, not *knew*, but suspected?" Christ, this was so undignified, but I couldn't stop myself.

"Of course I would," she said quietly.

There is more than one school of thought on this issue, of course, and some contend that it takes two to do the hurting: the one who cheats and the one who tells. Telling may have more complicated motives than simple friendship, I admit. Still, I put those who would rather not know in the same category as those who would want their doctors to lie to them about their terminal diseases. I say call the cancer a cancer and skip the paternalistic bullshit.

"I know that," I told her. "I'm sorry. It's just sort of a shock."

"It might not be anything to worry about. Maybe he wanted to talk to him about something entirely unrelated to the two of you. But if it isn't . . ." She paused. "I just didn't want you to be unprepared."

"I am unprepared. I don't even have a lawyer yet."

"That's what I mean."

"But if I get one, and he hasn't really done anything yet, then I'll be forcing his hand, won't I? I might be rushing into something."

Her silence, which was tactful, nevertheless told me what she was thinking.

"It's hopeless, isn't it, Susan? He's never coming back, is he?"

"I can't answer that, Caroline," she said firmly. Her tone, which was matter-of-fact and not at all pitying, was exactly right. "Do you want him to?"

"Probably not," I confessed. "Not after all this. I'm not sure we could put it all back together again. But he is the children's father. And besides, I'd like it to be my choice, not his."

She laughed. "Well, that's honest, at least."

"So what do you think I should do?"

"Do I really have to say it?"

"You think I should call a lawyer."

"I think you should call a lawyer," she agreed.

"Maybe I'll call the person who represented Eleanor," I said, "as long as Jay Thompson might be representing Steve."

Silence again.

"I was kidding," I told her. "I have someone else's name."

"I hope so." She took a breath. "You want to stay

miles away from any association with her."

I thought this was carrying it a bit far. "Susan, she's dead."

"So is Hitler."

I laughed.

"I'm not kidding. They were furious with her around here. You can't imagine. You don't want anyone to put you in the same category. I know it seems ridiculous, but you don't want this to become a revenge thing." She sighed. "That's why I was warning you about the box."

"Susan, Steve knows I'm not after his balls, or whatever it was they accused Eleanor of. He knows me better than that. As long as he doesn't try anything unreasonable . . ." I tried to sound confident, but when I reviewed some of our recent conversations, I wasn't so sure.

"Maybe," she agreed, "but if he's retained Jay Thompson, it won't be Steve who's calling the shots. Besides . . ." She hesitated.

"Besides?" I prompted her.

"Well, in the end Eleanor really did get screwed, didn't she?"

Five minutes later, the phone rang again. It took me a while to answer it because I was in the throes of a digestive upset I don't particularly want to describe. Stress always went directly to my midsection. The body that could process a slice of Brie or a chocolate eclair, sending it uncircuitously to my outer thighs with maximum efficiency, completely lost it when it came to handling pressure.

"I almost forgot," said Susan. "I assume you don't want to go to the play, but I didn't ask you."

"The play?" I asked blankly, and then I remem-

bered. The firm outing. Dinner under the stars. "Oh,
yes . . . why not?"

"Well, everyone will be there," she said bluntly.
"I thought you might—"

"Susan, it's *Much Ado About Nothing*!" I cried.
"It's my favorite Shakespeare."

"Have you thought of just renting the movie instead?"

"Why don't you think I should go? I don't have
to sit with Steve."

"No, but what if he shows up with a date?"

"He wouldn't do that to me. Not at a firm event.
Not when we're not even divorced."

"Caroline, the world is full of women whose very
last thought before the bastard pulled some egre-
gious shit on them was 'He wouldn't do that to
me.' "

I remembered her fiancé and the canceled wedding party, and I wondered if she had told me the
whole story. At the moment, I didn't much feel like
asking her.

"I don't care," I told her. "I can't be hiding from
him for the rest of my life. The people in the firm
are—or at least used to be—my friends." Besides, I
thought, what better way to prove that I was rational, in control, and not reduced to a quivering
wreck by such a small thing as an impending divorce?

Everyone knows that after a woman has crossed
the Great Divide—suffered the "Big D," as they say
in La Jolla—she gets ostracized by the still-to-all-
apparent-intents-and-purposes-blissfully-married
sector of her acquaintance. The higher her ascen-
dance on the social ladder, the more precipitous the
fall. This appears to have not much to do with the
state of her bank account, wardrobe, or store of wit.

It's as if all those "just girls" lunches at the La Valencia Hotel suddenly become inappropriate and threatening if one of the girls doesn't have a husband to go home to. And the women's organizations—the upper tiers of social groups with Spanish names who organize the charity fund-raising events where everyone wears dresses that make them look like popped soufflés—are pretty much sisterhoods of one half of a couple.

Still, I didn't move in those circles or even aspire to them, and while I did expect some diminishment of attention from our married friends, I couldn't believe I would actually be unwelcome at group events. And it was *Much Ado*. I didn't see why I should give up my life just because Steve was, as he so euphemistically put it, moving on.

"I'm going," I told her firmly, inspired by the notion of feisty Beatrice. "I don't care if Steve brings Madonna to it; I'm not going to stay home and mourn my marriage while everybody else is enjoying Shakespeare."

"Bravo," said Susan. "Or is it 'brava'? Anyway, if that's what you want, go for it."

"You sound like a self-help book. 'Be all you can be.' 'Get in touch with your inner elf.' "

She shuddered. "God forbid. I haven't been in California *that* long." She paused. "Elf?"

"I think it's like your inner child, only more quixotic."

"Caroline, tell me you haven't been reading that shit."

I laughed. "No, I just read the titles in the book review."

"Well, if you feel the urge, promise me you'll see a good shrink instead. It costs more, but at least you won't end up sounding like a recruiting poster for psychobabble summer camp. Anyway, what about the dinner?"

"Sign me up," I told her, feeling reckless. "After all, how much worse could things possibly get?"

8

FOR THE RECORD, I am not one of those people who believe in Fate, so, theoretically at least, there can be no such thing as tempting it. The expression "knock on wood" is almost as repulsive as the act itself. It smacks of Santería or sacrificing chickens or some such thing, all of which doubtless have their place in certain cultures but are only marginally relevant, if that, to twentieth-century La Jolla.

Still, I have to say it. Asking "How much worse can things possibly get?" was a dumb move.

On the morning after I talked to Susan, I called up the lawyer whose name Gene had given me and made an appointment for a preliminary consultation. I made cookies for a bake sale that Megan's choral group was having. Then I put Melmoth out, locked up the house, dropped off the cookies at the school, and went shopping for something to wear to the play. You might think that such a trite and trivial activity would be the last thing on my mind in the midst of so much domestic chaos, but the image of myself in some devastatingly chic and colorful outfit, disporting insouciantly among the lawyers, was the only tonic I could think of for the depression and fear that made me want to pull the covers over my head and sleep till it all blew over. If you're thinking that was shallow and silly, you might be right, but I have to say it worked for a while. And anyway, in the end I got punished for it.

I parked the car in the driveway and unloaded my packages. The door was still locked; I remember that. I turned off the alarm and put the packages down at the foot of the stairs, crossing into the kitchen.

The card, gilt-edged and slick, was lying on the kitchen table. It read "Sunlight Realty" over an agent's name I didn't recognize. I knew it hadn't been there when I went out because I'd cleared and wiped the table after breakfast. Maria, the house-cleaner, was coming in the afternoon, and I always picked up before she got there. I stared at it stupidly, thinking of how the door had been relocked, the alarm reset. It could only mean that Steve had given someone a key and permission to show the house.

I started hyperventilating. I picked up the phone and dialed the number on the card. The agent, chirpy and unsuspecting, took my call.

"Oh, Mrs. James," she gushed before I could say anything more than my name, "my client *adored* your house. Such a lovely neighborhood, and so beautifully kept. I'm sure we can get a good price for it. The only thing is—"

Despite myself, I couldn't help asking. "What's that?"

"Well, frankly, dear, my client was very interested in seeing your garage, but it was such a mess I couldn't show it."

"My garage is not a mess," I said defensively.

"Whatever you say, dear. But if you are really serious about selling the house, I suggest you clean it up."

I drew in a breath. "That's just the thing. I'm not."

"Not what?" she inquired, her tone a shade less friendly.

"Not serious about selling the house. In fact, for the moment I have no intention of selling it at all."

"I see."

"And furthermore, if you come into my house again without my permission, I will inform the police."

"Mrs. James, there appears to have been a misunderstanding. We obtained the key from Maxine Dorfman. I understand that your husband has given her the listing," she said patiently. Her tone said she understood very well what was up.

Stay calm, I told myself. "Well, there has been a mistake. I am half owner of the house, and I'm telling you it is not for sale." I said the words very slowly and carefully. Mentally I was running through the cost of rekeying all the locks and changing the master code on the alarm system.

"Certainly, dear," said the agent in a placating voice. "I understand how it is. But when the time comes, I hope you'll consider using—"

I hung up on her.

When the time comes. I could turn the house into a fortress, but how long could I hold out? Steve had promised that he would wait and not push me. The inevitability of losing the house, which I had refused to concede, suddenly became a lot more real. And if I could lose the house, maybe I could lose the children, too. Things were moving too fast. I had never felt more powerless in my entire life.

Still, I wasn't completely brain-dead. I called Maxine and explained the situation to her candidly, pointing out that I could still end up with the house as part of my settlement, and it would scarcely be good for business to alienate me by showing it against my will. She sounded genuinely shocked and apologetic, which may or may not have been an act but made me feel better. She promised to hold off showing the house until she heard something "definitive." I decided to leave it at that.

Then I started thinking about my garage, which was a definite improvement over thinking about my divorce. The last time I had seen it, which was when I pulled the car out in the morning, it had probably not qualified as a mess. Sure, there were a few too many boxes of old *Connoisseurs* and *Gourmets* stacked up underneath the workbench and turning into spider condos (thank God Steve had taken three years of back issues of *Photography* when he left), but it wasn't *that* bad. Now and then I would get visions of my old age in which, like one of my octogenarian neighbors, I lived out my days surrounded by stacks and stacks of unread reading material, making my way to the bathroom and kitchen down paper corridors. Following these epiphanies, I always threw out the past few years' accumulations, and I was pretty sure I'd gone on such a binge within the last year. So how bad could it be? I pushed the button of the door opener inside the house and looked out.

My garage was a real mess.

The boxes were tumbled out of their careful stacks, their contents spilling all over the floor and blocking the entrance from the driveway. The storage cabinet doors stood open despite their earthquake latches. I ran to the side entry. The chain was dangling from the frame where the door had been forced open. It wouldn't have taken much—one good shove could do it. We'd always meant to install a dead bolt and hadn't gotten around to it. I looked around, wondering what the burglar had taken. The kids' mountain bikes were still leaning against the far wall, apparently untouched. The tools, the sports equipment, even the wine storage unit had not been disturbed. What, then? I shifted some boxes gingerly, mindful of lizards and arachnids, neither of which tops my list of desirable companions. Some of my old college term papers and books, things I hadn't seen in years, were at the bottom of the pile. I tried to envision a bibliomaniacal burglar, obsessed with other people's reading material. It didn't make sense.

Next to the book pile was a vaguely familiar-looking roll of material, which I unwrapped gingerly with the aid of a garden hoe, wary of unwanted surprises. The material turned out to be an old comforter which I thought I had long ago given to the Cancer Society Thrift Store. Enclosed within it was a pillowcase I did not recognize containing a pillow I did. It had belonged to Megan, and it had taken me years after it had become a lumpy, misshapen eyesore to get her to finally put it away. I think it languished in a closet for a year or two before it ultimately, by our mutual agreement, made it into the trash. That I did remember.

The pillowcase also contained something that looked like a baseball with gangrene, which I identified, after the first wave of horror, as a somewhat geriatric orange. Next to it were an unopened sack of corn chips and a can of carbonated grape drink. I hadn't been able to ban those commodities from the household, precisely, though for aesthetic reasons I wouldn't have minded, but the kids' indulgences were generally colas (sugar-free for Megan) and, good Southern Californians that they were, tortilla chips. And while I was ready to fault Steve for many things, it never for a moment occurred to me that this dismal stash could be his.

That left the decidedly unwelcome possibility that, in addition to trashing my garage, a homeless person might have taken up residence there.

Living down-and-out in La Jolla is not the oxymoron it might seem. Dumpster-diving at the two downtown supermarkets is likely to yield up a menu Alice Waters might not disdain (particularly now that edible compost is de rigueur), if you don't mind a few bruises or a little mold on your arugula or chanterelles. The beaches are reasonably safe and comfortable for sleeping, and the climate makes a New York kind of desperate contrivance like camping out on the grates largely unnecessary. Rumor even had it that some ex-socialites, newly divorced and down on their luck, lived in their cars but managed to keep up appearances by having free makeup demonstrations at department store cosmetic counters.

Still, it is one thing to be basically sympathetic, to experience the reflex frisson of guilt (or, in the case of the socialite divorcées, fear) in the face of the HOMELESS/WILL WORK FOR FOOD signs, but it's something else entirely to confront the possibility that some wild-eyed dérangé has taken up residence in your garage. And why would he vandalize it and not steal anything? My blood pressure went up alarmingly. I lifted the quilt and the pillow and the food with a pair of tongs and dropped them into an open garbage bag. I tied the bag up with a twistie, stuffed it into the garbage can and dragged it out to the curb, though it was two days till trash day.

Then I walked into the house and called the police.

I didn't really expect them to do anything about it. San Diego, like every other major urban center, is short on police, and its residents seemed to feel that the funding for more of them ought to come out of the pockets of welfare cheats or cutbacks in the libraries. Consequently, there weren't enough to handle even the major crimes, and if you suffered, say, a purse-snatching or a stolen bicycle, the most you could hope for was a sympathetic phone conversation with a precinct clerk. A break-in in the garage (particularly where nothing was stolen) or routing the homeless, even from La Jolla, was probably not a high priority.

I was surprised when the pleasantly efficient voice on the other end of the line informed me that someone was already in the area and would stop by within the hour, if that was quite convenient. Then I started wondering why someone was *in* the area, and then I closed the garage doors, picked up Melmoth (What if the vagrant was a cat-murderer, too?), reassured myself that I did not need to pick up Jason and Megan from their respective after-school activities for at least three hours, and bolted myself inside the house.

The doorbell rang about half an hour later.

I peered cautiously through the peephole. Then I laughed and opened the door wide to Kenny Henson, Rob's ex-stepbrother (if I have got that right) and present lover.

Kenny, particularly in S.D.P.D. uniform, could have been the Platonic ideal of a Roman centurion. With his surfer-blond hair, tanned and muscled body, and cerulean eyes, he wasn't exactly Marcus Aurelius, but he had a sweetness and an ability to sum up character that made him immensely likable and, in an odd way, a perfect mate for Rob, whose edges were altogether sharper.

Kenny flashed me a thousand-watt dazzling smile. "Hi," he said casually, stepping into the house. "I heard you had a break-in in your garage, so I thought I'd come over and check it out."

"Thanks," I said fervently. "I found an old blanket and pillow, and I know I had already thrown them out. There was some food tucked out of sight, too. I think the guy that trashed it might have been living there." I told him about the moldy orange, and the papers all over the floor, and the puzzling fact of nothing being missing. I said I knew it had happened this morning because a friend had tried to get into the garage and found the way blocked. I didn't mention real estate agents. Rob would have a fit if he thought someone else had been showing the house, even without permission.

"Have you seen anybody?" he asked, sounding concerned. After all, his and Rob's house was equally vulnerable, and all of us wanted to know it if a stranger had taken up residence in the neighborhood.

I shook my head.

"I haven't, either. I'll keep a lookout, though. How was the garage broken into?"

I told him.

"Let's go take a look," he said.

"I already threw out the stuff," I told him.

"I'll just take a look," he said kindly.

"Do you want to see the pop and the corn chips and the orange?"

"No," he said with a shudder.

*   *   *

"Was all this stuff stored in here?" he asked, surveying my boxes with a critical eye. I knew he disapproved, because Rob and he maintained a garage whose neatness and sterility was surpassed only by a Swiss W. C.

"I'm cleaning things out," I told him.

He smiled. "Get a dead bolt for the door," he said, inspecting the ruined chain. "Don't use it for a while; just go in and out with the opener." He stepped outside and looked around. "Have you been using the spa?"

"Now and then." Steve had wanted a pool, but even though I liked to swim, I argued that unless you were willing to spring for twenty-four-hour heating, the water would never get warm enough to be really comfortable. About half of La Jolla had pools they used three times a year, all of them in August. Besides, when the kids were younger, I didn't want the hassles, so we had compromised on a hot tub. I didn't really like it; the water made your skin prickle and the interior was too slick, like the underside of a snail. Still, sometimes it was nice to climb in at the end of the day and watch the sun go down behind the Torrey pines, a glass of Chardonnay in hand.

"Well, don't," Kenny said. "At least not at night. And not for a while."

I thought of sitting alone in the water in a bathing suit. It made me feel extremely vulnerable and defenseless. I shivered. "Like Eleanor," I said aloud.

"What?"

"I was thinking about how Eleanor Hampton died. It's scary to think about how hard it would be to protect yourself."

He frowned. "Maybe, but Mrs. Hampton offed

herself. No homeless psycho shoved her under the water while he emptied her wine bottle."

"How do you know?" I asked him.

"Because there was no evidence that anyone else was around. The housekeeper had gone home for the night, and there wasn't anybody else on the property."

"What I meant was, how do you know she killed herself? I always wondered."

He shrugged, a gesture that seemed to imply lack of knowledge rather than interest. "We don't, really. It could have been an accident. She might have just doped herself up too much on pills and booze and passed out. If you're far enough gone, slipping into the water might not rouse you before it's too late. People have done it before." He stopped, shaking his head over the folly of mankind. You probably did that a lot if you were a policeman.

"Well, then?" I prompted him.

He raised his eyebrows. "You know, I'm not sure I should be telling you all this."

"Why not? It's not a murder investigation."

"Well . . ."

"Come on, Kenny. You know Rob will tell me if you don't."

He smiled then. "What makes you think I tell Rob everything?"

"Because he'd make your life a living Hell if you didn't."

"You're right. And anyway, as you say, the investigation is closed. Your husband's law firm saw to that."

"Eastman, Bartels?"

He nodded. "They were very big on the suicide theory, too. Brought us some letters and some evidence that your Mrs. Hampton was off her rocker.

It seems she thought the entire legal world was in conspiracy to get her, personally. She was planning to write some kind of a book about it, but it looks like she just got fed up and couldn't take it anymore."

"She wrote that to someone?"

"She apparently told several people that it was costing her a fortune in legal fees to fight Mr. Hampton, and she was sure she would get screwed in the end anyway."

"That's probably true," I admitted.

"Well, the law firm was eager to get the whole thing wrapped up as soon as possible. They didn't want to embarrass Mr. Hampton with his messy ex-wife any longer than necessary. That's probably why they handed us the whole thing on a platter. It seemed to fit, and since there was no evidence of what the public likes to call 'foul play,' we went along with their version." He cleared his throat. "I'm being a little too candid here. Please don't quote me on this."

I swore as much discretion as if I had been Bob Woodward protecting Deep Throat.

"The only thing is, I can't imagine offing yourself dressed—undressed, I mean—like that. I mean, she looked *terrible*, even for a corpse. And I've seen some bad ones, especially when I worked the Southeast."

I told him I had thought the same. "Does anyone know where Barclay was at the time of her death?" I asked him.

He cocked a golden eyebrow. "What's that supposed to mean?"

"Nothing much. But Barclay was acting strange at the funeral."

He shook his head.

"I know it's not an indictable offense, but I expected him to act all smug and smarmy, the way he usually does. Instead he was sort of . . . distraught."

He looked at me. "It's possible he was genuinely sorry that she killed herself."

"That's not what I meant." I struggled to pin down the thought into words. "He seemed more worried than upset."

"People always act weird at funerals. You can never tell if somebody's guilty or not by the way they seem. Didn't you see *A Cry in the Dark*?"

"You mean where the Meryl Streep character was convicted of killing her child because she seemed so unemotional, and it was really the dingos that did it?"

"Right." Rob and Ken had seen every movie since *The Birth of a Nation*. "And anyway, Mr. Hampton was at his office at the approximate time of his wife's death."

Oh. "The firm told you that?"

"They confirmed what Mr. Hampton told us." He folded his arms. "Why does this bug you so much?"

I sighed and wondered if I would ever come up with a satisfactory answer to that question. "I'm not sure," I told him honestly. "But I felt sorry for her. She was probably certifiable, but nobody should have to die like that." I paused. "I just can't stand the thought of Barclay Hampton secretly gloating over all this, after everything he did to her. He treated her a lot worse than anyone realizes. I just want to be sure he didn't have the tiniest thing to do with her death, like threatening to take the children away or to cut her support check in half. I just want to know that he didn't somehow pressure her into suicide."

He shrugged. "I can't help you there. But at least you know he didn't murder her."

I looked down at the jumble at our feet. "Kenny," I asked him after a moment, "do you think whoever left the food and things in the garage was the one who did all this?"

"My professional opinion?"

"Sure."

He shrugged. "Maybe, but probably not. The stuff in the sack sounds like it's at least a few days old. If somebody was hanging around your garage, why would he trash it and not steal anything? It doesn't make sense." He shook his head. "Not that some of these guys need a sensible reason for what they do. Still, this could just be kids, or—" He stopped.

"Or what?"

"Well, this is really a bizarre explanation, but to tell you the truth it looks like somebody was looking for something." He smiled at the absurdity of the idea. "You aren't by chance hiding something out here that somebody wants pretty badly, are you?"

"I'm not sure," I told him curiously, I couldn't help remembering how I had implied to Steve that I'd put the rest of Eleanor's materials out in the garage. I don't know why I hadn't thought of it right away. I couldn't help believing there was a connection, somehow. Eleanor had said she was getting screwed by Barclay, and everything pointed to the fact that not only was she right, but she was trying to get evidence to force him to behave honorably. Maybe Barclay wanted a look at that evidence; it would, to say the least, be embarrassing if it got out. Still, breaking into my garage might be carrying things a little far. I knew that if I confronted Steve, he would tell me *I* was certifiable. Besides, if I did anything like that now, he could use it against me later, in court. I would have to have proof or keep silent. I shivered. "If somebody did break in to look for something, what about the stash?"

He raised his eyebrows. "A coincidence, maybe. Who knows?"

I shivered again. "Kenny, will you come take a look around the house? Just to make sure it's as burglarproof as possible?" As soon as he left, I was definitely calling the locksmith and the alarm company.

He looked at me with concern. "Okay."

When I opened the back door, Maria was standing at the sink, going round the edges with a toothbrush laced with stainless steel cleaner. None of my accumulated dirt ever escaped her notice, and standards would definitely decline after her departure. She had arrived after I had gone out to the garage with Kenny, but I never had to worry about giving her instructions or supervision. I was really going to miss her when I could no longer afford household help—a day, I realized, that could not be postponed much longer. It wasn't that I minded doing all my own housework so much, although I can't say that the prospect of scrubbing out toilets myself seemed particularly attractive or virtuous, but the idea of this gradual shrinkage of affluence was painful, a constant, niggling reminder that I hadn't really paid for (read: deserved) my former privileges myself.

Maria looked up when we entered, toothbrush poised for another stab at sink slime. Her hand stopped in midair, and while only in drugstore novels would you have described the implement dropping from her nerveless fingers, that is pretty much what happened. She gasped and gave Kenny such a stricken look that I wondered if I had been mistaken about her integrity after all.

"Maria," I prompted her, "you remember our neighbor, Officer Henson."

She bent over and picked up the toothbrush. "*Sí, señora,*" she said, uncharacteristically, in Spanish.

"This is Maria Castañeda," I reminded him. "Her cousin Manuel works at Eleanor Hampton's house."

Maria, who had been regarding Kenny as if she would have liked to ward off the evil eye, started. "Oh, no, señora. He went home."

"Home?"

"*Sí.* To Mexico. His mother was very sick."

"Oh, I'm sorry," I told her. "You should have told me. When did he leave?"

She shrugged. "*Hace rato.*" Her eyes did not meet mine.

"Well," I said, puzzled, "Mr. Henson is here because we had a break-in in the garage. There may have been someone sleeping in there, too. Have you seen anyone? Anyone at all," I stressed.

She lifted her hand. Her eyes grew big. "No, Mrs. James, I see no one."

"We think it might be a homeless person," said Kenny. "Mrs. James is going to keep the garage door locked. I'm pretty sure there is no danger, but be careful if you go out there by yourself. And if you see anyone, let someone know right away, okay?"

Her face was closed, as inscrutable and resigned as the Oaxacan Indians who had been her ancestors. "Yes, sir," she said and gave the grout another vigorous jab with the toothbrush.

9

PATRICK DUNN CAME around from behind his football-field-sized rosewood desk to greet me, his hand pumping mine with enthusiasm. "Gene Stewart told me you might be coming," he said affably. "I'm happy to be of assistance, if I can. Gene is a very close friend." He pulled out a chair for me to sit down. "And of course I know your husband as well."

I was paying him a rather hefty consultation fee, so I'm not sure why he made it sound like he was doing me a favor because I was lucky enough to have such illustrious connections. "You know Steve?" I inquired.

He nodded. He sat down again, smoothing his suit coat as he did. It fit him flawlessly, like an anchorman's. "We've worked together on a few projects," he said offhandedly. "Eastman, Bartels refers some business to us now and then, because we work in a very specialized area of tax law."

Judging from the looks of the place, they probably set up offshore insurance funds in the Caymans. Patrick Dunn had a sleek look, too, rosewood made flesh. But what about my divorce? "Aren't you a family law attorney?" I asked him.

"Oh, ha ha," he said jovially, as if I'd made a wonderful joke. "I *used* to be, but now I only handle special cases." He winked. "Like yours, I hope."

"Won't it be a problem for you?" I asked, leaning forward in my chair to keep from sinking deep into the comfortable cushions.

"Oh, no," he said with a smile. "It's like riding a bicycle—you never forget. Besides, there is a great deal of tax law involved in these issues, so I like to think I have a leg up. I can assure you, you're in very good hands."

I couldn't help looking at his. They were very white and perfectly manicured. I sighed. "I meant to say, would it be a conflict of interest, because my husband's firm sends you work?"

He stiffened and pushed the edges of a stack of papers on the desktop into perfect alignment with the palms of his hands. When he looked down, I could see that he had the beginnings of a double chin. "I prefer to think of myself as a mediator rather than simply an advocate," he said at last, when the pile was perfectly precise. "If I do my job, you and your husband will stay friends, and the usual adversarial role a divorce lawyer plays will not be necessary."

"You mean that Steve will be happy with the terms of the settlement," I translated.

"Mrs. James, in this state we have no-fault divorce," he said patiently, as if I were an obtuse young associate. "You ladies wanted that—fought for it, even. However, there are certain realities we have to face. Women are no longer helpless creatures who can't support themselves, so now we divide the property pretty much equally and go from

there. I'm not saying we can't get you a nice settlement, but there are no more free rides."

Oh, great, a reactionary. "I'm not looking for a
free ride," I told him, trying to stay calm.

"I'm glad to hear it," he said with a benign smile.
"Look, there are lawyers out there who will advise
you to fight for every last dime, who'll start up the
war by filing liens on the husband's property or getting court orders to copy documents. We lawyers
like to win and we don't like to get sued by our
clients, so it's natural to go for the jugular." He
stretched his arms over his head. "Needless to say,
that is a *very* expensive approach." He looked virtuous, as if such a strategy would never have
crossed his mind. "I always tell my clients, why not
buy a Mercedes for your wife instead of for your
lawyer? Be generous, and you can get out sooner
and get on with your life." His smile slipped. "Oh,
I'm sorry. That was tactless. But I'm sure you see
what I mean."

"I do, but what if my husband doesn't see it that
way? He's already hinting strongly about asking for
custody of the children, and—"

He folded his hands on the desk. "Asking for custody is often a bargaining strategy. In my experience, if you show that you are reasonable, that
you're willing to be flexible and generous, the issue
rarely comes up."

"But what if he insists?" I was starting to feel
panicky. "What if he manipulates his assets so that
my portion isn't fair? What if *his* lawyer doesn't believe in generosity?"

He reached across the expanse of gleaming wood
and patted my hand, no mean feat. "My dear, for-
give me for saying so, but aren't you being just a
little bit paranoid? I know that a separation brings

out hostile feelings, but don't forget that I know your husband well enough to have faith in his *reasonableness*, even if you are temporarily blinded by your anger at him."

Boy, was I getting tired of that word, "paranoid." "Do you know Barclay Hampton, too?"

His expression grew more wary. "Why, yes. Why?"

"Do you think *he* would have done any of those things?"

"Of course not. But we are not discussing—"

"Well, *I* think he did. As a matter of fact, I'm certain of it. His ex-wife was collecting evidence against him before she died."

His mouth shriveled into a little *moue* of distaste. "The dreadful Eleanor, I know. The case is famous. It's one of the reasons so many of us have left family law for less stressful practices. My dear Mrs. James, let me caution you against repeating any such thing about Barclay Hampton. You should not take anything Mrs. Hampton might have said quite so seriously."

I took a deep breath. "Well someone took it seriously enough to try to steal some documents she left with me out of my garage," I said, a bit recklessly. I sketched briefly the story of the break-in.

He heard me out with growing impatience. "Do you seriously believe that your husband or Barclay Hampton or someone from Eastman, Bartels would stoop to something like that?"

"I don't know for sure," I confessed, feeling it incumbent upon the circumstances to be scrupulously honest. "But there is too much coincidence for comfort."

He folded his arms into the classic body language of rejection. "Preposterous. In fact, absurd."

"Why?" I fought the urge to stick out my tongue at him.

"There's no reason for anyone to take such a stupid risk. Even if everything you say is true, at this point—although such revelations are undoubtedly embarrassing—they're not criminal. Barclay would just say it was a misunderstanding, and after a while no one would care. Nobody," he added firmly.

"But wouldn't it be fraud? Couldn't he go to jail or at least be forced to reopen the settlement or . . ." I just couldn't believe that no one would really care.

He sat back so far in his chair that he almost hit the window. "Mrs. James, I fear you are in ignorance of the law. The relevant section of the Family Code does provide for setting aside final judgments on the grounds of perjury. But you have one year to file your case. After that, nada. Zip. *Rien*. Do I make myself clear?"

I nodded, stunned. I had been so sure that someone wanted Eleanor's documents back, someone who wanted to protect Barclay from what they revealed. But if Patrick Dunn was right, the documents were useless once more than a year had passed since the divorce and settlement. No matter what Barclay had done, he had been safe from any legal recourse on the part of his ex-wife.

Maybe he and Gene and Steve were right after all. Maybe Eleanor was just crazy. Maybe I *was* getting to be paranoid. Maybe . . . I lifted my head. Maybe there was something *else* among those papers, something I had overlooked. I had been over almost everything in the box, but there was a sheaf of legal and financial documents that put me to sleep every time I looked at them. I had no idea

whether they were significant or not. Maybe there
was something damaging there. . . .

"Mrs. James, did you hear me?" Patrick Dunn
said, recalling me from my reverie.

"I'm sorry?" I said, blinking at him.

"I said I'm afraid that based on our discussion
here you might not be a very good candidate for
mediation," he said briskly. "Has Steve engaged a
lawyer yet?"

"He hasn't informed me officially, but I have reason to believe he is talking to Jay Thompson," I told
him.

He flinched. He tried not to let me see it and
turned away quickly, but I did. My stomach turned
over. "Well, ahem, I think the best thing for you to
do might be to get another attorney," he said hastily. "It's like a marriage—somewhere out there is
the perfect match for you." I thought this was sin-
gularly tasteless under the circumstances, but he
continued undaunted. "If you call the Bar Association, they have a referral list." I knew about that. It
wasn't very helpful; they just gave you the name at
the top.

He rose. So did I. "And naturally, we will waive
today's fee," he said, apparently a practitioner of his
own strategy of generosity. Or maybe he was so
anxious to be rid of me, no price was too high.

"Thank you," I told him.

He gave me a cheery little wave as he saw me
out. "Good luck," he intoned solemnly and closed
the door behind him.

Now that Patrick Dunn had fired me as a client,
I was panic-stricken about finding someone to represent me before Steve and Jay turned their legal
ammo in my direction. I was afraid of what would

happen if I didn't have a lawyer soon. I was afraid of what would happen when I did have a lawyer.

What I didn't count on was how hard it would be to actually get one. I had a list of every family law attorney I had ever heard of, but after a while I began to wonder if I should cast my net wider, say to Los Angeles or Orange County. Nobody in San Diego wanted to touch me with a ten-foot pole.

"I'm so sorry, Mrs. James," the first person I called told me, "but I've worked with your husband on bar committees and I just wouldn't feel right about going up against him in a divorce action." You would have thought they had been bosom pals from law school, supporting each other through all the hours of preparation for a moot court triumph. As far as I could remember, Steve hadn't served on a bar committee for at least five years, because he was too busy making money at Eastman, Bartels.

Another, a starchy-sounding inmate of Pompous, Self-Important, and Tweed, told me his wife had once worked as a paralegal at my husband's office and he would feel "conflicting loyalties."

After a couple more of these, I began to get the picture. Thanks to Naturcare, Eastman, Bartels was a rising star in the corporate-service firmament, and a lot of divorce attorneys weren't terribly eager to take on one of its partners, particularly not one represented by a heavy hitter like Jay Thompson, in court. Eleanor had warned me; it had happened to her.

The last name on my list was a woman one of my friends had recommended when we met in the produce section of Jonathan's. It was a very unscientific way of going about finding an attorney, but she was so careful about holding each organic tomato up to inspect it for blemishes that I figured she wouldn't just be talking off the top of her head. By the time she had sorted through every oyster mushroom in the bin, I was doubly convinced.

I dialed fast, as if the clock were already ticking on the legal fees.

Rachel Fenton, however, was in Florida visiting her mother. "We expect her in a day or two," her receptionist told me on the phone. "She hates the humidity, so she never stays long. Can I have her return your call?"

I liked the sound of it—friendly, but not desperate for business. "Please," I told her and gave her my name and number. As an afterthought I added, "Do you think she would mind taking on a case where she'd have to go up against Jay Thompson?" I didn't really expect that she could give me an answer. Still, I didn't want to waste two days on a hopeless prospect.

The receptionist laughed. "I imagine she'd relish it," she told me.

Dear Caroline, Eleanor had written in the letter she enclosed in her box of materials, *Maybe you haven't been separated long enough to understand what I was trying to say to you the other day, but sooner or later you'll find out. If you do decide to write something about how lawyers screw their ex-wives along with their clients and the general public, you'll find plenty here of interest.*

People are always telling me to pick up the pieces and move on, to forget about what that cocksucker Barclay Hampton did to me. They advise me to join a singles group, for God's sake, and go out on dates. They say there are lots of divorced women out there who have made new lives for themselves.

Well, I have seen those women at the singles table at the ball, with their too-tight dresses and their bleached

*hair, and I can tell you right now I AM NOT ONE OF
THEM. I WILL NEVER BE ONE OF THEM. I would
rather die than spend my evenings wondering if some
new man will overlook my stretch marks and my cellu-
lite. So I will not join a singles group. And I WILL NOT
FORGET.*

I hope this helps you, she concluded. *Call me when
you have finished reading the contents, and we'll talk
about where to go from here. Yours sincerely, Eleanor
Mary Hampton.*

I put away the phone book and took two aspirin.
I was too spent to call any more lawyers, so for the
moment I was pinning my hopes on Rachel Fenton.
It was time to get on with the next order of business.
Where to go from here . . . The kitchen was empty except for Melmoth, who was snoozing on his cat
blanket in the corner. The cat blanket, a hand-
knitted wool throw inherited from Steve's mother
years ago, had been appropriated by Melmoth at an
early point in his history, and his ardor for it was
so intense nobody had the heart to take it away and
return it to the closet. It was supposed to stay out
of the "public rooms" in case of drop-in visits by
my in-laws, who presumably would not take kindly
to its current use, but Megan had a habit of laying
it out wherever Melmoth plopped himself down.
The last time I had seen it was upstairs in one of
the bathrooms.

The cat blanket reminded me that Steve's parents
hadn't been over to see the kids in some time. I
hated calling them and getting into all the awkwardness of a conversation in which the chief areas
of interest couldn't even be broached, much less discussed. Their idea of tact was to withdraw completely, so that the people who had insisted I call

them "Mom" and "Dad" for more than a decade, whose birthdays and Christmases I had shopped for, and who had been at my bedside after the birth of my children, were now more remote than strangers. I don't think they sided with Steve particularly, but it was easier to deal with the pain by cauterizing it, so in effect they cut me off. Still, they had been close to their grandchildren, and even if Megan and Jason occasionally groaned and rolled their eyes at the prospect, they were happy enough to see them. Another pang of guilt smote me, and I vowed that I wouldn't put off calling them for more than another week.

I needed time. Time to pick up the pieces of my faltering family life, to comfort my children and patch up their emotions the best I could. Time to figure out what I was going to do to earn some money. Time to discover why somebody had broken into my garage. Time to deal with the contents of Eleanor's files and decipher their secrets, piled up like little volcanoes all over my office floor.

Sighing, I bent over to put on my running shoes. If I'd been wearing socks, I would have pulled them up. My back protested. I really would have to take up yoga again before age and osteoporosis set in and cemented my posture into a permanent vertical.

I locked the door carefully behind me and crossed the street to Rob and Kenny's.

As always, Rob overwhelmed me with feelings of inferiority. He answered the door in a perfectly pressed shirt that screamed "Ralph Lauren" and jeans that displayed what he assured me was a very cute ass to suitable advantage. He wore such outfits for cleaning out his garage. "Hi," I said to him. "Is this a bad time?"

"Not at all," he said, eyeing my round-the-house clothes with small enthusiasm. "I'm charmed by your informality. Come in." He opened the door wider.

Had he not succeeded in selling very large houses to people with incomes to match, Rob might have made it as a decorator. The interior of the house was in various shades of white—white rugs, white walls, white Haitian cotton couches—that served as the perfect frame for the spectacular view of the Pacific coastline outside his oversized picture window. His genius came in the little touches—terra-cotta pots with orchids, tropical wood frames on perfectly selected artwork—that he mostly made up himself out of things he found anywhere from Cost Plus to Rodeo Drive. As he read absolutely nothing that didn't have big celebrity pictures on the front cover, despite his intelligence and background, there were no messy books or newspapers to mar the perfection of the decor.

"Can I get you anything?" Rob asked me.

I didn't want anything, but the kitchen was so beautiful that I considered asking for something just so I could go in there. I resisted the temptation to ask for passion fruit iced tea or whatever the giant ivory-colored side-by-side might disgorge. "Nothing, thanks," I said regretfully.

Rob looked at me expectantly as I settled in for the long haul on the sofa. It was fabulously comfortable. I did not let my running shoes touch the fabric. "Is Kenny home?" I asked him.

"Certainly not. No self-respecting policeman is home in the middle of the day."

"What about real estate agents?" I asked with a smile. Rob was notoriously quixotic about his hours, but he would get up at three in the morning if some client wanted to see Cassiopeia from a prospective backyard.

He made a face. "I was supposed to take someone out today, but she wanted to look at houses in Rancho Las Golondrinas, for God's sake, so I sent my assistant instead."

"Where is that?" I asked him. The pace of development had slowed down since the eighties, but these communities could sneak up on you almost overnight, like particularly fecund jungle plants.

He waved a hand in a vaguely northerly direction. "Up there, where all the second-rate 'Ranchos' are. They think that if they have four floor plans and a Spanish name with a 'Rancho' in front of it, people will think they're getting the real thing instead of Levittown with tile roofs. I won't sell anybody property in one of those developments. It would wreck my reputation with the clients who count."

"But you'll take a cut if your assistant sells it, right?" I asked him.

He raised his eyebrows. "I may cling to my principles, Caroline, but I haven't taken leave of my senses."

"Good. I came to ask your advice, and I want you to be as cynical and world-weary as possible. I wanted Kenny's input, too, but I guess I'll have to wait."

"Kenny is never cynical, much less world-weary; you know that."

"Yes, but he is a policeman."

He sat back a little, looking surprised and amused. "Are you thinking of pursuing a life of crime?" Then, before I could say anything, he stopped smiling. "Oh, God, Caroline, I'm sorry. Is there some kind of trouble? It's nothing to do with Jason, is it?"

"Relax," I told him. "It's nothing like that." Now that I had arrived at the point of telling him what it *was*, I wasn't sure how to begin. "It's Eleanor Hampton," I said finally. "I told you Barclay screwed her on her settlement. I think she might have proof of something pretty awful about Barclay, and now somebody wants it back. The trouble is, I think *I* have it, whatever it is." I shrugged. "Or maybe not."

He blinked at me. "You aren't making any sense."

At least he hadn't said I was paranoid, or not yet, anyway. I gave him an edited account of my conversation with Eleanor, her hints about Barclay, and a summary of the contents of the box.

He was most interested in the lurid details of their correspondence. "Did she really throw an ashtray at him at the Sport and Water Club? It sounds like a Tracy and Hepburn movie, without the style."

"Rob, you can't tell anybody. It wouldn't be fair to Eleanor."

"Not to mention Barclay and Tricia."

"Well, okay. Tricia, at any rate." I tried to explain my theory that Eleanor's box was the target of the burglary in my garage. "The trouble is," I told him, "now that I know it can't be evidence of Barclay's fraud against Eleanor that someone's after, I don't know what it *is*. I've been through everything else in there and I can't make heads or tails of the legal and financial documents, so I have no way of knowing if this is real or all in my head. Like the governess in *The Turn of the Screw*."

He pushed a piece of invisible dust off the tip of his impeccably shined loafer, ignoring the reference.

"I'm curious to know what it is you plan to do with this information—or this theory, at least—and what it has to do with me."

"I was hoping you would go through the papers with me and see if you could find a motive for blackmail or something that makes Barclay look really bad, since you know so much more about business matters than I do," I told him. "I'd ask a lawyer, but Eleanor already tried that, and she couldn't find anyone who'd be willing to use the information against Barclay. Besides, I can't think of any lawyer I'd trust with the knowledge that I'm investigating this." I didn't tell him my old friend Gene Stewart had shrunk in horror from the prospect. "So, will you help me?"

"Caroline, let Uncle Rob give you some advice," he said, in a tone that was far more serious than his words. "Drop the whole thing. It's ridiculous. It's not important. Find some other adventure to embark on."

I shook my head. "I'm not sure I can just leave it alone. I thought I could, but I sort of feel like I owe Eleanor something. Even if I don't do anything about it. I'll like to know what really happened. I just can't stand the idea that her death lets him off the hook. Maybe she was vindictive and a harpy and all the things you've said, but there's something about losing your husband, your friends, your income, and your place in life that might make you a little obsessed. If she was paranoid, Barclay did his best to make her that way."

"That is unadulterated bullshit," he said, smiling a little. "But I'll accept it, if you'll accept that I want absolutely nothing to do with any of this. And I'd appreciate it if you left Kenny out of it, too."

"Don't you feel even the slightest commitment to finding out the truth?"

"Jesus, Caroline, I'm in real estate, for Christ's sake. If you have some fixation on Eleanor Hampton, for reasons that appear to me to be largely unhealthy, it's none of my business."

"Okay, I get the message," I told him.

"Fine." He uncrossed his ankles. "So what will you do next?"

"I thought you wanted to be left out of it."

"I do. Right after this conversation."

"I don't know," I told him truthfully. "I guess I'll have to find someone else discreet to look over the papers."

He raised an eyebrow. "If a lot of them have to do with business, you might consider someone who smells out financial rats for a living."

I frowned until I realized whom he meant, and then I blushed. "Oh, Rob, I couldn't ask him. Not after the way I acted last time."

"Oh, Rob," he mimicked. "I thought you were serious about this. You can't be a shrinking violet if you want to pin something nasty on one of the most prominent lawyers in town. David Sanchez is an obvious choice to review your materials, if you can get him to agree to it."

"But what could I say to him? I hinted around about it, and he said he doesn't do that sort of thing. And then I practically insulted him to his face."

He shrugged. "Are you charming?"

"Not very."

"Attractive?"

"In certain lights, if you don't use a magnifying glass."

He made a face. "How about smart, then?"

"Probably," I conceded. "But only about some things."

"Then think of something. What good does it do you to know what happens in *Tristram Shandy* if you can't do what you want in life?"

"Nothing happens in *Tristram Shandy*," I told him.

"I know," he said. "I read the Cliffs Notes once. How could you write fifty pages of summary and analysis of a book where nothing happens?" He looked genuinely puzzled, so I knew he couldn't have been an English major. "Anyway," he said with a shrug, "I rest my case. Call him tonight."

"I can't tonight. I have to go to *Much Ado About Nothing*."

He raised an eyebrow. "I am going to exercise a great deal of restraint and let the opportunity to remark on that pass. But don't push me too far."

I laughed. "Okay. Anyway, it's my debut as a single woman still in command of her wits. I have to go just to show the crowd at Eastman, Bartels that I'm not crazy."

He shook his head. "First thing in the morning, then." He stood up signaling, if not the end of the interview, at least a change of direction. "Sure I can't get you something?" he asked.

"How about passion fruit iced tea?"

"I'll check the refrigerator," he said.

10

THE OLD GLOBE, like the La Jolla Playhouse, offers a variety of plays from the obvious Shakespeare to the avant garde. The theater scene is generally considered superior to other artistic endeavors about town, and plays are often performed as dry runs before moving on to Broadway. The Old Globe, in addition, has the advantage of a superb location in Balboa Park, which makes it a favorite site for corporate outings. The Eastman, Bartels, and Steed pretheater dinner would take place in the adjacent Sculpture Garden, under the stars.

I had decided to follow Signor Eduardo's advice and dress with a bit more flair than caution habitually dictated. I was trying to hold the essentials of the makeover together, but it was like attempting to stop entropy with your hands. Still, I was not wholly displeased with my efforts. A green silk shell under a suede jacket combined with a floral, broomstick-pleated skirt seemed youthful and exotic. For good measure, I added Navajo silver earrings inlaid with coral and opal.

147

"You look nice, Mom," Megan said, looking up from her book with a smile.

"Thanks," I told her gratefully. "I'll be home late, so don't wait up. I gave Jason money for some pizza."

She sat up, visibly annoyed. "You should have given it to me," she protested. "Jason always wants anchovies. *Gross!*"

"Well, get two of them. Put the extras in the refrigerator, and we'll have the rest tomorrow night."

"Okay." She hesitated. "Will Dad be there?"

"I imagine so."

She smiled again. "Good. Have a good time then."

There were place cards at the Sculpture Garden café, so I fussed around looking for my table in order to get over the awkwardness of arriving alone. It was less easy than I had imagined. A number of people smiled and waved at me, but nobody came over to talk. After a few moments, heads turned toward me and then quickly swiveled away again, so I knew that Steve had arrived. I looked down with ferocious determination to find my name, and fast. I just hoped that whatever secretary had arranged the seating had placed me with a congenial group.

She hadn't. My place card was across the table from Jonathan and Meredith White. Jonathan was a partner in trusts and estates, a dull, fairly pompous man with silvering hair and an expanding chin. Meredith, on the other hand, was third-world thin and so perfectly preserved she seemed to be coated in Lucite. She had the habit of making apparently affable remarks that were really digs of a minor or major nature, depending on the accuracy of her intuition. Despite this unfortunate tendency, she was rather popular. It seemed prudent to invite her to social events, as long as you made sure you didn't leave the party first.

To my left was Jeff Grayson, who passed, for lack of a better candidate, for firm Lothario. He was handsome in a dissipated, Kennedyesque sort of way and had been divorced twice. He did a lot of the work on the Naturcare account, and he had bragged to Steve that just one weekend's worth of billables had bought him a second Rolex. He was wearing it now.

To my right were Tricia and Barclay Hampton.

It wasn't quite the dinner party from Hell, but it was hot and uncomfortable nonetheless. Meredith gave me a little wave full of malevolent good cheer which I interpreted, correctly, as glee at having found such a perfect target. Jonathan smiled politely and looked profoundly uninterested. Barclay looked up with the unwelcoming astonishment one usually associates with discovery of the monster in a horror movie, so I knew someone had been talking about my involvement, such as it was, with Eleanor. Tricia, to do her justice, make a kind attempt at civility, but since she wasn't very adept at small talk and I was by then thoroughly embarrassed, we didn't get very far.

Worst of all was my acute consciousness that anything stupid I did or said would be bandied about the firm, and maybe used against me. I might have been determined to show the world that I was not an Eleanor wannabe, but the deck was already stacked. I even wondered about myself. I liked Barclay no better than before, but as I looked around, I could see why my suspicions seemed so ludicrous to Patrick Dunn. It was a real stretch to think of

Barclay, resplendent in his Armani suit, rooting around amid the rubble of my garage.

The only person who acted natural was Jeff Grayson, who might have been a practiced seducer but at least managed not to behave as if I were the carrier of a particularly loathsome but unmentionable disease. I felt like Fergie dining with the Queen, but the difference was that I was blameless—no toe-sucking orgies or flagrant infidelities—and everyone had still blatantly sided with Steve. I hadn't even known sides were necessary, but there it was.

"What are you doing with yourself these days?" Meredith asked me, her shrimp poised in midair on its little fork.

Studying nuclear physics by correspondence. Submitting designs to REBUILD LA. What did she think? I shrugged. "Oh, the usual," I told her. "Reading. Writing some articles. Going to Megan's soccer games. Things like that."

The article part was a lie. Why did I always feel like I had to sound like the chairman of 20th Century-Fox in front of a bunch of women who hadn't worked for pay since their first child was born, on the average of fifteen years before? The really intimidating ones, the female lawyers, were seated at other tables.

Meredith didn't exactly coo "How nice for you," but I wasn't bathed in a wellspring of warm acceptance, either. I felt prickly with sweat, which owed more to my anxious state than to the warm fall night. Worse, I could see Steve out of the corner of my eye sitting next to Linda Williams. Linda was a very bright associate in the firm whose manner toward the male partners had always included laughing immoderately at their witticisms and resting her lovely blond head on their shoulders. All in jest, of course. Ha ha. Steve always said I overreacted to her flirtatiousness. I loathed her. Still, it didn't look like a date. And it could have been worse.

I decided to try Tricia. "How are the kids doing?" I asked her. A safe topic. Barclay looked away and began a conversation with Jonathan and Jeff about finding a name for a client's mail-sorting business that wouldn't infringe on someone else's copyright in all fifty states. When I was forced to listen to conversations like that—and I'd heard a lot of them over the years—I put aside any latent regrets I might have had about not having attended law school and gone for the big bucks.

The Hampton children did not seem to be Tricia's favorite topic. She lowered her sable lashes sadly. "Well, Jennifer is at school, of course, and she seems to be okay. But the boys . . . well, they are having a lot of trouble adjusting to their mother's death. Eleanor spoiled them, and . . ." She glanced uncertainly at Barclay, who by this time was so enthralled with his topic that if the table had levitated, he would have pushed it down and talked on. "Barclay's never home," she hissed, with a vehemence that surprised me. "He doesn't come home till late, and he brings work with him. He worries all the time. He doesn't sleep."

I nodded sympathetically. "They do that," I agreed.

"But he leaves everything to me," she protested. "The boys, their discipline, the house, everything." She shook her head. "It's too much. I can't cope with everything by myself."

Poor Tricia. I wondered how long it had been since she had unburdened herself, since I was, to say the least, an unlikely target for confidences. I sighed. "I know what you mean. Steve was the same way."

She looked alarmed, as well she might. She looked over to where my husband was playing "life of the party" and frowned. "But Steve—" She broke off and blushed.

I knew what she was going to say. Steve wasn't working himself to death these days. He looked tanned, prosperous, and sleek, like a man who is getting plenty in the sack. As a matter of fact, his offensive good looks in the face of our separation were like a slap in the face.

"Have you tried talking to Barclay about it?" I whispered.

"Of course. He promised me he would try to cut back. We wanted to start a family—"

I noticed that past tense. "Wanted?"

"Now he's putting it off," she said, digging her nails into her palm.

"What about the judgeship?" I asked her, sotto voce.

She bit her bottom lip, which would have looked adorable if she hadn't been so agitated. "I don't know," she said, and I was amazed at her frankness. In all our married life, I would never have owned up to ignorance of a matter of such importance to Steve. "He won't *talk* to me. But something's bothering him. I just can't get him to tell me what it is." She lowered her voice even below the whisper she was already using. "I think it may have something to do with *her*."

I started to ask "who?" though of course I knew who she meant, but just then I looked up to see Barclay glaring at us. Too late, I realized that the best way to attract attention to yourself is by lowering your voice. Barclay definitely did not like the

idea of his wife exchanging confidences with someone who might be harboring sympathy for the late,
unlamented Eleanor.

"Tricia," Barclay said, in his plummiest accent,
"Meredith was asking what we think of the dyslexia
program at Harold Greer. Her nephew might be interested in going there." Harold Greer was an exclusive private school currently charged with the
unenviable task of educating the Hampton twins.
Our children were in public school, because in a fit
of antielitism I had countermanded Steve's decision
to take them out in the fourth grade after some
classmate had threatened to punch Jason's lights out
over an argument at the drinking fountain, which
Steve attributed both to the socioeconomic mix of
the student body and the school's Lack of Control.
It wasn't that I had anything against Harold Greer,
but I didn't have anything to contribute to the conversation, so I sat there, excluded, until Jeff, who
had apparently solved Jonathan's name problem,
rescued me.

"Having fun?" he asked, with a wink.

"Sure," I told him.

"Right," he said. "For the record, I think it was
brave of you to come."

I shrugged, displaying an insouciance I was far
from feeling. "I didn't think so, until I got here."

"It's rough. I know. I've been through it twice."

He sounded earnest—sincere, even—but it was
hardly the same. Besides, from what I'd heard, both
his divorces had been his idea.

"Thanks," I told him.

"Do you have any plans?"

Christ, not again. I wondered if Steve had planted
him to ask me, to find out if I was secretly studying
to become a neurosurgeon in order to figure it into

his calculations with Jay Thompson. Or maybe he figured he had asked me too many times himself, and thought if I heard it from someone else I might get my ass in gear.

I sighed. "Well, I want to keep on writing, of course, and—"

He laughed and waved his hand dismissively. "No, I meant after the play. Would you like to have a drink with me?"

I looked over toward Steve's table. Linda's aquiline nose was about a fourth of an inch from his sleeve. He looked like he was loving it. "Sure," I said, "if it's not too late. My kids are home alone." I hoped I sounded as casual as the invitation, and not as if I expected handholding in the dark and furtive glances across the table.

"Good," he said. "I'll talk to you after the play."

Another thing I learned in the course of that awful evening is that the fix you're in, whatever it may be, reorders the universe. I even had a new take on *Much Ado about Nothing*, which I had hitherto regarded as a rather snotty but delightful comedy about the war between the sexes. But with Steve sitting next to me (he was not, after all, able to do anything about fixing the ticket), his arm pulled so far into his lap, away from his armrest, that another person (albeit a pretty thin one) might have squeezed in between us, I was suddenly sensitive to the play's darker side. It was all about lies and deception. I certainly had never felt like crying when I had watched or read it before, but when Friar Francis told Hero, "Die to live," and said:

> . . . *what we have we prize not to the worth*
> *Whiles we enjoy it, but being lack'd and lost,*

Why, then we rack the value, then we find
The virtue that possession would not show us
Whiles it was ours. . . .

I was very close to tears.

That might have been the lowest point in my whole life. My favorite play was ruined, at least temporarily, but that was only a symbol. I didn't have a life. All I had were some relicts—like my "friends" at the firm, and the house Steve was threatening to sell—of the life I had lived till my husband left me. I didn't have a job or new friends or anything to look forward to except (hopefully not too soon) grandchildren. How did I let myself get into a fix like that? I was smart! I knew Shakespeare! I couldn't even reach into my purse for a tissue because then Steve would have seen me, despite his resolute concentration on the stage. That would only have confirmed his view that I was hysterical or menopausal or crazy or all three, and I didn't want to hand him that ammunition on a plate. All I could think of was, has it really come to this?

It had, apparently. After the play, Steve nodded briefly to me, as if I were someone he had once run into at the car wash, and then exited the row without speaking. We had barely spoken a word to each other the entire evening, and although I realized this was not the time to bring up putative fishing excursions in my garage, I was frustrated by his stony silence. I have to admit that I was scarcely in the mood for a drink with Jeff. Or anyone. From two rows back, I saw Meredith giving me the eye and bending over to whisper something to Jonathan. His expression didn't change, but his head swiveled my way as well. Henry Eastman and his wife, Pamela, approached me anxiously, the senior partner eager to shower kindness on the lost sheep.

Henry took my hand and whispered, "How *are* you, my dear?" with so much courtly compassion that I almost lost my composure. Sympathy is often harder to handle than derision, however much I might have needed it. *Oh, great*, I thought. I was giving serious consideration to disappearing out the side door and into the park when Jeff leaned over the back of my chair. "Where are you parked?"

His breath was warm in my ear. It tickled. I tried not to squirm in my seat. "The organ pavilion." I hoped he would not take it as an invitation.

"So am I. Do you want to follow me?"

"Where are we going?"

"It's a surprise."

If he had leered or half-closed his eyes or given a suggestive little chuckle, I would have backed out right then and there, but his smile was perfectly frank and genuine. "Okay, but—"

"I know," he said. "You have to get home early."

Mission Hills is where old San Diego money lives if it doesn't live in La Jolla or Rancho Santa Fe (new money lives in Fairbanks Ranch, plus everywhere else). It is a charming area, near the park and downtown, and full of beautiful old trees. What it is not full of is places to get a drink.

I wondered where Jeff was taking me, but since I had no way of asking him, I had only two options: keep following his BMW or head for home. I didn't want to be rude, so I kept behind him. My manners were impeccable. If he'd driven all the way to Tijuana, I probably would have followed him right over the border.

Somewhere short of Margaritaville, he stopped

the car. We were in the middle of a residential area, quiet as a rodent siesta. Dark, too. He got out of the BMW and came round to where I sat in my Honda, the lights still on. He put a hand on the door handle. "Coming in?" he asked.

"Is this your house?"

"Yes. I have something to show you."

"What is it?" I asked, hoping I didn't sound as if he'd offered to show me something nasty behind the shed.

He laughed. "Books," he said.

I switched off the car lights.

The last Mrs. Grayson, a brittle blonde whose years in the sun (before all the skin cancer warnings drove everyone to sun block) had left her with a perpetually parched look, had received the Point Loma house where Steve and I had once attended a party for summer associates. The associates, many of them from the harsher climes of the East where a bug zapper is de rigueur for enjoying even a ten-minute sojourn out-of-doors, were always impressed with beachside living and the mildness of the San Diego summer. It was usually the top selling point for the firm, since you could scarcely make the case based on great artworks or riotous nightlife. (The zoo is outstanding, though.)

Jeff's new house was vintage Old California on the outside, but the inside was nouveau bachelor—polished hardwood floors, buttery Roche-Bobois leather couches, Navajo rugs on the white walls, high-tech entertainment center. The kitchen had soft mauve tiles and was as big as an operating theater. It was also very attractive. "It's great," I said admiringly.

He took my hand. "I want you to see my study,"

he said, drawing me through the door.

I was expecting a tufted leather couch with metal studs, an oversized desk, and acres of law books. When he switched on the light, I saw that the only thing I'd been right about was the oversized desk, which was French and exquisite, instead of massive oak or rosewood. The rest of the room looked like the library at a stately English home—imposing, but inviting. And the books! Instead of all the dingy, capacious volumes of case law I was used to seeing around lawyers' offices, there were shelves and shelves of English novels all the way back to Defoe, most of them beautifully bound and deckle- or gilt-edged. There was not a paperback in sight. There were also old travel books, a particular passion of mine, from every era and on every area imaginable.

I pulled one down from the shelf. It was a nine-teenth-century guide to Rome, illustrated with beautifully tinted drawings.

The library had to have cost a fortune. The firm must have been doing better than I realized, or else Jeff had inherited money. "Wow," I said.

He seemed to have read my thoughts. "My late Uncle Oscar was very big in a high-tech start-up company," he said quickly. If he'd made it off of Naturcare, he had wit enough not to confess it to a partner's-about-to-be-ex-wife. "Like it?"

"It's fantastic," I said sincerely. "I didn't know you collected old travel books. Did you have them at the other house?"

His expression wilted just a little. His jawline, I noticed, had become slightly puffy with the years, and there were the beginnings of pouches under his eyes. "I have to confess I didn't collect them," he said with a shrug. "My decorator bought them from a dealer in Los Angeles. Most of what I had before was business books and paperbacks. I still have those in the bedroom."

His sheepish look was somewhat disarming, though I had been far more impressed when I imagined him going through Volitions—a La Jolla used-book store where the clerks had meaningful discussions about Catholic guilt versus Jewish guilt, and Dickens would not have felt out of place—volume by volume. Fake libraries inevitably conjure up images of Jay Gatsby in his white suit, hungering after acceptance into East Egg. Still, it could have been worse. Jeff had at least furnished his shelves with a great reading selection rather than, for example, leather-bound copies of *Gray's Anatomy*.

"I remembered that you're a writer," he said, without the verbal quotation marks Steve always put around the word when it applied to me (in fairness, I put them there myself), "so I thought you might be interested in seeing what I bought. I wish I'd thought to ask your advice beforehand."

"Your decorator's dealer did a wonderful job," I assured him. It was so flattering to be taken seriously, even in this small capacity. It was even flattering that he'd remembered my interest in books. "Even Henry and Pamela Eastman don't have a study like this."

He sighed happily, so I knew I'd said the right thing. "Drink?" he inquired.

I nodded, and he poured cognac from a decanter on a silver tray into two cut-crystal glasses that screamed Baccarat. It was so Noël Coward. So what if you risked lead poisoning? What a way to go.

"Do you want to go into the living room?" he asked me.

"Could we stay here?"

He grinned, a high-voltage smile full of boyish

charm that had probably melted the defenses of countless females with armor tougher than mine. "I knew you'd like it."

I did. I also liked it when we sat on the couch sipping our cognacs, and he asked me about my travels, my writing, and, with the greatest of tact, my impending divorce. He wanted to know who was representing me, what my plans were, how I felt. He was persistent, but he probed so gently that I was not offended. He seemed to be offering a kind sympathy I apparently needed more than I realized. His gaze was earnest and sincere, his interest intense.

I lost my head completely.

You might wonder why the relatively simple act of paying attention to me should prove so seductive. It wasn't that no one ever did; I was reasonably bright and an adequate raconteur at cocktail parties, so people usually listened to what I said. I wasn't desperate for notice or anything like that. But when the man you've lived with for years, the person who knows you best in the whole world, decides he doesn't want to be with you anymore, it knocks a pretty big hole in your confidence.

When we were first married, we used to talk about everything from apartheid to Zen, but over the years our conversations had increasingly become monologues. Sometimes Steve would read me a newspaper article from start to finish, without even asking whether the topic interested me or expecting any response. Now and then a subject of mutual appeal would animate a discussion, but Steve's rhetorical posture was invariably argumentative, and I never excelled at debate. What I wanted from conversation was affirmation and sharing; what Steve wanted was to knock down every point I raised.

Anyway, I was definitely vulnerable to a man who apparently hung on my every utterance. I started focusing on the little beads of perspiration over his full lips, the way his hair had grown down over his collar, the little freckles on the backs of his hands. I caught myself wondering if he would have a lot of chest hair, and if so, what color. I was definitely having trouble concentrating on the substance of the conversation.

I suppose I should have been grateful that that part of me, previously comatose if not vegetative, was waking up again, but as a matter of fact I was far more frightened than delighted.

I looked at my watch ostentatiously. "I ought to be going," I told him.

His hand slipped down the back of the couch onto my shoulder. "Stay a little longer," he said and kissed the back of my neck. Waves of delectable sensation traveled down my spine and arms, rendering me immobile and, apparently, inarticulate. All the warnings that were going off in my head—This is one of Steve's partners! . . . you'll make a fool of yourself! . . . Protection! AIDS! Herpes! Warts! VD!—didn't seem to make it all the way to my mouth.

"I've always thought you were so attractive," he murmured, before he snaked his tongue into my ear. Oh, Christ, I didn't want to fall for that. But I was clearly plummeting. In fact, it was more like free fall without a parachute.

Jeff seemed to take my silence for consent and got busier.

My lips opened, perhaps to form a protest, and were covered by his for their pains. His tongue filled my whole mouth, and I began to think about how uselessly restrictive all my clothing was.

He had blond chest hair, touched with gray. Despite the workouts, racquetball, and tennis games requisite for a middle-aged man of professional status, there was loose flesh around his middle, and his ass was no longer kouros-boy firm. The lines were blurred and softened by the years. Since gravity had done its work on me as well, it made me like him better. So did the box of condoms in the bedside dresser, for all their implication of practiced seduction. At least I wouldn't be playing Saturday-night roulette.

If Jeff's library was vintage Blenheim Palace, the bedroom was late space station: all high tech and black lacquer. A second full-screen entertainment center took up one whole wall. There was a whole row of Kronos Quartet CDs. The bedspread looked like Paul Klee on a bad day, with little fishy things that were strongly suggestive of sperm.

But I was too beside myself for details. Well, not so beside myself that I didn't wish I'd spent more time at the gym attempting to subdue the parts of my body that tended to go one way when I went the other. Or so out of it that I didn't fold my clothes neatly and put them over the back of an enormous, high-backed wooden chair. Whatever happened, I would still have to go home in them. But I couldn't take much more. I was getting dizzy, and I wanted to lie down, but I didn't know if you were supposed to wait for the host. Finally, I arranged myself as decoratively as possible beneath the covers.

Jeff strode unashamedly around the bedroom, putting on music and setting the stage. At last he lifted the sheet—perfectly clean and soft as silk— and slid in beside me.

I put a hand on his chest with little feathery movements that Steve had always liked in happier days. I felt sure that my sexual technique was horridly outdated, but years of monogamy are not conducive to staying au courant on such things. In fact, when I read articles or books that referred to "innovative practices," I was never quite sure what they meant. Steve and I never did it with rings or hanging from baskets or anything like that. I never read the *Kama Sutra*. Maybe if I had, he wouldn't have left.

I started to descend to more productive regions. Jeff grabbed my hand and stopped me.

"Wait," he said, in a rougher tone than he had used all evening.

Of course I stopped. He pulled back from me a little, and I saw what the trouble was. What had been rather awesomely tumescent before he got under the covers was now a shrinking violet in every since of the word. The only thing performing was the Kronos Quartet.

He ran an experimental finger down my stomach and below. "Christ," he said, "you're too dry. At this rate it'll take as long as the mad scene in *Lucia di Lammermoor*."

I wasn't, but I wasn't about to argue. They never cover this one in articles on dating etiquette, but I gathered I was supposed to offer up my readiness to salve his ego. Maybe I was supposed to be glad that it was a high-class put-down, evoking opera. Ha, ha.

"It's probably been a long time for you, hasn't it?" he asked with just a slight edge of nastiness. I might have mistaken simple embarrassment for blame, but I didn't think so.

I looked at my watch, which I had placed on top

of the bedside dresser. It read twelve thirty. I swung my feet out of the bed onto the floor. "Yes, it has," I told him.

He noticed my upright posture. "Where are you going?" he asked as I reached for my bra.

"It's late. I have to get home."

He propped himself up on his elbow. "That's not very tactful, you know. And anyway, I think you should stay. I could help you with your problem."

My problem was that I had gotten myself into an embarrassing situation because of a moment of adolescent yearning, but I didn't think he could help me with that. Though this was clearly the point at which one of us should have kissed the other gently and said "It doesn't matter," the atmosphere had obviously turned a little unpleasant. The moment had passed, and both of us knew it. It didn't really matter whose fault it was. "I'm sorry," I told him.

"Maybe you should see a therapist," he suggested.

If he wanted to punish me, he would have to stand in line. "Do you mind if I use the bathroom?" I asked, gathering up my clothes.

I didn't wait for the answer. The bathroom gleamed at me when I turned on the light. I squinted into the mirror while I ran some water. Christ, it was so trite to examine your face in the mirror after you've just done something you wish you hadn't, but I couldn't help it. I wondered if my children would look at me in disgust. I didn't feel disgusted myself, just very tired. And unsatisfied. I didn't even want to think about what this would do for my future sex life, on the remote chance that there ever was one. I didn't want to think what they would say about this one around the conference table at Eastman, Bartels, and Steed.

I hunted around for a tissue. A pearl earring with a gold stud fell out of the Kleenex box when I picked it up. I doubted it belonged to the maid. I wondered if Pearl Studs had had better luck. I wondered if I should leave something of mine for the next one to find. I decided against it.

I stayed in the bathroom a good fifteen minutes, until I knew every miniscule bit of overlooked mildew on the grout. It took a certain amount of courage to come out again, but I couldn't hide in there all night. I turned out the light and opened the door quietly.

"I'll just be going," I said in my breeziest voice.

No answer. I looked over at the bed, where he was, apparently, asleep. I felt a momentary pang for the days of my youth, when your dates held your coat for you and walked you to your door.

"You don't have to see me out," I called softly and closed the bedroom door behind me.

The kitchen light was on when I got home. Looking right and left nervously as I left the garage, in case our unwelcome lodger had returned, I dashed up to the door, hoping my innocents had remembered to lock it. They had. I fumbled with the key, expecting to encounter a sink full of dirty glasses, crusts from half-eaten pizza slices, and other detritus of the adolescent appetite. Instead I found Megan sitting on a stool by the bar, watching me, her eyes wide.

"Megan, it's after one in the morning!" When you're a mother, such statements come out of your mouth automatically.

She rubbed her eyes with her fist like the child she had been till very recently. "I couldn't sleep," she said wearily, but she looked as if she'd been trying to force herself awake.

"Do you want to try now? You look tired."

"Mom . . ."

"I could make you some warm milk."

"Yechh!" She made a gagging noise. "Why do people always suggest warm milk?"

I shrugged. "Because it's supposed to work, I guess."

"Mom . . ." she said again.

I waited. Her eyes searched my face. I wondered what she saw there. I tried not to look guilty. "Yes?" I prompted her.

"Were you with Dad?"

I crossed what was left of the space between us in quick steps and put my arm around her. "Oh, Megan, honey, no . . . I sat next to your father at the play, but he left right afterward."

Her eyes looked up at me, dark, angry, and accusing. "Then where have you been?" She stressed each word, pronouncing them slowly and emphatically.

I let out a breath. There were undoubtedly guidelines for handling this scene in some of those self help postdivorce manuals, but I hadn't had the heart to get around to them yet. "I was having a drink with Mr. Grayson, one of Daddy's partners," I told her, in the most matter-of-fact tone I could muster.

She shrank away from my touch. "You went out on a *date*?" she cried, with as much horror as if I'd confessed to grave robbing or shoplifting from Saks.

"Megan, it wasn't a date. We had a drink and we talked." I wondered how much she could sense, even if her mind hadn't yet articulated her real suspicion.

"Where?" she asked dully, avoiding my eyes.

I swallowed. "At his house."

She flushed crimson. I wasn't sure what the correct response was, but I didn't want her to have to deal with anything more. "Megan, nothing happened."

She did look up at me then. *"Liar!"*

My mother would have slapped me, and did, for such an infraction, but these were different times. I took a breath and counted to ten. "You will go up to your room and go to bed this instant," I told her. "I don't want to talk about this anymore tonight."

She looked at me, still angry but with the beginnings of regret. "Sorry," she mumbled, and averted her eyes.

"Get some sleep," I told her.

Easier said than done, of course. My heart was going into overdrive and my skin itched all over, sure signs that unconsciousness was several hours away. I had never seen more than a few dozen sheep in my whole life, and I was fairly certain that attempting to count them would be futile.

My mind unrolled the day's scenarios like text on the computer screen. Meredith White pointed a lacquered finger at me, accusing me of insignificance. Steve glanced at me, looked away with indifference. Henry Eastman patted my arm with unnerving compassion. Jeff—was Jeff laughing at me behind my back, certain that I'd fall for anything that looked at me with a slow burn, that ministered to my vanity and my need for male attention? Was I so undesirable I had made him literally shrivel? The images made me thrash on the bed. I turned the pillow over to the cool side and tried to think of anything but the evening's embarrassing events.

I had to stop this. I was trying to hold on to my old life, and I was clinging to stasis like a scared child. It was time for reinvention. Change had come to claim me: My husband had left, my children were growing up, and some of my friends had metamorphosed into acquaintances. There was no going back; it was silly to hold on to the firm like a reef in a storm when most of the people there were, and always had been, Steve's colleagues. It was stupid to start a relationship, even a one-night stand, with one of the partners. It was time, as Eleanor's friends had urged her, to get on with my life.

Braver people than I actually did this to themselves, put themselves at risk again by leaving their secure jobs or moving to Costa Rica or whatever just to see how things would turn out. It was asking too much to be grateful for having my old life jerked out from under me like a rug, but at least I should be moving forward. If I didn't, I could end up like Eleanor.

I pondered that a little and wondered if I could wind up drowned in a hot tub, having offed myself on pills and expensive wine. The wine part would be difficult; Steve had taken most of the good bottles out of the Eurocave when he took off, claiming that he had selected them specially and I wouldn't know the difference anyway. Most of what was left was the white zinfandel we had laid in for a party of family members whose powers of discrimination were no more acute than mine.

I didn't feel so confident about the pills. I didn't take anything, but what if Eleanor had had trouble sleeping, too? When I had known her, she had seemed angry and purposeful, not overly medicated. Still, I could see the appeal of gulping tranquilizers—it was better than living life in the grips of a constant, relentless rage.

You had to sort of admire a woman like that, someone who wouldn't bow to change or give up, but you wouldn't necessarily want to be that person. I contemplated Eleanor, threatening her husband unless he gave her old life back to her. Trying to drag the firm into it until even gentle Henry Eastman was irritated with her scenes. I bet that more than once Barclay had wished Eleanor was dead.

The thought caught me up short.

Of course he had wished her dead. And now he was paying for it with a pronounced sense of guilt.

No, that didn't hold water. Barclay Hampton was about as introspective as a tomato. Nothing more complex than a middling case of midlife crisis had ever ruffled the waters of his tranquillity, and when he left Eleanor, cheating her out of her rightful share of their assets, it had been with a chilling display of sangfroid. If he was guilty or disturbed, as I had seen at the funeral and as Tricia had indicated, he must really have something to be guilty or disturbed about.

Like killing his ex-wife.

The thought sprang full-blown into my head and refused to go away. I didn't exactly sit bolt upright in bed, but all thought of sleep vanished in an instant.

I turned the idea around in my mind to examine it. I wanted to be objective, to discover the reasons why the vision of Barclay as killer seemed so satisfactory, so *right*. The truth is, I think I must have believed it, deep down, all along. Ever since I had learned what he did to Eleanor, how he had destroyed so much of her safety and happiness, her cause had taken possession of me to a far greater extent than could realistically be explained by my (not unjustified) fears that I might find myself in the same predicament. I didn't want to be objective about why I found the notion of Barclay the murderer, literally as well as figuratively, emotionally attractive. I would deal with that later.

I kept coming back to the image of Eleanor's bloated body, naked in her hot tub, washing her pills down with Bâtard-Montrachet '85. As a scenario for suicide, it had always troubled me. It didn't square with my impression of Eleanor or with what I would want for myself.

Just for a moment I would go with my instincts and assume that the suicide theory was wrong.

That left only two options. Accident was one of them.

The other was homicide.

Half a lifetime of watching *Mystery* on PBS and dipping into detective fiction from Christie to Cornwell brought the protocol of murder investigations quickly to mind. First you had to have a method and a motive.

The first issue, means, was easy enough. Eleanor was alone and defenseless. Did he slip pills in her drink? Did he hire a hit man to inject her with drugs? Well, probably not, much as I would have liked to imagine him placing a transatlantic phone call to one of Tricia's remote Sicilian relations. It just didn't fit with the Barclay I knew, and I was winging this whole thing on the strength of gut feeling alone.

The motive part was even easier. My mind raced ahead to the obvious conclusion, but I forced myself to backtrack, to take just one step at a time. Everybody who had met Eleanor in recent years had wished she were dead at one time or another, even if only half seriously. Wanting to stop that tidal wave of impassioned revenge would be reason enough. How much would it take before you would give anything to rid yourself of a person who told your friends, your business associates, and the world in general that you had stolen her life, that you had engaged in legal and emotional terrorism, and that you were a ridiculous, middle-aged fool in love with a hot numero half your age? And even if the goods Eleanor had on him were no longer legal tender, so to speak, he could scarcely have been thrilled with the idea of what she could put into circulation.

Still, wanting to shut people up, while understandable, was probably not sufficient motive for murder unless you were in the Cosa Nostra or had a lot more to hide than a new wife and a hair transplant. Barclay had shown every sign of exasperation and disgust, but so far none—at least to my knowledge—of murderous rage.

What about a financial motive, then? You might argue that Eleanor was costing him a lot of money, that with her out of the picture the savings in alimony payments alone would pay for a cozy villa in the south of France or at the very least a princely condo in Palm Desert.

However, I couldn't really buy that one, either. The gist of Eleanor's box of materials, condensed into one vociferous howl of outrage, was that Barclay had lied about his assets in the first place, and then he and his attorney, Jay Thompson, had bludgeoned her into a pared settlement that was only a fraction of what she deserved. As Patrick Dunn, the Great Mediator, had explained to me, no-fault divorce was a repudiation of more idealistic times and the rather courtly notion that the man had to pay for breaking up the home. No-fault divorce, and Barclay's duplicity, had left Eleanor up the creek without a paddle.

If Barclay was suffering from the loss of income his support of Eleanor had created, he certainly hadn't shown any signs of it. In fact, he had made noises about becoming a judge—which, if I was not mistaken, would reduce his income stream by somewhere between two-thirds and three-quarters. A guy with a yen for expensive cars and a high number on the waiting list for membership in the Fairbanks Ranch Country Club could not be contemplating a move like that unless his financial security was independent of the annual sum he grudgingly paid out to his ex-wife.

With a growing sense of both certainty and dread, I had to face the obvious conclusion, the one at the end of this path of speculation. I already suspected that Eleanor must have been blackmailing Barclay with something she learned he had done. Maybe it was bad enough that he had killed her over it.

Suddenly I saw Eleanor standing in her pink suit, her hand clutching my arm in hot despair. "You won't believe what they've pulled," she'd said. "It will help when your turn comes." Well, my turn had come, and she had clearly believed she was handing me some leverage in negotiating my divorce.

She'd gone through the firm files, she'd told me, but her attorney, Barclay's racquetball partner, wouldn't let her use what she had.

A matter you've misunderstood entirely, Barclay had written. Could that be it? I had thought she was referring to the fraud he had perpetrated on her, but Barclay of all people would know that the statute of limitations had run out. If Eleanor was black-mailing her ex-husband, it had to be with some-thing else she had discovered in his files, something that would damage his ambitions enough to make it worth getting rid of her.

There were so many illegal things lawyers could do, it boggled the mind. All you had to do was look at the summaries of disciplinary actions in the pages of the old *California Lawyers* for confirmation. And these weren't errors and oversight sorts of problems, like I-accidentally-missed-the-filing-date-and-cost-my-client-a-million-dollars-as-a-result. These were the biggies, like my-client-was-a-widow-with-Alzheim-er's-and-somehow-all-the-money-from-her-trust-fund-of-which-I-was-the-sole-trustee-ended-up-in-my-investment-account-in-Grand-Cayman. You get the idea. It might be something like that. These days it would be much more difficult to blackmail somebody for personal reasons, because there is hardly anything you can do that other people would strenuously object to.

The thing that chilled me, lifting up the little hairs on my neck, was that I didn't know *what* it was, but I certainly knew where it was, if it existed. Down-stairs, locked in a drawer in my office. If Barclay had killed Eleanor over something that was in the box, he wouldn't think he was safe so long as there was a possibility I might have it. Somebody had already broken into the garage. What was next? Whatever happened, the only way I could protect myself was to find out the meaning of Eleanor's pa-pers, and fast.

Means, and Barclay's alibi, were matters for the police, although I did think I could do a bit of sleuthing to determine whether anyone could actually verify his presence at the firm on the evening of her death. Still, all I had was a theory, and not one shred of evidence. Nobody with a badge would want to talk to me unless I had more than that, especially since the popular and more comfortable view was that she had drunk and drugged herself into such a stupor that she had drowned herself, either accidentally or on purpose. I couldn't even get help in crossing the street unless I had more than a strong suspicion that the victim's ex-husband had something to hide.

It was far too late to do the sensible thing, which would be to forget all about it and get on with my life. That's what everyone had told Eleanor, and look where disregarding their advice had gotten her. And resurrecting the Woman Scorned from her unquiet grave hadn't made me all too popular, either, and that was before I'd thought up the murder theory. Still, the status quo didn't look so safe anymore. I was going to have to find out if Barclay killed Eleanor, and why.

I'd wanted a new direction, and now I had no choice. Reinvention. Well, why not?

11

PERSONALLY, I HAVE always thought that Wordsworth was full of it about that "emotion recollected in tranquillity" business. All right, he produced some great poems, and maybe he did them after reflecting on what he experienced rather than in the heat of passion. But I've always thought it was more a metaphor for settling, for forgetting about your love affairs and sinking comfortably into a life of orthodoxy and conservatism. The late Wordsworth might have found himself very much at home in La Jolla.

Anyway, what I was after was not poetry but truth, and despite the exaggerating influences of scratchy sheets and a fevered imagination, I was inclined to trust the insights of my late-night epiphany. If I'd rushed to my desk to write down a sonnet, no one would have thought twice about it, but a common sense solution to a problem that had bothered me for some time probably required a daylight review.

The prospect of tackling the mystery of Eleanor's death, which I'd previously found too depressing to contemplate, now reanimated me with vigor. I

would call David Sanchez without delay. I would
look into Barclay's alibi. I would ... well, I would
do *something* important, even if I wasn't sure what
it was. Still, it didn't do a lot for the bags under my
eyes. It had been a number of years since the loss
of even an hour's sleep didn't manifest itself in deep
antigravitational hollows above my cheekbones. I
trudged downstairs in my jeans and an old shirt of
Steve's to make Sunday breakfast, a remnant of
family tradition from happier days.

There was a note from Jason on the counter, along
with an empty juice glass and cereal bowl. "Working on video with Danny," he'd scrawled. "Back
this afternoon to do homework." *Homework* was un-
derlined twice, so I'd get the point of how responsible he was being. The video was something he and
Danny were working on as a semester project for
their English class. Its contents were a bit of a mystery, but it seemed to require a lot of shooting at
the beach.

Megan was sitting at the counter, too, in almost
the same position as the night before. She looked as
if she hadn't slept well, either. She was listlessly
pushing the remnant of a piece of toast around her
plate.

I abandoned any ambitions I might have har-
bored for French toast, *huevos rancheros*, or home-
made muffins. "Would you like anything else to
eat?" I asked her. "I could pick up some croissants
or some bagels."

She pushed her hair out of her eyes and looked
at me. "No, thanks, this is enough." She shoved her
plate aside. "Mom . . ."

I poured some instant coffee into the bottom of a
cup. When Steve was home, we'd always had fresh-
ground, in some hyphenated flavor redolent of the

Spice Islands. Now it was too much trouble for one person; the coffee just got stale sitting around in the thermos all day.

"I'm sorry about last night," she said.

I topped off the coffee with low-fat milk and one and a half Equals. "Apology accepted," I told her. I set the mug down on the counter and sat down to face her. She tensed, the way I always had whenever my mother had displayed such clear indications of an impending heart-to-heart.

"Look, sweetheart, I know this is hard on you and Jason. It's hard on Daddy and me, too. I don't know what to tell you. I think we'll probably get a divorce."

She looked at me in that numb, stricken way animals do before you run over them with the car. We'd been over this before, but it still broke my heart.

"You don't want to get back together, then?" she asked carefully, almost casually.

"I don't know, Megan," I told her honestly. "A lot of things have happened. I'm not sure it would be possible, even if we both wanted it."

She nodded, trying to understand. I thought it was a brave gesture.

"I want you to know there isn't anyone else. It's nothing like that. I'm not even . . . interested right now. As far as I know, your father isn't seeing anyone seriously, either." I cleared my throat. I wanted to look down at my cup so I gazed right into her face. "But that doesn't mean I won't ever want to date, to see anyone else. I can't promise you that, and I don't think you should ask it of me even if it hurts you."

"In other words I don't have a choice," she said moodily.

I reminded myself that she was moody about a lot these days; it went with the territory. "Look, you're growing up," I told her. "You might get married; you might not. You might have six children or none. You might eventually decide to live with someone. Would you want me to make those decisions for you? Even if the decisions you made might hurt me?"

"I guess not," she said reluctantly. "But it's different."

"Yes, it is, a little," I acknowledged. "But not entirely. People who love each other give up a lot to make each other happy, but nobody should ask too much."

"How do you know what too much is?"

"Too much is giving in to Jason's demand that we send you back to the hospital after you were born," I told her.

She laughed. "Did he really want that?"

"Well, yes. We thought we had him all prepared—we'd showed him all the pictures and read him dozens of books about little brothers or sisters. He seemed pretty warm to the idea till we actually got you home and offered to let him hold you. I think he thought a baby was more like a puppy. He let us know in no uncertain terms that he didn't approve of all the fuss being made over the newcomer and wanted you sent back right away."

She laughed again. "That's just like Jas. Did he throw a fit when he didn't get his way?"

I smiled at the memory, although, as anyone new to sibling rivalry can tell you, it was a thoroughly exhausting period. "As I remember, he developed stomach aches that required lots of special attention."

"So what did you do, Mom?"

"The best I could, Megan. That's just about all you can do."

There was a moment of silence in the kitchen. It was the right moment for the phone to ring, or a clock to strike, but nothing happened.

"Mom?"

My antennae went up. Sixteen years of parenting made you acutely sensitive to a change in tone. "Yes?"

"You might be hearing from one of my teachers."

Dropped so casually, the statement was unlikely to be good news. The school's teachers, a dedicated and overworked lot, did not have time for phone calls in order to discuss the weather or the prospects for success of a referendum on the voucher system. "Oh?" I replied, with, I thought, admirable restraint. "Which one?"

"Mrs. Fletcher."

Christine Fletcher taught career and family studies, a sort of life skills course that covered everything from birth control to reading the stock pages. I couldn't believe Megan would be having trouble in the class; she showed so much enthusiasm for virtually every lecture and paper topic. "Are you going to tell me why I might be hearing from her, or do you want me to be surprised?" I asked her.

She managed a sheepish grin and then turned suddenly serious.

"I had to write this essay on my family," she said, not meeting my eyes. "And I wrote about, you know, the separation." She sighed gustily. "Mrs. Fletcher got pretty upset about it."

I gripped the countertop hard with my left hand while trying not to rattle my coffee mug with the other. Only those who have experienced firsthand a typical teenager's reckless disregard for scrupulous fidelity to the facts in favor of the temptations of dramatic exaggeration will entirely understand the frisson of dread I felt at that moment. I wondered if a visit from Child Protective Services was just around the corner. I tried not to think of the probable outcome of Steve's custody suit if that happened.

"Why?" I asked her. "What did you say?"

She shrugged, a little too nonchalantly. "I don't really remember. I guess I was . . . uh . . . pretty unhappy that day, and I might have come on pretty strong about how bad I was feeling."

"I see. And what did Mrs. Fletcher say to you about it?"

She looked away, embarrassed. "Well, usually Mrs. Fletcher's pretty cool. But she was like . . . crying."

"Oh Megan," I said, dismayed.

"I'm sorry, Mom."

What could I say to her? That I was angry (which was the truth) that she had aired the family linen at school? I felt too guilty at having been the cause of her pain, at having driven her to seek sympathy from her teachers. "It must have been some essay," I told her.

"Would you like to see it?" she asked, brightening.

"Sure," I said, as casually as I could manage. "Why not?"

"Okay. I'll get it back from Mrs. Fletcher."

I felt a little better. I didn't think she would have offered to let me see it if I'd come off a close second to Joan Crawford in the "Mommy Dearest" competition. Still, she had felt compelled to write *something*. "Megan, would you like to see someone,

someone you could talk to about your problems?"
I asked her.

She looked horrified. "You mean a *shrink*? Do you
think I'm crazy?"

"Of course not. I was thinking more of a kind of
counselor. Maybe we could all go."

She regarded me with disbelief. "Daddy, too?"

"He might be willing. He doesn't want you to be
unhappy, either."

"I don't think I want to, Mom. But thanks anyway."

"We'll let it rest a while, then. But why don't you
keep a diary, put your thoughts down on paper? It
might make you feel better."

She smiled at me. "Thanks for the suggestion,
Mom, but I already do."

I was a mother before I started investigating
crimes, and it was clear that I needed to keep my
priorities straight. Instead of calling David Sanchez,
I picked up the phone to call Christine Fletcher. I
might have been a shrinking violet about detective
work, but I guess I could be a Venus flytrap where
my kids were concerned.

"Thanks for your time," I told her when I had
navigated all the obstacles involved in getting hold
of a teacher in a public school. "Megan told me
there might be a problem with an essay she wrote
for your class, and I wanted to clear things up if
there was anything you wanted to discuss."

There was a silence on the other end of the line
while she mentally sifted through the 180-odd papers she had no doubt corrected in the last couple
of weeks and retrieved the information on Megan's
Career and Family Studies confessional.

I could almost hear her click in. "Oh, yes." Silence again. Finally: "Have you read it?"

"No. She said you still have it."

"Oh, right, of course. That's true."

"Should I read it?"

She sighed. "Well, you know that teenagers can be very emotional. They think everything in the world is about them. Basically Megan just wrote a very affecting essay about how your domestic situation is impacting her. It will probably make you unhappy to read it, but I guess I would anyway as long as you remember it's undoubtedly an exaggeration. Does she seem to be adjusting well at home?"

"I think so. But sometimes it's hard to tell what's normal teenage dreadful behavior and what's a reaction to the separation. She's a pretty good kid, though, most of the time. I just don't want to see her suffer in school or get anorexia or anything like that."

"I'll try to keep a closer eye on her than usual and let you know if I see any danger signs," she said quietly. "It's better to catch things before they go too far." She paused. "I'm divorced, too, so I know how hard it is. You can wear yourself out trying to meet everybody's needs."

She'd certainly put her finger on it there. I noticed that I had twisted the telephone cord round and round my finger so tightly that it had almost cut off the circulation. I let it go. "Do you think anybody ever has a good divorce?" I asked her.

She laughed. "I heard of one once. But the same person who told me about it assured me that Charles and Di would never split up for the sake of the monarchy, so who knows?"

"My husband and I haven't even begun the legal

proceedings yet, and we're scarcely speaking. I
hope things don't get a lot worse, especially for the
children's sake."

"Well . . ."

"That's naive, isn't it?" I asked her.

"Yes."

"I was afraid it might be," I conceded.

"Look, Mrs. James, getting a divorce is a little like
being pregnant—as soon as people get wind of your
condition, they can't wait to tell you their horror
stories."

I remembered that. When I was carrying Jason,
perfect strangers would clutch my arm in the check-
out line at the supermarket and tell me about their
sister/niece/granddaughter/cousin who had la-
bored thirty-six hours without anesthesia to produce Siamese twins joined at the head. It was
enough to make me want to stay indoors for the
duration of my pregnancy with Megan, particularly
since by then I realized that however optimistic
one's frame of mind, labor was not a prospect one
could easily contemplate with good cheer.

"I know what you mean," I told her.

"You probably don't yet, but you will," she assured me. "But one thing I'd like to tell you—to
warn you about, really—is that even when you
think it's settled, it isn't. It's never really over for
you as long as you have any financial dealings with
your ex-husband."

"What do you mean?"

She gave a self-deprecating little laugh. "This is
what I meant about everybody wanting to tell you
their stories."

"Please. I'd like to hear what you have to say, if
you want to tell me."

"Well, I guess what I want to warn you about is

that there's no such thing as a done deal, even if you've agreed on your settlement, your custody arrangements, and everything else." She cleared her throat. "I had a friend, a handyman, rent out my garage apartment after my husband left. I was lonely, and it helped with the rent, but it was really dumb because we had a brief romantic relationship that my ex-husband found out about. The next thing I knew, my husband was taking me to court, suing to eliminate my alimony because I had a 'de facto' marriage with this man who he claimed was in effect supporting me. It was completely specious because my friend moved out as soon as we ended our little fling, and my lawyer told me my husband didn't have any kind of a case. My lawyer also told me it would run about two thousand in legal bills," she said bitterly.

"And then there were depositions from my children, delayed hearings, and all kinds of expenses my counsel hadn't predicted, even though he still kept assuring me that Jack—my ex-husband— didn't have a legal leg to stand on. He told me he was very sorry, but he thought his original estimate for his fees would be too low."

I could hear her sighing into the phone. "You know, Mrs. James, I sat in his offices with his expensive paneling and his walnut desk and some oversized leather chair crafted for minor royalty, and all I could think of was 'I'm paying for all this.' I was, too. By the time the judge had concluded that Jack had no basis for his claims, my bill had reached about fifteen thousand. My lawyer asked that the plaintiff bear the cost of the proceedings, but the motion was denied. So the money had to come out of my savings for the kids' college fund, and I didn't get one damn thing out of it." There was a catch in her voice. "Sorry," she added.

"That's horrible!" I told her, full of indignation.

"You think so and I think so, but it's how the system works," she said more briskly. "If your ex-husband stops paying you or arbitrarily cuts your support in half, it will cost you three, four, maybe five hundred dollars just to talk it over with your lawyer and decide what to do about it." She sighed again. "This year Jack left his company to open his own business, and now he wants to reduce my child-support payments because his income has gone down as a result. He's put me on notice, he says, and he'll take it to court again if I don't agree to a voluntary reduction. Depending on how much less he wants to give me, I think I have to go along with it because I can't afford to pay another lawyer to battle it out in court. I just can't stand to lose any more."

"I don't know what to say," I told her. "I'm overwhelmed." I paused. "At least it's good to know that I'm not paranoid to be worried."

"No," she said firmly. "Definitely *not* paranoid. You might look into a support group while you're going through the process, and afterward. It helped me a lot. I guess I'd also suggest that you get as much as possible in real property and stocks, things you can sell if you have to. Don't trade them for the promise of high support payments."

"I really appreciate your candor," I told her. "You've given me a lot to think about."

"I'm glad if I can be of help," she said. "Anyway," she added, very much the teacher again, "Megan's a very nice girl, and for the most part she's happy and well-adjusted. I'd like to see her stay that way."

*   *   *

I called David Sanchez's Newport Beach office
while the brave mood was still upon me. I was not
destined, however, to ride the wave on to victory.

"Mr. Sanchez is out of town at the moment," his
secretary told me.

"I'd like to schedule an appointment, then," I told
her.

This was clearly unusual. "Are you a prospective
investor?" she asked. "We have prepared background information on our fund and its performance over the last ten years, and we'd be happy
to send you—"

I cut her off. "I have some information that might
be of interest to Mr. Sanchez, and we require his
assistance in evaluating it," I said starchily. I hoped
it sounded as if I had somehow gotten the goods
on GM. I thought the "we" sounded more authen-
tic. Steve had once had someone schedule an appointment with him because she was sure her
enemies were pursuing her with lasers through the
open windows. He had almost fired his secretary
for letting her sneak by. I had pointed out that anyone who had seen *Three Days of the Condor* four
times should not have been so cavalier in dismissing the possibility, but at that point in our relationship, he no longer found my jokes a thrill.

I had apparently succeeded in quelling the alarm
of David Sanchez's secretary, however, because she
granted me access on a day and hour not too distant. I gave her my name, perfectly sure he would
not recognize it in any case. I hardly wanted to
identify myself as someone who had been rude to
him at a prior meeting, particularly when I wanted
him to do me a favor.

*   *   *

Stasis was the enemy of progress. The phone was still hot and heavy in my hand. I stared at it for a minute before taking out my address book. Then I wiped my palm on my pants and dialed.

"I was wondering how you're getting along," I said, a little breathlessly. "Actually, if you're free, I was hoping you might like to get together for lunch one day this week."

Tricia Lindera Hampton sounded surprised, as well she might be, since our previous contacts, if you don't count Eleanor's funeral, were pretty much limited to a few seconds of pleasantries at firm social events. "I'm not sure . . ." she began, polite but hesitant.

I took the offensive. "I know we don't really know each other all that well, but you did seem as though you might need a friend when we talked at the play the other evening. And I thought you might like to get out of the house. I remember what it's like to have young children around all the time," I added shamelessly. Actually, if I had had parental responsibility for Randy and Barry Hampton, I not only would have gotten out of the house, I would have left the state altogether. In fact I was surprised that the phone lines were still functioning at Château Hampton, which was probably in ruins by now.

"Well . . ." I could tell she was weakening.

I played my trump card. "And of course I need to get out as well. Since the separation, I've lost touch with a lot of people in the firm, and I really don't want to write off all the wonderful friendships I've enjoyed over the years. I've always been sorry I didn't have more opportunities to get to know you better."

I felt more than a little guilty about appealing to

her sympathy (all right, pity) this way, but I had to get her to talk to me somehow. I knew she'd been ostracized by the remaining first wives in the firm, for whom the sight of a partner's wedding ring on a paralegal's finger was far from reassuring, so I hoped that even an outcast's acceptance might retain a little bit of allure. I didn't think I'd get more than one chance at it.

"Actually," she said in a quiet voice, "I'm free today."

"Great," I told her, hoping I sounded pathetically grateful. "Neiman Marcus?" I inquired. I really liked their lime and cilantro shrimp salad, though what I always lusted after, but never ordered, was the baked Brie.

"Could we go to La Valencia instead? It's closer."

"One o'clock," I told her.

The La Valencia Hotel is in the heart of the village, a beautiful old (by California standards, anyway) building painted a color somewhere between hot and salmon pink. The view from the tile and wood interior encompasses the sweep of the ocean and the terraced grounds descending to the shore; the patio, outfitted in wrought iron and potted plants, faces Prospect Street. It is a quintessentially California place, both elegant and casual. Celebrities (Greta Garbo) and wannabes (Marion Davies) have loved it ever since its opening in 1926.

The patio, while enjoying the favor of discriminating tourists and a few lucky businessmen in suits, was also a favorite of the Ladies Who Lunch, those whose pictures appeared in the social pages of the newspaper wearing big hats and surgical smiles for the opening day at the Del Mar Racetrack (the West Coast answer to Royal Ascot). It was the perfect refuge for those with trust funds and sedate good taste.

I had intended to arrive early and people-watch from the patio while I planned my interview, but I was too restless. Instead I skipped the valet parking and found a spot a zillion miles away (it was never too late to start economizing) up a street whose residents were cursed in perpetuity by the perennial scarcity of parking spaces in the downtown area. I walked down Prospect, past the mélange of trendy shops, tourist traps, and art galleries. Next to the little boutiques with two-hundred-dollar beaded T-shirts were clothing stores whose windows offered skirts and sweaters, soft, rich, and comfortable. There was none of the frantic luxury of Rodeo Drive, and there hadn't been even at the height of the eighties. Nobody honked a horn, imperiously summoning a salesperson to a car window; no one paced through the stores clutching a cellular phone. It was all quite relaxed and a rather good-humored acknowledgment that those who shopped there, like the residents, were improbably fortunate.

I arrived at La Valencia's patio approximately one and a half minutes before Tricia, who ran up breathlessly in a charming little black suit and heels, clutching a sheaf of papers. Every man in the place turned to look at her. She had the kind of body that would have them colliding with each other in over-populated places like airports, their heads swiveling one way and their legs continuing another. Even some of the women were openly admiring.

"Sorry I'm late," she said, though she wasn't, much. "Barclay's redecorating his office, and he wants me to pick out some artwork for the walls." Eleanor had done his last decor in, if I recall correctly, a style that might best be described as Seventies Modern, right down to the Eames chair and the metal sculptures. It probably looked tired now, and I didn't blame him for wanting to change it.

"That's great," I assured her.

"I've just been at the galleries," she added, when the hostess had shown us to our seats. She handed me the pamphlets and papers she was still clutching. "What do you think of these?"

I thought she was more interested in preventing an embarrassing lull in the conversation than in soliciting my opinion about paintings and lithographs for Barclay's walls, but it did present me with an awkward dilemma. What should I say to her? The truth was that for real art you had to go to Los Angeles. Some artists made brave attempts in their spartan lofts in downtown San Diego, but there wasn't enough big money in the city to support a thriving community of serious art independent of sales to tourists and decorators.

Most of what you found in La Jolla was the visual equivalent of Barry Manilow: easy looking. There were undemanding scenes of French provincial life painted in a vaguely Impressionistic style. There were Southwestern landscapes featuring cute Indians and charming buffalo. There were Nouveau Art Nouveau statues favored by those with newly acquired upper-middle-class incomes and large Cadillacs.

Somehow, I didn't think Barclay would appreciate any of them, though it was hardly my place to say so. In fact, I wondered if he didn't deserve to have me steer her toward something truly hideous. I looked hopefully through her handouts, but what she had collected was too innocuous to afford an appropriate revenge.

"Ummm," I procrastinated. "It's really hard to

choose art for somebody else. It's really all a matter
of individual taste." God, that was such a cop-out.
So much art was pretentious nonsense, like the
sculptures that moaned at you and did everything
but clutch your arm (an artistic genre much favored
by the Whitney in New York, if I remembered correctly) or the man-sized hippopotamus on roller
skates I had once seen in a gallery in the desert.
"Are you an art lover?" the salesperson asked
everyone who came in the door. As if anyone would
dare to say no. As if only that discriminating quality
would enable you to appreciate the company of life-
sized jungle animals in the living room.

"I know what you mean," she said, folding the
papers and putting them away. "I think I'll get the
decorator to show me some things before I make
any decisions."

I wondered if Van Gogh would have done better
if he had lived in a world inhabited by decorators.
Probably not—a neurasthenic one-eared genius
would be a hard sell even now.

"That's probably best," I agreed, reluctantly
abandoning the fantasy of some updated Odalisque
hanging above the volumes of tax codes in Barclay's
office. "Then you could coordinate the colors with
the carpet."

She looked at me to see if I was serious. Apparently satisfied, she peered at the menu. "I always
have the scallops," she told me.

I sighed and handed mine to the waiter. "I'll have
the spinach salad with the dressing on the side." I
looked at her. "Would you like a bottle of wine?"

She hesitated. "I guess so."

"What would you like?"

The waiter stubbed his toe on the chair leg in his

rush to get her the wine list, but she wouldn't choose. She shrugged delicately.

I might have disgusted Steve with my wine philistinism, but I knew enough to pick a California Chardonnay. I wanted to impress her and relax her enough to confide in me, so I picked Grgich Hills, which everyone in the entire oenophilic world had heard of. I trusted the hotel to pick the good years, but I doubted whether either of us could have told the difference anyway.

While I was busy with the wine rituals, she took out a little compact and darted a quick look at her face, as if to reassure herself, "That's me." Whenever I looked in the mirror, even before the makeover, I always thought, "That can't be me." That's probably the difference between beautiful (young) women and the rest of us.

I raised my glass and saluted her. "I'm so glad you could come," I told her, oozing solicitude. "I know this must have been a hard few weeks for you."

She bent her head in acknowledgment.

"How are the children adjusting?" I asked her.

"Pretty well, I guess." She still didn't look up. "Actually, they're sort of unhappy."

"Naturally, losing their mother so recently."

Her head snapped up. She looked as if she were about to say something, but she broke off a piece of bread and chewed it daintily. "I'm sure they miss her," she said when she had swallowed. "But it's more than that. She gave them anything they wanted. Really. You can't believe it. Now they complain about *everything*. What we eat. What we buy them to wear. What I let them see at the movies. Everything. It's never as good as what she got for them or let them do. It's never enough." She shook her lovely head sadly. "Sometimes I think they hate me as much as she did."

I murmured something sympathetic, but there was no point in protesting too much. Any thought I might have had about Tricia doing Eleanor in was rejected on the grounds that she had clearly had a powerful motive for keeping her alive. If she didn't, she had stood to inherit the children, and it was worth putting up with the occasional thrown ashtray to avoid that. I wondered if she'd inquired into a good boarding school.

"Of course she would have been jealous of you," I told her.

Her shrug of indifference would have seemed perfectly natural to another stunning twenty-five-year-old. "Well, she was old and—"

"Not that old," I couldn't help interrupting.

She looked at me again. "Okay, but she was so *fat*, and Barclay didn't love her anymore. At first I felt sorry for her, but she just wouldn't accept that he had moved on beyond her. I think she went sort of crazy. She called him all the time and wrote him letters. She just wouldn't let go."

"Did the letters and calls upset him?"

"Not at first. We used to laugh when the phone rang, because you could always tell when it would be Eleanor. She always called at eight o'clock, just when she knew we'd be having dinner. Finally we'd just let the machine pick up, and then she'd get *really* mad. She said, 'What if one of the kids had an emergency and you missed it because you wanted to be alone with your—' Well, you get the idea."

"But later on, he got more upset?" I prompted her.

She nodded. "That's when he started getting real

angry, you know? But he wouldn't say anything. It was like he was holding it all inside. Then he started having trouble sleeping and . . . and all the other stuff I told you about. I made him go to the doctor. He got some pills, but they didn't help."

Just then the waiter emerged from the kitchen with our lunches, so I was prevented from pressing her on it. I wondered if by chance Barclay's prescription had found its way into Eleanor's digestive system, but I couldn't think of a way to ask that wouldn't seem too obvious. We toyed in silence with our food while I racked my brain for a way to get back to Eleanor and Barclay. I wondered if journalists and detectives had better covers than that of nosy voyeur.

"I thought I'd be glad when she was dead," she said frankly, spearing a scallop on the end of her fork.

She must have seen my expression alter. "Sorry," she said. "I know she was a friend of yours, but—"

"She was not a friend of mine," I said quickly and truthfully. "Where did you get that idea?"

She looked down at her plate. "Barclay told me so the other night, after the play. He said you took her side of things because—" She stopped, and a look of horror crossed her face.

"Because my husband left me, too. It's okay." The spinach tasted suddenly dry in my mouth. I wondered if her agreeing to have lunch with me was in some way a small rebellion against Barclay's recent neglect of her. "You know, I don't think Eleanor really had any friends," I told her. "She was so obsessed with the divorce that she drove them all away. Nobody could stand to be around her. You had to feel sorry for her, though," I added incautiously.

She twisted her wedding ring round on her finger. It held a stone worthy of a Gabor sister. "I didn't feel sorry for her," she said angrily. "She wouldn't leave us alone. She wanted to make Barclay pay for leaving her, and she was never satisfied with what he gave her. I don't think she ever would have been satisfied. She'd always have wanted more."

"Wasn't Barclay"—I chose the word carefully—"relieved when he learned she was dead?"

She looked at me oddly. She might have had an IQ only slightly higher than room temperature, but she knew something was up. "Why do you ask?" she asked coolly.

It was my turn to squirm. "Well, you mentioned that he was angry with her and taking some kind of medication. I was just hoping things might have gotten better after she died."

She narrowed her eyes. "My husband is a very compassionate, caring man," she said emphatically. "He had some feelings for her; she was the mother of his children. Of course he was upset when she died."

"People have always admired him for that," I reassured her hastily and hypocritically. "It must have been hard for him when he got the news."

"Well, the police came to our home right after Juanita—our housekeeper—found the body when she took the twins over there. Fortunately, the boys were inside the house and didn't have to see their mother . . . like that. Anyway, by the time Barclay got home, they had already heard the news at the firm, so I wasn't with him. But he was *very* upset."

"He was working the night she died, too, wasn't he?"

"Yes." She pushed her plate away abruptly. "Do you mind if we don't talk about this anymore? It's really been hard for all of us, and I'd just like to forget about it for a while."

"Right. Of course. I understand how you feel."

"I mean, it's not like a normal death, or anything."

"Oh. Why not?"

"I really don't want to get into this, Caroline. I think enough's been said on the subject."

"Fine," I told her. "We can just drop the whole thing."

"I mean, she committed suicide. It's like she wanted to pin the blame on Barclay one last time for what he did to her. It's like she was saying, 'Look how miserable my ex-husband and his new wife made me. I couldn't take it anymore, so I had to kill myself.'"

"I'm sure no one thinks—" I began.

"Sure they do. They look at us and they feel sorry for *her*, just like you do. Eleanor turned herself from something spiteful and pathetic into some kind of martyr just by taking her own life. Saint Eleanor," she said, her lips curling bitterly to form the words. "The bitch tried to ruin everything for him—for us—and now it's like she's reaching out from the grave. Why couldn't she just get run over by a car or something easy like that? She made a big enough target. Why does she have to make our lives so terrible?" Tears trembled at the edges of her magnificent dark lashes. She would never look ugly when she cried.

"Do you think that's why Barclay's been depressed?" I asked her.

"I'm sorry, Caroline, but I have to say it really isn't any of your business," she said and dabbed at her lips with her napkin.

"I'll get the check," I said.

12

I WASN'T SURE what I had gleaned from my lunch with Tricia other than flecks of spinach on my teeth and the conviction that Barclay probably wouldn't allow her within ten feet of me again once she reported the gist of our conversation. I was sure he was hiding something, but there was no way to prove what it was. You could hardly hang a murder rap on somebody for being glad his ex-wife, a harridan of almost mythical stature, was finally out of the way, and that was really all she'd confessed to. If he'd been openly jubilant, I would have been much less suspicious. What I didn't buy was Tricia's explanation of his misery, although hers was clearly unfeigned.

What was I doing trying to wring information out of a harassed second wife who was doing the best she could to deal with a rough situation? I should have been offering to babysit, not faking sympathy for her plight so she would spill the family secrets. What did I expect her to do, confess that she had wondered how Barclay's suit pants had gotten wet up to the knees on the night Eleanor died? That he had rubbed his hands together with glee, chortling that their problems were over at last? I hadn't really learned much of use, and I had probably tipped my hand.

Still, even if Barclay had renounced any further interest in the contents of Eleanor's box and had left the state with his devoted wife in tow, I wasn't going to relinquish this investigation. Maybe it was the thrill of defying Steve that appealed to me. Maybe I wanted to humiliate Barclay and, by extension, my own husband. Maybe my motives would have given a psychologist a field day. Everything I had told Rob was true. I still wanted to know, and I was kidding myself if I thought I was going to give up on it now.

The office of Rachel Fenton, my would-be attorney, was perfect. The chairs were severe but not uncomfortable, the table and desk no-nonsense and functional. There was nothing to give potential clients the fear that expensive interior appointments would be coming out of their bills, no burnished wood paneling or oversized floral bouquets. The parking lot had been full of middle-sized Japanese cars, nothing a car-jacker would give a second glance.

Rachel Fenton, like her furnishings, was direct and unpretentious. Her business suit was Wall Street blue, her hair stylishly short, her makeup light. She shook my hand firmly but not in that overly hardy way some women use to prove they are "one of the guys." She explained her fee schedule, the retainer, et al., in a manner that did not make me wince. Then she seated herself calmly, prepared to listen.

I told her I was somewhat embarrassed at initiating the process when I had not yet heard officially from Steve. "But I know he's been in contact with Jay Thompson, and I'm pretty sure it wasn't just to set up a tennis date," I added.

She smiled. "Jay Thompson doesn't play tennis. He does these iron-man triathalon events almost every weekend."

"Do you know him well?"

"We've met in court a lot. If Jay's representing him, your husband's got himself a top-notch lawyer." I liked the way she said it—confident but not cocky.

"What do you need to know from me?" I asked her.

She pulled out a pad of paper. "I need as complete an inventory of your assets as you can give me: stocks, bank accounts, the house, and any separate property you might have—that's property that came to you before the marriage or might have been given to you specifically, say by your parents."

"I know what those things are. You can't be married to a lawyer for eighteen years without some of it rubbing off."

She sighed. "Well, that's the easy part. The hard part will be putting a value on your husband's share of the practice, among other things. Did you work to put him through law school?"

"Sure," I told her. "But it wasn't much. Stanford gave law school wives—there weren't as many husbands then—sort of time-filler jobs around the campus as a kind of courtesy."

She raised her eyebrows. "It helps to have a big endowment, I suppose." Nevertheless, she scribbled something down on the pad. "Now, what was your income last year from your writing?"

I told her, blushing as I did so because the grand total was scarcely enough to keep my family in hot dogs for a month even if you compromised and bought something other than Hebrew National. "It isn't much," I said apologetically.

"You'd have a hard time living on it, even in Bangladesh," she admitted. "But I'm still impressed. I always wanted to write something, but I never found the time."

Another closet author. "Well, don't give up your day job," I told her.

She smiled. "Okay. Now, do you know what your husband's partnership draw was last year?"

I gave her a ballpark figure. "But I'm not sure," I said sheepishly.

"Don't you sign your tax returns?"

"Yes, but I never really look at them. Steve always takes—took—care of that." I almost hung my head. I felt I had let her down. "I was foolish, I know."

"Too trusting, maybe, but you're not alone; I can tell you that. Anyway, it's no problem getting hold of your returns, even if you don't have copies. Do you know if Mr. James regularly gets a bonus?"

"He got one last year. It varies from year to year. But this year should be another big one, because the firm took an important client public not long ago and"—I had a brief vision of the library in Jeff Grayson's house—"everybody's talking about how much money they're making."

She laid her pen down on the pad. "Has your husband mentioned that he expects a big bonus?"

I considered. "No, I don't think so."

She sighed. "Well, I have to warn you that sometimes it can be pretty hard to pin it down. I'm not saying it will be true in your husband's case, but most partners in a firm have a certain amount of flexibility about moving money around and hiding it from their about-to-be-ex-wives. It's sort of 'catch me if you can,' and if you don't happen to ask the right questions, you won't get the right answers."

I was so relieved I could have hugged her. At least she wouldn't dismiss my concerns, gleaned from the knowledge of what Barclay had done to Eleanor, as paranoid ravings. "I've heard they can lie about their bonuses," I agreed.

She shook her head sadly over human frailty. "It's been known to happen. I just need to warn you, but let's not borrow trouble before it starts." Her expression said she nevertheless expected it would.

I cleared my throat. "I want to talk about . . ."

"Yes?"

My heart started to thud in my chest. My voice was so tight I could hardly get out the words. "The children are living in the house with me, but Steve is talking about . . ."

"Suing for custody?" she asked briskly, to help me along.

"He hasn't said so in so many words. But I feel he's threatened it. I feel very pressured to go along with whatever he suggests because if I don't, he'll demand custody."

She gave me a level gaze. "Does he have any reason to remove them from your custody?"

"Not at all," I said firmly. "Right now, he sees them on occasional weekends, but that's it. The kids would like to see more of him, but I think they're happy living with me."

"Then it's probably fair to say that it's just a negotiating tactic, like a move on a chess board. He probably can't get sole custody, so you don't have to cave in on his other demands. However," she added gravely, "I can only say that some form of joint custody is usual in these cases. I have to tell you that if you can work out something you are both happy with, without getting your lawyers involved, it will save you a lot—and I do mean a lot—of money and grief. Some kind of specious custody battle could run through your assets in no time flat."

"Just present you with a fait accompli, you mean?" I asked her.

"If you can. Trust me; there is nothing you could do that would be more beneficial to yourself or your children than to settle it without a fight." It was the same advice, in essence, that I had gotten from Patrick Dunn, but it sounded better coming from her.

I looked at the picture in a little silver frame on the desk. Two kids, a little younger than Jason and Megan, with their arms around a pleasant-looking dark-haired man in a Hawaiian shirt at the beach. "I believe you," I told her. I just wasn't sure I could do it. I wondered how anyone could stay unscathed and sane dealing with matrimonial law all the time. I didn't see how you could avoid getting singed by all the anger and disappointment, but I didn't know her well enough to ask, and I didn't want her to think I expected her to function as my psychiatrist as well as my lawyer. "The only thing is, what about the house, then? He's trying to sell it out from under me, and if he's using the kids as a negotiating tactic . . ."

She frowned. "When I see the list of total assets, I'll have a better idea how to advise you. I can probably get you the house, but you'll have to give up something in exchange. And I can't promise you won't have to sell it eventually."

"I can live with that," I told her. And, surprisingly, it was true. I remembered Christine Fletcher's tales of constant renegotiation and blackmail and decided I would rather give up everything than live like that. It might have been stupid, but it was very liberating.

She glanced at her watch and stood up. "Good. The worst thing that could happen would be not to be able to come to any kind of agreement, so that your husband can press for a bifurcated divorce. In that case, he would get his freedom before you settle your finances, and we would lose a lot of leverage. Trust me, you don't want that. So if you'll put together that information for me, we can get the ball rolling." She looked down at the paper on her desk, then up at me. "Do you want me to go ahead and get a date for a temporary support hearing, even if your husband and Jay Thompson haven't initiated any action?"

My fingernails were probably making indelible marks in my palms, but I held her gaze. "Yes."

"Okay. The legal separation and the temporary support are usually pretty straightforward. It's the divorce that can get sticky." She looked at me assessingly. "You know, I can't promise you this won't be a grueling ordeal. You can split up the money, but the legal system still has to work out problems it was never designed to solve. It can be pretty tough."

I took her outstretched hand and shook it. "You mean like the fact that somebody once promised to love you and doesn't anymore?"

"Yes," she said sadly. "Like that."

"Tell me some bad things about New York," Susan said when I called her at home. "Hurry."

"Susan, you lived there. I didn't," I protested. "All I know is the basic stuff I read in the papers.

Donald Trump. Muggings. Things like that."

"Okay, then tell me some of the things I've told you over the years. And after that, tell me some good things about La Jolla. Think. I really need this."

I searched my brain. "All right. In New York they have to buzz you into the exclusive stores, and you can't get in unless you're white."

"Good one," she said. "Nobody has to get buzzed into surf shops. Keep going."

"Okay, didn't you tell me that when women go to Mass at St. Patrick's, they clutch their purses when they kneel so no one can lean over the pews and steal them? What kind of a place is that?"

"I didn't tell you that; you must have read it somewhere. How would I know? It was a stretch just to go into the place, and when I did, my eyes were on the stained glass. Chalk up another one for San Diego, though; after you've testified in New York, this is where they relocate you on the Witness Protection Program."

"How about this one, then? 'Southern California is where people get to do what they're too inhibited to do in Manhattan.'"

"That won't work," she said, sounding regretful. "Nothing's too outrageous for Manhattan."

"I give up," I told her. "I can't think of anything beyond the obvious, like the climate and crime. I mean, we can't compete on a cultural basis. All La Jolla had was Dr. Seuss, and he's dead."

"It's true," she said mournfully. "Philip Roth, Susan Sontag, E. L. Doctorow . . ."

"And you haven't even touched art, architecture, or music," I added. "Not to mention bookstores. I don't suppose you'd care to tell me why we're playing, would you?"

"The Surfing Gynecologist asked me out."

"Oh, God." The Surfing Gynecologist was a minor media star, a local doctor who had held on to his surfboard more successfully than his youth and managed to appear in local publications once or twice a year framed against the sunset and purportedly exemplifying all the virtues of the La Jolla good life. The publicity had apparently made him the big kahuna of local gynecology and led to all sorts of speculation as to whether he really uttered "Cowabunga" when he slipped a gloved finger into an exposed orifice. "Are you going to go?" I asked her, although I already knew the answer.

"Of course not," she snapped. "Boogie boards for two is hardly my cup of tea. But it's a bad omen. There's something else, too. . . ."

"What?"

"I got this really terrific job offer today from a law firm in New York. A *big* firm. Casey and McDonald. And a big salary to match."

"Wow." It was all I could think of to say. "What are you going to do?"

"I don't know. They want to fly me back to talk about it. I was hoping you'd talk me out of going."

"Well, if you don't want to go . . ."

"I'm not sure how I feel. I left . . . all that . . . a long time ago, and I promised myself I would never go back. I've made a new life here, and for the most part I like it. But the truth is, I miss New York. Sometimes I think that if I hear the term 'laid-back' one more time I'll scream. I hate the whole *concept* of laid-back. New York is not laid-back," she said wistfully. "And it is a very good offer."

"Then I think you should at least talk to them," I said firmly, although I couldn't imagine what I would do if she moved away. "How did they hear about you, anyway?"

"I have a friend who's a headhunter and thought I'd be just perfect for the job," she said, as mournfully as if she'd just been told she'd lost her savings in the latest S&L scandal.

"Well, you don't have to sound as if you've been invited to a morticians' convention just because somebody's recognized your excellence," I said with a laugh. "Go to the city. Have fun. Get buzzed into boutiques. Hold on to your purse in the synagogue."

"If I do go . . ." She paused. "Would you be interested in coming with me? New York is great in the fall. I mean, if you can survive to enjoy it, it is a kind of secular nirvana."

"Thanks," I told her sincerely. "But I'm not sure I should spend the money. And I've got a lot going on right now. As a matter of fact, I—"

"Well, I just thought you might be needing a change."

There is little point to friendship if you can't read between the lines. Such cautious, kid-glove solicitude was as unlike her as interrupting me. "Susan," I said firmly, "what is it you're not saying?"

She sighed so gustily I could hear it through the receiver. "Okay. There's talk at the firm."

Then I knew what she hadn't yet told me. "Why don't you just ask me how I could have been so stupid?" I said.

"Oh, shit," she said. "Did you really go out with Jeff Grayson? I was hoping it wasn't true. How could you have been so stupid?"

"He asked me," I told her. "I know it's lame, but that's the truth. He asked me, and at the moment I couldn't think of a good reason why not."

"Caroline, if you can't say 'no' to anybody, you're going to have a very interesting life after your divorce. It might also be very short." She made a small gagging noise. "Jeff Grayson is even worse than the Surfing Gynecologist."

"Nothing happened," I said somewhat defensively and inaccurately. "Well, not much, anyway. We just had a drink at his house."

"You're not interested or dazzled or anything else, by chance, are you?"

"No." I shuddered a little at the memory of hiding out in his bathroom, at best a highly inauspicious reentry into the Dating Scene.

"Good. Jeff Grayson is a decent lawyer, and I'll grant you a certain measure of charm if you go for the dissipated type. But he's the kind of guy who'd like to go around with his dick hanging out of his pants, just so everybody would get the message about what a big stud he is."

I couldn't resist. "It wasn't that big."

She let out a whoop of laughter. "I thought you said nothing happened."

"It was a near miss," I said.

"Well, you'd better be prepared for a certain amount of snickering. I mean, this is a guy who sent 'Mission Accomplished' telegrams to the other partners on his honeymoon."

"Christ. How do you know that?"

"Caroline, I am the office manager. The secretaries know *everything*. They type the letters. They take phone calls. They sign for telegrams." She sighed. "Quite frankly, sometimes they snoop. That's what I'm trying to warn you about."

"I've learned my lesson; I promise. Is it really so bad I have to leave town?"

She laughed. "Maybe not, but I think you should

come anyway. It would do you good to get away from the pressure of deciding your future for a while. Besides, you've handed your husband a—well, not a weapon, maybe, but at least a water balloon to use against you, and you might as well let him cool down first."

"I can't, Susan. I'm on a quest."

"For what?"

"You won't like it."

"I already don't. Still, I admit I'm intrigued. What could be more important than swimming in the *au courant* on Madison Avenue in a stream of people who haven't been seriously outdoors since they went away to camp? Just think, you could lose your healthy tan and acquire an all black wardrobe to wear while waiting to expire from terminal despair."

"I thought you missed it," I told her.

"I do. And you're avoiding the question."

"All right. But first you have to tell me how you feel about snooping."

"You mean, other than the fact that it is entirely inconsistent with my position at the law firm and could result in my losing my job?"

"Yes."

"I'm opposed to it in something a bit more than principle."

I was not dissatisfied with this answer. Her primmest language was reserved for cases when she wanted to leave herself an out, as if the formality alone would entice the listener into failing to examine the small print.

"I want to ask you a hypothetical question," I told her. "What if somebody says he was at the office at a certain time when something else was taking place? Is there any way to tell for sure if he was really at the firm or not? I mean, could somebody sneak out without anyone knowing?"

"Is this your quest?" she asked, all seriousness now.

I took a breath. "I want to know what really happened to Eleanor Hampton."

"You mean you want to pin it on Barclay." She had accurately deciphered the import of my questions.

"No, I just want the truth." At least that's all I hoped I wanted.

"You're right. I don't like it. This could be incredibly self-destructive."

"Do you think I should see a psychiatrist and get my priorities straight?" I said it with a laugh, but I seriously wanted her opinion.

"Cut the crap, Caroline. I mean, if it gets out that you're doing a Samantha Spade number on Barclay, the whole firm will be out for your blood. And that could mean problems when you go for your settlement. I tried to warn you about that before."

"This is really important to me, Susan."

"Do you actually believe he had a hand in Eleanor's death?"

"There was something strange going on, and I want to find out what it is. And I promise to be very careful about throwing accusations around."

"You're sure I can't talk you into a culture orgy in New York?"

I said nothing.

"Okay." She sighed. "Then here's the answer to your question. If it's nighttime, people come and go with their keys as they please, but we're supposed to know where the lawyers are during office hours. If they leave for lunch or a board meeting or whatever, they're supposed to let someone know in case there's an important call. Then there are the phone slips and the record each attorney keeps of his or her billable hours. If someone says he was here, there could be an incredible paper trail to substantiate it."

"But? I heard a 'but' in there somewhere."

"Well," she conceded, "it's just that it all depends on the lawyer supplying his or her own record. It's not like they punch time cards. Nobody questions them. Well, sometimes partners write down—reduce—some associates' billable hours, but that's not what I mean. You can walk into a lawyer's office and if he's not there, he could be anywhere: the bathroom, getting some coffee, in another lawyer's office. The place is huge, so unless you think you know where he might be, you wouldn't go looking."

"So nobody could really prove he was in the office during a certain period of time?"

"Well, sure he could, if he was in a meeting during that time or attending a deposition or something like that. All you need are witnesses."

"Did Barclay have witnesses?" I asked her.

"I don't know," she said carefully.

"Can you check?"

"I could access his calendar and phone log and billing records and make some guesses, but that's about all. I can't go around asking people if they were with Barclay on the afternoon and evening his wife was killed, not even for you."

"Will you do what you can, then?" I asked, not wanting to pressure her but wondering what I would do if she refused to help me.

"I can get you that information," she said slowly, "but I'm having a little trouble with the ethics here.

I'm not sure how much more I can do unless you come up with a *very* convincing case."

"I won't ask you to do anything unless it's really important," I promised her.

"Good. Getting fired might be a little hard to paper over when I talk to Casey and McDonald."

"Cowabunga," she said the next morning when she called me back.

"Is that the password?"

"I thought it not inappropriate to your up-the-establishment project. I got the information you wanted."

"Can you tell me now?" I said, lowering my voice conspiratorially.

"I don't imagine the phones are tapped, so I don't see why not." She sounded amused. "Here's what I found out. Barclay billed ten hours to Naturcare on the day Eleanor died. That's a lot, so it probably means he worked into the evening. He didn't have any meetings scheduled. There were a number of phone calls, all of them billed to the same account."

"So it means he might have been there, and he might not have. There's nothing conclusive."

"Well, I checked with his secretary—very discreetly, of course—and—"

"You did it! You really asked!"

"Would you like to hear what she had to say?" she asked calmly.

"Sorry," I told her. "Shoot."

"Well, Martha and I were just commiserating about how hard things have been for poor Mr. Hampton lately, and I asked her what she might have remembered about his schedule that day, in case he had been so upset later he had forgotten to record all his billings. Nobody would think twice about worrying about that; it's all anyone thinks about around here. Anyway, she said that Mr. Hampton was in his office all afternoon working, but that he said she could go home early because her son had an orthodontist's appointment, so she wasn't there after about four o'clock."

"That's great," I told her. "It means his alibi is shaky. It means he might have had opportunity."

"It could mean that," she agreed, "if you concede there was a homicide in the first place."

"I'm working on that," I told her.

"My, you're sounding more like Nancy Drew by the minute. What's next in the investigation?"

"Motive," I told her in my best Samantha Spade growl.

13

DAVID SANCHEZ GREETED me with
that little start of unpleasant recognition, quickly
masked over, that I had once encountered in the
maître d' of a three-star French restaurant who
couldn't find the transatlantic reservation we had
made weeks before at great expense and even
greater effort. Immediately afterward, he had recovered himself sufficiently to lead us to the Gallic
equivalent of Siberia, but that instant had been
enough.

David Sanchez, however, did not have the option
of seating me next to the kitchen door or the men's
room and then abandoning me to my fate, so he
schooled his expression into politeness and waited
for me to explain my invasion of his turf.

To counteract the impression of our last meeting,
I had rejected the black-clad "you touch me, you'll
be sorry" look in favor of something softer and
more colorful. Signor Eduardo would have ap-
proved of my turquoise and green pleated skirt; it
had the added advantage of not wrinkling in the
course of the hour-plus drive to Newport Beach.

Newport Beach may well have the highest per

capita number of financial sleazeballs in the state of
California, and maybe in the United States—with
the possible exception of celebrated portions of New
Jersey. It was, therefore, an excellent location for
one who made his fortune unmasking and profiting
from the exposure of the Ponzis and the Pyramids,
along with lesser frauds and ineptitudes. It was also
quite beautiful, with a charming harbor and a perfect climate, like a cross between Switzerland and
the south of France.

Sanchez Associates, however, was in the business
corridor near the freeway, in one of those buildings
that reflect back the light in interesting colors depending on the time of day. His office itself was
done in generic wealthy: everything understated,
from the chair (body by Scandinavia, leather by It-
aly) to the Tamayo lithograph on the wall, which
featured one of his coyote-wolf-like things squinting
malevolently at the artist. It was rather disturbing.

However, I had not come to critique David Sanchez's taste in art. "Thank you for seeing me," I said
in a tone I hoped was as far from desperate as possible.

"My secretary said you might have some financial information of interest," he said politely.

I didn't blame him for being dubious. He had already correctly pegged me as Ms. Suburbia, the
leather briefcase at my feet notwithstanding. His indifferent civility made me realize the absurd futility
of trying to convince him to help me, but I plunged
in anyway. "I'm not sure what I have," I said truthfully, "but I'm hoping you can help me evaluate
some financial information." I sketched, very
briefly, the background of the materials and my be-
lief that something in the box might have been the
source of blackmail. "I've looked at the papers my-

self, but I need someone with the background and resources to interpret them."

The corners of his mouth turned down slightly. "These are legal files?" he asked.

"Among other things." I had brought most of the letters, too, in case there was something hidden that I had missed.

"Your possession of them might not be strictly legitimate," he suggested.

"I think almost everything is a copy," I told him.

He opened one of the folders, gave it a cursory glance, and then looked harder. I peered at it across the desk; it was one of Eleanor's haranguing letters. His nose wrinkled. "This is rather distasteful," he said, his eyes widening.

Too late, I realized that I should have organized the contents more carefully. "I know," I told him. "Some of the personal letters are really awful, but I wasn't sure if I should leave them out. The business papers are in the next folder."

He folded his hands on the desk in front of him. "I'm sorry," he said somewhat curtly, as if I were a panhandler blocking the entrance to his favorite restaurant. "I just don't think there is anything we can do for you. I thought I told you when we first met that we don't review personal financial documents."

"Look," I told him, trying not to sound desperate, "when I first asked you about it, my motives *were* personal. I was very worried about my own divorce settlement, and I wanted to know if there was, shall we say, a precedent at my husband's law firm for deceitful dealings. But this is more important than that. I think there might be something in these papers that somebody wants back pretty badly. Now that I know it can't just be that Barclay Hampton manipulated his assets to cheat his wife out of a fair settlement, I figure it has to be something I've over-looked." I took a deep breath. "And I think Eleanor might be dead because of whatever it is."

He gave me a look of polite incredulity. "If you think this is a matter of blackmail, or, if I under-stand you correctly, homicide, it's a criminal issue. You should probably take it to the police."

"I'm prepared to," I assured him, "but first I need a coherent story to overcome their theory that this was a suicide or maybe an accidental drowning. I need to put all the pieces together."

"Would it be unfair to ask why you are so inter-ested in pursuing this? What do you stand to get out of it?"

"Apart from wanting to see justice done, you mean?"

He smiled slightly. "If you like."

I told him about the break-in in the garage. "I don't think it's safe not to know what happened, and why."

"I see." He sounded perfectly equable, but of course he didn't see. He thought I was a loony. It was written all over his face. I decided to abandon my cool businesswoman posture, since he had clearly made up his mind not to help me in any case. "Look," I told him angrily, "the last time we met, I was rude to you. I—"

"True," he said, with another glint of a smile.

"I apologize. Getting divorced does weird things to you. That's not an excuse; it's an explanation. Anyway, please get it through your head that I don't want anything personal from you other than a few hours of your time, which I'm prepared to pay for. All I need is your help. I just want you to understand that this isn't some elaborate ruse to see you again or anything like that." I was talking too fast, and my palms were sweating. *Calm down*, I told myself.

"Relax," he said, the smile now extending to his eyes as well. "Stop worrying about hurting my feelings. I accept that your motives, whatever they are, are noble. It's okay."

It wasn't. He thought I was a crazed premenopausal Fury out on some personal vendetta. "Don't humor me," I told him.

He laughed, a broad, rich sound. "What do you want me to say?"

"That you don't believe I'm so in the grip of my idée fixe that I've lost all perspective. That I'm really not some vengeance-seeking sicko trying to get a thrill out of pinning a murder on a blameless innocent. But even if you believe that, the death doesn't have to be your concern. Everybody in the world has said 'good riddance' about Eleanor Hampton, and there's no reason you should be an exception."

"I'm almost sorry I didn't meet this woman," he said meditatively.

"You wouldn't have liked her," I assured him. "No one liked her."

"Except you," he offered.

"*I* didn't like her," I said, surprised at the suggestion. "I'm not even sure I blame Barclay for dumping her for someone else. But he could have been kinder, personally and financially, especially when he made so much money on Naturcare. And I do blame him for that."

He shifted his posture ever so slightly and leaned forward over the desk. "Naturcare?"

He said it blandly, but nevertheless I thought I had caught the first real glimmer of interest in the conversation. Interest, if not enthusiasm, in his line of business had to mean something. "You've heard something?" I asked him.

He sat back in his impressive chair and put his fingertips together. He frowned. "Do you remember when you suggested that just investigating a company might have the desired effect, at least from my point of view, and drive the stock price down, whether or not there was any real financial basis for concern?"

"Did I?" At this distance I was a little vague on our former conversation.

"You did," he assured me. "When you're in this business, everybody and his mother is looking for tips." He sighed. "I never mention company names if I can help it, not even to the shoe repairman or the grocery clerk. It would be totally irresponsible, not to mention unethical."

"In other words, I didn't hear what I thought I heard."

"Correct." He rubbed his temples with his slender fingers; he looked tired. "Look, if you'll promise not to read anything into it, I'll make you a deal. Right now I'm so busy I don't have time to eat dinner, much less anything else. But if you'll leave your materials with me for a few weeks, I'll try to have one of my associates look them over for you. I can't promise they'll find anything more than you found yourself, but their eyes are better trained than yours to spot irregularities."

I envisioned some sneering Yuppie whippersnapper trying to get through my files in record time because his boss said he had to look at them to humor somebody. Besides, I didn't want to leave them anywhere for weeks and weeks. There wasn't time for that. "But it would only take a few hours to get through them," I protested.

He took off his reading glasses and massaged the end of his nose. "It's the best I can do; sorry."

I stood up and gathered the files into a pile. I swept them into the briefcase. "Thanks anyway," I told him. "I think I ought to find somebody else, then."

"You're sure? It wouldn't necessarily be more than a couple of weeks. I just don't want to make any promises."

"No, it's okay," I told him. "It's not your fault; I'd be skeptical, too, if I were you. But I think I need to find somebody who hasn't already made up his mind."

"Look, I never said—"

"Don't worry about it," I told him, extending my hand. He took it gingerly; his clasp was warm.

"Okay," he said. "Good luck."

Back on the street, clutching my briefcase full of inscrutable information, I pondered my next move. Of course there were other people who could look over the material, but I had counted on David Sanchez. I wanted him to do it, not some kid just out of business school with suspenders and aspirations. I sighed and put the case in the backseat of the car. A Mercedes sports car with the license plate TIME4FUN had parked so close to me that I couldn't open the driver's side door without nicking its paint or, worse, setting off the car alarm. I imagined David Sanchez leaning out the window, annoyed.

I felt like crying, an overrated pastime that nonetheless has its satisfactions. Instead, I opened my purse, extracted a quarter from my wallet, and marched over to a phone booth I had seen just inside the building lobby.

"Sanchez Associates."

"Mr. Sanchez, please," I said in my best imitation of a Texas accent. I was hampered by a lifetime aversion to *Dallas* reruns. "Please hold for Mr. Perot."

This was not, apparently, so remarkable an event as to excite suspicion. "I'm putting your call through," the receptionist told me.

"Ross?" David Sanchez's warmth threatened to ooze all the way down the line into the lobby. He was going to be pissed when I undeceived him.

"Sorry," I said sincerely, "it's Caroline James."

The warmth turned to ice. "Is this some kind of a joke?"

"No, of course not. I couldn't think of any other way to get you to answer, because I knew you wouldn't pick up if I told you the truth."

His silence told me that he acknowledged the justice of this.

"Look, I said I was sorry. I'm desperate," I told him.

"What can I do for you?" he asked, after a minute.

"I have a proposition. Just give me two hours of your time, and I'll fix you dinner. I'll pick you up and bring you back. You can choose the menu. I'll pay for your time, too. You won't be out that much because even though you said you don't have time to eat, you know you have to. After that I promise I'll never bother you again."

I could almost hear him weighing the inconvenience against the certainty of getting rid of me once he did as I asked. "One hour," he said finally.

"An hour and a half."

"How good a cook are you?"

"Very," I told him.

"Okay, it's a deal. Do you have a car phone?"

"No," I said. I managed not to tell him that I thought they were pretentious, if not dangerous.

"Then I'll drive myself down." He paused. "I'm free on Tuesday."

"Great." I gave him the address and directions. "Do you really know Ross Perot?" I asked him curiously.

"Are you really a great cook?" he countered.

"See you Tuesday," I told him.

The back door was open, and I could hear Maria moving around in the kitchen. A tiny pile of entrails, the remains of something I would rather not have known about, rested tidily on the bricks. I was always amazed at the cat's ability to consume all of his victim except this apparently distasteful remnant. Melmoth usually wanted praise for his kills, so I obliged him, but I wished his self-esteem had not necessitated bringing them to our doorstep to dispatch. I went to get a spade to dig yet another hole in the flower beds. If there were a tribunal for feline serial killers in the afterlife, our backyard was damningly full of evidence.

Intimate contact with the flower beds, which I avoided as often as possible, forced me to confront the fact that the weeds had made a number of daring incursions since the last time Jason and Megan spent an afternoon "cleaning up." They were supposed to take care of the yard in exchange for the astronomical allowances they commanded, but all of our standards had declined since their father had left, though the allowances, of course, had not. I just didn't have the energy to nag them about it.

The yard wasn't exactly an eyesore, but it was a little shabby around the edges of the landscaping Master Plan. Spurge, the most tenacious of weeds, had extended green tentacles in an alarming number of directions, bent on conquest. I considered the prospect of marshaling my family for an assault on the overgrowth and immediately wondered if it was worth it to pay a gardener to come in and clean things up.

I briefly considered hiring Manuel, Maria's cousin, who had worked for the Hamptons, till I remembered that she said he had gone back to Mexico. Then I grabbed the spade, electrified, the guts quivering on the point over the hole I had made. I should have remembered Manuel earlier. What if he had seen or heard something before he left? Even if he had gone home before Eleanor died, he might be an "inside source" about goings and comings at the house, and he had been right under my nose all along. He did have the minor, annoying problem of not speaking English, so it would be too much to hope he had overheard anything of interest, however careless Eleanor might have been in her talk. Still, it might be worth getting in contact with him, if Maria could arrange it.

Maria was washing the crystal. I hadn't used any of the glasses in at least six months, so they were covered with the film that the combination of sea air and dust causes to coat things in coastal communities. It made me sad that they were dusty with disuse, and the useless cleaning ritual, repeated every few weeks, reminded me of polishing my mother's enormous silver spoon collection as a child. No one ever used those, either, but you weren't supposed to, so it was okay. The alternative to the futility of cleaning was letting them gather cobwebs untouched, like Miss Havisham's wedding feast, and that was infinitely worse. There were only so many symbols of ruined expectations I could handle.

Jesus, was I ever feeling sorry for myself. The mood came and went like fainting fits. I remembered the sense of purpose with which I had entered the kitchen and tried to recover it.

Maria smiled warmly at me when I went in. "How are you, Mrs. James? Jason said to remind you, you said he could go to Danny's to work on his movie, and Megan has football practice."

I smiled back. "Football?"

"I think so."

I thought. "Oh, soccer. That's *fútbol* in Spanish, isn't it?"

"*Sí.* I forgot."

"Well, girls play every sport these days, so football is probably next. Anyway, I wanted to ask you something. About Manuel."

The smile faded. She set the last glass down next to the sink very carefully and looked at me.

"I'd like to know where he is." I was about to say that I wanted to know how to get in contact with him, but to my surprise, she burst into tears.

"I'm sorry, Mrs. James," she said, hiccuping a little. "I swear he's gone back to Mexico now. I swear it."

"Why, what's the matter?" I asked her, confused. "Is something wrong with him?"

She ignored the question, wiping her eyes on her wrist. "It was only a couple of days. He didn't have no place else to go."

"Maria, I don't understand what you're talking about."

She stopped, wiping her eyes, and sniffled.

"About Manuel," she said patiently, as if I were slow-witted. "He only stay here two days, then he go. That's all, I swear."

"*Here*?"

"*Sí.* In the garage."

Much, as they say, was now made clear. "You mean it was *your cousin* who left the blanket and the food?"

It dawned on her that she had made an unnecessary confession. Her eyes widened. "You did not know?"

"I had no idea," I assured her. "Did he . . . did he break into the garage, too?" Obviously, if Manuel was the burglar, I was going to have to reevaluate my hypothesis.

Maria drew herself up with indignation. "Of course not. Manuel would never do such a thing. Besides, he go home long before." She looked at me suspiciously. "If you did not know it was Manuel in the garage, then why did you want to know where he is?" she demanded.

"Wait. First tell me why Manuel was sleeping out there, and why you didn't say anything about it if he needed a place to stay."

She stared mulishly at her feet.

"Maria?"

"He was scared, señora," she said at last. "He made me promise." She looked up. "He didn't steal nothing."

I remembered the orange and the corn chips. "Oh, Maria. I know that. That isn't it." I paused. "What was he afraid of?"

"Señora?"

"You said he was scared. What was he scared of?"

She averted her eyes. "I don't know," she mumbled. I didn't think she was telling me the truth.

"Did Mr. Hampton do something to him? Or Mrs. Hampton?"

She stepped backward, but the sink prevented her retreat. She shrugged. "She was dead."

I felt a surge of excitement, as if the word "clue" had suddenly descended from on high in neon letters, flashing and whistling. I tried to sound calm. "Please, Maria, won't you sit down for a minute and tell me about it?"

She looked trapped, the way Melmoth did when he saw the cat carrier that always meant a trip to the vet. "Okay," she said reluctantly. I felt like a bully.

"Coffee?" I offered, to show that my intentions were benign.

She shook her head. "No, thank you."

I faced her across the kitchen table. "Maria, please tell me the truth. This might be important. Did Manuel's leaving have anything to do with the death of Mrs. Hampton?"

She studied her fingers, with their bitten nails and swollen knuckles, as if they were the most important objects in the world. "*La Migra.*"

"Pardon me?" I asked her.

"*La Migra*, you know." She waved a hand in a wide circle. "Immigration. Manuel was"—she lowered her voice—"illegal."

"Is that what scared him?"

She looked at me assessingly. "I can't tell you that, Señora James."

"Maria, did Manuel do something wrong?"

"No!" She seemed outraged at the suggestion.

"Then if you tell me the truth, he won't get into any trouble. Does he know something about Mrs. Hampton's death?"

"You promise?"

"Yes, I promise."

She sighed and rested her elbows on the table. "Manuel . . . he see—saw—somebody," she said quietly.

"Saw somebody when? You mean when Mrs. Hampton died?"

She nodded.

"Who was it?" I hoped my voice wasn't trembling.

"A man. He did not know who. He was far away."

"Mr. Hampton?" I prompted.

"I don't know," she insisted. "Manuel did not see." She studied her wedding ring with little enthusiasm and sighed. "He came back. He went home and then he remember he left a—" Her eyes looked upward, searching for the word. She shrugged and gave up. "I don't know, some tool. He leave it outside, in the yard, and Mrs. Hampton get very mad if the gardeners leave tools out. So he came back." A natural storyteller once she got going, she paused for effect. "Then he saw this man, bending over the pool. He saw the señora's head, above the water. It was far away, but the light was on. The señora—she wasn't decent, Mrs. James. Sometimes she wear no clothes in front of Manuel. So he look away. He put away this—thing—and he went home. That is all."

"And then the next day they discovered she was dead?"

"Sí." She put her hands up to her face. "¡Ay, que miedo! Manuel did not want to talk to the police, so he came here. He want to stay with me, but I could not permit this, because of the children." She looked down. I wondered whether Manuel might have

been something more to her than—or other than—
her cousin. "I told him he was *estupido*, because if
she was murdered the police would think he did it.
He was very afraid. He want to go back to Mexico
right away, but he did not have money for the bus.
So I said he could stay here until I could give him
the money." Her eyes filled with tears again. "I'm
sorry, Señora James."

I touched her arm. "It's all right. I'm glad it was
Manuel, and not some homeless—well, I'm glad it
was Manuel. What happened next?"

"We wait for news. Manuel, he gets up in the
morning very early and takes a bus to the park."

"The park?"

"*Sí*. The big one in San Diego. Balboa. He meet
many people who speak Spanish there. Some of
them are living there, too, so some days he sleeps
in their camp with them." She shook her head
sternly. "That is not a good way to live, Mrs.
James."

I nodded agreement. "I know. Go on."

"After a day or two, it is obvious that the police
are not looking for Manuel. They say the señora's
death was an accident or—"

"Suicide?" I suggested.

She crossed herself hastily. "Yes. So I tell Manuel
it is safe to look for another job, but he say—said—
no." Her eyes grew big. "He say that if he is the
only person who knows about this man, this visitor,
it is dangerous to have this knowledge, no matter
what the police say. So I gave him the money and
he went home."

"Where is he now?" I asked her.

"I don't know," she said firmly.

"Maria, I have to get in touch with him. I have
to know more about this man he saw."

Her eyes widened. "No, señora! You promised."

"I promised nothing would happen to him. I meant it. But you must see that if he knows something important about what may turn out to be a murder, it is his duty to come forward."

She shrugged. "The police are not interested, señora. Did not your friend tell you so?"

"Well, yes, but they didn't know about Manuel."

"And if they did, how can you promise that they will not accuse him? The very best thing that could happen would be that they would bring him back here, question him, and send him back to Mexico again. The worst, well . . . why should Manuel go through all that?"

"Well, couldn't he at least talk to me?"

She shook her head. "Impossible."

"Maria," I began.

"Impossible," she insisted. "I do not know where he is."

"I thought you said he went home to your village in Mexico."

"That is so," she agreed, "but by now he has left again."

I sighed. "Where has he gone?"

She spread her hands wide. "Texas, maybe. Or New York. Chicago. He might have gone to Los Angeles. I do not know. He will contact me when he is ready."

Whether she was telling me the truth or not, I had to acknowledge defeat, at least temporarily. I wouldn't get any more out of her, at least about Manuel. "Okay," I conceded. "But when you do hear from him, would you at least consider asking him if I could ask him some questions about what he saw?"

She got up, the victor in this skirmish. "Sí,

señora," she said with a little smile. "I will *ask* him."

"Thank you," I said, forced to be content with what was probably an empty promise. I got up, too. She started to carry the crystal out to the dining room, but I stopped her. "Maria? Just one more thing."

She turned, the tray of glasses in her hand.

"Did Manuel happen to see what this man was wearing?"

She thought, then nodded briefly. "*Un traje*," she said firmly.

"Pardon me?"

She paused again. "A suit, Señora James," she said at last. "The man was wearing a suit."

14

ON SUNDAY I took Jason, Megan, and Danny to a Chargers game on Steve's turn at the firm's newly acquired season tickets. He was extremely unhappy that a last-minute "legal emergency" over the weekend prevented him from using them, but as he had already promised to take the kids, he couldn't get away with giving the tickets to one of his tennis buddies or a valuable client. It made him particularly mad that I remained oblivious to the game's finer points, despite his efforts, in better days, to educate me. Hence my unworthiness to benefit from his largesse.

There were many unelectrifying stretches for the untutored, and after a while I stopped paying attention and started worrying about what I was going to serve David Sanchez for dinner. It was easy to decide what not to fix—anything that might cause heart attacks or gas, which left out an entire repertoire of enticing edibles from Brie to black beans. It was far harder to pick something, despite the 151 (I counted them once, during a particularly dull phone conversation) cookbooks residing imposingly on the built-in shelves in the family room.

I sat with my yellow pad, poring over menus.

You have to take this food business fairly seriously, although not as seriously as you did in the eighties. The most stressful organization of that decade had to be the "food group," where several couples got together and prepared dishes each designed to outdo all the others in terms of rarity and difficulty of preparation. The more exotic the ingredients, the better; roasted woodcock heads were a stretch but not an impossibility. Food groups kept a lot of peripheral agents in business for a long time: charming little produce stores that sold edible flowers and blue-corn tortillas, butcher shops/restaurants/mail-order outfits that would send Maine lobsters, Virginia hams, Texas pecans, or Long Island ducklings winging around the country in time for Saturday night dinner.

Once, in the grip of a particularly virulent bout of Food Group Mania, I went into a veterinarian's office on the main street of town and begged them to let me cut down two leaves from the giant banana plant outside in the parking lot. The receptionist nervously nodded assent. I figured it was a strange request, but I didn't see why she was so jumpy until I looked down and realized I was clutching my paring knife. I looked for a place to put it, but I couldn't find one. "Sorry," I told her apologetically.

I wanted to tell her that it wasn't my fault, that I had ordered the banana leaves from Jonathan's across the street, who got them from the produce market in L.A., who got them from the Philippines or someplace like that, and somewhere along the line the order got lost. Still, she didn't look like a Foodie, although you couldn't always go by appearances, but I thought that trying to explain why

I was in desperate need of a couple of banana leaves might make me look even weirder, and possibly dangerous.

In case you're wondering, what I wanted them for was *cochinita pibil*, a pork loin marinated in citrus juices and achiote and cooked for a very long time in a slow oven. You can wrap it in something else, but in the Yucatan they do it in banana leaves. If I do say so myself, it was delicious.

Still, you'd want to be careful about fixing something like that for someone who was virtually a stranger. Excessively elaborate food is like overdressing; you look like you're trying too hard. There was danger in "diner food," too—meatloaf and mashed potatoes and all the things your mother fixed at least once a week and you hoped you'd never have to eat again after you grew up. That was the problem; you didn't want to seem like somebody's mother (or wife). Besides, how many people have a really good recipe for meatloaf?

After weighing all these factors, I decided that ossobuco, and maybe some pasta beforehand, was trying just hard enough. You're supposed to serve the veal shanks with risotto, but that requires all this fetishistic ladling of broth onto the rice, and at least half the time it turns out gummy. Besides, without the risotto you can do most of it in advance, so you don't have to be bumbling around in the kitchen in front of your guests. A salad and some kind of fruit ice for dessert (no cholesterol) would be plenty to complement the meal.

The Chargers won, and Jason elbowed me in time to watch the winning touchdown. We celebrated with hot dogs and potato chips.

*   *   *

On Monday I packed up all the relevant documents to launch my legal separation and dropped them off at Rachel Fenton's office. She promised to have the papers to sign in a couple of days, as soon as I gave her the go-ahead to let Steve know what was going on. I didn't much want to think about it, so I immersed myself in preparations for a guest of Important Stature—dusting the tops of the cabinets, scrubbing all the toilet bowls and showers, hiding my well-worn copy of *Scruples* in the back of the bookshelf. I have never actually known anyone who inspected the tops of other people's cabinetry or the interior of their plumbing fixtures, although I myself often scrutinized their libraries. On the other hand, you never could tell. If David Sanchez was a zealot on the subject of cleanliness and high-minded thinking, no doubt he would be impressed by my thoroughness.

Or maybe not. I have always wished I were one of those hostesses born with the gift of casualness, the sort of person who throws a newspaper over the grease spots in the carpet and happily invites guests in for a month. I didn't ask myself why it was so important to impress David Sanchez, period, with as much effort as you might put into a visit from, say, the Queen, and more than you'd exert for Prince Charles.

Consumed by these labors, I almost let the machine pick up the phone when it rang, but it was the middle of the day, and it might have been the school calling.

"It's me," Steve said curtly. "Can I see you this afternoon?"

He did not sound as if he had a passionate reconciliation on the chaise longue in mind. "I'm busy," I told him.

"Is someone there?"

"No," I admitted reluctantly.

"I'll be there in half an hour," he said and hung up.

In the almost-two decades we'd been married, Steve had been really angry at me a number of times and vice versa. We'd yelled at each other, slammed doors, and once, on the road to Whitney Portal in Northern California, I had punched his arm really hard with my fist. He had responded by elbowing me in the stomach, knocking the wind out of me. When I recovered my breath, we'd both been appalled at this physical brawling, and it had never happened again. Still, there had been some life to the relationship, some flame that could flicker into hot anger.

Over the years, even before things got bad between us, I sometimes imagined myself at his funeral, trying to think of how it would feel. Now, instead of the man, it was the relationship that was dead. The spark was out, and there was a glacier in its place.

"Come in," I told Steve as he pushed past me into the living room. He looked tired and strained, and the skin around his mouth was taut and white.

"The kids?" he inquired brusquely, jerking his head in the direction of the upstairs.

I still understood his marital shorthand. I shook my head and pointed to my watch. "Of course not. They're still in school."

He looked confused, as if it had been ten years since he'd had to consider such a thing. "Oh, right. They okay?"

"They're fine. Jason's getting an A in history, and Megan's reading *Daddy-Long-Legs*."

Despite his apparent determination to get right

down to his agenda, he couldn't help asking "What's that?"

I shrugged. "A classic. What did you want to see me about?"

He settled himself into the cushions of the couch, crossing one leg over his knee so that I caught the shine of his gleaming Church's loafer. His hands were clenched. "I think you know, Caroline."

I imagined there was a laundry list, but I wasn't going to help him. "Why, how could I?" I asked innocently.

His look was hard, unblinking, and ungenerous. "Look," he said with exaggerated patience, "what you do with your personal life is no longer any of my business. I would have thought—well, never mind."

"You're right," I told him. "It's not."

He looked momentarily taken aback. "What?"

"My personal life," I said helpfully. "It's not any of your business."

"Fine, have it your way," he said angrily. "If you don't have any more sense than to get involved with one of my *partners*, for God's sake—"

"I am not involved with one of your partners," I said in a calm voice that I knew would irritate him more than an angry rebuttal.

He stared at me while a number of more grown-up variations of "Oh, yeah?" apparently crossed his mind. "That's not what I heard," he said at last.

I shrugged. "It's true, but I don't really care whether you believe me or not." I shifted position and tucked my feet up under me on the couch, leaving a moat between us. "Come on, Steve, you didn't take time off from work to come over here in the middle of the day and ask me about having drinks with Jeff Grayson. What's going on?"

"Drinks?" He was still unwilling to let it go.

I said nothing.

"All right, Caroline," he said, marshaling his forces for a frontal attack, "then suppose you tell me what the fuck is going on between you and Barclay Hampton."

"My, you do give me a lot of credit," I said lightly. "Do you think I'm chasing all the male lawyers in the firm?"

I thought for a moment I had gone too far. His hands clenched into white-knuckled fists. He looked at them for a moment and then spread his fingers wide. "Cut the shit, Caroline. I want to know why you've been asking Tricia a lot of questions about Barclay's state of mind since Eleanor's death, and what he was doing on the day before they found her body. You scared the poor girl to death."

"I didn't think she was quite such a delicate flower as all that," I said snidely but with some qualms.

"You're lucky Barclay didn't come here himself. He's *beside* himself, Caroline. He thinks you're implying that he had something to do with Eleanor's death. I told him he had to be mistaken, that I'd talk to you about it."

"All right, you've talked to me about it."

"And?"

"And nothing. What do you want me to say? I did *not* imply to Tricia Hampton that I thought Barclay had killed Eleanor. I merely made what I thought was a solicitous inquiry into his state of mind, since his own wife professes to be worried about him. I wonder why. Barclay is acting a little paranoid, don't you think? Do you suppose he has a guilty conscience about something?"

Steve ignored the question. "I certainly hope you

didn't. There are libel and slander laws for things like that."

"Okay, Counselor, you've done your job. You can rest assured that I know better than to throw accusations around without proof." I decided to hit him a hard ball. "By the way, did you ever find that file you wanted?"

"What file?" he asked before he thought.

"The one you tore up my office looking for." I watched his expression. "You didn't by chance extend your search to the garage in my absence, did you?"

He blinked. "I don't know what the hell you're talking about."

I couldn't tell if he was lying or not.

His eyes narrowed. If I could read him, he could read me as well. "Caroline, what the fuck are you up to?"

"Relax. I'm just doing a little investigating, that's all. It's no big deal."

"Investigating what?"

I effected an approximation of a Gallic shrug, as if the matter were a minor distraction from a life full of electrifying adventures. "Eleanor's life, I suppose. What she was thinking. Why she died."

"Have you lost your fucking mind?" he shouted. Melmoth darted out from underneath one of the chairs and streaked for the kitchen.

"You scared the cat," I told him.

"Fuck the cat," he said, but he lowered his voice. "You know why she died, Caroline; she killed herself. What are you trying to prove?"

I said nothing, not only because I didn't want to tip my hand completely but because it was complicated to explain.

"I asked you this once before, and this time I

want an answer. Why are you so interested in Eleanor Hampton?"

"I'm not sure I can tell you the answer to that," I said truthfully. "Maybe it's because I feel sorry for her, maybe it's something more. She sent me a lot of papers, and I just got interested, that's all."

"Those goddamn papers again. What was in them?"

"Nothing much. As a matter of fact, I've destroyed them," I lied. "But it started me thinking."

"It's fucking sick, that's what it is. If you want to feel sorry about something, why don't you take on Bosnia or Somalia as a project? Or why don't you get a goddamn job? Do something useful."

"Let me ask you something, Steve: If everybody at the firm is convinced Eleanor killed herself, why are they so threatened by questions about it? What if she had a little help in getting to the other side? Wouldn't you want to know the truth, even if it wasn't very pleasant?"

Steve's expression changed from anger to one of horror or perhaps fear. He leaned over the gap between us and took my wrist between his thumb and forefinger. "I don't care what mad things Eleanor Hampton might have said or written," he said in a deliberate voice. *"It is not in your best interest to pursue this."*

"Are you threatening me?"

He sat back. "Don't be melodramatic. Of course not. But speculation and innuendo could hurt the firm, and if the firm is hurt, it will ultimately come out of your settlement."

"And the truth can go hang?"

"I'm talking about conjecture, not evidence. There's something else, too. Whatever happens between us, I still have feelings for you. I'd hate to see you turn into an object of scorn and disgust among the people at the firm—our friends, Caroline—the way Eleanor did. And if you attempt to carry on some kind of personal vendetta or a one-woman crusade, that's exactly what will happen."

"And it wouldn't be much of a help to your career, either."

He fetched up one of his "I'm being as patient as I can but don't push me" sighs. "Whatever you say, Caroline; I'm tired of arguing. If you don't want to believe I have your best interests at heart, then don't; I don't care. But if you would stop short of embarrassing me, yourself, and the children, I'd really appreciate it. Also," he said, clearing his throat, "if you persist in this, I really believe the children would be better off with me. At least until you come to your senses."

I was furious that he would drag Jason and Megan into it. He knew my weakness. I certainly didn't want him to see that he had scored. "Bullshit," I told him.

"Wh-what?" He seemed taken aback.

"That's crap, Steve. You're just trying to bully me into agreeing to whatever you say."

"Well, I guess we'll just have to see about that," he replied, so confidently that my heart began to beat in alarm again.

"Have you said what you came to say?" I asked coldly, to mask the fear.

"Not quite." He coughed and looked at me. "I wanted to tell you something else, too. I'm glad the kids are out of the house." He hesitated. "I hope you won't be too upset."

"What is it?" I prompted.

He looked away. "I've instructed my attorney to file for divorce," he said to the vase in the corner.

He produced a card from his inside coat pocket. "His name is Jay Thompson. Here's his card." He handed it to me, still without looking at me directly. I was glad that Mr. Don't-negotiate-till-you're-sitting-on-their-chest James, Esquire, had enough conscience left to find it difficult to face me. "When you get an attorney, have him contact Jay. You should do it as soon as possible," he added.

I got up without speaking and went into the family room. I'm sure he thought I was struggling for composure, going in search of a tissue. I silently blessed Susan for her advance information, which had given me time to prepare. Did he really think it would come as a complete surprise?

I walked back into the room and handed him Rachel Fenton's card. "This is *my* attorney," I told him. "Why don't you ask Jay Thompson to contact *her*? She's working on the separation agreement now."

I confess that, painful though the moment was, I enjoyed his stupefied reaction. "You already saw an attorney?" he asked me.

"Of course," I said. "Isn't that what you wanted?"

He blinked. "Yes, that's what I wanted." He stood and looked down at me. "There'll be a lot to work out. The house, the kids . . ." I hoped I was imagining the slightly menacing tone.

"Yes, but not today," I said, determined to stay in control of the interview. "We've already been through too much, and it's better if we don't do this when we're angry."

He hesitated, then nodded. "Soon, then?"

"Yes," I told him. "Soon."

15

ON TUESDAY MORNING, armed
with an ecologically correct reusable shopping bag,
I set out to find a bottle of wine to go with the ossobuco. If you know what you're doing, you can buy
at a discount house, but if you don't, the alternative
is one of the wooden-floored specialty stores that
look as if the casks are aging in the very next room.
I confess to a certain fondness for those places, despite the many tedious hours I had spent listening
to Steve and some clerk hyperventilate about the
merits of the latest botrytisized Johannesberg Ries-
ling or whether the Pinot Noir grape could ever
really be made into a great California wine. I heard
perfectly normal-looking people say that a wine
was mean, pinched, and watery, and that was just
the smell. I found it impossible to enter into a conversation in which a liquid was described as
"fleshy."

Still, if you can get past all that, a wine shop (with
or without the final "pe") is undeniably attractive.
The fact that, historically at least, the contents of all
those beautiful bottles are occasionally and notoriously unreliable (the Austrians added antifreeze to

boost the alcohol content, the French packaged *vin ordinaire* as a *cru* considerably more grand than it was, and the Italians . . .) does not detract from the comfortable, cozy atmosphere, something like a good bookstore. Besides, a lot of work went into the designer labels, so if nothing else you could always admire those.

The clerk, a youngish sort with the serious mien of a novice monk, suggested an Italian red—a Barolo or a Chianti classico.

I shook my head. "Too heavy," I said. Steve would have debated the reliability of Italian wines, but I just wanted to make sure my guest had his mental faculties unimpaired when it came time to consider my documents. I was only going to get one shot at it.

The clerk frowned in concentration. "The dish, I believe, requires a strong wine to accompany it," he said with the patient air of one used to dealing with novices and Philistines. "If you want to go with something white, I might suggest one of the big California Chardonnays. Or perhaps a French wine, such as a white Burgundy. . . ."

All those years of being an unwilling eavesdropper on oenophilic bibulo-babble suddenly paid off. "White Burgundy?" I asked him. "Like Le Montrachet?"

He was far too classy for such a vulgar reaction as salivating, but let us say that the prospect of selling a two-hundred-dollar bottle of wine acted as a significant tonic upon his enthusiasm. I, of course, had just discovered another agenda.

"Our Montrachets are over here," he said, not quite tripping over his feet in an effort to reach the locked cabinet in which these treasures reposed. "We have 1990, which was a very good year, along with '88 and '89. The '86 is considered the best of the last decade, but some people are afraid it's too old," he said regretfully.

"Aren't there other kinds of Montrachet?" I asked uncertainly.

He looked a bit crestfallen but recovered quickly. "There is only one Le Montrachet. It is the top, the crème de la crème. But there are other vineyards nearby with hyphenated names like Puligny-Montrachet, Chassagne-Montrachet, Bâtard-Montrachet. . . ."

"Bâtard-Montrachet!" I exclaimed as if I had just remembered it. "I had a friend who recommended that very highly. What's the difference between that and Le Montrachet?"

He smiled. "About a hundred dollars and a few steps—literally—across the road. There is, of course, a difference in taste, but the Bâtard is also a very good wine."

I smiled back. We were almost there. "My friend particularly enjoyed it, I remember. I'm fairly sure she bought it here. Perhaps you know her. Eleanor Hampton?" It seemed worth a try. Most of La Jolla used the store at least occasionally.

The smile slipped a little. "Why, yes. The Hamptons were very good customers. But surely she— Mrs. Hampton—didn't I hear that she passed away recently?"

I wondered why so many people felt the need to avoid saying "died." "Passed away" seemed so wispy and unsubstantial for the ultimate certainty of death. "Yes, she did," I told him gravely, in keeping with the mood. "As a matter of fact, I believe she had been drinking a bottle of Bâtard-Montrachet when she d—passed away."

He blanched. "I'm sure there was no connection . . ."

"Oh, no, of course not. She seems to have been
quite happy with her selection. Just an accident,
that's all."

He looked relieved. "Good. I mean, she did seem
happy. At least I think so. She seemed to be antic-
ipating some sort of celebration."

"You waited on her?" My voice sounded
squeaky. I couldn't believe my luck.

"Well, I think so, yes. She often ordered by
phone, and she came in now and then to pick up
just a bottle or two. I remember that she bought a
bottle of the Bâtard-Montrachet a number of weeks
ago because she made so many jokes about 'Bâtard'
meaning bastard," he said a little apologetically.
"People do often mention it, but she was more than
usually interested in the name. In fact, I had the
feeling that was the main reason she chose it, although of course it would have been a wonderful
bottle of wine."

"Did she say why 'bastard' was appropriate? I
mean for right then?"

He shook his head. "I gather she was divorced,
wasn't she? She seemed very angry." He sighed. I
supposed Eleanor Hampton was not the only angry
or lonely divorcée he had dealt with. La Jolla was
full of them.

"But you said she mentioned a celebration?" I
prompted him.

"She didn't *say* anything," he said thoughtfully.
"It was just a feeling I got. She came in asking for
a good bottle of wine—like you," he added, showing high-maintenance teeth, "and when she saw the
Bâtard—well, as I mentioned, she wouldn't hear of
anything else."

I would have liked to reward him for his help by buying a Bâtard myself, although I didn't much like the parallel it implied, but my budget wouldn't stretch to accommodate such a noble gesture. Instead I descended many rungs on the price scale and bought an Aligoté, a perfectly decent white Burgundy I had always liked. The clerk took it in good part. Having shared an Eleanor story made us temporary confrères.

"Was the Bâtard really her last bottle of wine?" he asked curiously as he wrapped my purchase.

"The police found the bottle beside her body," I assured him.

He permitted himself a small smile. "Empty, I hope."

I smiled back. "I assume so." I looked around the vast assortment of wine varieties in the store. It was hard to imagine all of it coming from something so unadorned as a grape. "What would *you* choose, if you knew it was your last bottle?" I asked him, out of curiosity.

He looked up quickly, reddening a little. "Well . . ."

"Really, I'd like to know."

"Okay," he said sheepishly. "I guess I'd probably choose a white zinfandel. You're not supposed to, but I really like them." He handed me the bottle, wrapped in paper inside a plastic sack. I put the whole package into my reusable shopping bag.

"Don't tell anyone," he implored, as if he'd confessed to a preference for pedophilia instead of just an ordinary blush wine.

His secret was safe with me. "They can tear out my fingernails," I assured him.

He smiled feebly.

*　　*　　*

On Tuesday evening, early, I gave Megan and Jason a pizza and an entreaty to spend the evening upstairs unless a life-threatening misadventure required their descent.

"Now hear this," I reiterated. *"This is not a date."*

"Oh, Mom," said Jason, rolling his eyes.

"I am not kidding. This is a business dinner. Important financial business. I am paying for this man's time, so please don't get any ideas. This is like having someone over to help with your homework. This is like studying for a test. This is like—"

"We get the picture, Mom," Jason interrupted. "We'll stay out of the way, won't we, Megan?"

My daughter, who realized why I was making such a fuss about the issue, looked embarrassed but nodded her assent. "Sure. It's fine, really."

"Well, you don't have to *hide*. You can introduce yourselves if you want to. It's not like I'm ashamed of you."

They exchanged looks. "Relax, Mom," Jason said, patting me on the shoulder.

But I couldn't. I was so keyed up by the discovery that Eleanor's mood on the day of her death was far from suicidal—almost exultant, in fact—and by what I had learned from Maria, that I could scarcely wait to see what evidence the box would turn up. I just *knew* it had to be in there somewhere.

First, however, I had to get through dinner, and I was more than a little tense about that, too.

David Sanchez was attired perfectly in a blue pullover sweater—a little too formal for fried chicken and coleslaw, and less than what was required for, say, coubiliac of salmon or caviar mousse. He had apparently judged the occasion and the menu correctly. He was brisk and businesslike. I was relieved.

"Would you like to eat first or start work first?" I asked him, to make sure he knew I remembered the purpose of his visit and hadn't lured him there to reenact the food scene from *Tom Jones.*

"If it's not too much trouble, I'd like to eat first," he said, following me into the kitchen. "It's been a long day, and I don't think well on an empty stomach."

Jason and Megan stood in the doorway like the chorus in the middle of some particularly bloody Greek tragedy, hands at their sides, vigilant against hubris. "These are my children," I told him, no doubt unnecessarily. "My daughter, Megan, and my son, Jason. This is Mr. Sanchez."

He smiled and extended a hand to each in turn. Megan looked shy. Jason looked grave.

"I've cleaned up all our dishes," Jason informed us. "I think I'm going to go upstairs now. I have a lot of homework." He looked at Megan.

"Oh, right," she said. "Me, too. We know you have business to talk over."

"Fine," I told her. "Come down if you want anything. We won't be too late."

Jason had clearly decided to exert himself to make a good impression. He extended his hand again. "Nice to meet you, sir," he told David.

I hid a smile. We'd done our best to teach him good manners, but I hadn't heard a "sir" out of him since he'd hit adolescence some years before. In fairness, I probably had his coach to thank for his knowing how to use it now.

"Nice kids," David said, when they had gone upstairs.

"Thanks," I told him. "They are, actually, even if

they're showing off for company. At least I'm relieved that they know how."

He laughed. "You mean you don't have to pay them? Everything I read in the paper suggests that kids are a lot more assertive these days."

I shook my head. "You have to pay for it, but not with money," I told him. "Sooner or later they'll call in the chits. You don't have any children, then?"

He hesitated just a split second too long for comfort. "No." His eyes shifted around and then looked right at me. "My wife died."

"Oh. I'm so sorry."

"It's okay. It was a long time ago. Eight years."

Cancer, I thought, or an accident. "Drink?" I asked him uncertainly.

"Not if we're working tonight. Some water would be nice."

I crossed to the refrigerator to get out the San Pellegrino.

"Just tap water would be fine," he told me. "With some ice, please."

"It's terrible here. It tastes the way that stuff they put on athlete's foot smells."

He laughed. "Okay," he agreed. "Can I help?"

I wasn't sure about the ethics of this, but it was nice to have a man around the kitchen again, so I let him cut up the things for the salad. I liked the way he did it, without fuss and without expecting to be praised at the snip of every carrot.

Over the pasta with roasted eggplant and peppers (I had a porcini mushroom sauce to die for, but it used heavy whipping cream and I didn't want his arteries to stiffen till I was through with him), we made breezy, desultory conversation about La Jolla, the food, the public schools, anything at hand. I was trying very hard to be politely impersonal. I didn't make any jokes. I wasn't snide. I didn't mention Eleanor Hampton. I behaved beautifully.

"You were right," he told me.

"About what?"

He smiled. "You are a great cook."

I smiled back. "Thanks," I told him. "And do you really know Ross Perot?"

He shrugged. "We've met." He smiled again. "But we haven't shared ribs in the Board Room."

Over the veal, he mentioned that he had recently come back from visiting his parents.

"Where do they live?" I asked him.

He expertly extracted a bit of marrow from the bone. "San Miguel de Allende. That's in Mexico."

"I know where it is," I said. "I've been there. It's nice." It was, too, although there might be a few too many colorful characters and artsy Americans for strict authenticity. Still, that hadn't stopped me from writing a travel article about how quaint and picturesque it was.

"Are they retired?"

"For the most part. Basically they just went home."

"Home to San Miguel?"

"Home to Mexico."

"Didn't you grow up here?" I asked him, surprised. Everything about him was ostentatiously north of the border.

"Sure," he said. "But my father's . . . um . . . work meant we had to move around a lot. You understand. So my parents never really had a home of their own to go back to."

I thought he was deliberately making it sound as if his father had followed the crops and he had grown up in migrant-labor camps. I also had the feeling it was very probably untrue, that this was some kind of test. If I believed his father had been a *bracero*, I would never in a million years ask what he had done for a living.

"What did your father do?" I asked him.

He grinned. "Actually, most recently he's been a consultant for the World Bank."

I knew it had been a trap. I wouldn't give him the satisfaction of reacting. "And don't he and your mother find San Miguel a little quiet?" I asked him. "As I recall, there isn't much to do there except shop."

"Well, my mother's an artist. But really, I think they moved there because my grandparents came from Dolores. That's nearby."

"Your grandparents are still alive?"

He shook his head. "Oh, no. It's hard to explain why they would go back. I think they were afraid of losing Mexican values."

I saw that he was serious. "What are those?" I asked him.

"Family, land, the village—it's better defined by what it isn't. Mexico is afraid of becoming too modern, too American. There is too much freedom here. Like the Garden of Eden, after the fall." He looked up. "Sorry. I don't know why I'm talking like this."

"Please, go on. I'm interested."

He spread his hands wide. His fingers were long and slender. "The other thing is that America is too Protestant."

I thought of the huge Latin population of Southern California, the missions, and all the Catholic churches. "Even here?" I asked incredulously.

"Sure. In Mexico you're Catholic just by inhaling. Here, well, the ethic is all different. You are what you do. Work is what's valued, achievement is what lifts you out of what you are and makes you rise above your father. A Mexican doesn't necessarily want to rise above his father. Work is a curse. He works very hard, but he isn't defined by it. His family, his friends, his leisure—those are the things that make him what he is."

I wondered what it was like for him, growing up with a foot in two camps. "Is it really so different?" I asked him. "It sounds as if you've given it a lot of thought."

He laughed. "I just read Richard Rodriguez, like everybody else. But I think he's right."

"What about you?" I couldn't help asking.

"I got the worst of both worlds. I don't do anything but work, but I don't necessarily enjoy it." I couldn't tell if he was joking or not.

Over coffee and sorbet, he told me a little bit about his marriage. He and his wife had been introduced by their families, "the old-fashioned way," he said, but there was nothing forced, only the suggestion that they might be very well matched.

"We were, too," he said with a distant smile. "We liked the same movies, the same books, the same—" He stopped and shrugged. "Well, we were pretty young, and it's much easier to mold yourself then. We were happy for a long time."

"What happened?" I asked him gently.

He sat up straighter on the couch. "We didn't have children. Elena took it very hard. There were endless tests." He spoke quickly, as if speeding through the topic would render it painless. "She was coming back from the doctor's office when she—she was in an accident. The car was totally

demolished. She never woke up." His face was
drawn, his eyes filled.

"God, how terrible. I'm sorry."

"Thank you. I used to wonder if things would
have changed between us, if she'd lived." He
looked at me. "You understand."

I certainly did. I nodded.

"I should just be grateful for what we had. But
when a relationship ends like that—when someone
dies—there's so much unfinished business. It took
me a long time to get over it."

I wanted to know whether the unfinished business had been strong enough to keep him from getting involved with anyone else. Eight years is a long
time, and he was an undeniably attractive man. But
the conversation had already gotten far more personal than he might feel comfortable with. David
Sanchez had said more about his feelings in one
evening than Steve had confessed in a year and a
half. Steve had tried introspection once, and he
didn't like it.

David seemed to come to a somewhat similar
conclusion. There was a lull, like one of those dramatic pauses in a Chekhov play where the characters mentally take stock and then go off in an
entirely different direction. He looked at his watch.
"I seem to be talking too much, and we have your
papers to get through. Did you want to work here?"

"I've set things up for you in my office," I told
him. "There's better light, and you can close the
door. I'll leave you the coffee pot."

He grinned. "No distractions."

"Right." I thought of the files I had left for him
on the desk. Suddenly the thought of exposing
someone who cherished loving memories of his
dead young wife to the Hamptons' marital poison

filled me with qualms. Worse, I didn't want him to
think I was interested in it because my relationship
to Steve had been anything like Eleanor's to Barclay.

"Look," I told him as I gathered up the cups,
"I've put the legal and financial documents on top,
but some of the other things in the file are
pretty . . ."

He raised an eyebrow inquiringly.

"Pretty ugly," I finished, after due consideration.
"And personal. I left them for you because I didn't
know what might be important. That's the only reason all that stuff is in there."

He nodded. "I know. I saw a sample when you
brought the files to the office, remember?" He
shrugged. "It makes me glad I didn't go to law
school and become a divorce attorney. Dealing with
Wall Street sleazeballs looks a lot easier."

"Okay. I just wanted to warn you."

"Relax," he said shrewdly. "I won't hold it
against you; I promise."

I led him into the office, showed him where the
bathroom was, and then I closed the door and left
him alone on the theory that hovering would not
be productive of insights. I took down an old copy
of *Pride and Prejudice*, which had never, in the eight
or so times I had read it, failed to engross me no
matter how turbulent my state of mind.

A pleasant hour later I looked up from the party
at which Elizabeth exchanged confidences with Mr.
Wickham regarding Mr. Darcy to find David Sanchez watching me from the hall, a dazed and inscrutable expression on his face. He looked as if his
reading had been considerably less enjoyable than
Jane Austen.

"How's it going?" I asked, trying to keep it light,
although in reality I was somewhat panicked be-

cause there was only half an hour left on the meter.

"I'm just taking a break," he said. He rubbed his eyes. "Jesus, the poor woman," he said, shaking his head. "She was certainly determined, wasn't she?"

I nodded. I wasn't sure what to say. I still didn't know if she was determined and right or determined and wrong, and time was running out.

He went back into the office and I tried to go back to Jane Austen, but this time I couldn't concentrate. I kept looking at my watch, wondering how he was spending the last few minutes he had promised. Finally I got up and began clearing the table. If all else fails, you can always take refuge in domesticity. The half hour passed. Then another fifteen minutes. He was on overtime. I was on the last piece of silver, putting it into the drawer, when he came into the kitchen, carrying his empty cup and the carafe of coffee. We looked at each other.

"Ummm . . ." he began.

My heart sank. "It's okay," I said quickly, to mask my disappointment. "You gave it your best shot. I can't ask any more than that."

He took off his reading glasses, folded them, and put them away in his pocket. Then he crossed his arms and looked at me. "You really are a pessimist, aren't you?"

"If you expect the worst, you won't be disappointed."

"You should be in my business," he said with a smile. "Look, it's late, and I should be getting home. But if it's all right with you I'd like to take these with me and finish them up in my office. I need to check on a couple of things. I promise I'll Fed-Ex them to you tomorrow or the next day. Unless you have a fax machine?"

"Certainly not." I hesitated. "Are you just being

noble because of the ossobuco, or did you really find something?"

He laughed. "Actually, it was the blackberry sorbet. I'm not promising anything, but there are some papers I'd like to take a closer look at. I don't want to say any more than that until I've thought about it. Look, I know you don't want to let these things out of your sight, but I can't really do them justice here. If you could trust me with them for just a day or two, I could be much more thorough about investigating them."

I wondered if he thought I'd forgotten that only a few days before, I'd had to wheedle and bribe him to take a look at the papers at all. I knew something had to be up. "I guess that would be okay," I told him, "if you'll promise me something first."

He looked amused. "What's that?"

"That you won't use anything you find in those files without getting permission from me first."

He seemed taken aback, and then he laughed. "Jesus, you're a tough one," he said.

"Yes, I am."

"Okay," he sighed. "It's a deal." He extended his hand.

I took it. "Great," I told him. "I'll help you collect them."

He stopped me. "Caroline?"

"Yes?"

"Whatever else turns up, thank you for the dinner. I really did enjoy it."

I helped him put the files into his briefcase. He turned and strode to the door. "Bye," he said. "I'll be in touch." He turned back. "Say good night to Jason and Megan, please. I enjoyed meeting them."

"I will," I said. "Good night."

* * *

When the door had closed I went to the window and stood behind the curtain, holding it back with my hand and looking out onto the street, like a character out of *Rear Window*. He was sitting behind the wheel of his car, looking at papers, with the interior light on. The car was something sleek and comfortable-looking, but I couldn't tell what it was in the dark. I could ask Jason in the morning. He always noticed people's cars.

David seemed to stare into space for a few minutes, as if he were thinking. Or maybe he was just tired.

After a while, as I was about to let the curtain fall from my hand, he switched off the light and drove away.

16

THE DOORBELL RANG with the persistence of missionaries or Greenpeace. It was eleven o'clock, and I was up to my elbows in laundry. My arms were extended as wide as possible as I tried to subdue the disorder of some clean sheets. My mother could fold them effortlessly into precise rectangles, but I had never, even after so long, gotten the hang of it. The fitted ones were worst of all.

"Coming," I called as the doorbell sounded again.

I looked out the peephole into another eye, large and malevolent, peering in. I drew back.

"It's me," said a muffled voice.

I figured a homicidal maniac wouldn't announce himself with "It's me," so I opened the door. Still, if you think about it, it might have been a clever ruse.

"You certainly took your time about getting to the door," Rob said, striding past me into the living room. "I've got an appointment in half an hour, so I don't have long."

Rob's entrances were rarely self-explanatory, though he usually acted as if they must be. I waited.

"Well?" he demanded.

"Well, what, Rob?"

"Well, how was your date? Your evening. Whatever. Don't try to be coy. I saw David Sanchez's delectable ass moving up your walkway last night. How was it?"

"How was it?"

"Jesus, Caroline. Don't make me beg. I'm practically salivating, and you're playing dumb."

"What do you do, Rob, watch the neighborhood with binoculars? Get a life."

"Cute. You've made your pro forma protest in the name of good taste. Now are you going to tell me or not?"

I plopped down on the couch. "There's nothing to tell. It wasn't a date." I saw his expression. "Really, it wasn't. He's looking over those papers of Eleanor Hampton's. You remember."

"Honest to God. You really did it. I didn't think you'd have the nerve."

"What are you talking about?" I asked him, alarmed. "It was your suggestion that I get him involved in the first place. All I did was ask him to help."

"Well, it was a great way to get him to your house," he said admiringly. "Did you by chance fix him a home-cooked meal, too?"

I blushed. "Rob—"

"Aha!"

"Rob, will you stop it? You make it sound like the opening stratagem in Lovelace's campaign to seduce Clarissa."

He made a face. "Must you throw around that English major bullshit all the time? You're just showing off."

"I'll have you know that *Clarissa* is probably the most boring book ever written," I sniffed. "If I can't throw out apt references to it now and then, what's the point of having had to suffer through more than a thousand interminable pages?"

"Is this the advantage of an expensive education? So you can bore all your friends, too?"

"Are you bored?"

"Exceedingly. Or at least I will be, if you don't come clean about last night."

I sighed. Sometimes it was just easier to give him what he wanted. "It was only dinner, Rob. The kids were upstairs. We talked for a while, and then—"

"What did you wear?"

"Pasties and a G-string. For Christ's sake, Rob, this reminds me of high school."

"Why should that bother you?" he asked indignantly. "I adored high school. Anyway, you're deliberately leaving out the good parts."

"You mean the part where he puts down his violin and I lick champagne off his bare chest as we lie entwined on the dining room table? Grow up!"

He grinned. "You may laugh, but if you don't make at least a tiny push to interest a man like David Sanchez, you're an idiot. He's rich, he's good-looking, and he's apparently normal, which has got to make him a hot commodity in the marketplace. He's certainly better than another glowering workaholic lawyer. Take my advice and don't go prosing on about Eleanor Hampton all the time, or he'll run the other way, fast."

"That's going to be difficult, since he's the one going over her papers," I said coolly, to demonstrate how indifferent I was to whatever direction David Sanchez might run. "Besides, I haven't told

you my latest theory about Eleanor and Barclay. I
think he might have killed her."

His reaction was disappointing, to say the least.
"Oh, really?"

"Do you want to know why?"

"Not in the least. Didn't we have this conversation already?"

"Yes, but that was before I uncovered all the
things you don't seem to want to hear about," I told
him.

"Don't pout. Tell Uncle Rob all about it, if you
can condense it into five minutes or less." He
glanced at his watch.

I did, but he was still unmoved. "Don't you even
care?"

He shrugged. "This is your crusade, not mine. If
I saw him stab her with a Henckels Four-Star, I'm
not saying I wouldn't turn him in, but you don't
have a shred of evidence even to suggest she was
killed, much less by her husband. So what if there
was a man in a suit leaning into the hot tub? Maybe
it was the meter reader with a hot date. And even
if you do find out she was blackmailing him, so
what? You still don't have any proof the police
would listen to."

His casual dismissal deflated me, but I persisted.
"Well, actually, I was hoping Kenny could tell me
if there was anything the police might have over-
looked."

He frowned. "Look, Caroline, I love Kenny; I
really do. Aside from our sleeping together, he was
the only one in the tangle of snakes that comprise
my successive step-families who behaved halfway
decently and didn't try to take my mother for everything she's got. He's sweet. He's a hunk. He's the
best thing that ever happened to me." He sighed.

"But you have to realize that intellect is not his strong suit. He may have been there on the day they found Eleanor's body, but what they mostly have him doing is handling complaints down in the village, like when some hapless tourist spends too long on the benches outside McDonald's and the Ladies Who Lunch get up on their high horse about uppity riffraff."

I smiled. The presence of a truncated version of McDonald's on Prospect, the tony street running along the edge of the sea, was an acrimonious controversy in the village, particularly after the installation of the benches, which presumably would lead to crimes like Loitering with French Fries and besmirching the sidewalk with ketchup smears.

"You can laugh," he said, "but you don't want him blundering around the Homicide Department with a lot of impertinent questions. It could get him in a lot of trouble." He crossed his legs meditatively. "And you, too, for that matter. Let's just say it would hardly be wise to go around accusing a partner in a major law firm of murdering his wife, particularly when the police have closed the investigation. There are libel laws for situations like that. Barclay could sue you for any little thing Steve leaves behind after he takes you to the cleaners in your divorce. And even if he didn't collect, your lawyer would. Christ, Caroline, you were married to one for a decade and a half. Didn't you ever learn to think defensively?"

"Apparently not. I always hated that mentality." I didn't tell him that Steve had just warned me about the same thing.

He looked exasperated. "I presume you've spun this theory for David Sanchez, too?"

I nodded.

"And?"

"He hasn't said. He's studying the documents right now."

"He's probably humoring you. Listen, Caroline, if he doesn't find any dynamite evidence that will send Barclay up-river for twenty-five-to-life, just drop the whole thing with him, all right? If you don't, you'll blow any prayer of a relationship before it has a chance to get off the ground.

"Rob, I'm not in the market; I've told you that already."

He shook his head. "Bullshit. You'd like to be, but you're too scared."

"I am not scared," I lied.

"Fine. Admit you'd really like to screw the guy till you both drop dead from exhaustion, and I'll believe you're not scared."

"I would *not*—"

"Then at least admit you're interested," he interrupted. "You can go that far."

"I am not—"

The door bell rang. I froze. "Who could that be?" I asked.

"Well, it's decades too late for the Fuller Brush man. I suggest you have a look."

I sidled up to the viewer and quickly ducked back. "It's him!" I hissed.

"Really?" asked Rob in an interested tone. "I could have sworn the company stopped door-to-door sales a long time ago. In fact, I wasn't even sure they were still in business."

"*Not* the Fuller Brush man," I informed him in a whisper. "David Sanchez."

He grinned wickedly. "Oh?"

"Rob, promise me you won't say anything to embarrass me. I mean it!"

"I thought you weren't interested," he said.

"Shhh. He'll hear you! Rob—"

The doorbell sounded again. Rob folded his arms and raised an eyebrow in inquiry.

"Rob," I said desperately, "I am not kidding!"

He sighed. "All right. Since you're so pathetic, I promise. Unless you'd rather I fled out the back door? Although," he added thoughtfully, "I can see how that might lead to the wrong impression, so—"

"Will you shut up?" I asked him, through gritted teeth, which I hoped David Sanchez would interpret as a friendly smile.

I'm not sure what he thought; when I opened the door he was studying the wood as if it might contain termites. "I thought you weren't home," he said. He was wearing jeans and a sweatshirt, but he carried a briefcase big enough to impress even a litigator. Rob eyed it speculatively, and I feared the worst.

"Come in," I invited him. "You remember Rob Holland?"

"Of course." They shook hands.

"Nice case," Rob told him. "We thought you might be the brush salesman."

"Rob—"

David didn't blink. "Do they still make house calls?"

I laughed. "Not that I know of, but Rob does. Don't you, Rob?"

He consulted his watch. "Yes. Some distance away, I'm afraid, and I'm already late. Good thing you reminded me." He leaned forward to kiss me on the cheek. I tried to step on his toe, but I missed. "I'll talk to you soon, Caroline," he said, with something very nearly approximating a leer.

"Good to see you again," he told David.

"Sorry," I said when the door had closed on him.

He smiled. "I'm the one who should apologize. You weren't expecting me, and I have the feeling I was interrupting something."

I laughed, secretly vowing that at the first possible opportunity I would nominate Rob as "Bachelor of the Month" in *San Diego Woman* magazine. "Well, you weren't, though I can see how you might get that impression. Rob's a wild card; you never know what he's going to do or say. Can I get you some coffee?"

"Please."

I was absurdly pleased to see him for a complicated variety of reasons. He had to have found something important to come all the way down from Newport Beach again so soon, but somehow it didn't seem right to press him. This morning's atmosphere was much more relaxed, and we headed naturally into the kitchen. I was glad I'd cleaned up the breakfast dishes and swept away the toast crumbs. There was a blob of jam on the countertop; I wiped it off with a sponge and he set his briefcase down. I poured the coffee and handed it to him. "Sugar?" I asked. He had had it the night before.

He smiled. "Not this morning. I'm too wired already." He looked at me over the rim of the cup. "Aren't you going to ask me what I'm doing here?" He sounded disappointed, so I knew something in the box had hooked him.

"You forgot the recipe for blackberry sorbet."

The smile widened. "Guess again."

"You came back to sweet-talk me into letting you use whatever it is you found."

"Jesus, Caroline. Give me some credit."

"Am I wrong?"

He lowered his eyes and looked amused. His lashes were a foot long, and dark. "Not entirely. But it's complicated, and I'm not ready to move yet in any case. I want you to talk to me, and don't spare the details. If I'm going to help you, I want to know what started you on this quest, and what you've learned on your own about the Hamptons, Naturcare, everything." He paused. "Tell me what you would have told me when you came to my office if I hadn't behaved like such an asshole."

"You weren't an asshole," I protested, although he had been perilously close to it. "You were naturally skeptical. Do you believe me now?"

"I was, but thanks anyway. Let's just say I'm considerably more interested. Talk to me, Caroline."

So I did. I told him about the makeover and my conversation with Eleanor about the perfidy of lawyers in general and Barclay in particular. I skipped the part about getting my hair tinted and being told to brighten up my drab fashion sense, since he had seen me only in my new, presumably more colorful, incarnation. I told him about Mike and Cindy's Naturcare partioc. I told him how Barclay had acted at the funeral, and how the firm and everyone else seemed determined to believe that Eleanor had killed herself out of depression. I told him about Manuel's seeing someone standing by the pool on the day Eleanor had died, and how she had told the clerk at the wine store she wanted the Bâtard-Montrachet for a celebration. I told him that Tricia was worried about Barclay, and that his alibi on the day of Eleanor's death was full of holes. I told him, last but certainly not least, that I felt a responsibility to Eleanor to find out the truth, whatever it was.

He stared out the kitchen window, apparently

watching the peppertrees shed, which they did at an alarming rate. "I can understand why you'd feel that way," he said at last. "But I'm not sure I understand why Eleanor Hampton sent the box to you."

"Oh, because she wanted me to write it up," I told him. "I'm don't know what she envisioned— something between self-help and *Heartburn*, I guess—but she was determined that I could shape it into something." So then I told him about being a writer, too. He didn't laugh or gasp or make too much of it, but it still made me uncomfortable to talk about it too much, so I added, "Besides, I think she gave the box to me because she thought we had something in common."

He set down his coffee cup. "I sincerely hope not."

I choked. "So do I. But you'll have noticed, now that you've read her letters and notes, that she had a sort of hobbyhorse about lawyers who leave their wives and children and then use their professional knowledge to intimidate them into accepting a less favorable settlement. I'm afraid in the end she saw just about everyone as a victim, no matter what the circumstances."

"She wasn't entirely wrong, even if she went overboard."

"No," I agreed. "She wasn't."

He turned his level gaze on me. "What went wrong with your marriage?" he asked me.

I looked out the window into the garden. "Is this part of your background interrogation?"

"I'm sorry," he said. "I had no right to ask."

I shrugged. "No, it's okay. You told me about yours last night." Except that he had lost his wife before he had lost his marriage, and in my case it was just the reverse. I looked into my cup for inspiration. "I don't really know what to tell you. It's not that I haven't thought about it; for months I didn't do anything but second-guess. But it just . . . died . . . for my husband, and I didn't even realize it. That's the worst part of it: A whole section of your history isn't what you thought it was. I know that sounds like I was naive or stupid or blind. Maybe I was all three."

"No, it doesn't. But it is sad," he said gently.

"Stop sounding so sympathetic," I told him. "Too much sympathy is bad for people in a divorce. They start to feel sorry for themselves."

He laughed. "If you say so."

"I know it," I said, only half kidding. "Look at Eleanor. Even if she was right about everything, no one could stand to be around her, so then everyone agreed that she deserved to get dumped. And anyway, maybe we just expect too much out of marriage. Maybe it's too much to ask of one person that he or she be best friend and coparent and witty conversationalist and hot stuff in bed for fifty years, especially when all the evidence suggests that we're really just animals made to act on every passing genital fancy."

"Do you really believe that?" he asked.

"I don't think so," I told him. "But I'm still looking for answers."

"Your husband was a fool, Caroline," he said quietly.

Something woke up then, stretching and stirring like a cat after a nap. I shook my head to clear it. Why was I thinking about animals? He still hadn't told me what he had learned from Eleanor's papers. I felt like Pandora: Once I had opened the box, all sorts of uncontrollable things had been unleashed.

"Thank you," I said. It seemed like the simplest answer.

"You're probably wondering what I found in the papers," he said after a while.

"It crossed my mind," I said lightly. "Did you find a smoking gun?"

He laughed. "Do you by chance have a passion for detective novels?"

"Only the most literate kind," I assured him. "Dorothy Sayers, Amanda Cross, Elizabeth George . . ."

"Much," he said, "is now made clear."

"I am being extremely patient," I reminded him.

He grinned and cleared his throat. "Okay, the . . . er . . . smoking gun. I have to know more, of course, but right now it appears that if our friend Eleanor was blackmailing her husband, she might—and I stress *might*—have had something pretty good to do it with."

"Hot shit! Really? What was he doing to her?"

He looked blank. "To her? Nothing. At least nothing more than what the investigator uncovered, and we already knew about that."

"Well, what, then? You mean it doesn't even have anything to *do* with Eleanor?"

He sounded apologetic. "Well, I have to do some checking first, as I told you, and, frankly, I'm not even sure whether Eleanor meant to include it in the box, because otherwise—"

"David!"

"Sorry." He crossed one foot over the other. He was wearing extremely high-tech running shoes, the kind that will do your entire workout for you if only you pay enough. "You remember that Naturcare recently went public?"

Of course I remembered. Half the firm's new

found affluence was founded on it, and it had elevated Barclay to Big Legal Cheese. However, the question seemed rhetorical, so I just nodded.

"Well, when a company offers its shares to the public, it has to put everything into a registration statement—its assets, its debts, what contracts it has, everything. If you misrepresent anything deliberately, it's fraud. Big-time fraud."

My breath caught in my throat. "Wow! Did Naturcare lie about something on its registration statement?"

He lifted a hand in warning, but he was still smiling. "Let's not jump to conclusions, okay?"

"I will be the very model of dispassionate restraint, if that will satisfy you." I sounded like one of my Regency heroines. Next I would be urging him to "cut line" and tell me everything.

He looked dubious but reached into the voluminous case to extract a glossy, expensively printed set of papers without comment. "Here is the Registration Statement," he said without handing it to me. He opened it several pages in and pointed. "And this is where it discusses the contracts Naturcare has for going into the major department stores with their product lines."

I looked at it; the print was tiny, and it looked as if it had been written for people who really loved the chapters on how to process the parts of the whale in *Moby Dick*. "I'm with you so far," I told him.

"Good." He suddenly looked very intense and serious, full of silent, coiled tension. His presence was nonetheless extremely physical. I thought this must be how he looked at work. I wondered why it was that women always found a man's involvement with his work so sexually attractive, when they knew how much trouble that same involvement was bound to cause them later on.

"Now *this*," he said, removing another document from the case, "is what I found among Eleanor's papers." He held it as if it might scorch his fingers. It was a few pieces of ordinary paper, stapled together and rather battered-looking.

"What is it?" I asked, in tones of appropriate reverence.

"It's a copy." He sounded disappointed. "It would be better to have the original, because he could always argue that this was just a draft. There's probably some confirming documentation somewhere, but it will be really tough to find. . . ."

"David," I interrupted, exasperated.

"Sorry." He shook his head ruefully. "I'm getting ahead of myself. What it is, is a document called a 'side letter.' It's a sort of unattached appendix to another document like an agreement. It's what it says that could be really important here. What it says, in effect, is that the agreement with Blandings Department Stores is conditional, and what it suggests is that all those agreements with department stores we just saw laid out in the Registration Statement are conditional."

"I don't get it. Conditional upon what?"

He spread his hands expansively. "Upon the department stores' being in existence. Being solvent. It doesn't matter. Look, you know how many stores have gone belly-up in the last couple of years?"

I nodded. Hard times had driven a number of department stores out of the market altogether, or at least into bankruptcy or into mergers that essentially restructured their identities.

"Apparently some of the stores refused to make an agreement with Naturcare without the stipulation that the contract was cancelable at any time. That way, if you suddenly found yourself a bargain-basement outlet instead of a high-end retailer, you wouldn't necessarily be stuck with a line of beauty products designed to appeal mostly to a very affluent clientele. The cosmetics business is notoriously crazy—some stores don't buy the products at all; they just lease out their space and take a cut on what's sold. There are all kinds of ways of doing business. But this..." He pushed his reading glasses up on his forehead. "Some suppliers make contracts like this with school districts, because the schools never know how much money they're going to have from day to day." He shrugged. "There's nothing wrong with it, but you are absolutely not allowed to list those contracts on the profit/income side on shareholder information. A contract is an asset only if it isn't cancelable. Do you see?"

"I think so. Then you think Barclay drafted this letter and still permitted the client to submit a Registration Statement that he knew was wrong?"

"Well, it's only a copy. But I think so, yes."

"So what happens if that's the case?"

He rubbed the tip of his nose with his forefinger. "If it came to light, the most likely scenario would be a big drop in the stock prices, followed by a very big shareholder lawsuit, followed by a gigantic malpractice action against Mr. Hampton and the firm."

"Oh, my God," I said.

"Of course, your malpractice insurance is almost always void in the case of deliberate fraud, but the rest of the lawyers would be covered as long as they didn't know anything about it."

"Oh, my God," I said again. "Surely it's too big a risk. Why would Naturcare do it? And why would Barclay agree to go along with it?"

David shrugged, the gesture of someone whose dealings in the business world had not left him with substantial faith in its innocence. "Well, it's a risk, of course, but Naturcare products are really hot right now, and most of the stores are going to want to carry them if they possibly can. And if someone defaults, you just make less profit, but as long as the side letter doesn't show up, you probably wouldn't get caught." He sighed. "You know, most businesspeople think their legal advisors are unnecessarily conservative in their advice, just a lot of fuddy-duddies standing between them and their profits. Some of them can be very headstrong. And the accountants are vigilant, but they're trained to look for irregularities, and on the surface there's nothing here to trigger a closer look."

"And Barclay?"

"Let me ask you this: How much did it mean to him to get Naturcare as a client?"

I thought of his car, his house, his beautiful new wife, and his enhanced prestige at Eastman, Bartels, and Steed. "A lot," I told him.

He nodded solemnly. "That's what I would have guessed. If Naturcare told him they wouldn't make the deal without the side letter and the Registration Statement that conveniently overlooks its existence, do you think he would have gone along with it?"

"As much as I'd like to say 'yes,' how can we really be sure? He makes some reference in a letter to something Eleanor 'misunderstood.' Still, he must have done something, or why else would he go to such lengths to cover it up? He could have just told her to forget it and then let her go on and expose him, if it wasn't anything that would hurt him."

He chewed the end of his pen thoughtfully.

"Maybe . . . but it's a big mistake to jump to conclusions. All we have at this point is a bunch of conjecture. There's something else, too."

"What?"

"Mike and Cindi Meadows would have as much or more of an interest in seeing that this doesn't get out."

I had a brief, satisfying fantasy of Cindi Meadows behind bars before I was forced to relinquish it. "Maybe, but they were ballooning in Burgundy when Eleanor was killed. They didn't even make it back for the funeral, and Susan told me Barclay was really hurt." Something he had hinted at earlier was worrying me. "You don't think anyone else in the firm knew about it, do you?"

He put down the pen and looked at me. "My guess is that it's the last thing in the world he'd want them to know. The risk might be worth it to Barclay because of what he stood to gain, but I just can't see it for the rest of them, no matter how big the client is. It could bring down the firm and cost all the partners most of their assets." He shifted his gaze away from my face, toward the window. "Are you divorced from your husband?"

"Not yet."

"Legally separated?"

I nodded, but he was still looking away, so I said, "My lawyer is drawing up the papers this week."

"Sign them soon. Tomorrow, if you can." He sighed. "It would probably be better if you were divorced."

"I'm working on it," I said, trying to smile. His meaning did not escape me. "They'd come after me, too?"

"If your husband knowingly participated in a fraud, his malpractice insurance wouldn't cover him. In a shareholder suit, they go after every-body."

I must have looked a little green because he said, "I really don't think you'll have anything to worry about. In my business you always have to think about the downside of every action, but I doubt it's a big risk in this case." He peered at me. "Still want to go ahead?"

I shut my eyes and tried not to think of living in a run-down studio somewhere far from La Jolla, trying to make it up to the children for having lost the money for their college educations. I punted. "What's next?" I asked him, without actually making a commitment.

"Have dinner with me Saturday," he said.

I wish the state of being forty, reasonably intelligent, and of a cynical turn of mind had not chosen that moment to intrude itself upon my notice, but I couldn't help it. "Are you trying to sweet-talk me into agreeing to let you use the stuff you found out about Naturcare?"

He looked away.

I felt remorseful. What was I doing, driving away the only man who had been nice to be with since my salad days with Steve? It was a rerun of the way I had acted when I'd gone to his lecture. Maybe Rob was right.

"I'm sorry," I told him. "I didn't mean to be rude. I told you once that getting divorced brings out the worst in you. I guess this is one of those times."

He studied me as if I were a company whose price–earnings ratio was giving off a sell signal. Then he smiled. "Actually, you're probably right to be suspicious. Sometimes I'm pretty ruthless when I'm conducting my research."

I had enough sense not to ask him what he was researching now.

"So, first," he went on, apparently deciding to abandon any plans for socializing after all, "the important thing to remember is not to tell anyone about this. Nobody. Rumors could wreck everything. You told your husband you threw away the contents of the box, right? That was smart thinking. We can probably count on his mentioning it to Barclay." We probably could, but I shivered a little anyway to think of what Barclay would do if he knew what I had.

"We don't want *anybody* to know you have this," David continued. He frowned. "It would be nice to know if an original of this side letter exists somewhere in some legal file, but my guess is that if it does, it's in a place where we might not ever find it. Why don't you just sit tight and let me do some investigating on my own? I'll put some of my people on it, and we'll go over Naturcare with a fine-tooth comb. That might turn up something."

"If you had any subtlety, you wouldn't do the 'let-me-relieve-the-little-woman-of-her-great-big-burden routine," I told him.

"Is this another manifestation of the 'worst' we can blame on getting divorced?" he asked, looking amused.

"Certainly not," I said. "This is you trying to shut me out."

"I'm not. Really. If I could think of anything for you to do right now, I'd suggest it." He crossed his heart and grinned. "Honest."

"Good, because I feel dumb enough already."

He seemed surprised. "Why?"

"Because I missed the big picture. I was so sure this was all about something Barclay was doing to

Eleanor, I didn't even look for anything else," I confessed. "I personalized everything too much."

To my relief, he didn't ask me to explain further.
"Don't be too hard on yourself," he told me. "You
know what they say about a prophet without honor.
And anyway, look what you've uncovered so far."

"What if you don't find anything?" I asked him,
somewhat mollified.

"Then at least we have a motive. That's what you
wanted, isn't it? If nothing else, we can always start
from there."

Before I could think of anything to say, he picked
up his cup and saucer and took them over to the
sink, the perfect guest. Then he picked up the mammoth briefcase and headed toward the door. "I'll
talk to you soon," he said.

"Fine." I paused. "Thank you, David. I really
mean that."

I walked him to the door and opened it. He
reached out and touched my cheek with his free
hand. His fingers were warm. "I don't want to rush
you, Caroline," he said. "I can wait."

17

        I CAN'T BELIEVE you just asked me what I think you asked me," Susan said, eyeing me over her second glass of wine. "I'm going to pretend I didn't hear it."

We were having lunch at Gregory's at the Bay, and the food was so perfect, the view so breathtaking, that I felt guilty for spoiling it. Besides, I'd asked her to lunch under false pretenses. She was leaving for her interview in New York in two days, and I had to move fast. I took another sip of wine.

"Look, I know you think this is some demented psychological obsession—" I began.

"That's putting it mildly."

"Fine. But can't you just accept that this is important to me? I need your help."

She pushed a radicchio leaf around her plate. "Sure, I can accept that it's important to you, even if I think it's for the wrong reasons. What I can't accept is that you want me to do something that is a breach of every ethical duty I owe the firm, and you can't even tell me what you're looking for."

"Susan, you don't have to do anything. Just let

me in and show me where the files are, and I'll do the rest."

"Is that what you call not doing anything?"

"Don't make me beg," I said. "Don't you want to see Barclay punished if he had anything to do with Eleanor's death?"

"I'm more interested in seeing him punished for the way he lords it over the office staff," she reflected.

"Well, then?"

"This is starting to sound like *9 to 5*," she said with a smile. "But seriously, Caroline, whatever this mysterious document is that you're looking for, your chances of finding it without a reference number are close to zero. For some of the clients, there are literally hundreds of pieces of paper, not to mention what's in the computers."

I took a spoonful of black bean soup. It was delicious. "I know," I conceded. "But I have to try."

"And you won't even give me a hint as to what's in it?" she persisted.

I looked at my plate. "I can't," I told her. "I promised I wouldn't reveal anything about it."

She wiped her lips delicately with her napkin. "My, this is getting interesting. Who did you promise?"

"David Sanchez. He's a money manager up in Newport Beach. He's been . . . helping me."

"Is he managing more than your money?"

"Susan!"

"Sorry, but if you're trying to hide it, you really shouldn't blush and twist your wedding ring whenever a man's name comes up."

I looked down at my hand. "I didn't realize I was still wearing it. I suppose I ought to make some really dramatic gesture like throwing it into the ocean or burying it in the backyard at midnight, but I'll probably just put it away in a box," I said.

"And David Sanchez?" she prompted.

They don't say *"in vino veritas"* for nothing. "I think I want to have an affair with him, and it's scaring me to death."

She laughed. "Caroline, you're such a Calvinist. It isn't an affair if you're not still married. What you're looking for is a relationship."

"Okay," I agreed. "I think I want to have a 'r-elationship' with him, a relationship with sex in it."

She settled back into her chair. "Well, thank God for that. That's the healthiest thing I've heard you say in a long time. What are you scared about?"

Without thinking, I reached down and pinched a fold of skin just below my waist. My fingers were a long way from meeting.

Susan saw me doing it and grinned. "Relax," she said. "You look great. Really. Especially since your Svengali from Naturcare got a hold of you and put a little cha-cha in your cucaracha. You used to dress like Hester Prynne, you know."

I shook my head. "Susan, your Spanish is hopeless. *Cucaracha* is a cockroach."

She flicked her fingers dismissively. "Whatever. Linguistic verisimilitude isn't the issue here, is it?"

"No," I conceded. "And neither is my weight, although lately I've actually been thinking about working out." I took another spoonful of black bean soup. "It's either that or a starvation diet." I put the spoon down. "But . . ."

"But?"

I looked down at my plate. "It's the sex thing."

"My God, Caroline, you sound positively virginal. You were married nearly twenty years."

"That's the problem," I said, casting a furtive

look around the restaurant to see if anybody might be listening. Nobody was. "Sex with Steve was ... fine, I guess, for most of that time. It was better than fine at the beginning. But it got sort of—you know—perfunctory." I lowered my voice. "I mean, you read in books about people weeping and scratching each other's backs with their fingernails. And I've never screamed, not once in my whole life." I toyed with my fork, expanding on my subject. "I've always wondered what people meant when they talk about techniques and learning new tricks. I mean, what could you learn that was new? You stick it in, you move up and down, you have an orgasm or you don't, and out it comes."

Susan wordlessly extended the wine bottle toward my glass. "I've had too much already," I told her. She poured some anyway. I took a sip.

"What I really think is that people invented this mythical sexual paradise where sex never happens the same way twice and they wear penile rings"— the waiter, pouring water for the couple at the next table, glanced at me oddly, so I lowered my voice again—"or hang from baskets while they explode with no fewer than seven orgasms in a row, just to make everybody else feel inferior. It's like those stories they used to tell about the incredible ecstasy you would feel if you hit the G-spot, only it turned out the G-spot doesn't exist." I put down the spoon resolutely. "That's what I think. But what if I'm wrong? Besides, my one near-sex experience post-Steve turned out to be a disaster."

"You mean Jeff Grayson?" Susan said with a delicate snort.

I nodded.

"You shouldn't count that. The only person Jeff can really get it up for is himself. Anyway, you should hear yourself. 'Near-sex.' You make it sound like 'near-death.' " She raised a finger in the air, and the waiter brought coffee without being asked. "Do you think this David Sanchez is interested in you?" she asked when he had gone.

I shifted my gaze and blushed again. "I don't know. He might be, but—" I didn't want to tell her I really feared that my chief appeal might be that I offered access to the Naturcare documents. I shrugged. "He did say that he was willing to wait till I was ready."

Susan poured half a pitcher of cream and two Equals into her coffee cup. She saw my look. "It's my indulgence, instead of dessert. Anyway, this Sanchez person sounds reasonably sensitive. I suggest you stop worrying and just see what comes up. Nobody's going to expect you to be mistress of arcane sexual technique. It doesn't matter. If it did, Dr. Ruth would be the most sought-after female on earth."

I laughed. "Thanks," I told her.

"Let me ask you one thing," she said when the waiter had brought the check, "Does your wanting to break into the firm's files have anything to do with David Sanchez?"

"In a way," I conceded. The truth was, I was so jumpy imagining Barclay lying in ambush around every corner that I just had to do something, but I had to admit, if only to myself, that there was an element of wanting to prove to David Sanchez that I could move things along on my own. "I'm just so tired of waiting for other people to take charge. I started this, and I want to see it through to the end myself."

"Did he ask you to do it?" she said.

"Oh, no," I told her, surprised at the question. "He'd be horrified if he knew."

"Good." She sighed. "Could we possibly postpone all this till I get back from New York?"

"It's urgent," I pleaded.

She waved aside my bills and put her Gold Card on the plate. "I certainly hope they still want me for the job, then. I could be needing it."

Eastman, Bartels, and Steed occupied an entire floor of a high-rise building in downtown San Diego. In order to enter off-hours, Susan had to use her identification card and her real name. I considered registering as Elizabeth Bennet, visitor, but she convinced me that if I were seen it would be much harder to invent a story to cover my presence if I were found to have checked in as a Jane Austen character. It was 10:30 at night, so even the most ardent associate would probably have gone home. It was too big a risk, Susan said, to show up much later than that unless you were a litigator. Everybody knew they did odd things at night. If anyone asked, we were on our way home from the theater when Susan remembered something important left undone. My presence was an unavoidable embarrassment.

The reception area was dark and silent, the carpet thick as lawn. The couch and table were Italian and very expensive, probably purchased with Naturcare money. I hadn't seen them, because they had still been on order when Steve moved out. A large floral arrangement was displayed on a marble end table. I would have liked to look over everything more closely, but this was hardly the time for furniture shopping.

Susan lifted the wastebasket behind the recep-

tionist's desk and inspected it. "Empty," she said in
a whisper. "That means the cleaning staff has already been through."

We stepped into the hall leading to the lawyers'
offices and the file room. It was lit. I drew back.

"It's okay," Susan told me. "The hall lights are
always left on at night." We reached the file room
and she took out her keys and unlocked the door.
We stepped inside and turned on the light. The air
was metallic and stuffy. The air conditioning went
off at seven o'clock. "This is the safest place in the
whole firm to hide out," Susan said with satisfaction. "The lawyers hardly ever come here."

"Then how do they get things out of the files?" I
asked her, surprised. I knew there were file clerks
who came around with little carts every half hour
or so to put things away, but I hadn't realized there
were so many barriers between a lawyer and his
papers.

"They send somebody to pick up what they want.
Half of them couldn't find anything in here anyway.
The whole place would collapse without the staff."
She looked at me. "All right, I've told you about the
different-colored folders for each client. If you
wanted correspondence, for example, that would be
in a blue folder under the client's name and the file
number. Documents are filed by date of receipt."

"Suppose," I said carefully, "I was looking for
documents on Naturcare. I'm not asking, of course,
but just for example, where might they be?"

Her eyes widened. She crossed the room and put
her palm against the edge of a shelf, patting a series
of brown accordion files. "Naturcare, for example,
is found in this area," she said primly. She glanced
at her watch. "How long do you need?"

I glanced helplessly at the contents of the room,

which probably totaled more than the entire inventory of the Library at Alexandria. "All night," I told her.

"One hour, okay? I'll be in my office." At the door she turned around again. "And please, Caroline, put everything back as you found it. We still have the business to run, and if they can't find their documents, the lawyers get pissed off and blame the file clerks."

"I'll be careful," I promised.

"You know I'm really trusting you on this one, don't you?" she added grimly.

"I know. I really appreciate it."

Twenty minutes later, I knew that the side letter was not in the file. I hadn't thought it would be because it didn't have a file number, and I didn't think Barclay would have left it where everyone else in the firm had access. Still, I went through by date and checked, just to be sure. When I was reasonably certain I had been through everything important, I went to the door of the file room and looked out. The corridor was deserted.

What I had to do was get into Barclay's office and check there. For obvious reasons I had refrained from telling Susan this part of my plan. It was bad enough to go through the firm's client files—a gross breach of confidentiality—but breaking into a partner's desk was beyond the limit. They might do worse than fire you for that.

I have to say right now that the confidentiality bit concerned me less than it probably should have. When we were still talking, Steve had shared details of just about every interesting matter he was working on, up to and including a juicy paternity suit against the CEO of a well-known company the firm represented. If you wanted to be really scrupulous about it, he shouldn't have told me anything, but if he hadn't, we would have had even less to talk about than before. It's hard not to share something you're immersed in eleven hours a day, six days a week. I suspect we weren't alone, either. Probably the only way to insure complete confidentiality is to engage a law firm of Trappist monks.

Fortunately, the partners never locked their offices. I walked noiselessly down the hall, past doors opening onto rooms as varied as the people themselves. The firm's premier tax attorney, Dora Green, surrounded her delicate French Provincial desk with so many stacks of paper she should have been number one on Earth First's hit list. Across the hall, Simon Bartels's (Italian walnut) work surface was so clean and empty you would never have guessed that he accounted for more billable hours than anyone else in the firm. My one fear was that Barclay had switched offices since I had last visited, boosted into a coveted corner with its two sets of windows and a view no one had time to look at anyway, although presumably the clients enjoyed it. The fights for corner offices were ugly, almost as bad as the ones over who got into the firm name.

Barclay was a heavy hitter, but he had yet to make the starting lineup: His office was still in the same place. I looked at my watch. Fifteen minutes. I opened the door, closed it behind me, and felt for the light switch.

Tricia had been hard at work. Barclay's office looked like the members' room of a men's club in London. A Regency hero, one of the powerful-thighs set, would have felt right at home. The green leather couch was finished with visible stitching and little brass nails. A cut-glass decanter stood on the credenza, doubtless full of single-malt Scotch whisky. A painting of a horse, school of George Stubbs, graced one of the dark-paneled walls. The background looked like the Del Mar Racetrack, but otherwise it was pure Epsom Downs. I wondered if Barclay and Tricia had acquired shares in a race-horse. I wondered if the fox and hounds would come running through any minute.

I wondered if Barclay's desk drawers were un-locked. My bravado nearly vanished then. This was worse than my historical attempts at snooping—reading someone's letters while baby-sitting, or opening Steve's mail from his mother to see what crimes I had committed before I passed it on. I for-tified myself with the knowledge that my motives for going through his files, unlike Eleanor's, were pure: She wanted to blackmail him; I only wanted to see him tried for murder.

The file drawer slid open with so little effort I knew it was almost empty before I looked into it. There were a few manila files, most of them with client names printed on the tabs. I virtuously ig-nored everything but the Naturcare file, which con-tained only one disappointing memo. I glanced at it, but although it was intriguing, I couldn't make heads or tails of it. "Please destroy the earlier memo with regard to the way Naturcare does business," it read. "It should be removed from any client files or document files." It was dated several weeks ear-lier.

There was nothing too remarkable in this; law-yers have been known to purge a client's files before the regulators get a shot at them, though nobody admits it. I imagined it was more unusual to purge a memo from your own files. It was too big a risk to go down the hall and copy it, so I had to leave it or take it with me. With more than a few qualms, I folded the paper up and put it into my wallet. Even the most amateur detective had to know it wouldn't be admissible as evidence, but I just couldn't leave it.

Almost of its own accord, my hand drifted up to the top drawer of the desk. It was filled with Mont Blanc pens in enough different styles to write out the whole *Encyclopaedia Britannica* without running out of ink. There were breath mints and a travel-size vial of Ralph Lauren men's cologne. Best of all, there was a pocket calendar, the kind lawyers can't live without. Steve always carried his inside his suit pocket, so that if he had to schedule an appointment while he was at a board meeting, for example, he wouldn't have to phone his secretary to find out if he was free.

I flipped through the blue calendar pages. The handwriting was execrable, but as near as I could make out there were business meetings and lunches two or three times a week along with the odd appointment with his doctor and hairstylist. There were play dates for Torrey Pines golf course and twice weekly notations for the gym. I hurried through until I reached the day of Eleanor's death.

I don't know what I expected—tearstains or bloodstains would have been nice—but there was only a smudge and a single perfect "E." I couldn't exactly exclaim "Eureka," and I would have felt better if the smudge, which might have been another letter, hadn't preceded it, but that "E" cheered me no end. True, it might have been Elke, his personal Swedish masseuse, but I felt sure it was Eleanor he had planned to meet, covering his tracks by billing Naturcare for the entire afternoon and evening. And if it was, I had the goods on him.

I turned over a few more pages. "E Funeral" was scrawled across the page for the Saturday following her death. I wondered what kind of man had to remind himself of the date and time of his ex-wife's funeral. What had he felt when he wrote that entry? If I knew the answer to that for sure, I wouldn't have to ask any more questions.

I ripped out the calendar page and stuffed it in next to the memo. It was another big risk, but I had already taken so many that it seemed pointless to worry.

I looked at my watch again. I had six minutes left on the hour. I could stop now, and unless Barclay was compulsive about the contents of his calendar, I was pretty sure I was safe. I closed the door, turned off the light and stepped into the lighted hall again. Five minutes.

I'm a little ashamed of this next part. There was no excuse for it, at least none I'd care to admit to. I walked a few paces farther down the hall and went into Steve's office. I'm not sure what I hoped to find—a life-sized boudoir portrait of Linda Williams, evidence of orgies on the desk—but I just had to see it again.

It looked just the same, professionally bland and eminently tasteful—no discarded champagne bottles or gargantuan piles of American Express charge slips detailing lustful encounters in elegant beach-front hotels. The only thing I could see that was different was that the small sterling frame was missing from the desktop. I'd given it to him for our tenth anniversary, with a picture of the two of us on top of a Mayan pyramid in Tikal. Some fellow tourist had taken it, and it wasn't perfectly level, but we had looked very happy and pleased with our adventure. I wondered what he had done with it—if he had thrown it away or just put it in a box somewhere, like my wedding ring.

I stood there gripping the side of the desk, feeling immeasurably sad over what we had lost. I couldn't resurrect that feeling of happiness, even though I remembered we had had it. I thought of how naive I had been, how unprepared. I should have known better. The world was full of middle-aged women looking over their old photographs and anxiously wondering, "Did he love me then?" That was the worst thing about it—it made you doubt your own experiences.

I can't say for sure whether lack of scruples would have led me to go through Steve's desk as well as Barclay's. Before I had a chance to decide, the door to the office opened. Henry Eastman, the senior partner of Eastman, Bartels, and Steed, was regarding me with an expression of evident surprise. Behind him, in varying states of amazement and disgust, stood Jeff Grayson and Barclay Hampton.

18

IT WAS A few moments before I could get breath enough to speak.

"Jesus God," said Jeff Grayson. "What are you doing here, Caroline? You scared us half to death." He was holding a large sheaf of papers in his hands.

Barclay stared at me wordlessly. It was worse than facing a firing squad. The saliva evaporated from my mouth, and my throat felt epoxied shut.

"We saw the light on, under the door," Henry said courteously, but in a tone that nonetheless demanded an explanation.

"I'm sorry, Henry," I said, when I could find my voice. I focused on his face because I couldn't bring myself to look at the others. "I was looking for the bathroom and I just . . . came in here." As a matter of fact, I was clamping my legs together to keep from adding an embarrassing accident to my other sins.

"The ladies' room is in the other direction," Jeff said with satisfaction. His voice held a note of amusement. Christ, what a sadist. How could I ever have thought him attractive?

"Thank you," I said and started to move toward the door.

"Henry—" Barclay began, but Henry silenced him with a wave of his hand.

"Wait, Caroline," said Henry. "Please sit down for a moment." He gestured toward Steve's overstuffed client chair. Henry was a gentleman, and his demeanor with the firm wives had always been avuncular, or fatherly. He was still gentlemanly, but for the first time I saw him as a young associate might—as a thoroughly formidable figure.

I sat. He took the chair behind the desk, facing me. Jeff stood in the doorway, and Barclay took up a position behind me. I could feel his eyes boring into my back. "I really think you should tell us what you're doing here," Henry said in his cultured voice.

"It's difficult to explain," I began.

Jeff gave a soft laugh from the door. "I'd love to stay and hear this, but I'm outta here," he said gleefully. "I've got an early tennis match tomorrow. Nice to see you again, Caroline. We'll tell Steve you stopped by."

He would, too. I didn't answer him.

"You were saying, Caroline?" Henry prompted.

"Susan and I were at a play, and—"

"Susan Goldman?"

"Yes." Susan would *kill* me. "And she remembered something she'd left undone here. You know she's going on vacation?"

He nodded.

"I don't know what it was," I said truthfully. "But I was waiting in her office, and I needed to find the ladies' room, and I got turned around. Then I saw Steve's office." I sighed. If they wanted to see me squirm, I would do it. It was a small price to pay to extricate Susan from the mess I had gotten us into. Mentally I retraced all my steps, praying that I had left everything as I had found it. If Barclay caught a whiff that I had been in his office, he would know for sure that I was onto him, whatever I might have told Steve about throwing away the contents of the box. It was bad enough as it was.

I looked at Henry in what I hoped was a wistful fashion. "I don't expect you believe this, Henry, but all I wanted to do was come in and look around. I expected things would have changed somehow, but they haven't. I can't come here anymore in ordinary circumstances. But the firm was a big part of my life, too, for a long time, and I just had to see it again."

I had told him something not so very far from the truth after all. I saw at once that I had taken the right tack, appealing to the paternalistic loyalty— no, love, more likely—he felt for the firm he had founded.

He reached across the desk and patted my hand. "I understand it must be difficult," he said kindly, "but you really mustn't wander around in here at night."

"I know that," I told him. "I promise it won't happen again."

"Excuse me, Henry, but that is unadulterated bullshit," said Barclay explosively from behind me. "You know what she's here for. It's just like Eleanor," he said hoarsely. "Ten to one she's been looking through Steve's files, trying to find leverage for the divorce."

I almost breathed a sigh of relief. Bad as it was, it was better that he believed that than the truth. I continued to look at Henry as I spoke. "Henry, I swear to you I never so much as opened a drawer

in here. I was just standing here, remembering."
Thank God it was the truth. A few more minutes
and I might have been caught with my hands in the
filing cabinet.

"Christ, Henry, you're aren't going to believe
that, are you?" inquired Barclay in a desperate tone.

I turned to face him. "What do you want, Barclay? A body search?"

"I'll leave that to Jeff," he said nastily. "Henry—"

"Leave this to me, Barclay," Henry interrupted
him. "I'll take care of it."

Barclay made a choking sound. His hand was at
his chest. "Do you want to start all this up again,
Henry? *Do you?*" He was as pale as I was flushed.
I could almost have felt sorry for him, if I didn't
know what he had done.

"I said I would take care of it, Barclay," Henry
told him in a quiet tone that nonetheless might have
excited envy in General Patton. "Why don't you go
on home and get some rest?"

Barclay turned wordlessly and left the room. If he
threw me a last withering look, I didn't see it. I kept
my eyes demurely on the desk.

"I'm afraid Barclay's not himself these days,"
Henry said regretfully. He said it lovingly but with
exasperation, like the Prodigal Son's father. "Not
since Eleanor died."

I wondered if Henry, too, had wondered about
Barclay's involvement in Eleanor's death and how
much he knew about what had gone on at Naturcare. "Maybe he was fonder of her than he realized," I suggested.

He put his hand lightly on my wrist. His skin was
dry and papery, and his nails were manicured. "*She*
came here, too, one night," he said, looking away.

"She said it was the only time, but I'm sure she wasn't telling the truth."

"Who?" I asked him. I thought it best to seem ignorant of other office-breakers.

"Eleanor." He uttered it with a little shudder of distaste. "She had it in her head that Barclay was hiding the true amount of his bonus from her, and I believe she crept in with the idea of looking through his files."

"Was he?" I couldn't help asking.

His eyes traveled back to my face. To his credit, he made no rash protestation. "Not to my knowledge," he said calmly. "In the ordinary way, of course, the firm doesn't get involved in such things, but I imagine I would have heard about it if that had been the case." He sighed. "I'm very old-fashioned, you know. I think people nowadays divorce too easily. But whatever happens, I believe a man should stand by his obligations."

"I know you do, Henry," I told him sincerely. "That's what I've always admired about you."

He smiled. "Yes, well, I'm afraid the trouble is that poor Eleanor was really quite mad. I tried to assure her that the firm would have no part in any kind of fraud against her and that she was putting herself in a very grave position by breaking into the firm's files. She wouldn't listen to reason." He shook his head sadly. "In the end I had to threaten her with prosecution."

I hoped this wasn't a parable, that he didn't realize how uncomfortable he was making me. "Did she listen then?" I asked him, swallowing a lump in my throat.

"As a matter of fact, she died before the issue was entirely resolved. I can't tell you how relieved I was not to have to go through with it. Barclay was livid, of course, but I couldn't help feeling sorry for her no matter how dreadfully she acted. It must be terribly hard for a woman when her husband gets bored with her and wants to leave."

"Yes," I said neutrally, "it is."

His grip on my wrist tightened. "Oh, my dear, I'm so sorry. I didn't think."

He looked so sincerely worried that I wanted to reassure him. "It's okay, Henry. Really. I'm doing fine."

"I'm glad to hear it." He let me go and picked up a pen off Steve's desk. It was a gold-filled Cross; he hadn't graduated to Mont Blanc. "Still, I'd like you to know I meant what I said about standing by our obligations. I'll be happy to be of service in any way I can. I'm particularly interested in seeing that your children—there are two of them, aren't there?—don't suffer."

"Thank you, Henry."

"I tried to tell her the same thing," he said, gazing off into space again with an injured look, as if he found it hard to believe anyone could have doubted his good intentions, "but she simply wouldn't listen." He sounded so sincere that I couldn't believe he had been a party to Barclay's fraud. He sighed. "I'm sure you're a great deal more reasonable."

"I hope so," I said.

He folded his hands together on the desktop and regarded me seriously. "Good. And you'd tell me, wouldn't you, if there were something bothering you?"

My heart thumped. "Something bothering me?" I squeaked.

"Something to do with the firm. If there were something, I'd do everything I could to help; I hope you know that."

I wondered if he had some sort of uncanny lawyer's instinct about ferreting out what hadn't been said. "Would you really want to know, if there were something awful about someone in the firm? Something you couldn't do anything about?"

He gave me a searching look. "Are you speaking about your husband?"

It was a natural assumption. "I'm speaking hypothetically," I told him.

"Of course." He chuckled. "Is there anything you want to tell me?" I had heard the way he spoke about Barclay, and I thought that he could never be convinced that one of his flock would do anything so dastardly as murder. Besides, there was the business of Naturcare and all the resulting ramifications. Still, I looked at him with his gentlemanly composure, his perfect stillness, his fatherly compassion, and I was tempted to tell him the whole story.

He looked at me expectantly.

"I—" I'm not sure I would have lost my head and told him anything, but in any event I never got the chance to find out. For the second time that evening, the door opened suddenly, startling us both.

Susan had a stricken expression on her face, but her voice was firm. "Here you are, Caroline," she said, her hands clenching a file and her purse with equal ferocity. "I've been waiting for you in my office." I could see her swallow. "Hello, Henry."

"Good evening, Susan," said Henry pleasantly. "Working late?"

I prayed she would remember our story. She did. "Oh, no. Didn't Caroline tell you? We were just at the theater, and I wanted to pick up the recruiting lists for Stanford and Boalt. I had a little trouble finding them," she finished lamely.

"Well, my dear, we appreciate your dedication,

but you don't have to do that sort of work at home," Henry told her.

"I don't usually, but I'm going away for a few days and I didn't want to leave it for Cheryl."

"Yes, of course. Well, I won't keep you." He turned to me. "Perhaps we can finish our conversation another time," he said as if we had just met at a cocktail party. "In the meantime, I hope you'll remember what I've said."

What he'd said about threatening to prosecute Eleanor for breaking into the firm or what he'd said about coming to him with any problems? It was like Henry to leave you guessing. "I will," I told him.

Susan was livid. Her hands gripped the steering wheel so hard I thought she was going to yank it out of its mounting. I could feel the heat of her wrath all the way across to the passenger's seat. I rolled down the window an inch; the night air was uncharacteristically warm from the Santa Ana wind that blew hot air off the desert. Fall, so revered elsewhere, is the ugliest season in Southern California; the natural vegetation has finally given up the ghost after months of no rain, and the smog colors the horizon with a smudge almost as brown as the hillsides. Even at night, the air smelled metallic and combustible.

Susan was uncharacteristically silent. "Talk to me," I begged her. "Yell at me. Anything."

She barely glanced at me. "I'm not mad at you," she said virtuously. "I'm mad at myself."

"That's bullshit," I told her. "You're furious at me."

"You're right," she admitted. "I'm mad at both of us. But I'm the one who let you in."

"Look, I'm really sorry I went into the partner

offices without telling you, but I knew you wouldn't approve."

"You were right about that."

"I don't want to have some big philosophical discussion about whether the end justifies the means here, but I promise you it was absolutely necessary to have a look at Barclay's desk."

She sighed. "I know you believe that, Caroline. That's what scares me."

"You think I'm going too far?" I asked her.

"Don't you?"

I thought about it. "Actually, no. I haven't been this certain about anything in a long time. Not about Barclay, necessarily, but about the importance of finding out the truth." I looked into my lap, struggling to find the words to tell her how I felt. "Since . . . since Steve left, I've been almost asleep. Maybe even before that. I've just been drifting along. God knows enough people have told me I have to get on with my life, but I couldn't seem to manage to do it. I know it may seem like what I'm doing here is hanging on to Steve and the firm in a kind of perverse way by trying to get at them through Barclay, but I honestly don't think that's the case."

"I think I should remind you that the Crusades did not come to a happy conclusion," she said tartly. Susan had studied history at Barnard. Still, she sounded less angry.

"I don't want to retake Jerusalem," I told her. "I just want to know what really happened to Eleanor. I'm getting close, too. Barclay's calendar had—"

"I don't want to hear about it."

"—an 'E' beside the day of her death," I persisted. "At least I think it was an 'E.' I mean, I know it was an 'E,' but I'm not sure it was only an 'E,' because there was a blob in front of it, so it might have been 'something E,' if you know what I mean."

She looked at me incredulously. "I most certainly do not."

I shrugged. "Well, what it boils down to is that Barclay may have had an appointment with Eleanor on the day she died, when he said he was working on Naturcare all afternoon and evening." The car pulled up in front of my house. "Coffee?" I asked her.

She shook her head.

"I don't suppose I could interest you in looking at the memo I found in Barclay's office, just to see if you might know anything about it?" I suggested.

"I'm not a secretary, Caroline. I don't type memos."

"Is that a 'no'?"

She sighed. "Let's see it," she said.

I took it out of my purse and handed it to her. She reached up, turned on the overhead light, and squinted at it in the dimness. Then she looked at me. "Now I'm embarrassed. I did type this."

"Really?" I couldn't believe my luck.

"Well, sometimes partners ask me to type something confidential if they don't want it to go to the regular secretarial pool. I remember him asking me to do it, but now that I look at it again, I can't think why. There's nothing in it that I can see. Anyway, I doubt it has anything to do with whatever it is you're looking for."

"We can't be sure. If Barclay—"

"No, no. That's what I wanted to tell you. Barclay didn't write this memo. Henry Eastman did."

"Oh," I said, disappointed. "I'll have to think

about what it means." I looked at my watch. It was half past midnight. "I should let you go," I told her. "I'm really sorry about tonight. I hope you have a great trip to New York."

"Thanks. Well, look at it this way—this whole business may force me to do something I've probably wanted to do for a long time."

"You mean go back to New York?"

She nodded.

"I'm happy for you if that's what you want, but I'm sure Henry isn't going to fire you or anything like that. He seemed to understand that it wasn't your doing. And I don't think he has any idea I went into Barclay's office, since he found me in Steve's."

"And what are you going to say to Steve about it when Jeff Grayson runs into him on the courts and tells him all about your little visit? He will, you know."

"I know. It's not a criminal offense to be standing in his office, reliving the past. I'll tell him I was looking for the picture of the two of us at Tikal. He might even be flattered. At least he can't use it against me."

"Was it there?"

"Not anymore."

I tried to say it lightly, but Susan wasn't fooled. "Sorry," she said.

I shrugged.

"You didn't take anything out of Steve's office, did you? Honestly?"

"Cross my heart." I didn't tell her it was mostly because I hadn't had the chance.

"Good," she breathed. "Because if I know Henry, he'll have Steve go over it with a fine-tooth comb."

I shook my head. "Really, Susan, he was very nice about it. He seemed almost sympathetic. I don't think he was that upset. Barclay is the one who hit the ceiling." I shuddered. "And Jeff."

She touched my arm. "Look, I know Henry comes on like some kind of geriatric Atticus Finch— all wise and scholarly and benevolent—but don't carry it too far. He also drinks too much vodka in the afternoons and his wife looks as if she were dressed by the Fauves, but he is definitely not a comic figure. He is one very tough lawyer, so don't go assuming he's some gooey marshmallow who's going to go all soft on you just because you shared some kind of tender moment, or whatever it was."

"Okay. I'll keep it in mind." I opened the car door and looked at her. "Are we friends again?"

"Sure. If I move to New York, I'll bequeath you my sunblock."

"Greater love hath no woman," I said lightly, stepping out of the car.

She called me back. "Caroline?"

"Yes?"

"Even if I don't agree with you, I really admire your guts."

I liked that image of myself as some kind of gutsy crusader. I even, with a curious lack of the self-deprecation that had dogged me for years, recognized that it was true. I was so elated that I marched right into the house to call David Sanchez, until I remembered that it was nearly 1 A.M. and that he was out of town for a few days anyway. Before my courage could fail me, I dialed the private office phone number he had given me and left a message on his tape machine. "This is Caroline James," said the bold new me. "If you'd like to take a rain check on dinner, I'm free this weekend."

"*Brazen*," said my mother's voice in my ear.

I smiled.

19

"YOU DID WHAT?" David's fingers were holding a spring roll that threatened to slip from his grip into the sauce. A sprig of coriander slid unheeded to the plate.

I poured myself another cup of tea, ignoring his stare. "Maybe I should have waited till after dinner," I murmured.

"At least until after the crab," he agreed. He took a bite of the spring roll. "Delicious," he said, licking a bit of sauce off his fingers. "I'm glad you suggested this restaurant. But Caroline—"

"David?"

"You should not have broken into the law firm's offices."

"I didn't break in. Susan has a key. I just . . . went in with her."

"Right. What about Barclay Hampton's desk?"

"It was unlocked." I tried to say it with bravado, but I lowered my eyes.

He grimaced. "If you really think he killed his wife, hasn't it occurred to you that letting him know you're onto him might be dangerous?"

I shook my head. "He may suspect that I know

something, but I think he thinks I was there looking for the goods on Steve. Projection, you know. Anyway, I'm not his biggest fan, but even I think it would take more provocation than I've given him before he turns into some slavering serial killer. I just can't see it."

"You watch too many bad movies. You don't have to slaver to want to protect yourself if you're threatened."

"Well, okay, I admit I'm a little nervous about it. But at least he doesn't know for sure what I know."

"Yet."

"Yet," I agreed. The waiter came and put two plates of stuffed crab down in front of us. "Do you eat these with chopsticks?" I asked David when he had gone.

"Not me. I know my way around the dessert forks, but chopsticks elude me. I can't seem to figure out what to do with my fingers. I just pick up the crab with my hands, like this." He demonstrated.

I laughed. "This reminds me of Leslie Caron learning to eat ortolans in *Gigi*."

"What are ortolans?"

"Some kind of very expensive French bird, I think."

He looked at me curiously. "Does everything remind you of something out of a book or a movie?"

"Frequently," I admitted. "Especially when I'm nervous."

"Are you nervous now?"

"Very."

"Why?"

"You know why, David."

"Tell me."

I sighed. "This makes me nervous," I told him,

making a sweeping gesture that included the rice bowls, the crab, the table, him.

"Vietnamese food makes you nervous?"

"Of course not." I was about to say that this was like a scene from a Woody Allen movie when I caught myself. "I meant dating. Dating makes me nervous."

He smiled. "Dating makes everybody nervous," he said. "At least I'm glad you aren't so caught up in your quest for the truth that you haven't noticed we are dating." He made a face. "Actually, I hate the word. It sounds like Frankie and Annette going down to the local drive-in."

"Now who's making movie references?"

He wiped his hands on his napkin. "I'm nervous, too. I admit it. Look, I'm interested in you. You're pretty and smart and—"

"And I gave you the Naturcare information." Why did I say things like that? It made me sound so insecure.

He looked at me. "And you're still vulnerable." He grinned. "Actually, you're a smart-ass. It's not exactly the culture I grew up in, but I like it."

"Latinas don't make jokes?"

"Sure, but the man is still the *Queso Grande*."

"The 'Big Cheese'? Is that a real Spanish expression?"

"Certainly not."

"Is it true?"

He shrugged. "Pretty much."

"Uh-oh," I said.

"Uh-oh?"

"I've had enough big cheeses to open a fondue restaurant," I told him. "Actually, I was thinking of going vegetarian."

He laughed. "How about a taco stand?"

"I love tacos," I admitted.

"Well?"

" 'Well,' what?"

"Are you interested in me?" I stared at him. "Come on, Caroline. This isn't a conversation about food. Be brave."

I folded my hands together to keep them from wandering manically around the table or in the air. "I'm interested," I told him at last.

He smiled. "Good. Want to change the subject?"

"Yes," I said, relieved. I hadn't felt so awkward— or so elated—since Ricky Fowler asked if I wanted to wear his letterman's jacket for the day in eighth grade. Besides, all those reactivated hormones were making me dizzy. "What shall we talk about?" I asked him.

He looked amused. "Our mutual project?" he suggested.

"Oh. Right."

"Let's talk options." His eyes were very dark, very intense. "Caroline?"

I forced myself to concentrate. "I'm with you."

"Okay. As I see it, there are two separate issues here. One is the murder. That's your specialty." He smiled. "The other is the financial fraud. That's mine. So let's talk about what we have."

"You first."

"Okay. We don't have the 'goods' on anybody, but I think with the memo and the financial stats I've compiled on Naturcare, not to mention the goings on at Eastman, Bartels, and Steed, we have enough to convince the SEC that Mike and Cindi Meadows might have been trying to pull a fast one on the public. They'll at least want to look into it. If the terms of that side letter are in force, then somewhere there will be a record of it. The SEC can find that 'somewhere' better than anybody else. If it doesn't exist, then the Registration Statement is accurate, the contracts are binding, and they're off the hook. And so is our friend Mr. Hampton, at least in that regard."

"But you doubt it."

"I doubt it," he agreed. "I'm going with my gut on this one. Anyway, that's one thing. Another is whether or not I can make any money off this issue. I'm getting my lawyer's opinion on whether using the information to short the stock would be insider trading or not, but I don't think it will be. If someone inside the company had passed on the tip, it might be different, but I think this is okay. Still, it's better to get an opinion, just to be sure."

"What would happen if the SEC decided it *was* insider trading?" I asked him.

"In this case, you'd just have to give back the money you made. No penalties. It's my issue, though, not yours. What have you got?"

I ticked off the evidence on my fingers: the motive of blackmail, the threats, the mysterious suited man beside the hot tub, the Bâtard-Montrachet, the notation in the calendar. "Not enough to convict," I said sadly.

"Perhaps not," he conceded. "But possibly enough to interest the police, at least. You'll have to decide what you want to do with what we've got. It's too bad we didn't get more written documentation at the firm, but I don't think we're going to turn up any more."

"You don't think I should try to scare a confession out of Barclay?" I asked with a laugh.

"Don't even joke like that," he said seriously.

"I thought you liked a smart-ass."

"With the emphasis on *smart*. Threatening Barclay would be dumb."

"Do you really think I should go to the police?"

"I think you should decide this one on your own. It's your quest."

"Thanks for not saying 'obsession.' What if they don't believe me, or they can't prove anything, either?"

He sighed. "If we go to the SEC and they find that Barclay knowingly went along with a fraud, he's ruined anyway. It might not be as satisfying as hard time in San Quentin, but he could lose everything he's got, and he might get disbarred."

I thought of Tricia and the boys turned out on the street, of Jennifer having to leave the university, and shivered. "That's rough."

He nodded. "There's something else you should think about. It won't do the law firm a lot of good to have it revealed that one of its partners did something blatantly illegal. The firm will probably get sued, and while the insurance would cover any judgment against the innocent partners, they'd lose some significant business, at least for a while." He hesitated. "That could affect your financial future too."

"You mean you think I should just do what's best for me?"

"I didn't say that. But before you jump off the bridge, don't you want to know how deep the water is? It's foolish not to count the cost."

"Spoken like a true portfolio manager," I told him with a smile. "But you're right; I know you're right." I sighed. "Still, it makes you think. When Steve was in law school, he used to sit around with his friends talking legal issues. That's natural, right? They were immersed in it about eighteen hours a day. But you know what they talked about?"

David glanced at me, smiled, and shook his head. "What?"

"Public policy," I told him. "They spent a lot of time in all this earnest conversation about what's best for society, and how the law could take you there. It wasn't even boring," I added, remembering how I had listened from the tiny kitchen as I made sandwiches and opened beers. "What I'm wondering is, how does all that looking at whether something is good for society or not turn into just focusing on what's best for the client? What about what's fair or right in the big picture? Maybe it's that kind of ethic that leads somebody to go along with whatever a client asks him to do, no matter how uncomfortable it makes him."

"They're not necessarily all like that, Caroline."

"Maybe not." I shrugged. I picked up the fortune cookie, a depressing concession to Anglo confusion about Asian cuisines and traditions. Still, I couldn't stop myself from opening it with attentive interest, as if I were expecting a personal message from the cookie factory: "Revenge his foul and most unnatural murder" or "Le Ly Haslip is a good read." What it said was "Sing before breakfast, cry before night." It sounded as if my grandmother had written it.

The bill hovered on the plate between us. More uncertainty: Did the man still pay?

He saw me eyeing it and grinned. "My treat, remember?" He took out his wallet and laid some bills on the plate. Then he looked at me. "So, where do we go from here?"

I studied my hands, searching for an answer. "I'm not sure," I told him finally. "Before I do anything, I have to figure out what the right thing is—

not just the expedient thing, but the right thing. Give me a day or so to sort it out, and then—"

"Caroline?"

"Yes?" I asked, surprised.

"That's not what I meant."

I looked up quickly, then down at my plate again. "Oh." I fiddled with the clasp of my watchband, and then I raised my eyes to his. "Steve has the children this weekend," I told him.

"Let's go."

The house was completely dark. I opened the door hesitantly, turning off the alarm and switching on the light in the hall. I sensed I was half expecting one of the kids or Steve or someone to come out of the darkness and stop what I was pretty sure was going to happen. It seemed inevitable. Even the doorknob had an erotic charge.

"Can I get you anything?" I asked him when we had gone inside. "Coffee? A drink?" My voice sounded hoarse.

"No, thank you." He smiled and touched a finger under my chin. "Caroline, you look so stricken. If you feel uncomfortable, I'll go home right now and that will be the end of it."

"The end of it?"

"For a day or two. I have to go to a conference in Rio in the morning."

"How early?" I put my arms around him and gave him a small, soft kiss on the mouth.

"Late. Very late." He pulled me close and kissed me back, a long, deep, fervent kiss. Our bodies seemed to rub together of their own accord. His warm breath was on my ear, my cheek, my throat. I moaned a little. His tongue found the inside of my mouth.

I managed to find my voice before I reached the point of no return. "I was married a long time," I told him in a whisper, "but I'm not very experienced." It seemed important, somehow, to say it.

"I'm not interested in experience," he said softly. "Can we go upstairs?"

Melmoth was dozing on the hand-painted bedspread, an illicit pleasure he accomplished by hiding in the closet when he was supposed to be outside. He blinked at us sleepily, so deep in some feline dream of raccoon-sized rats that he didn't even make his usual guilty lunge for the door. "Can I put him out?" David asked.

I nodded.

He picked him up, put him over his shoulder in a fireman's carry, and then set him down gently in the hall. An experienced cat handler.

He closed the door and turned to me, extending his arms. It seemed natural, inevitable, to step into them.

He stroked my hair softly. His touch was very light, and I felt safe and protected. I sensed that he was waiting for me to signal when I was ready for something more.

I took his hands, kissed his fingertips, and lifted them to my breasts.

Then I unbuttoned his shirt, very slowly, and pulled his undershirt up to his shoulders.

He pulled it off and dropped it on the floor. Then he helped me out of my dress and slip and bra. "You're beautiful," he told me, his voice husky. At that moment I believed it myself.

I reached for his zipper, but he stopped my hand. "You'd better let me," he said. "I don't need much more, and we don't want to rush."

I didn't need much more, either. I savored the delicious sensation of brushing my breasts against his naked chest as if it were the most rare and exquisite pleasure on earth. I clutched him and made small, low noises.

He led me to the bed and pulled down my underpants gently, with two fingers, before taking off his own. I was so moved by his tenderness. I looked at him and thought how foolish I had been to worry.

With his mouth, he traced a feathery line down my chest to my stomach and below. I pulled him up, twisted, and sought him. A wave of sensation caught me, and I stopped analyzing. My defenses were down. And that's when I learned that there were no tricks, no studied technique that mattered—only the lack of anger, and resentment, and fear. I could have wept with gratitude and joy.

"You're perfect," I told him afterward.

His lips brushed my forehead in the darkness. "So are you."

"We're both perfect," I said blissfully, extending my toe out through the bottom of the disheveled covers. "At least tonight."

"Caroline?"

"Mmmm?" I felt luxuriously sleepy and very sleek, like Scarlett O'Hara on the morning after.

"I want to stay, but I have to get up early tomorrow to pack, and I don't want to disturb you."

I turned on my side and touched his beard stubble with my finger. "If you want to go, go."

"I don't want to go." His hand drifted down along my hip.

"I'll set the alarm," I said.

20

    DEAR BARCLAY, Eleanor had written in the last, and saddest, letter in the file, *Except for the children, I am all alone. You have taken everything from me. You have destroyed my home, my possessions, and my family. You continue to attack me. My friends are all gone, and my dignity is in shreds. So what more do I have to lose? Your threats mean nothing to me. A law degree does not give you license to destroy, nor does it give you immunity from punishment. And you will be punished . . .*

The letter wasn't dated, and I didn't know whether she had ever sent it or not. I could imagine Barclay reading it, shivering with dread despite his manly bravado. It made me shiver, too. The utter hopelessness gave the last line a fateful certainty, an invocation of doom that Jeremiah might have envied.

Still, in the end the doom had been Eleanor's. Maybe Barclay would be punished and maybe not, but look what a price she had paid. If I was going to take over the role of avenging angel, I would have to be sure it didn't cost me as much. Unlike Eleanor, I did have something left to lose. I had to decide what to do next, and the next step could be a big one. Did I go to the police with nothing more than circumstantial evidence and a pile of hints? The SEC?

I even considered talking to Steve first, on the grounds that I might owe it to him in spite of everything, but on second thought I figured that would be foolhardy, and I had promised David I would be careful. Still, I'm ashamed to say that it also occurred to me that I might be able to trick him into admitting something. I had been turning the matter over in my mind ever since early morning, when David had kissed me good-bye and extracted my assurance I would not do anything rash in his absence.

"Why do you assume I'd do something rash?" I'd asked him.

To his credit, he forbore mentioning my breaking into the firm's legal files. "I know you, Caroline; you're dead set on proving how self-reliant you are," he told me. "Just swear to me you'll be careful."

"There's nothing wrong with being self-reliant," I protested, simultaneously flattered and annoyed. Still, I promised prudence. He gave me a number where I could reach him in Brazil, in case I needed him. I thought that a distance of many thousand miles would scarcely make him a very effective savior in the event that, for example, Barclay showed up at my door with a machete, but somehow the gift was still enormously comforting.

I wasn't sure whether it qualified as rash to try to pump the man I'd been married to for more than a decade, no matter how shabbily he'd treated me. Confronting the killer would be rash. Breaking into Naturcare's corporate headquarters would be rash.

Trying to pass myself off as a prospective buyer so I could get a real estate agent to let me into Eleanor's shuttered house in order to snoop around would be a little rash, although I considered it.

I rejected the idea regretfully because I remembered Barclay had told Eleanor's brother that after her death the firm had taken charge of all her documents to help "settle her affairs," so it would be pointless even to look. Besides, what was there left to find? David had said that somewhere there would be additional documentation of the side letter agreements, but I doubted they would be reposing in Eleanor's attic. More likely they were locked in the wall safe behind Mike and Cindi Meadows's stunning oversized Natkin (*their* decorator had good taste in paintings) or in some super-private legal file, safe from secretaries' prying eyes.

Talking to Steve probably wouldn't net a thing because I was sure that if he knew anything, he would stonewall it. Still, I was tempted, at least until I remembered that I hadn't spoken to him since the Three Musketeers had caught me red-handed in his office. Now *that* was odd. By rights he should have come storming in (well, I'd had the locks changed, but he would have at least pounded on the door) full of righteous ire. Why had I been spared that?

I began to wonder if something more sinister were afoot. Maybe he was gathering evidence against me, as he had hinted. Maybe Barclay, Henry, and Jeff (I winced at the thought) would give depositions about my instability. Henry would shake his head sadly, reluctantly disclosing that I had seemed so *upset*, so irrational on the subject of my husband. Jeff would say that I had developed nymphomaniacal tendencies brought on by excess book lust. Barclay . . .

The phone rang. I was almost relieved at the interruption. I glanced at my watch. At this hour it was probably too early for the weekly telemarketing blitz, an onslaught that usually drove me to turn on the machine. "Hello," I said briskly, just in case.

"Caroline James?" The voice was male and not fawning enough for a boiler-room operation. In fact, it sounded vaguely familiar.

"Speaking."

"This is Barclay Hampton."

My knees buckled and I sat down on the stool at the bar. My throat was so constricted I could barely squeak out a response. "Yes?"

"I'd like to talk to you." His voice was heavy with dislike. My blood was slamming in my ears, and I was finding it hard to breathe. The fight or flight syndrome had definitely kicked in.

"Wha-what about?" I asked unsteadily.

"Not on the phone," he said curtly. "I'd like to see you."

Flight, definitely. "No!"

"Why not?" He sounded exasperated, as if I were a truculent child. What had he thought I'd say— Sure, come on over; I'll jump into the hot tub? I wondered how he could possibly think I'd want to see him, knowing what I suspected him of. Well, maybe he didn't know as much as I thought. That comforted me, at least a little.

"I'm busy," I said, as firmly as I could. "I mean, I've got people here." A platoon of marines from Camp Pendleton, I wanted to tell him. A squad of jujitsu experts.

"Tomorrow, then."

"I don't think—" I began, trying to think of a

convincing way to say I was fully occupied until at least the year 2015.

"Oh, for Christ's sake." I heard a voice in the background, then his hand covered the receiver and he mumbled something. "Somewhere public, I meant," he said, returning to the phone. His voice lowered. "I can't talk now. Tomorrow. One o'clock. The Shorebird Café. It's important."

He hung up before I could tell him I would prefer to lunch with Jeffrey Dahmer, had he not been permanently indisposed. I held the receiver in my hand and punched in the firm's number. "Barclay Hampton, please," I asked the receptionist.

"Mr. Hampton is in a meeting," his secretary told me when the call had been put through. "Can I take a message or have him return your call?"

I was about to leave a message whose meaning would be unmistakable when I paused. If he meant to fillet me with a boning knife, he would probably not have called first to announce his intentions. I could put him off forever, or I could try to find out what he wanted. Maybe he was on a fishing expedition. Maybe I could learn something useful, something more to document my case.

"Hello?" said the secretary.

"No message," I told her.

If I were cautious, how dangerous could it be to meet him in a public place? All the same, I wanted backup. David was in Brazil, and I could hardly call Steve or anyone else in the firm. I absolutely refused to involve my children, and anyway, Steve was taking them to their grandparents'. I was entirely on my own, and while that thought didn't scare me as much as it once would have, it was hardly comforting, either. I looked out my front window, frowning. Across the street, Kenny was shirtless and bent over, apparently applying compost to the flowerbeds in precision doses. Even putrified plant matter looked tidy at Rob and Kenny's.

I raced across the street. "Hi," I said enthusiastically, despite Rob's warnings not to involve Kenny. "I'm glad I caught you home."

He straightened and smiled. "As a matter of fact I have the next couple of days off. What's up?"

I explained about meeting Barclay at the Shorebird Café. "I was hoping you could have lunch there—on me, of course—and just sort of keep an eye on things. Barclay wouldn't connect us, and I'd feel a lot better if I knew you were there."

"I guess I could do that," he said soberly. "Why did you agree to meet him?"

"I'm hoping he'll let something slip."

He raised his eyebrows. "It only works that way in the movies."

"Still," I insisted, "it's worth a try."

He shrugged. "Okay, but don't get your hopes up."

I looked at my feet. "There's something else."

He reached over and plucked his shirt from a low-hanging branch of the melaleuca tree. He put it on. "What?"

"I need a bug, or something like that." I was afraid to look at him.

"*What?*" he said again.

"I've got to get something down on tape, Kenny. I don't have enough evidence otherwise."

"Why don't you just ask to borrow my gun while you're at it?"

"Don't be angry. I'm desperate."

He sighed. "I'm not angry, Caroline." He wasn't, either. He was too good-natured. "But what you're asking is impossible. I can't give you police equipment to illegally record a conversation, no matter how justified you think it is, so don't ask me, okay?"

"All right," I agreed reluctantly. "Sorry." I would have to think of something else.

" 'S'okay." He picked up the trash barrel full of compost.

"The garden looks nice," I told him. I looked away, across the street at my house. Some of the bushes needed trimming, and the geraniums looked like they had bud worms. I sighed. "Are we still on for tomorrow?"

He grinned. "Sure. We'll go separately, and afterward I'll meet you in the parking lot."

"Thanks," I told him.

He hoisted the can with one muscular arm and walked toward the side of the house, opening the gate with his free hand. I turned to go home. "Caroline?"

"Yes?"

"Check out Radio Shack."

He disappeared around the side of the house before I could thank him again.

"I'm writing a mystery," I told the clerk at Radio Shack, "and I'd like to know how to record a conversation across a restaurant table without being detected."

His eyes glinted but his tone was pious. "I have to inform you that you are required by law to obtain the consent of the person being taped," he said.

"Okay," I told him, "but how would I do it?"

"Well," he leaned across the counter conspiratorially, his duty discharged. He looked like a devoted reader of science fiction novels. "For the really advanced technological stuff, you could go to the Spy Factory. They have everything."

"The Spy Factory?" I couldn't believe there really was a place with that name.

"Sure," he said enthusiastically. "Their equipment is *very* sophisticated. But you don't really need anything fancy." He walked over and picked up a tape recorder about the size of a pack of cigarettes off a shelf and handed it to me. It was heavy, but not uncomfortably so. "You could just put this in your pocket, press the button, and—" He spread his hands, palms up.

"No wires, no microphone?" I asked him.

His smile told me I was in the technological Dark Ages. "The microphone's built in, right there, see? That's all you need."

"And how far away will it pick up a conversation?"

He gestured at a partition about ten feet away. "At least to that wall," he said.

"How much?"

"One hundred fifty dollars."

"I'll take it."

He looked at me oddly.

"I want to study it," I added lamely, "for artistic accuracy."

"I'll ring it up," he said dryly.

I woke up Sunday morning after a largely sleepless night. I'd spent an unproductive few hours rehearsing various scenarios in my mind, all of them distinctly unattractive. I saw myself with my throat cut by Barclay's steak knife, strangled with Barclay's tie (Italian silk, naturally), or pierced by a bullet from Barclay's hit man (I gave him some credit).

Rational, daylight revision told me what I had told David—that however much Barclay disliked me, I couldn't quite see him as a stalker or some sort of homicidal maniac. If—when—he killed Eleanor, I imagined it must have been a spur-of-the-moment thing. I doubted he'd marched over to her house with a bunch of tranquilizers to jam down her throat, so maybe Eleanor had done most of the work for him already by doping herself up on booze and pills.

Maybe she taunted him with the side letter. I saw him standing over her in his perfectly tailored suit, disgusted with her bloated body, goaded to fury by all the trouble she had caused him and would cause him in the future. So he stooped.... Maybe he grabbed her feet and pulled her under, or just gave her a little shove as she was about to slide in anyway, like Gene shaking Finny off the tree limb in *A Separate Peace*.... Jesus, why was I thinking about literature at a time like this? Maybe David was right.

On the other hand, David had reminded me that threatened people are dangerous, and Barclay was definitely threatened by what I knew. He wouldn't have called me if something weren't up, and it was important to keep my guard up, whether Kenny was there or not.

Eleven thirty. Only an hour and a half to go.

I tried out various wardrobe articles for their efficacy in concealing recording devices and finally settled on a sweatshirt with front pockets over the stomach so I could slip my hands in and out without arousing attention. The sweatshirt was navy blue with a gold anchor logo, so I rounded out the nautical look with white pants and tennis shoes. It looked jaunty, and okay for the Shorebird Café.

Eleven forty-five. The phone rang. Kenny had promised to call to check in before we left so we could "synchronize our watches." I picked up the receiver. "Hi," I said. "I'm all set."

"Caroline?"

Not Kenny. "Yes?" I said impatiently.

"This is Henry Eastman. I'm afraid I've caught you at a bad time."

He caught me off balance. "Well, actually, I was just about to leave the house," I told him.

"I'm sorry. If you can spare me a few minutes, this won't take long."

I sat down on the chair, holding the phone gingerly. I felt as if I'd been caught by the principal. "Okay," I said, hoping I didn't sound as guilty as I felt.

"We didn't finish our conversation the other night." His voice was neutral, but my heart sank. The reckoning had come.

"I didn't realize—" I began lamely.

"I invited you to tell me if something was bothering you, and I haven't heard from you."

I hadn't realized it was a command performance. "There really isn't anything . . ."

"Caroline, I accepted your explanation the other night because you were obviously embarrassed at having been caught in Steve's office after hours, and I didn't want to make an issue of it in front of Barclay and Jeff. However, both of us know there was more to it than that, and I really must insist on an explanation. I've discussed the matter with Steve, and he seems to feel you might have been searching his office for documents or something of that nature." He lowered his voice to a serious whisper that was far more effective than a shout. "Your husband thinks it might have something to do with something Eleanor Hampton told you before she died."

"You—you talked to Steve?" was all I could manage to ask. I hadn't realized it till that moment: I'd had an absurd hope that somehow he wouldn't find out.

"Yes, and he was rather upset, as you can imagine. But don't worry, Caroline, I've calmed him down. I've told him I will handle it. But you must see that I have to get to the bottom of this, *now*."

As a matter of fact, I did see. The thing was, what was I going to tell him? I wondered if he had learned about the side letter and wanted to discover if I knew about it, too, if that was what this was really all about. I'd toyed once with the idea of telling him about it anyway, but it was my ace in the hole, and as long as I didn't know who was guilty of what, there was no point in tipping my hand. On the other hand, he clearly wasn't buying my story about my visit being a nostalgia excursion—Steve had seen to that—so I was going to have to tell him *something*. I took a deep breath.

"Henry, I swear to you—I *swear*—that all I did in Steve's office was look for a picture of us that used to be on his desk." Thank God that much at least was perfectly true. I fetched up a regretful little sigh. "But you're right; there is more to it than that."

"Go on," he said.

"I'm not sure where to start," I told him.

"Take your time," he said kindly, "but the beginning is usually best."

I drew a breath. "I know you are aware that Eleanor thought that Barclay was"—I almost said "screwing," but it seemed a little too crude for Henry—"mistreating her financially, with the connivance of the firm. She was certain that the amount of his compensation was artificially lowered so that the formula used to calculate his support payments to her and the children would be reduced. You probably realize she got more and more obsessed with the idea of lawyers and how they sc—mistreat their spouses in general."

"Oh, yes. She certainly made no secret of her feelings," Henry said.

"No, she didn't. And I met her—entirely by accident—at the end of the summer, and she seemed to feel that . . . well, that I might share those feelings. Steve and I had recently split up, and I think she wanted to warn me that what happened to her could happen to me, too." I shrugged, a little embarrassed. "I think what she really wanted was to convert me to her point of view."

"And did she?"

I hesitated. "Not entirely. She became so obsessed that she clearly lost perspective. But I have to tell you, Henry, I've learned a lot since I started looking into this, and one of the things I've learned is that she wasn't completely wrong, either. People who have an edge—and you definitely have the edge if you make the money and you know how to tweak the system to get what you want—can't always be trusted not to use that advantage unfairly."

"You're probably right," he admitted sadly.

"Anyway," I continued, "she sent me a whole box of materials documenting what she perceived were Barclay's injustices. She wanted me to write it up somehow, maybe as a warning to other women in the same situation. Quite honestly, I really didn't want to get involved in anything like that at all. It made me very uncomfortable. I'd tried to put her off, but in a few days the box arrived anyway. I didn't even open it until after she died." I looked at my watch. It was noon. I was going to have to hurry this up.

"I take it you found something in this box that caused you some concern?" Henry asked gently.

"Well, yes. Mostly there were embarrassing letters to and from Eleanor and Barclay and their respective lawyers, but some of the documents had to do with his compensation and his bonus." I waited to see if he would react, but he didn't say anything. I could not shake the suspicion that he was not hearing all this for the first time. I cleared my throat. "What I believe is, Eleanor was right about what Barclay had done." I lowered my voice conspiratorially. "Henry, she had private investigator reports."

There was a long silence. "That is outrageous," he said finally.

"You mean—"

"I can't be sure until I examine the documents myself, but if what you say is true, it's despicable." He sounded genuinely disgusted. "No wonder you were so angry at her funeral."

I hadn't known it showed that much. Now that he was somewhat more sympathetic, it was time to segue into my nocturnal ramblings at Eastman Bartels. "Well, it's too late for Eleanor of course. But the thing is, Henry, you can see how I might worry that the same thing could happen to me. Other women warned me, too. So when Susan said she had to stop in at the firm that night, I thought maybe I could find something in Steve's files about his bonus or . . ." I sniffed a little. "I'm so embarrassed, Henry. I was thinking about going through his drawers. But I promise you I didn't do it." I let out a breath of relief. Everything I had told him was more or less true, and I hoped the story would be enough to satisfy him.

"I'm very glad you told me, Caroline," he said in a much more friendly tone. "You can see that I had to find out the truth."

"Yes, of course," I told him.

"And *I* can see how you might have been worried," he conceded. "Naturally I don't wish to interfere in your personal relationship with Steve, but if you will trust me to handle certain things for you, as he has done, I think I can guarantee that what appears to have happened to Eleanor will not happen to you. I've tried to say as much to you before, but I can see now that you might have had cause not to believe me. I'm very sorry about that."

"Thank you, Henry. That's very kind of you. If it's all right with my lawyer, it's all right with me."

Silence. I wondered if he'd forgotten I would have one. "Well, that's that, then. Case closed. I assume, of course, that this will put an end to any further investigations as well." He said it lightly, but I nevertheless heard the warning note.

"There wouldn't be much point, would there?" I countered.

"None whatsoever," he said firmly.

I glanced at my watch again and discovered I was going to be late for my meeting with Barclay if I didn't leave in the next thirty seconds. "I'm so sorry, Henry, but I really have to run. I'm already late as it is."

"Lunch date?" He sounded amused.

"Something like that," I told him.

When he had hung up, I dialed Kenny. "Sorry. I got tied up. I'm out the door."

"Okay," he said calmly. "No problem. I'm leaving right now." He paused. "Relax, Caroline. You're breathing so hard I can hear it over the phone. It's not too late to change your mind."

I shook my head, then realized he couldn't see me. "No, I want to go," I told him.

"Right. Meet you there."

As I was stepping out, the phone rang again. I hesitated, then shrugged. "Screw it," I said and closed the door.

21

THE SHOREBIRD CAFÉ was funky and unpretentious, with a world-class view of the yacht harbor and the open water. The food was nothing special, standard fare for restaurants where people come more for the atmosphere than the cuisine. Still, on a Sunday afternoon it was a popular lunch spot, and I had to wait ten minutes to get a table. Kenny was more fortunate. He was sitting with his back to the window, facing almost the entire room, a perfect site for surveillance. I could see him from where I sat, studying the menu while the waitress studied him.

By the time I was seated, Barclay was fifteen minutes late. I toyed with a cup of coffee for a while until the frequency of the waitress's visits to inquire if I was ready to order became impossible to ignore. I ordered a chicken salad, one of the oriental kind with sesame dressing. By the time it came, Barclay was more than a half hour late.

The salad wasn't bad, but I didn't feel much like eating. Across the room, Kenny consumed what appeared to be an extra-large club sandwich and french fries, though without my glasses I couldn't be positive. I twirled my fork around and around on my plate and thought about what I would say to Barclay if he showed up. I doubted if he would oblige me by confessing on tape, but maybe he would let something drop that would help persuade the police or the SEC that they had a case. At least he hadn't become a judge. There was still enough vestigial respect for the bench that it would have been even harder to convince anyone then.

There was something about the judge business that troubled me. If you thought about it, all the talk about becoming one is what had set Eleanor off in the first place. She was outraged. Judges don't make as much as big-time corporate attorneys, and Barclay had rubbed her nose in the fact that now she was going to have to accept less in support. That was probably when she started looking for something to use against him, and somehow she got hold of the Naturcare side letter. Maybe she had found it when she searched the firm's files, but I doubted it. More likely she copied Barclay's personal files before he moved out, or broke into his new house and stole it from there. I wouldn't have put anything past her.

Anyway, once she had something to blackmail him with, she must have threatened him with exposing his fraud if he didn't come up with a significant amount of money. The trouble was, he wouldn't *have* a lot of money if he left the practice and took judges' robes, even if you consider the tidy sum he'd already socked away as a result of Naturcare. He could hardly ask the firm to pony up more without confessing, and he most certainly wouldn't have wanted to do that. It was clear that his continued prosperity depended on staying in the corporate game, and what troubled me was that

I really couldn't understand why he'd wanted to leave it in the first place. He was Mr. Big Shot at Eastman, Bartels, and Mike and Cindi Meadows weren't about to blow the whistle on him. More likely they would steer even more business his way.

I didn't buy the story about wanting to spend more time with Tricia and the kids, either. Tricia was admittedly a pretty luscious type to spend time with, but Barclay just wasn't a hearth-and-home kind of guy. Over the years I'd heard a lot of male lawyers complain about not having enough time to be with their families, but it seemed more like a mantra than an expression of true regret. If Barclay had had more time off, ten to one he would have spent it on the tennis court. It was the life he was meant to live. But I just couldn't see him consorting with felons and scofflaws, even from the right side of the bench.

I didn't have the answer. I looked at my watch. Barclay was almost an hour late. The waitress came and cleared my plate away, along with the extra place setting. She gave me a pitying look and asked if she should bring the check. I nodded. It was bad enough to be stood up, but being stood up by a *murderer* had to be some kind of lifetime low.

I suppose I should have been grateful, but what I really felt was depressed. I'd been sure this was a break, a chance to get something on tape that would help my case. Even a threat would have done nicely. Now I was back to where I was before Barclay called: wondering what to do.

I paid the bill and went out into the parking lot. Kenny was already there. "Sorry," I told him. "I wasted your time."

He smiled. "No problem. It was a great sandwich."

I fished into my purse and handed him fifteen dollars. "Will that cover it?" I asked him.

He put up his hand. "No, really, Caroline, I don't want it."

"I insist," I told him glumly. "My treat."

"Don't take it so hard," he said soothingly. "If you're going to play detective, you have to be prepared for disappointments like this." He put his hands in his pockets. "To tell you the truth, I'm sort of relieved. I didn't much like the idea anyway." He pulled out his keys. "Is there anything more you want me to do?"

"No, that's it. I appreciate this, Kenny; I really do."

"Right. I'll take off, then, if you don't mind. I got a call to come in this afternoon after all, so I have to get going."

"Okay. Thanks," I told him.

He opened the car door. "Caroline?"

"What?"

"Go straight home, okay?"

"In case Barclay's really lurking around like Dracula with a defective watch?"

He didn't smile. "Just . . . in case. It would make me feel better."

I made an X over my chest with my finger. "Cross my heart and hope to—" I laughed. "Well, anyway, I'm going," I said.

I meant to go straight home; I really did. I didn't think Barclay was going to show up an hour and a half late, but I wasn't about to court disaster, either. Or at least I didn't plan to. But I was walking toward my car, keys in hand, when it occurred to me that the Shorebird Café wasn't more than a few hundred feet from where the firm yacht was moored. And the firm yacht had a very large filing cabinet.

The *Legiti-mates* (I know, I know. It's corny, but it's better than *Counselors-at-Sea* or *Sea-Legals*, or some of the other candidates. In general, though, I react to boat names like personalized license plates: When people are most convinced they're being cute, they usually aren't.) was ostensibly for entertaining clients in luxury and privacy, like a private club. It was fitted out with all the appurtenances of the office—fax, phones, computers, and a little bunk area for the secretaries—as well as the usually yachtish things like a nice galley and a lot of gorgeous wood. The main enclosed area had been made into a conference room with a scaled-down table and chairs.

Most of the "business" conducted on board seemed to be done with wine glasses and hors d'oeuvres in hand. Like other notable law firm business meetings—the Acapulco cruise, for example, or the Aspen ski weekend—the work agenda seemed to be dispensed with rather quickly, although, for tax purposes, the ritual was always diligently observed. The pure entertainment functions, the partners insisted, really saved the firm time and money over expensive and unpredictable restaurants and hotels. I had always suspected that a certain amount of extramarital hanky-panky occurred on board as well, but I couldn't prove it.

The truth is, I didn't want to go anywhere near the *Legiti-mates*, but I knew I would despise myself as a coward if I didn't. Nobody was going to want to act on my story without some hard evidence, no matter how suggestive the circumstances or enticing my theory. David might be able to convince the SEC to look into things, and that was certainly a plus, but I didn't really think much beyond that would happen without something more than what I already had on Barclay. I wasn't sure what the likelihood would be of finding anything worthwhile in a place so accessible to all the partners in the firm, but I didn't have anything else going in the investigation department, and I was frustrated by my inability to get the goods on Barclay at lunch. Besides, if you wanted to meet with a client clandestinely, the yacht was the perfect spot.

For my purposes, the best thing about it was that I wouldn't even have to break and enter, at least not until I got to the files. Henry and Pamela Eastman mostly used it as their private yacht, but in the name of, if not democracy, oligarchy at least, all the partners had keys. Said key was still reposing on my key ring, the relict of happier times. So I could just slip on board and peruse the files for anything Barclay and the Meadowses might have cooked up on Naturcare, particularly something that tied him more definitively to the side letter. It would take ten minutes, max. My nerves were shouting "flight" again, but I had to at least try it.

It was Sunday afternoon and the boat docks were crowded. I slipped my key authoritatively into the lock on the gate and joined the rubber-soled throng carrying ice chests and hampers for parties on board. There were a number of boats leaving the dock under power and heading out into the harbor, but the *Legiti-mates* was still moored in her slip. I scanned the deck for possible occupants, but the boat was empty-looking and quiet. If there was a tryst going on below decks, I would have to take my chance on bluffing it out.

On the theory that the best way to avoid attracting attention was to avoid slinking along as if I were up to something, I stepped smartly up to the yacht and hoisted myself over the low railing onto the deck. I unlocked the door without difficulty (a Grand Banks is like a Mercedes—everything works) and closed the door behind me, descending the steps into the cabin. It was dark and apparently uninhabited. I let out a big breath of relief. I went to the window on the side away from the dock and pulled back the curtain to let in some light.

The filing cabinet was at one end of the conference table. It was three legal-sized drawers tall, so with luck I could look through the contents in under half an hour. I didn't even hesitate. Maybe it was just easier the second time, like sex and murder. I reached for the top drawer and pulled.

It was locked.

Damn. So much for Nancy Drew. Forcing it open or picking the lock was out of the question; I lacked the strength or the skill for either. If I couldn't find the key somewhere on board, I would have to give up. Still, I was not unhopeful. Nobody would want to carry a file key around all the time, so there was a good chance it was someplace close at hand. I put my purse down on one of the chairs and scrutinized the room for possible hiding places. I looked in the drawers, under the cushions, anywhere I could think of. Finally I tipped over a leather pencil holder, spilling a pile of pens and paper clips onto the table surface. Sure enough, a file key was in the bottom.

The Naturcare documents were right there in the top drawer, stuffed into a brown accordion file that looked thick with possibility. There was a copier on board, too, so I could just look through, copy anything I thought might be helpful, and replace the file. It was going to be easy. My hand closed around the file and pulled it out of the drawer. . . .

The yacht, unmistakably, moved.

The dockside portholes and windows were still covered with curtains, so I couldn't see anything, but the boat's movement could mean only one thing: Someone had jumped on board. I looked around wildly for someplace to hide, slamming the file drawer shut with my elbow as I turned. I pulled one of the curtains back across the porthole, but I had to leave the other. It was too late to do anything about the unlocked door. The best I could hope for was that it was just the caretaker or someone checking things out.

The only reasonable hiding place was what—for reasons that are unclear—in nautical parlance is called "the head." Despite the yacht's luxurious appointments, it was incredibly cramped. I put the lid down and planted my feet as best I could around the toilet, still clutching the sheaf of Naturcare papers. Fear and proximity made me yearn to use the facilities, but I didn't dare. I was scarcely breathing as it was.

Minutes passed, filled with muffled noises. I could feel, as much as hear, someone moving about the boat. After a while I heard the door open, and footsteps descending the steps. I held my breath and shut my eyes, as if that would prevent my being seen. My muscles were knotted and tense with the effort of holding still in my foxhole, but in spite of my efforts my knee started shaking. I opened my eyes and regarded it clinically, like a stranger I had no relation to.

The footsteps paused and a light switched on. I could see it around the edges of the door. More muffled sounds. The footsteps came closer.

I breathed a prayer. *Don't let it be Barclay.*

Silence.

The footsteps retreated. The light went out.

Relief left me sweating and feeble. I slumped against the bathroom door, taking the pressure off my twitching knees.

I only had a minute or two to enjoy it. I heard the clink of cable and metal and seconds later the *Legitimates's* engine came to life. I stood there, trapped, while the boat lifted and settled into a steady thrum of vibration. The yacht was leaving the dock and heading out toward the open sea.

22

~I FELT SO incredibly dumb, like one of those heroines in Gothic novels who get themselves into idiotic situations because of their failure to heed the warning signs. *Think*, I told myself, but I couldn't. I couldn't decide whether to make a break for it and jump over the side while we were still close to shore, stay in the head and hope nobody on board consumed too much Chardonnay or soft drinks, or emerge and try somehow to brazen it out. I wasn't pleased by any of the scenarios. Barclay Hampton topped the list of people I didn't want to find myself on the boat with, but I couldn't imagine encountering a single individual from Eastman, Bartels—even someone presumably more favorably disposed toward my person—without the most hideous embarrassment. What was I going to say, that I had had a sudden yearning for one more spin around the harbor on the firm yacht?

On the other hand, as big as it was, the *Legitimates* wasn't exactly the QE2, and I doubted I could just slip off the stern undetected. Besides, every minute I hesitated made that a less attractive option.

But if I stayed, sooner or later, he (or she) might need to use the head. . . .

The air was definitely getting stale inside my water closet, and my muscles were screaming for relief. I began to realize that it might not be possible to last out an entire cruise in my hiding place, whatever else might happen. After a few more minutes, I was sure of it. I might pass out if I stayed there much longer.

I heard a faint voice calling my name.

It seemed too early for an angelic summons, but hallucinations were definitely in the realm of possibility. I decided to open the door and get some air, no matter what greeted me on the outside.

I lifted the handle and pushed it open about six inches. I heard it again: *Come out, Caroline*.

No hallucination. The jig, as they say, was definitely up. For good measure, I closed the door again and used the toilet. I wasn't sure about flushing it inside the harbor, so I put the lid down and left it.

I still had the Naturcare documents in my hand, but when I tried to put them away, the cabinet was locked again. I almost left the file on top, but then I took it topside with me. In for a penny, in for a pound.

Henry Eastman was standing behind the wheel, holding my wallet in his hand. I let out my breath. Bad enough, but not as bad as Barclay. My heart slowed down a little. My purse, whose existence I had forgotten until that moment, was open beside him on the seat.

"I'm sorry to have gone through your purse, Caroline, but you left it on one of the conference chairs down below," he said levelly, without apparent irony. He dropped the wallet into the purse and handed it to me.

I considered answering him with some kind of ghastly archness, but I opted for simple shame instead. "Henry, I don't know what to say. I'm so embarrassed—"

He held up his hand to stop me and then extended it for the file. I passed it to him wordlessly. He glanced at it and then put the whole thing into a wooden locker at his feet. "Sit down, Caroline," he said politely.

The shore was getting farther away. "And now I've ruined your afternoon cruise as well," I said as brightly as I could manage. "After this, you certainly won't want me anywhere near you. I'm afraid you'll have to take me home." I was close to babbling, but the entire situation made me too nervous for fluency.

"On the contrary, I'm delighted you're here. It gives us an opportunity to talk, and I'm sure you'll agree there are some things we need to discuss." He didn't sound angry or sorrowful. In fact, he sounded vaguely amused.

"Henry, I—"

"Not now, Caroline," he said firmly. "And do, please, sit down."

I sat. This was his show, and I really didn't have any choice but to let him conduct it the way he wanted to.

"I've always loved boats," he said, looking out over the water. "When I was a young associate at a firm in New York, I used to get away to the island whenever I could so I could take one out. Anything, from Sunfish on up. There was a little place that would rent them by the half or whole day." He laughed. "I could only afford half-day, but I made the most of it." He looked at me. "I used to dream about two things: having my own boat and having my own law firm. Not necessarily in that order."

He seemed to expect me to say, "And now you've got both," so I did.

He smiled. "Well, technically the yacht belongs to the firm, but I suppose that's only fitting. In most of the ways that are important, I am the firm, or I should say that the firm is me. I don't mean that in some monomaniacal sense, that other people aren't vital to Eastman, Bartels, too. We all contribute. But when you put as much of your life and hopes as I have into something, it can't help but start to define you."

Under the circumstances I couldn't think of any reason why he should be cordially unveiling his life's ambitions, so I examined him closely for signs of tippling. He might be highly competent as a lawyer, but drunk driving in a Grand Banks yacht was not terribly dissimilar to drunk driving in a Bentley. In both cases, I would just as soon walk. His eyes were clear, however, and he looked tanned and alert.

He saw me scrutinizing him and chuckled. "I used to be in the Coast Guard, you know, before I went to law school. You'll be perfectly safe. Would you like something to drink? There are beer and soft drinks in the refrigerator. There's a sandwich, too, if you'd like it. And some pâté and crackers."

"No, thanks," I told him. His politeness was unnerving, as it was no doubt meant to be. I was glad I had worn a sweatshirt. It was cold out on the water. A sea lion swam across the bow and hauled itself up with some effort onto a buoy, displacing a smaller rival from the chosen spot. I watched it, waiting for whatever came next. I knew he was working around to an interrogation. I shivered a little.

Henry turned the boat slightly so that we were heading directly out of the harbor. I looked at my watch. "I can't stay out too long, Henry," I told him. "Steve will be dropping off the children in a couple of hours."

He shot me an amused glance but said nothing. Well, it was hardly a normal social occasion, so what could I expect? We sailed along in apparent amity, absorbed in the views of the skyline and the blue horizon. It was a war of nerves and he was winning.

Just when I thought I couldn't stand it another second, he asked me, "What were you looking for down below?" His voice was so bland he might have been discussing the color of one of Pamela's floral centerpieces.

I shook my head.

"I think you should know," he added almost apologetically, before I could say anything at all, "that I had already determined that the Naturcare documents were missing from the file cabinet."

I respected his delicacy in letting me know up front that there was no point in lying. I looked at him.

He met my eyes. "I could have you arrested," he said, abruptly changing his tone.

That's when I realized that Henry was using his litigator tactics on me. He was admittedly a master, but I decided to fight back.

"Bullshit," I told him.

He looked as if he had never heard the word in his life. "What did you say?"

"You heard me. All the partners have keys, Henry. I might have been stretching it a little to use the one Steve and I have, but I doubt you could get a conviction."

He raised his eyebrows expressively. "The file?" he suggested.

I shrugged. "I found it on the floor. Maybe someone was careless about putting it back. I brought it up to you because I thought you might want it."

To my surprise, he threw back his head and laughed. "My dear Caroline, I really do admire your nerve. I wish you would trust me. I've tried to tell you several times already that I honestly do have your best interests at heart."

"You mean you have the firm's best interests at heart."

"Well, certainly. But in this case it is apparent to me that the two are one and the same."

I said nothing.

"Come, Caroline, it is obvious by now that the late, unmourned Eleanor has bequeathed you something that has you very interested in Naturcare. That is the object of all this . . . ah . . . shall we say, 'amateur sleuthing,' isn't it?"

I still remained silent. I felt as if I was in the witness box, taking the Fifth.

Henry sighed. "Well, all right, then, Caroline, let's be honest. The only thing about Naturcare that could possibly be worth all of this interest is the side letter. I take it you've stumbled onto that."

"You know about it?" I asked. I wondered how long he had known and if he had guessed at the rest of it. If he had, would he protect Barclay?

"We'll get to that in a moment," he said impatiently. "Right now, I really need to know *what* you know and, more importantly, what you're going to do about it. I—we—all of us need time to prepare. I'm not sure you realize that doing something drastic could have enormous financial repercussions that could swamp your little boat along with ours.

Before you take any action, I think we ought to discuss it; that's all."

I decided to play along, at least a little. "I don't really know that much about it, Henry," I told him. "I just know enough to realize that it might get Barclay and Mike and Cindi in big trouble, and it would probably interest the SEC. I take it that's what you meant by 'doing something drastic.' "

I thought he looked a little pale. "That would definitely qualify," he said dryly. "I'd like to avoid that, if possible."

I just bet he would. "I guess it wouldn't look very good for the firm if one of its partners got that kind of negative publicity." The sun went behind a cloud and I shivered again. I put my hands in my sweatshirt pocket. My fingers touched the metal of the little tape recorder. Until that minute, I'd forgotten all about it. What a detective.

Henry ran his fingers through his hair. "There's a lot more to it than that."

I ran my thumb along the edge, feeling for the switch, just in case. "I'm listening, as long as the solution isn't that the whole thing just gets dropped."

He looked out to sea, where the Coronados, the offshore islands inhabited mainly by goats and crabs, loomed with a startling clarity. They were at least fifteen miles away but looked close enough to swim to. "What if," he began, in such a quiet, gentle voice that I had to strain to hear him, "this could all be taken care of without involving the SEC? What if, in fact, it has already been taken care of?"

"What do you mean, 'taken care of'?" I asked him. I pressed the recorder switch. Okay, maybe it wasn't strictly ethical, but this could be evidence, and I needed David to help me evaluate it.

"We are speaking hypothetically, of course." He looked at me. I didn't answer. He sighed. "You see, the problem with bringing in the SEC is that the issue could be a bit more complicated than you imagine. What if, for example, there were a particularly zealous young summer associate working on Naturcare matters who discovered the side letter you mentioned? It's not illegal, you know, to do business that way, so long as one doesn't get greedy and include these agreements as solid contracts so that it puffs up the asset column when you go public. What if, let us say, this associate, noting the arrangement by which Naturcare's agreements with department stores are cancelable at any time, in all innocence writes a memo to all the partners describing the way Naturcare does its business? Now, in the event of some"—his face darkened and twisted in a spasm of fury—"asinine attempt to jack around with the Registration Statement, it would appear that the entire partnership was in on the fraud."

"Even if no one but Barclay knew anything about that part of it?" I asked him.

He shrugged. "Naturally we would protest our innocence. We would point out that the memo did not circulate until after the Registration Statement had been prepared. But malpractice insurance companies, like your friend Eleanor, are notoriously unsympathetic to lawyers, particularly when it's an issue of millions of dollars in claims."

I remembered the memo I had found in Barclay's file, instructing the partners to purge their files of some unnamed earlier document. Susan had told me that Henry dictated it to her rather than to a secretary, although she hadn't seen anything in it that would necessitate such privacy. I thought I did, now.

"You could remove the offending memo from the partners' files," I suggested.

He looked surprised, then pleased, as if he had found me an apt pupil. "You could do that," he agreed, "but sooner or later it would come out. Too many people in a law firm get their hands on things." He looked at me speculatively. "Would you like to take the wheel? It's very easy to steer."

"No, thank you. And anyway, we should be turning back soon."

"Soon," he said absently. He drummed his fingers along the teak railing. A seagull flew past, swooping down briefly to see if we were giving any handouts. Disappointed, it sped on. "Do you know what would happen if the hypothetical matter we were discussing were somehow to come to the attention of the SEC?" he asked. "The first thing that would happen is that the stock price of Naturcare would fall, probably disastrously. That would be a shame because the company is very solid, and there is every indication that the contracts with the department stores will not be canceled."

He sighed. "The next thing would be a large shareholder suit against the company. People don't like to see the value of their shares plummet in the best of circumstances, and this would hardly be that. Mike and Cindi could be wiped out, of course. That wouldn't bother me too much—they probably deserve it—except that we have too much tied up in Naturcare as a client. But what would also happen is a suit against the law firm for malpractice, and if there is any evidence of our knowledge that would suggest collusion, we would never get the insurance company to cover us." He reached over and touched my wrist, briefly. His hand was very cold. "I'm talking *millions*, Caroline. It could wipe out everything we had. Not just Barclay, but everyone. *Steve*. Everybody."

I shuddered. David had warned me, but Henry made it seem much more real.

"And if by some miracle we could convince the insurance company that it was Barclay's fraud alone," he continued relentlessly, "what do you think would happen to the firm anyway? Our reputation would be tarnished forever. We'd look like either villains or fools. Think about it, Caroline. Would you really want that to happen?"

"Of course I wouldn't want it to happen," I told him, "but—"

"So *if* the matter could be settled without involving all those complications," he said, overriding my objection, "I'm sure you see that would be for the best."

"You *do* mean just forget about it," I said.

"Certainly not." He sounded indignant. "Certain . . . remedies could be taken to insure that the Meadowses would live up to their obligations in the future. An overeager young associate could be found a lucrative partnership at a firm in Honolulu. That sort of thing."

"And Barclay?" I asked him.

His face got red again. I thought he was going to burst a capillary, one already close to the surface from years of vodka tonics. I saw how truly, awesomely angry he was at Barclay for getting the firm into this fix. "Even if the client *insists*, threatens to take away its business, that is no excuse for—" He broke off suddenly, as if he were appalled by his unrestrained outburst. "Well, Barclay would be dealt with," he said after a moment. His emotions were once more under control, his voice steady. "Eased out, naturally. There should be an opening on the municipal court bench later in the year, and—"

"It was *your* idea to make him a judge?" I asked, almost dumbstruck by this revelation.

He looked startled. "Well, I couldn't have him compromising the law firm." He spoke entirely without irony. He seemed to take my silence for assent. "Look, Caroline, you are an intelligent woman. Reasonable, too. You must see it would not be in your best interest, or that of your children, to start something none of us can stop once it gets going. Why don't you trust me to set things right, to handle things in the best way? I know that you can expect a generous—no, a very generous—settlement from Steve, and I wouldn't want anything to jeopardize that. Not bringing up the matter before the SEC would certainly be worth something to the firm." He paused, to let his simultaneous offer of a bribe and blackmail sink in.

"Aren't you forgetting something?"

"What is that?" He sounded puzzled.

"Eleanor is dead."

"Ah." He swept a hand through his beautiful silver hair. "That is regrettable. But I don't see how it's germane."

I discovered I had a temper, too. "I'll tell you how it's germane, Henry," I said angrily. "I'll put *you* a 'what if.' What if Barclay killed her to keep her from telling anyone about Naturcare?"

"That's ridiculous." His face was ashen. I couldn't tell whether it was from anger or distress. His cheek muscle twitched.

I wondered if telling him my suspicions was really wise, but I had blurted it out before I thought. After I considered it, it seemed as if it might be a good way to see how much he knew, whether he could add anything to the blotter. The recorder was running. "I'm sorry, but it's not ridiculous. There is every reason to believe it's true. You've just given him a powerful motive, haven't you?"

"It's unfounded nonsense." He spat the words out, as if he could not bear to have them in his mouth any longer than necessary. "If everyone who had a motive to murder someone else were brought to trial, the courts would be backlogged for the next century and a half. There isn't a shred of evidence to suggest that the woman didn't just combine too many happy pills with a fine bottle of wine. If I were drinking a Bâtard-Montrachet '85, I'd make damn sure I finished the bottle, too." He wiped his forehead with the back of his hand. "Maybe it was an accident; maybe she intended it. Maybe she only half intended it. She was certainly miserable enough, God knows. We'll probably never know for sure. But I do know that there is no reason to believe Barclay had anything to do with it, even if he prayed out loud for her death in the middle of Prospect Street every single night."

My pulse accelerated rapidly, so that I felt a little dizzy. I hoped I wasn't going to get seasick. "He was there on the afternoon of Eleanor's death, Henry. He was seen talking to her by the hot tub."

He looked stunned. "Barclay was seen?" His voice was hoarse.

Something was bothering me about this entire conversation—that is, something more than having to tell Henry that one of his partners was probably a murderer and that the law firm that gave his entire life meaning was headed for trouble. I couldn't put my finger on what it was. It made me irritable. "Well, someone was seen bending over her while she sat drunk and naked in the water. Someone in a suit. Who else could it have been but Barclay?"

He shuddered. I could see it travel the length of his body. He looked out to sea. "Who else indeed?" he asked quietly.

All those synapses in my brain were working overtime, struggling to make a connection. The bytes of information were heading toward some great inductive synthesis. I could feel it. Suddenly my heart thudded so hard in my chest I had to sit down.

I had it now. *How had he known the wine was Bâtard-Montrachet '85?*

Henry looked at me with concern. "Are you all right?"

No, I wasn't. In my first conversation with Rob about Eleanor's death, he had made it very clear that the police weren't giving out details from the scene, like what kind of wine she'd been drinking or the fact that she'd flapped out to the hot tub in ghastly pink mules. He wasn't supposed to know it himself. If you didn't count the police force or the people Kenny and Rob and I had inadvertently told (like the wine shop clerk), the only person who could know about the Bâtard-Montrachet would be somebody who'd been at the crime scene himself.

Somebody like Eleanor's killer.

23

My FIRST THOUGHT was *How could I have been so stupid?* I'd been so obsessed with Barclay's treatment of Eleanor that I had yearned to pin her death on him, and I'd refused to consider any other possibility. Henry had just painted a gruesome picture of the firm's future after news of the side letter got out, and nothing meant more to Henry than the firm. He'd as much as said so himself. If I hadn't been blinded by prejudice and my own divorce jitters, I would have at least considered that his motive and opportunity were equal to Barclay's.

I remembered the letter in Eleanor's papers where Barclay tried to convince her she had "misunderstood the whole thing," meaning, as I now supposed, the side letter. He must have really been sweating. Maybe when he realized she wasn't going to back down, he panicked and told Henry that Eleanor had found out. Eleanor might even have told Henry herself; she certainly wouldn't have had any idea he already knew, and if she hoped to blackmail the firm . . .

"Caroline?" Henry was looking at me with concern.

I was trying to keep my face absolutely impassive, despite the images that were galloping through my brain.

My second thought was *Nobody knows I'm here.*

"Are you all right?" he asked again.

I forced myself to concentrate on sounding normal. "A little seasick, I guess," I told him. "If you don't mind, I'd really like to go back to shore now." I tried to keep the edge of desperation out of my voice. The wake of a passing trawler rolled the boat a little, and I shifted my footing. Henry remained immobile, watching me. We were almost to the mouth of the harbor, where the water was choppy around the end of Point Loma. It was the only place near the shore where people occasionally drowned if their boats capsized.

I remembered how, at Eleanor's funeral, Barclay had told Eleanor's brother that Henry had offered the firm's services in wrapping up her affairs. Were they looking for the side letter? Suddenly a wave of anger hit me right in the chest. After I told Steve that Eleanor had sent me some documents, he had made a search of my office, and then someone had broken into the garage. Even Jeff had interrogated me, under the guise of . . . had Henry orchestrated the whole thing? How much did Steve know? I tried not to hyperventilate.

"Caroline!" Henry commanded my attention.

I looked at him, and my anger shriveled into a cold lump at the bottom of my stomach, replaced by fear. His look had changed from concern to . . . what? "Calculation" was the closest I could come. *He knows,* I thought.

"When you've been in courts for as long as I

have, you develop a sixth sense about your witnesses," Henry said. He sounded calm, even serene,
but he started compulsively rubbing his left arm.
"You know when they're lying, when they're hiding something. You have to be able to look into their
minds and know *what they're thinking*, Caroline." He
looked so intensely into my face, I almost believed
he could do it. I had to struggle not to avert my
eyes.

"I'm not a witness, Henry," I said, striving for a
jocular tone. I failed.

"No, but you think you know something."

"I don't know what you're talking about," I told
him.

"Don't bother denying it, Caroline," he said with
artificial patience. "Ordinarily it would be pointless
to bring this up, but only the two of us are here,
and I can see quite plainly that I've said or done
something to excite your suspicions. I don't know
what it was right now, but no doubt it will come to
me presently. Right now you've transferred your
theory about Barclay to me, and there are some
things I need to make clear to you."

I thought about saying "Don't be ridiculous," but
the words crumbled in my throat. I clutched the
railing tightly with my hand, considering flight. I
didn't much fancy the idea of a long swim back to
shore or of getting dashed against the breakwater
rocks. On the other hand, the tape was still going,
and maybe Henry would confess, thinking we were
alone.

"Really, Caroline, you are being far too melodramatic about this entire thing," Henry said, observing my stricken countenance with apparent
amusement. "This isn't *Columbo*. No one is going to

gratify you by confessing to having a hand in Eleanor's death."

Jesus, maybe he really could read minds. I thought it prudent to remain silent.

"There is something called 'admission against interest' that could incriminate anyone who, for example, concurred in such an interpretation of the facts, even if no one else was around to overhear. Do not for a moment believe that that will happen." He was detached and authoritative, as if I were a young associate being instructed in the intricacies of the tax code.

"I am a very good lawyer," he continued. "This is not precisely my field, but nevertheless I am going to give you some excellent free legal advice. No matter what you think you have on me or Barclay, you do not have a case. 'Flimsy' would be a compliment for the sort of evidence you were talking about. Any D.A. who even considered taking it on would be laughed out of practice. First, there is no evidence of homicide. Second, if a man in a suit was seen bending over the hot tub, that doesn't mean he was a killer. In short, with regard to Eleanor's death, you have nothing whatsoever. Shall I go on?"

"No," I told him. Despite his assumption of command, he looked sweaty and rather gray. "Let's go back now."

"Not yet. There's something I want to make plain. If anyone were to make . . . accusations, I would be forced to protect my reputation by instigating an immediate libel suit. The person making the accusations would probably lose. At the very least she would be exposed as a lonely, paranoid, middle-aged woman with an ax to grind against lawyers, someone not unlike Eleanor herself." His voice was soft. "You must see that it would not be in either of our interests that such an action be brought. It could expose a lot of damaging things on both sides. But I would be *forced* to. I'd have no choice."

He was trying to bully me, but I was going to pretend to let him do it, at least till we got safely back to shore. I was just about to open my mouth when a swell caught the boat hard, causing me to lose my footing and lurch against the railing.

Henry's eyes were riveted on my midsection, but not in admiration. I looked down. The tape recorder was sticking out of my pocket, still turning away.

It seemed to have a galvanizing effect on him. One minute he was behind the wheel lecturing me on the law of libel, and the next he was lunging at me—or the recorder, I'm not sure which—in a rage. I'm not sure whether the murderous look in his eye would legally qualify as an "admission against interest," but to me it was as good as a confession.

I don't know if he really would have choked the life out of me with his bare hands right there on the deck. For one thing, he was pretty old for a wrestling match, even with a premenopausal out-of-shape female who definitely preferred books to the gym. Still, given the circumstances, I didn't want to wait and find out. My feet did the thinking for me before my head could react. They were over the rail and into the water before I could weigh the alternatives.

Boy, that water was cold. Even in the summer, when the four of us used to go snorkeling in La Jolla Cove, we always wore wet suits. If you didn't, you ended up exhausted in under half an hour, and your muscles trembled when you tried to stand up onshore. All your body's energy went into maintaining a safe temperature for its vital organs. It was a great way to burn calories.

Jumping overboard into an icy sea in November, however, could not qualify as a prudent weight loss plan. The nautical blue sweatshirt filled up with water like a leaden sponge, so that it was hard to move my arms. The recorder sank past my hands, heading for the bottom. My running shoes were miniature anchors pulling my feet down. Henry was shouting something that might have been, "Come back," although I couldn't tell for sure. Despite the cold, I didn't feel much like accepting his invitation. He circled me with the boat, coming uncomfortably (I felt) close with the engine. I kept going under, sometimes on purpose and sometimes because my clothes were so heavy I couldn't help it. He didn't throw me a life preserver, so I drew my own conclusions.

Finally he gave up. The last I saw of him, he was standing on the deck clutching his chest with a stricken look. I hoped he had a coronary that fell off the Richter scale. I bent over to try to take off my shoes, a maneuver much more difficult to execute in the water than it sounds. My hands were already so cold they fumbled at the wet laces, and I had to submerge my face and arms, which caused my whole body to sink. When I had finally pulled them off, I was already tired. I surfaced and blew water out of my nose. When I opened my eyes, I saw the *Legiti-mates* heading west, toward the Coronados.

But I didn't have time to worry about Henry. I looked around to get my bearings. Land was a long way away, and the shortest line to it would take me through the rough waters where the harbor met the open sea. I was a fair swimmer, but Mark Spitz would have opted out of that one. I decided that the best course would be to drift back toward the middle of the channel and try to reach the buoy that marked the edge of the lane. Maybe some passing sailor would pick me up.

It seemed like a good plan, except that I couldn't keep my head out of the water, and my movements were hampered by my wet clothes. I got out of my sweatshirt and watched it sink with regret. I couldn't get my pants undone, so I left them for the moment and relied on my arms to propel me.

This was the moment I had always read about when your life flashes before your eyes or, at the very least, you reorder your priorities. I was almost looking forward to it, but all I could think about was the chicken salad I had had for lunch, and how I wished I hadn't left half of it uneaten on my plate. I was probably hallucinating a little, too.

Apparently devoid of philosophy, I struggled on toward the buoy. Fortunately, it was big enough to be seen by a battleship, because your perspective from within the water is definitely distorted. My teeth were chattering and my legs and arms were numb, but I thought I could make it.

Finally, I drew up beside it. Hauling myself up on top of it looked like an impossible task, but I had to get out of the water. I reached out a hand to pull myself up when an enormous brown head popped out of the water beside me, right next to my face. If I'd had the strength, I would have screamed. The sea lion looked less surprised, probably because it had come up beneath me.

I had always thought they were rather cute at the zoo, but up close, "cute" was not the operative word. The beast was gigantic; that's all there was to it. Its face was all whiskery, and its breath was more than a little reminiscent of the can of rotten sardines someone had once thrown out in front of our house. The eyes, while intelligent, did not look friendly. In short, a monster.

He looked as intent on getting onto the buoy as I was. I feared it was too much to hope that he might recognize my superiority on the evolutionary chain and cede me the right of place. I chattered my teeth at him, the only sound I was capable of making. He regarded me with a bland contempt.

I had to pull myself out, without waiting another minute. If he went for me with his flippers, or whatever sea lions do, so be it. I turned my back and pulled myself onto the buoy, gasping and shivering. He watched me from the water and then let out a deep, throaty noise with his mouth wide open. It sounded peevish, but not seriously annoyed. With one final piscatory blast in my direction, he gave me a disgusted look and swam off.

Now that I was out of the water, there was good news and bad news. The good news was that there were a lot more boats out than I had realized, and some of them were sailing or motoring in my direction. The bad news was that I was nearly naked and soaking wet, and the wind was even less comfortable than the water had been. I clung to the rocking buoy with fingers that had all the flexibility of metal pipes and none of their strength. I concentrated on the boat that looked as if it would reach me first, a middle-sized sailboat making good way in the wind. I kept my eyes on it and plotted a visit to Death Valley in August in scorching detail.

Unfortunately, by the time my putative rescuers drew close, I could see that they had been making rather merry, so that the spectacle of a half-

drowned fortyish mermaid in the middle of San Diego harbor seemed more a source of befuddled
mirth than a call for immediate action. Their sweat-
shirts proclaimed them students of that large and
famous local party school that regularly ranks as a
top contender as a place to go to have a good time.
In general, I regarded such pursuits with tolerance,
if not approval, but now it looked as if they were
going to sail right by me with a cheery wave. I tried
to call out, but I couldn't. They grinned. Someone
opened another beer. Desperate, I hauled myself to
my knees, reached out my arm as far as I could,
and extended my thumb.

A half hour later, dressed in borrowed sweat-
pants and a Hussong's sweatshirt (Hussong's is a
hole-in-the-wall bar down in Ensenada. For reasons
no one has ever been able to explain satisfactorily,
it enjoys a certain cachet all over Southern California. The sweatshirt had seen maximum use and
minimum washing, but I regarded it with as much
reverence as if William Faulkner had worn it to accept the Nobel Prize.), I set foot on land again. My
rescuers had a thermos of coffee as well as beer, so
I'd warmed up a little. They wanted to give me a
ride home, but I had already spoiled their outing as
it was, so I said I would call a cab. When I insisted,
they gave me money for the phone and a twenty
just in case no one was home when I arrived. I collected addresses for the return of all these favors
except for the Hussong's sweatshirt, which the
owner pressed me to keep. It seemed ungracious to
refuse. I could have kissed them all and very nearly
did.

I propped myself up inside the phone booth.
Now that I was warmer and almost dry, my mental

faculties were starting to function again. I looked at the coins in my hand, deciding who to call first. I felt alert, calm, detached. I had this vision of the phone booth as my command center, from which I would direct the various segments of my life. It was exhilarating. I put in a quarter and got the operator to supply me with the number of the Intercontinental Hotel in Rio. I dialed it in, charging it to my phone calling card, but when they put me through to an English-speaking clerk, I discovered David was out. I left a message. I called Susan in New York, but she was out, too. I called my stockbroker. I considered calling the police, but I thought better of the effort involved. My "evidence" was at the bottom of the ocean. Finally, I called my children.

"Where have you been, Mom?" Jason asked me. "Dad was really pissed off that you weren't here when he dropped us off. He says he needs to talk to you about the settlement."

"Don't say 'pissed off,'" I said automatically. "Anyway, Dad will have to wait. Can you get someone to drop you over here? I lost my keys."

"Sure," he said. I could hear the hesitation in his voice. "Brian's over here right now. Is it okay if he drives me?"

Brian was a charming but not altogether trustworthy classmate of whose company I did not normally approve. He was rather too reminiscent of an updated version of James Dean for comfort. "Bring him," I said. "You can drive my car back. And Jason, order a pizza. The biggest one you can find. With lots of cheese. And pepperoni."

"Mom, are you okay?" he asked me. "You sound kind of funny."

"I had a little accident," I told him. "But I'm fine now."

*   *   *

The hot shower was invented for moments like this. I let it run full blast, oblivious of past or future droughts. I could never understand how anyone could prefer to sit in a tub, surrounded by soap scum and little flecks of skin. The shower was definitely the thing for making you feel new and clean again.

While I stood there, I thought about what had happened on the boat. If this had been a murder mystery, even a third-rate one, Henry would have confessed everything as soon as he realized the jig was up, and the harbor police would have been waiting to lead him away in handcuffs right after he finished. As it was, he had very carefully admitted nothing about his role in Eleanor's death, and if I accused him of lunging at me on the boat, he would probably just contend that he had lost his footing and slipped. Other than a deep-seated conviction that my days of dining chez Eastman were undoubtedly over, what did I have? I was left with a great theory and some circumstantial evidence. You can make books turn out to order, but life is something else.

I toweled off and put on a terry cloth robe, the thickest, warmest one I owned. The answering machine flashed at me, so I pressed the "Messages" button.

"Caroline, this is Barclay Hampton," began the message. "Something's come up." He didn't sound apologetic. I remembered the phone ringing just as I left the house. "I just realized Henry usually takes the boat out on Sundays, and I don't want him to see us together at the café." Now that I knew more of the whole story, I realized why not. He seemed to hesitate. "I have to talk to you," he said. "Since you're not home right now, I'll call another time to reschedule. Please don't tell *anyone* that I've contacted you. I—well, we'll speak later." He hung up.

I pressed the button and listened to the tape again, considering the problem of Barclay. Despite the fact that he was now only a second-tier player in Eleanor's death, I still didn't want to have anything to do with him. I remembered that Tricia was beside herself with worry because he was so distracted and couldn't sleep. I had taken this for a sign of his guilt, but maybe he felt guilty not because he had killed his ex-wife, but because he suspected Henry had. How? I wondered what he wanted to talk to me about. Was he trying to warn me?

Someone knocked on the bedroom door. I opened it.

"Mom?" Jason had a strange look on his face. "There's some guy from Dad's firm on the news. Mr. Eastman. They said he's dead."

I walked over to the bed and turned on the TV with the remote. Sure enough, there was the *Legitimates*, back in port. "What happened?" I asked Jason.

He was still looking at me oddly. "They found his body on the deck. The boat almost ran somebody down; that's how they knew. They think he might have had a heart attack."

I thought so, too. Fascinated, I watched the camera focus on the removal of the gurney while the newscaster overlaid intoned pieties about the tragic end of one of San Diego's leading legal lights. Right. The corpse looked stiff and uncompromising beneath its cover. Even in death, Henry observed the formalities.

"That's the same boat Dad took us on, isn't it?" Jason asked me.

"Probably," I agreed.

"It sure was a busy day down at the harbor," he said, his hands in his pockets, when the news had moved on to the canine frisbee tournament in Balboa Park.

Well, I had to tell him something when he picked me up at the marina, adorned with the Hussong's logo and smelling of seaweed and stale beer. I had come up with a preposterous account of having slipped off the end of the dock while taking a stroll among the yachts. Jason had looked dubious even then, but Brian had cried, "Oh cool!" and asked if he could have the sweatshirt if I was sure I didn't want it. I gave it to him.

"Mom, were you on that boat?" Jason asked me.

I thought about what I would say now, in view of Henry's death. I wondered if he had pitched my purse overboard before his heart gave out from stress and guilt and the exertion of trying to run me over with the yacht. On the whole, I thought so; it was like Henry to attend to the details. If not, I would think of something, but in all likelihood not the truth. This ending coming off the Celestial Word Processor might not be perfect justice, but it was probably close enough.

"Of course not," I told Jason, smiling. "It's just a coincidence."

24

HENRY EASTMAN HAD one of the biggest funerals in La Jolla history. Everyone who was anyone in the legal world was there, trading stories about all the incredible lawyer tricks Henry had pulled off in his prime. What a swell guy. Pamela, whose fashion sense had frozen with Jackie Kennedy in the sixties, wore a black dress with a hat and a veil. The news camera caught her going into the church, clinging to Jeff Grayson's arm.

Naturally, I was not among the mourners. Neither was Susan, because after I called her in New York to tell her what happened, she decided to fax the firm her resignation and stay on in Manhattan to hunt for an apartment. As soon as she found one, she was going to fly back and pack up her things.

I don't know whether our absence occasioned any comment, but I doubt it. Eastman, Bartels, and Steed, and Barclay in particular, had other things to worry about. David, with my blessing, took our documents to the SEC, and as soon as even the tiniest rumor leaked out, the shit hit the fan. Naturcare's stock price went south. The business section of the paper started running uncomplimentary articles about Mike and Cindi Meadows. Barclay, not surprisingly, did not return my calls. The engine was set in motion, and however long it took to get where it was going, I was content to leave it alone.

Well, almost. Steve called me the day after the funeral, spitting nails. "The whole goddamn firm's in an uproar," he yelled into the phone. "You did something, didn't you? You found some information, and you used it against us."

"I didn't do something; you did."

"I'm coming over."

"You are *not* coming over," I told him. "We will not enact this scene in front of Jason and Megan. They're upset enough as it is."

"If you're so concerned about them, why don't you think about their future, for God's sake? You're throwing it away."

"Steve, will you listen to yourself? When did money turn into the only thing that's important? What kind of future will they have if they grow up believing that?"

He was silent.

"You knew what Barclay did, didn't you?" I asked him.

"I'm not going to say anything about that." His voice was stony and flat.

"You don't have to. I already know. Henry sent you to look for that side letter here because he suspected I might have it. How could you do that to me, Steve? How could you abuse my trust and go through my things like that?"

"You don't understand," he said in the same uninflected voice. "You've never understood. You might have ruined us. We could lose all our money. And if I go down, you'll lose your child and spousal support; I can promise you that."

"I understand. It's been explained to me often enough. If it comes to that, I'll sell the house. I don't want my whole life to be a hostage to keeping my possessions. I'll stand by what I've done. All I ask is that you do the same."

His voice was thick with horror. "Are you so drunk with revenge you don't even *care*?"

"Of course I care. I'll tell you something else. You are Jason and Megan's father. Like it or not, we have a relationship. I'd like it to be a friendly one, but that's up to you. But whatever happens, I don't ever want to be dependent on you again the way I was. We've divided our property and made our deal. I hope you live up to it, but frankly, I don't want to worry all the time that you're going to cut my support or haul me into court to renegotiate it on whatever pretext you can dream up. I won't live like that. I did what I thought was right, and I'm prepared to take the consequences. I'm sorry if it hurts Barclay or the rest of you at the firm, but frankly, you brought it on yourselves. Jason and Megan and I will be all right. That's the bottom line. It can't be renegotiated."

"You're brave enough now," he sneered, "but how are you going to support yourself?"

"I'll have some money," I told him.

"How much?" he asked suspiciously.

"Quite a bit, actually."

He didn't exactly say "Oh, sure," but he meant it. "Where will you get it?"

"Well, I took my half of our investments and—"

His voice was hoarse. "What? What did you do?"

"I shorted Naturcare," I said.

A couple of days later, in the interest of truth (justice, I believed, having already been served), I confronted Maria in the kitchen.

"I'd like to talk to Manuel," I told her.

She looked up from scrubbing the grill on the Jenn-Air and then down again. "I'm still not sure where he is, Mrs. James."

"I understand," I said, "but if you should hear from him, you might ask him if he wants to come and work for me."

She straightened. "Here?"

"Yes—I need some help getting the yard back into shape. There would be several days of work at first and then a maintenance schedule." I took a deep breath. "Tell him . . . tell him that if he comes here to work, I will help him get a green card." I was letting myself in for an incredible amount of hassles dealing with the INS, but then we both knew I wanted more information from Manuel than how deep to plant the tulip bulbs.

Maria considered. As a bribe, it was fairly sizable.

"There is something else," I told her, before she could say anything. "The man in the suit . . . you know who I mean?"

She nodded. "*Sí, señora.*"

"He is dead. *Muerto,*" I emphasized. "So, if by chance Manuel should get in touch with you, I'd like you to tell him that."

"I will," she said, bending over the grill again. "If he calls."

Two mornings after this conversation, Manuel sat nervously on the edge of a kitchen stool, cradling a cup of coffee gingerly between his hands while Maria translated my assurances that no, I did not mind that he had slept in our garage for a couple of days and yes, wasn't it a delightful coincidence that he had called her so soon after I had indicated I wanted to hire a gardener. There are certain rhythms and rituals to such conversations, and I observed them, but eventually I brought him round to the day of Eleanor's death. Now that he hoped to be legal, and the threat of retaliation was removed, he seemed to savor the attention.

"Ask him to please tell me exactly what he saw," I said to Maria.

This required some discussion and handwaving, but eventually she said, "It was as I told you before. He remembered he had left out a tool—" She broke off and asked him something I did not catch, and then turned to me. "We do not know the name in English. It is small, like this, for digging holes."

"A trowel," I suggested.

She shrugged. "Maybe. Manuel came around the corner of the house. He saw the man with the suit, bending over the pool. The señora's head was above the water. So Manuel did not look at her, although he was far away, because she would not wear clothes like a decent woman. It is just as I told you," she said again, with satisfaction.

"And then what?" I asked her.

"He ran away, because he was afraid."

"Did he see anything else?"

She seemed to hesitate. "Please ask him if there is anything else he can tell me," I implored. "It is important, for Mrs. Hampton's sake, to know the truth."

She turned to him and said something in rapid-fire Spanish. He took a swallow of coffee, looked briefly out the window and then at me. His reply was animated.

Maria shrieked something at him and said, "He did not tell me this before, Mrs. James, I swear." She seemed quite agitated.

"It's okay," I said, as patiently as I could. "What did he see?"

"Manuel says the señora's head was back against the side of the hot pool, like this." She tilted her head backward, and Manuel nodded. "The light beside the water was on. The man in the suit put his hand out toward the wine bottle—Manuel thinks the señora was *borracha*—and then the man stopped, like this." She held out her hand, poised just short of the imaginary bottle. "Then he—" She turned to Manuel and asked him a question. He nodded. "He put his hand on top of the señora's head and pushed her under the water."

"Did she struggle?"

"Señora?"

"You know—did she fight?"

She asked him. "He says no. He says it was very peaceful, like sleep."

Well, thank God for that, at least. "Maria, did Manuel get a good look at the man? Could he identify him from a picture?"

This required considerable discussion, but in the end she was firm. "He says no. He says the man had his back to him, and then Manuel ran."

I could scarcely blame him for that. I had an inspiration. "Manuel said the man was definitely wearing a suit."

She nodded.

"Did he see what color his hair was? Was it brown, like Mr. Hampton's?"

She translated, and Manuel looked at me. "The man is really dead?"

Maria asked me.

"Most definitely. His funeral was last week."

She looked at Manuel expectantly. *"Plata,"* he said. *"Color de plata."*

I didn't need the translation. The man who killed

Eleanor had had silver hair. "*Gracias,*" I told them. "Thank you very much."

David and I had a private celebration of the end of my career as a private eye. Afterward we lay propped up on lots of pillows, eating winter grapes and talking about revenge.

"Doesn't it bother you that Henry will never be exposed for what he did?" he asked me.

I considered. "Not much. He's dead, and Barclay is headed for a very rough time. The firm, too. That ought to be enough, even for Eleanor." I put the grapes back in the bowl. "I've thought about it a lot, and I've put together the most likely scenario for what really happened," I told him. "I think Barclay had an appointment with Henry on the day Eleanor died. Remember the little blot before the 'E' on Barclay's calendar? I thought it meant that Barclay was going to see Eleanor that afternoon, but now I think the blot was an 'H.' I bet Barclay told Henry that Eleanor was going to expose the fraud if he didn't come up with a lot more money, and he wasn't going to *have* a lot more money now that Henry had discovered what he had done and was going to force him out of the firm. I think Henry went over to Eleanor's house to offer her a bribe and a threat, the way he did me."

I sighed. "It's so obvious, I can't believe I didn't think of it. Henry always took care of things for the firm. 'Trust me, I'll handle it.' He even said that to *me*, but I was so wrapped up in nailing Barclay I didn't see it. Barclay was beside himself afterward because he knew that if Henry didn't have anything to hide, he would have told the police he was at Eleanor's house that day, but instead he kept quiet. That's when Barclay realized that he might not have to leave the firm after all, because if Henry tried to ruin him, he could always take Henry down with him. Tricia told me at lunch that Barclay wasn't sure if he was going to become a judge or not. All the pieces were there, and I just didn't put them together till the end."

"Don't be so hard on yourself. Look how much more you found out than anybody else. Do you think Henry went over there intending to kill her?"

"Probably not, at least not consciously. I don't know what happened before Manuel got there, but I do know she'd bought that wine to celebrate her victory over the 'bastards,' so most likely he just intended to pay her off. Eleanor had a way of infuriating people. Who knows? Maybe it was the sight of her in that hot tub, such an easy target. Maybe the Bâtard-Montrachet was the last straw. Manuel saw him reach for the bottle and then stop. He must have decided at that very moment." I frowned. "The only thing that bothers me is that Henry wouldn't tell me anything, even though I think that in a way he wanted me to know he did it. He said that killers only confess in *Columbo*, and that wasn't going to happen."

"You mean you wanted him to grovel and weep, and he didn't."

I laughed. "Maybe. But my Clytemnestra days are over for good. I don't want to make a career as the avenger," I said. "Look where it got Eleanor."

He took my hand. "Now that it's over, why don't you come on a trip with me? I have a beach house in Puerto Vallarta. It's beautiful this time of year. You can practice your Spanish."

"I thought that was what I've been doing," I told him.

He laughed. "Well, then, you can meet my parents on the way back."

"I'd like that," I told him. "Susan wants me to visit her in New York, too, when she gets settled. But as soon as I can, I have to get down to work."

"On what?" he asked me.

"On a book. About all this, somehow. I want to write a book about how to move on after your divorce. Eleanor wanted me to write her story, but I think she might have been pleased if I could help other women avoid her fate."

"What are you going to say?"

"I don't know yet. I'm still working on the title. Something like 'reinventing your life,' but I can't quite get it right."

"You'll think of something," he said and reached for me under the covers.

How easy change is, but how final.